BENEATH THE HALLOWED HILL

The Power Places Series

Theresa Crater

Crystal Star
PUBLISHING

First edition Eternal Press, 2011
Second revised edition, Crystal Star Publishing, 2016
ISBN-10: 0-9971413-0-1
ISBN-13: 978-0-9971413-0-6

Beneath the Hallowed Hill
by Theresa Crater
The Power Places Series

Cover art by: Earthly Charms Designs

Crystal Star
PUBLISHING

For Aldrin

Prologue

Alexander Cagliostro balanced on the side of the yacht, then did a back roll and fell into the warm water. With a kick, he surfaced, tested the air flow in his special face mask, then took the extra air tanks from his assistant, Karl Mueller. He tied his on and looked around for Miriam. Another splash announced her arrival. He waited while she adjusted her own equipment, then motioned for them to submerge.

The turquoise waters of the Caribbean darkened to a royal blue as they swam toward the bottom. A yellow cloud of Spanish Hogfish turned as one and headed away from the two divers. When he could see the bottom clearly, Cagliostro leveled out and treaded water, quieting himself until he could feel the subtle currents of energy around him. Miriam floated a few feet below him, waiting. He dropped deeper into his finely tuned sense, feeling for the magnetic pull he knew would come. Two dolphins swam into view and circled the divers, keeping their distance. Cagliostro gathered his desire, holding it in check until it grew into an ache in his chest, then pushed it out into the water. He tracked the vibration as it radiated out, listening for the thought wave to strike its target and ping back to him like sonar. Quiet, quiet, then he heard it. Southwest. He didn't spare a glance for Miriam.

He angled down until he was about five feet from the ocean bottom, then followed the contour of sand and rock, kicking up over a small hill, then down the other side into a valley. The ping grew stronger. The bottom flattened and he slowed, passing over a stand of pillar coral. It had to be here. Another ridge of rock rose on the other side of this valley. He swam over to it and found scroll marks on the edge of a perfect rectangle. This was no natural rock. It had been part of a wall or building of some sort. He took out a compass, checked his tanks and waited for Miriam. She swam up beside him.

"They're here somewhere." The face masks he'd had commissioned allowed them to talk to each other.

"You're certain?"

"As certain as I can be," he snapped. "We'll divide the valley between us. We've got just over two hours of air. You start here. This ridge is your western edge. That thick growth of sea fan one boundary and the rough rock the other. We'll meet in the middle."

Miriam nodded, went back to the wall and started to swim over her territory. Cagliostro glided back to the other side of the valley, keeping his senses open as he passed over the relatively even sand. He felt it somewhere close, but now was not the time to get careless. He must be patient, follow protocol. He didn't think anyone had followed them, but if he just swam at random, they might run out of air and light. Then someone else better equipped might come down during the night and uncover it for their own lodge. He reached the beginning of the valley and forced himself to swim the edge, even though he knew what he was looking for was more to the middle. He moved back and forth, studying the ocean floor for any clue, an edge showing, a shape hinted at by the slope of the sand, all the while his senses receptive as a satellite dish.

They swam back and forth for about half an hour, slowly but surely making their way closer to each other, toward the middle of the valley. Then he saw a glint. Cagliostro pointed his flashlight at the light brown bottom. The light bounced back at him from something barely covered. He moved in closer, ran his hand over the sand and found rock. Smooth and straight. He took out a rubber tipped shovel and started clearing the sand away. At some point, Miriam joined him, traced the edge of the rock and started digging with a similar implement farther down. The gleaming flank of a long crystal slowly revealed itself. Cagliostro moved with care and a suppressed urgency, as if he were undressing the most beautiful woman in the world. The straight facet angled deeper, and he grunted in disappointment. They'd have to bring in heavier equipment.

Cagliostro pulled off his glove and fished under his neckline for a chain. With a tug, he brought out the crystal he'd taken from the dead body of Paul Marchant in Egypt. Pulling it over his head, he looked up at Miriam.

"Ready" came her clipped response.

Cagliostro quieted himself and created a sacred space around them. He began a chant in his mind, then dangled the small stone over the long stretch of crystal. He waited, continuing his inner song. Nothing. He focused again on the vowel sounds, pushing away other thoughts, relying now on years of honed discipline. After what seemed another millennium, Cagliostro felt a deepening in the floor of the valley, like the approach of a storm. A flash of light traveled the length of the crystal, lighting the inside of the stone, sending rainbows dancing through the cracks, no doubt caused when the crystal had fallen from the temple it had been placed in so long ago. Cagliostro kept up the pressure of his chant, but the crystal did not speak again. It lay dormant, as if one burst of light was all it could muster after all those centuries of silence.

Finally, he relented. He took out his GPS, noted the exact coordinates, then set his equipment to measure their ascent. Motioning to Miriam, the two started up. Cagliostro chaffed at the slow ascent.

1

"Careful." Anne tried to not to stare at the shoulder of the road as Michael pulled the black Vauxhall onto the road that led to Glastonbury.

"I'm used to driving on the left side," Michael said.

Anne hid a smile. She just hoped the tires were sturdy. "It always takes me a couple of days to get used to it."

Michael completed the turn with no scrapes, and Anne leaned back, willing herself to relax. She'd never been so nervous before, had even enjoyed driving with Thomas, infamous for speeding. A burning lump constricted her throat. The memorial service had only been last month. Thomas Le Clair's plane had been shot from the sky leaving Tibet where he had been tracing one of six crystal keys to the Hall of Records in Egypt. Although his body had not been found, he and the crew of his private jet were presumed dead. Anne reached for the bottle of Celtic Springs water, took a sip, and watched the green fields behind the hedges. A house with a thatched roof stood on one side of the road, the garden full of spring flowers. She turned back to Michael. "What's Glastonbury like? Just another small English village?"

He glanced over at her. "You don't know the history?"

She shook her head.

"You still surprise me sometimes."

"I'm still learning all this, remember?"

"It's been a long time since I was here. I spent one summer on a dig on one of the nearby heaths." He smiled like a man with a secret. "I think you'll like it."

"Yeah?" Anne rubbed her shoulder unconsciously.

"Still hurt?"

"What?"

"You do remember Egypt?"

"My shoulder is fine, but my ribs are still sore." She'd been kidnapped. Cagliostro's questioning methods had been anything but gentle.

Michael reached over and squeezed her hand. "I don't ever want you to be in danger again."

"Don't worry. We saved the world. Remember?"

"I do." Michael paused. "Do you miss it?"

"Saving the world?" She smiled, remembering the rush of energy filling the star gate when they had brought the six crystal keys together.

"No, in the temple, when we all merged, that moment of—" he searched for the right word, "—illumination."

Anne turned back to the road. Now they were driving through a tunnel of trees. "It was real, then."

Michael glanced at her sharply, then back at the road. "You didn't really doubt it?"

"You've had a lifetime of study. I'm still relatively new at this, remember. I never realized humans could have such experiences. It feels like a dream now."

Michael nodded.

Anne squared her shoulders. "I'm looking forward to this vacation, to spending some quiet time with you. Before the official wedding and that zoo." She reached over and traced his chin with her finger. "Well, maybe not quiet exactly."

"Your ribs are still healing."

"I think I'll be all right."

"I'll be careful."

Her belly flushed warm. She sat back and stretched out her legs. They drove for a time in companionable silence, the Vauxhall humming along, the trees giving way to a village.

"Look." Anne pointed ahead. "Is there a sale?"

"A sale?"

"Don't you see that spotlight?"

"What are you talking about?"

"There. That beam of light. It's like when they open a new store and have a huge spotlight turned up into the sky." She looked over at him.

"I don't see any spotlight."

Anne looked back, her eyes searching. "There."

Michael negotiated the next roundabout, then pulled over. "Show me."

Anne raised her hand to point, but stopped short. "I thought I saw—"

"That's the Tor."

"But—I thought I saw a light."

Glastonbury Tor rose out of the fields before them, its green slopes spiraling to a slightly rounded top, the stone finger of St. Michael's tower etched against the purple streaked sky of sunset.

"It's beautiful," she said.

"Told you that you were going to like it here." Michael smiled over at her. "Which way?"

Anne smoothed out the map in her lap. "Go up Street then left on Fisher's Hill."

"The Fisher King," Michael said.

Anne's face lit up. "Wait, you mean this is where it actually happened—Morgen le Fey, King Arthur?"

"Not all of it. I don't think Arthur and Guinevere are really buried here, but this is the Sacred Isle all right."

"Remind me about the Fisher King."

"You should know. This is your heritage. I'm the Egypt expert."

"There's bound to be a connection between Glastonbury and Egypt," Anne teased.

"Of course, but you're avoiding the question."

They passed a grocery store on the left and a slope of green on the right. "There's his hill now." Michael pointed.

"Okay, smarty pants, the Fisher King kept the Holy Grail. He had a wound in his thigh—probably higher. Percival came to dine and the king showed him the grail."

"Well, technically the grail was kept by the maiden, but a passing summary."

"Oh, thank you Professor Levy. Do I get an A?"

"You're my best student."

Anne dug into his side.

"Ouch."

"I'm the one with the sore ribs. Oh, turn here. Left."

The tires protested Michael's quick response. He drove up the street and negotiated the next roundabout.

"Now, watch carefully. Grandmother Elizabeth said it's easy to miss the next turn. It's really just an alley."

They drove beside a low stone wall. "This might be it. Yes, Wellhouse Lane. Turn left."

"You've got to be kidding."

"No, this is it. It doesn't look like much, but—"

"Your Aunt Cynthia owned a house on this road?"

Something in his tone made her turn to look at him. "Why?"

"See that?"

Anne squinted in the growing dark at a squat brick building with wrought iron gates over wooden doors.

"Do you know what that is?"

"An old garage?"

"That, my dear, is White Spring, one of the sacred twin springs of Avalon. Your aunt's house—your house now—is on the Tor. Smack in the middle of one of the world's major power spots."

Anne looked back at Michael. "I thought you said this was the perfect place for R&R."

"Glastonbury is full of peace." Michael pulled the car into a spot beneath the house and they climbed cracked cement steps toward a two-story stone cottage. The front yard lay in the shade of an ancient oak. Ivy and shade-loving flowers filled the front yard. The round stones of the house's foundation supported a white wrap-around porch. They arrived at an oak front door with a diamond paned window inlaid with red and white roses. The door swung open to a long hallway and set of stairs on the left.

"Hello," Anne called out. They stood listening in the hall on a blue Persian runner, but no answer came. She called again. They listened for footsteps, a voice, but the house was silent. "The housekeeper said she'd get the place ready." Anne found she was whispering.

They walked into the parlor on the right where a small fire burned cheerfully in the grate. "Looks like she did just that and took herself off. The perfect housekeeper."

"Well, she left the door unlocked."

Michael swung Anne into his arms and kissed her forehead. "This will be—" he kissed each eye closed "—an extremely—" he kissed the tip of her nose "—quiet—" he kissed her mouth lightly "—relaxing vacation." Anne pushed against him and the fire between them kindled. Michael's hand found the smooth skin of her back.

The sound of someone clearing her throat made them jump apart. "Excuse me, ma'am. I didn't mean to disturb you." A short, round woman stood in the hallway watching them quite frankly. Her brunette hair hung in a long braid down her back and matched the brown of her eyes. Fine lines at the corners hinted at her age.

Anne pulled at her blouse. "Tessa?"

"Yes." The woman walked into the parlor.

"I'm Anne Le Clair, Cynthia's niece."

"Tessa Harden." She extended a reddened hand, which Anne shook. "Welcome to Glastonbury. The house is ready for you. I've even stocked the fridge." She walked into the room to check the fireplace, then straightened a doily on the back of an overstuffed chair. "If there's nothing else, I'll be going now. I've left my number on the kitchen counter. But the phone's switched off." She went into the hall again and stood studying Anne.

"We've got our cells." Anne found herself blushing under the woman's gaze.

"Sir," Tessa inclined her head to Michael, then left.

After a minute, Anne said, "I guess the diffident servants of England are a thing of the past."

"Anne," Michael scolded, "You've never stood on ceremony."

"Not usually, but there was something—she acted like I was in her house."

"Well, she's been caretaker for a long time, hasn't she?"

Anne smiled at his turn of phrase. Michael was already picking up the question at the end of a statement so characteristic of the English.

"I'll get the bags," he said.

"Let me help." Anne followed him to the front door.

He held up a finger to stop her. "You're still healing."

She paused at the front door, then on impulse turned and climbed the stairs, trailing her hand along the golden oak banister. The third step from the top let out a rather loud squeak. Light at the end of the hall drew her. A large window inlaid with red and white roses cut to refract the light, echoing the ones on the front door, framed the Tor perfectly. Sheep grazed on the slopes in the last of the sunlight. The silence wrapped around her like a wool blanket

The step announced Michael's arrival. "Which one's our room?"

"I haven't looked yet." She opened the first door to find a bathroom dominated by a claw foot tub. The door directly across the hall revealed a small room with a low table in front of another large window. A futon stood against the wall. Colorful cushions lay scattered about. The walls started out a deep purple at the bottom, then faded gradually to almost white. The ceiling darkened again into a midnight blue with a splash of stars across it.

"Meditation room, maybe," Anne said.

They walked down the hall toward the front of the house and found a large bedroom with a canopied bed and marble topped bedside tables. Michael dropped the suitcases at the foot of the bed, and they turned to find that the room stretched the whole width of the house. Opposite the bed, a large chair and chaise lounge were drawn up to another fireplace laid ready. A gilded mirror hung above the mantel decorated with dried-up evergreen sprigs, holly with browned berries and pillar candles.

"Looks like she planned to celebrate here. Wonder why Tessa didn't take it away?"

"Maybe she misses Cynthia." Michael kissed her forehead. "I'll get the rest of our bags."

Anne turned her back on the sad mantelpiece and explored farther. What had once been a smaller room, perhaps the nursery, had been converted into a walk-in closet. Rows of drawers and hanging clothes ended in a cozy dressing room complete with a little table and mirror. Anne opened a small door on the left and found a water closet. The second, larger door led to the bathroom they'd first discovered.

Suddenly, Michael stepped up behind her and wrapped his arms around her waist. Winded from the steps, his breath blew warm on her neck. "Hungry?"

"What time is it really?"

"New York is five hours earlier, but it's really dinnertime here."

"Look at all this." Anne pointed to the full closet, then at the dressing room. Brilliantly colored Egyptian perfume bottles lined the dressing table. Silk scarves and necklaces hung from small gold hooks from floor to ceiling. "She must have spent a lot of time in this house."

"I don't blame her." Michael closed his eyes for a moment. "Do you feel it?"

Anne stretched her senses. "It's so quiet. Not like Giza. I couldn't sleep there."

"Glastonbury is full of peace," Michael repeated, then his stomach rumbled and they both laughed. "Let's go to town. There are some good restaurants and the walk will work out the kinks from the plane."

They hiked down Wellhouse Lane, then passed the stone wall dividing Chalice Well from Chilkwell Street. Past the Well, a row of townhouses crowded up to the sidewalk, the windows full of plants and sun catchers with pentagrams and Celtic knots now lit from the lamps inside. An orange cat ran from the garden of a larger house and paused to look at them. The mouse he'd been chasing took advantage of his hesitation and dove into a drain pipe.

They turned down High Street and slowed their pace, looking into shop windows. "There's Chinese takeout," Anne pointed to a sign in the window. They stopped and read the menu.

"Another night," Michael said. "I'd eat it before we got home." They passed a health food store, then noticed a regular grocer across the street. A young man with dreadlocks was just folding up his display blanket from in front of the St. John's Church. The store windows displayed their offerings to the tourists. Crystals filled one window, locally made clothes another, books and Tarot cards in a third.

"Here." Michael led the way into Café Galatea where they took an empty table next to the front window. Work from local artists hung on the walls and a variety of newspapers were strewn about. They ordered a large pot of tea and two sesame stir fries. The tea arrived, and with steaming mugs in hand, they watched the tourists and town residents parade up and down the street. After dinner, they strolled past Market Square and the haunted George and Pilgrim's Inn, down Magdalene Street along the wall of the Abbey, then up the hill back to the house. Michael lit the fire in the bedroom, and they sat in comfortable silence.

"I'm too tired to unpack." Anne pointed to the suitcases still piled at the foot of the bed.

"We'll settle in tomorrow. Then I'll show you around." Michael stifled a yawn.

Anne smiled. "Time for bed." They curled together between the smooth sheets, but sleep won over passion.

SOMETHING WOKE ANNE. She listened for a sound, but heard only the ticking of an old clock downstairs. She rolled over and snuggled down under the duvet, but sleep did not return. Rather than toss and turn, she crept out of bed, careful not to wake Michael. In the closet among Cynthia's clothes, she found some old jeans and a shirt. At the window, the dark sky held a faint promise of light. Birds twittered in the apple orchard. The earth lay suspended in that silent moment before the tides swing toward morning. Anne made her way down the stairs, avoiding the squeaky step, and found a woolen cloak and clogs next to the back door. She slipped them on and walked through the dark backyard. A rickety wooden gate opened onto the gentle green slope. Above her, Anne could just make out the long finger of St. Michael's Tower. She climbed the wet grass to the steps running up the hill. She stopped to catch her breath at a convenient bench, then pushed to the top and sat against the old stone tower facing east, waiting for the sun to rise. She closed her eyes for a minute and sank quickly into deep silence.

From the west side of the tower, a lone voice lifted in a wordless chant. She opened her eyes and half turned to see who else had left their warm bed to climb the Tor and greet the dawn, but instead of the tower, she found herself leaning against a tall standing stone. Anne leapt to her feet and backed away.

"Good morning, Cynthia," a voice called from behind her.

Anne whirled to find an older man walking up the last slope of the Tor, his breath steaming in the chill.

The chant cut off mid phrase. Anne turned back to look for the singer and almost rammed her nose into St. Michael's Tower.

"You're up early," the man said.

"What the—" Anne turned back to the newcomer. He wore a woolen cloak similar in make to the one Anne had grabbed from the back porch, but his was a darker brown, almost matching his hair.

"Oh, you're not— I thought—" He came to a halt.

"I'm Anne, Cynthia's niece."

He stood close enough now for Anne to see wisps of silver in his beard. She pointed behind her. "Did you hear someone chanting just now?"

"You heard chanting." It was a statement.

"Yes. And I thought—" She pointed to the tower, then shook her head. "Never mind."

"You thought?"

"The tower disappeared and I saw a standing stone."

He nodded. "Some people see a ring of stones, some just the one."

Anne gave him a closer look.

"When is Cynthia coming back?"

She hesitated. "You haven't heard?"

He shook his head. "Sometimes we are out of touch for months at a time."

She took a deep breath. "I'm afraid Aunt Cynthia died late last year in New York."

12

"Died?" He stepped toward her. "But, such a vital woman."

"It was sudden. A heart attack." No sense telling the world it had been murder.

The man stared at her, eyes wide. Then he shook his head. "Cynthia and I were . . . neighbors." He offered his hand and Anne shook it. "My name is Garth."

"I'm sorry to bring you this news."

He ducked his head and leaned on his walking stick. Finally, he looked up and studied her face. "Anne." He shook his head. "I don't recall—"

"She and my mother were estranged. Cynthia probably never mentioned me."

"Ah, so you're the one."

"Excuse me?"

"The niece she had so much hope for."

Anne stifled her surprise. "So I'm told."

"You've taken up residence?"

Anne nodded. "I inherited the house. We—my fiancé and I—we came to see about it. Visit Glastonbury."

"And you're an early riser?"

"Actually something woke me. Probably jet lag."

"I felt it, too." He turned back to the east and gazed out across the downs. The bright curve of the sun lit the horizon. The fields greened under his gaze.

Garth turned back to her. "I hope you and your fiancé will come to dinner. I would like to hear more about Cynthia's passing. Perhaps I can help you know her better."

"We'd be delighted."

"It was good to meet you." He walked into the middle of the tower, his shoulders bowed.

Anne walked back down the hillside, leaving Garth to his own meditations. The sun lifted fully from the horizon and the mists began to thin. She slipped through the gate, now seeing the flower beds in the morning light. The jonquils were fading, but tulips pushed up from the earth. She picked one with a bent stem, went into the kitchen and rummaged through the top shelves until she found a small vase. Setting the flower in the middle of the table, Anne shed her aunt's cloak and clogs, then climbed the stairs. The third step from the top protested her weight.

"Anne?"

She opened the bedroom door to find Michel looking up at her from a jumble of covers, his hair tussled, eyes still heavy from sleep. "Where were you?"

"I couldn't sleep."

He reached for her. "You're cold."

"I went for a walk." She shed the rest of Cynthia's clothes and crawled into the warm bed. Michel pushed against her and she wrapped herself around him eagerly. Afterwards, they slept again.

A CLATTER FOLLOWED by a muffled curse woke Anne this time. Nothing mysterious in that. The smell of coffee followed the sound up the stairs. Her stomach responded with a loud gurgle. After a quick shower, she slipped into the clothes she'd worn earlier and found Michael in the kitchen scrambling eggs.

"Good morning." He kissed her on the cheek. "There's coffee here, tea in the pot, cream and sugar on the table."

Even though the coffee had beckoned her, the china cup with its row of delicate rose buds around the rim called for tea. She added cream, then took a tentative sip. Perfect. The red tulip had opened in the warmth of the kitchen. Michael pulled scones out of a small toaster oven and placed them on the round table. Anne reached for one.

Michael held up an imperious forefinger. "Wait." He turned and rushed into a small nook, then came out with raspberry jam and Devon cream still in their containers. He rummaged through a cabinet looking for bowls.

"They'll get cold." Anne opened the containers, then spread cream and jam on a scone. "It's a good thing I climbed the Tor already," she said, then took her first bite.

"Is that where you were?"

She nodded, savoring the taste.

"Couldn't sleep?"

She told him about her experience.

"Having visions already." He tilted the pan to test the eggs.

Anne took a breath to deny it, but stopped short. How else could she explain what had happened? "I met a neighbor. He asked about Cynthia."

"He didn't know?"

"No, but I got the feeling they were close. He asked us to dinner."

"Maybe we'll learn more when we go over." He scraped the eggs onto a platter and grabbed a bowl of heated beans, then placed them like an offering before her. "One more thing." He took a small casserole dish out of the oven and with tongs lifted a cooked tomato onto each of their plates.

"So you want to open an English bed and breakfast?" Anne asked. "Where's the bacon?"

"I knew I'd forgotten something." Michael put another plate down, this one filled with soy strips masquerading as pork.

"How long have you been up?"

"About an hour."

They ate in quiet contentment, listening to the song of the birds in the orchard and the occasional bleat from the sheep on Chalice Hill. Finally Anne could fit no more into her stomach. She took her plate over to the sink, then sat back down. "Thanks for breakfast."

"You're welcome." Michael nodded. "I was inspired."

"I'll say. What's next on the agenda?"

Michael finished his last bite before answering. "You have to do the dishes."

Anne laughed. "And then?"

"Let's get some water from White Spring first, then we can go see the sights. You've already been on the Tor, but I'd like to climb up sometime today. We'll go to Chalice Well, maybe get over to Wearyall Hill. Tomorrow, we'll tour the Abbey."

"Sounds like a real vacation."

Anne filled the dishwasher, protesting he'd used every dish in the house.

Then they walked down to White Spring with a few gallon jugs they'd found on the back porch. A local man held his own plastic container under a trickle of water next to the brick building. He nodded as they walked up. "It's still sluggish."

"What is?"

The man glanced up when he heard Anne's accent. "On holiday?"

"We just got in last night," Anne said.

"Welcome to Avalon." He jutted his chin toward the stream of water. "White Spring is running slow. Has been for a while now."

"How long?" Michael asked.

"For a few years really, but worse since midwinter." He studied Michael for a moment. "It perked up around Imbolc for a few days, but then the flow got erratic again."

"Has this happened before?" Michael asked.

"White Spring's flow always changes, but it's been reliable for thousands of years. Now, we're not so sure of it."

Anne stepped past the two men onto a flagstone patio. Spirals and inlaid crystals decorated a moss green wall next to the brick building that was now the entrance to the spring. A few ferns had found footholds in niches in the rock. Water trickled down the wall and gathered in a small pool. Several silver containers of votive candles, now burned down, sat on the edge. A few colorful ribbons hung from crevices in the rock face and the branches of vines. Tiny green buds swelled along the stems. Anne turned back.

The local man tightened the lids on his bottles. "You know, there used to be a restaurant here. Some people just don't get it."

"Surely the damage isn't permanent," Michael offered.

The man shook his head. "One would hope not, but we must restore the flow."

Goosebumps spread up Anne's arms. "Restore the flow." It was the phrase that had been passed down over the centuries to explain the purpose of the crystal keys.

Michael touched the crystal hanging beneath his shirt. "What did you say?"

"Something needs to happen to balance the spring. We've done some rituals, but if White Spring fails, I don't know what that will mean for the world."

He loaded his bottles in the back of a Citroen. After he'd settled the last one, he smiled. "Sorry to be glum. Have a good visit."

"Thank you," Michael said.

Anne watched the car swing deftly around and head back to Chilkwell Street before she turned back to Michael. "Did he just say what I think he said?"

Michael shrugged, a small smile playing on his lips. "I'd tell you it was just a coincidence if I didn't know better."

"We already saved the world."

"Guess it's a two part job," Michael quipped. He bent to open their jugs. "We'll need water."

"I'm on vacation," Anne said, then held the first container under the pipe. "But, Michael—"

"Like you said. We're on vacation." He smiled at her. "Besides, there are plenty of Druids and witches around here. They can fix the place themselves."

2

Michael took deep pleasure in watching Anne discover the sites he had long loved, first Egypt and now Glastonbury. In Egypt he'd spent half the time under the shadow of suspicion that he'd murdered Cynthia Le Clair. The second half, they'd dodged the thugs hired by the Illuminati to steal their crystals and then their lives. They'd returned home to Thomas Le Clair's memorial service. Michael planned to take her around the world, but now he longed for peace and quiet.

He followed Anne down Chalice Well's cobble stone path under the oak pergola entwined with slender vines filled with spring green. She paused at the white stones inlaid in the path and pointed to the white line that ran through the middle. "Michael's sword?"

"You could say that, but swords stand for the element of air as well as the male balance to the female circles. Some say it's a staff. Wands are the other male element."

"I feel like I should understand this symbol, but I'm not sure I grasp all the subtleties."

Michael laughed. "It's no wonder. It's very complex. Let's go sit by the pool and I'll explain it." At the gatehouse, he took out his Companion Card and showed it to the man behind the payment window, who nodded. They continued along the path. The last time he'd visited, it had been late summer and all the beds had been dense with flowers, the tall hollyhocks and bushes creating private nooks for meditation. Now spring plants burst from the brown beds, eager for the sun.

Anne tried to look everywhere at once.

"Just relax," he said. "We'll be here for a month at least. It will all come to you."

She took his arm. "Lead on, gallant knight." They continued up the walk and the pool came into view. Anne stopped in her tracks.

"Beautiful, isn't it?" Michael asked.

They made their way down the stone steps. Anne bent and trailed her fingers in the water. A small stream emerged from a stone bowl shaped like some exotic trumpet flower and flowed down what could only be described as a series of labia, finally falling on a squat and impertinent stone toad stool.

"Lucky guy." Anne pointed to the mushroom-like phallus.

"He lives in the lap of the Goddess," Michael whispered in her ear.

Anne pushed him away playfully. "You're just like him."

Two overlapping stone pools received the offering. The water brimmed to the top of the two interlinked circles, creating a sense of fullness and peace, then flowed out of the other end where it meandered through a vorticular stone channel down the hill into a small stone pool and finally disappeared down a just visible pipe. Anne sat on one of the benches and Michael joined her, taking her hand. They listened to the gentle trickle of the water.

Michael finally broke the silence. "See this tree?"

Anne looked over her shoulder at a smallish tree with waxy green leaves.

"It's one of the Holy Thorns. Do you know the story?"

"If every bush and rock in Glastonbury has a story, we're going to need more than a month," Anne quipped, then turned her attention back to the pool.

"Point taken."

The corners of Anne's mouth turned up slightly. "All right, Mr. Museum Curator, tell me about the tree."

Michael launched into his story with obvious relish. "When Joseph of Arimathea first landed on Wearyall Hill—"

"Where is that?"

Michael pointed behind them. "The green strip you saw when we first came into town last night. When we were talking about the Fisher King."

She nodded. "Joseph was the uncle of Jesus, right?"

Michael nodded.

"What was he doing all the way up here?"

"Probably on a business trip. He was a tin merchant. According to the story, though, he brought his nephew with him at least once."

"Jesus visited Glastonbury?"

"Yes, Blake wrote about it. *And did those feet*," he started to quote the poem, then stopped. "Jesus probably came to study with the Priestesses of Avalon."

"I thought he went to India."

"That, too."

"He sure did get around a lot without jets."

Michael's forehead wrinkled. "Feeling cynical today?"

Anne sat for a minute gazing at the pool, twisting a strand of her blond hair around her finger. Then she turned to him. "I guess I'm feeling dense."

"What are you talking about?"

"I had one of the best educations money can buy, but you know about this whole world I'd never even heard of."

"Annie—"

Anne flinched.

"What?"

"That's what Thomas called me."

"It's ironic. He knew all this—and more."

"Mother didn't try to control him," Anne said.

"He was older than you. Already beyond her jurisdiction. And I don't think Grandmother Elizabeth would have allowed her to take both of you out of the family legacy."

"I suppose." Anne slipped off the bench and leaned against his knees. "Time to get on with my education. Tell me about the Vesica Piscis. There's no wand cutting across this pool. I suppose the little guy there is the male energy."

"See, you're pretty smart after all."

She nudged his knees with her shoulder. "Stop."

Michael took a breath and launched into his explanation. "This shape represents the process of creation. When creation first manifests from the void—"

"Nut, or the Black Madonna," Anne said.

"Right," Michael glanced down at her face and smiled. "The first manifestation is a sphere, energy shooting out in all directions."

"The Big Bang."

"That's the scientific view. That sphere duplicates itself, not like an amoeba creates a whole new separate cell, but an overlapping sphere. This shape is the Vesica Piscis."

He began to stroke Anne's hair. "It's a basic form in nature. Fertilized eggs follow this pattern. The first cell division creates this shape." He paused for a minute.

"One more thing. The folks here at Chalice Well explain that by drawing a line down from the Vesica Piscis, you get the fish symbol of the Age of Pisces."

Anne laughed.

"What?"

"Some people would call that the symbol of Christianity."

Michael chuckled. "Glastonbury gave birth to the earliest form of Christianity. There's another shape that grows from the Vesica Piscis. If you keep creating spheres from this shape, you get what's called a Flower of Life, twelve spheres around the central circle."

"Twelve," Anne said, "Don't tell me—twelve signs, twelve disciples."

"Exactly." Michael took a breath to elaborate.

"Enough." Anne stood up. "Obviously, Glastonbury is an encyclopedia of metaphysical knowledge. But now, I want to just walk to the Well and meditate. Dr. Abernathy always says to balance the intellect with direct experience." She tried for an imitation of her older teacher's voice.

"He's right. After all, we have a whole month." His cell phone rang. Michael frowned, surprised he hadn't turned it off, then looked at the display. "It's the museum. I should take this."

In the past month, Michael had wrapped up his job at the Metropolitan

Museum in New York. He'd been lucky enough to convince Stephen, a member of his spiritual group who was well versed in secret metaphysical history, to take the job. He had impeccable credentials, so convincing the hiring committee that he was the right choice had been no problem. They had even offered Michael a stipend if he remained on call as a consultant. He had stayed an extra few weeks to smooth out the transition and promised to help if anything came up.

"This is Michael. Could you hold for a second please?" He took the steps by the pool two at a time and walked down the path away from the gardens before speaking. "Okay, I can talk now."

"Sorry to bother you so soon," Stephen said, "but something's come up. We need your opinion."

"Certainly." Michael perched on the wall in the parking lot.

"You remember the experiments we conducted with the items you loaned us from the collection?"

"Yes." Michael smiled at Stephen's convoluted attempt at security. He was referring to an ongoing exchange Michael had set up with his spiritual group and the museum. Sometimes people who owned valuable metaphysical libraries or sacred artifacts asked Michael to find a home for their private collections as they neared the end of their lives, particularly if no one in their family shared their interest. About a year ago, Michael had been given an interesting collection of crystals from an Italian metaphysician who had lived in the Bay Area. He'd sent a collection of crystal skulls and a large clear quartz, plus a library of typed psychic sessions and some rare books. Robert had taken a few of the crystals at a time to experiment with. They'd then compared their own experiences with the typed sessions to try to verify the history of the stones. It seemed the man had given them some ancient Atlantean artifacts, and Stephen had been trying to track their history.

"They've been stolen. And there's something else."

"What happened?"

"I don't know how to tell you this, Michael."

"Just tell me the whole story," Michael said. Something in Stephen's voice set his nerves on edge.

"Robert was bringing the last batch of crystals back to the museum. He was very excited about some work he'd just done. Told me he knew the big crystal had been a sentinel for the Tuaoi Stone."

Michael straightened up. "Tuaoi Stone? Is he certain?" The famed Fire Stone, the center of Atlantean crystal technology.

"He was. I waited for him for over three hours. I thought maybe he'd done another meditation with the crystal and lost track of time. I called his house and his wife said he'd left the house right after he'd called me."

A shiver of alarm ran the length of Michael's spine. "What's happened?"

"The police found Robert—" Stephen's voice choked off.

"No."

"He's been murdered."

"I'll come right away."

"Good. We need you."

Michael ended the call and ran back to the Vesica Piscis pool. Anne glanced up, her face the picture of contentment. Until she saw Michael's. She jumped up and ran over to him. "What's the matter?"

"It's Robert. He's been killed. I have to go back to New York."

ANNE DROVE Michael to Heathrow the following morning. After he checked in, she went with him to security where they found a private corner to say goodbye. "Are you sure you don't want me to come?"

"You have work to do at the house, and I'll be busy with the group."

"But you've lost someone very important to you. You stood by me when I lost Thomas."

He kissed her forehead. "I knew Thomas, too. We'd shared research several times. But I don't want you in any danger."

Anne stepped back and looked at him in alarm. "I'm calling Arnold." He was head of Le Clair family security.

"But he works for your family."

"So what are you, chopped liver?"

Michael smiled for the first time since he'd gotten the news. "The police

23

are investigating. I'm sure they'll find the killer."

"Right," Anne said, then spoke in falsetto. "Officer, you see my friend was doing psychic investigations on crystals from Atlantis, and we're being trailed by this Illuminati master who is obsessed with uncovering Atlantean technology to take control of the world."

Michael took a sharp breath. "Do you think Cagliostro is involved in this?"

"I don't know, but it's possible, isn't it?"

"We've tightened security in the lodge. Arnold did background checks on everyone. How could Cagliostro have known about this?"

"Who knows? The point is, I don't think he's given up. We still have these." Anne lifted the silver chain holding her crystal that was hidden beneath her blouse.

"I hope you're just paranoid," Michael said, "but please do call Arnold."

"Good."

Michael's brown eyes were full of pain. "I don't know what I'd do without you."

They kissed goodbye. Anne called Dr. Abernathy as soon as she was back in the Vauxhall. Roger Abernathy held an unusual position with the Le Clair family that had been passed down through his family for generations. He was the current holder of an ancient trust originally begun with a group of monks known as the Knights Templar. Over the years the position had become secular, but he still considered his position of Protector of the Bloodline a sacred duty. Anne told him all the details, then asked if Arnold was available.

"Actually, he's on vacation, but I'll bet he'll come when I tell him what's happening."

"I hate to interrupt him."

"We need him. I'll call you as soon as I have more information. Tell Michael I'm sending a car to pick him up."

Anne dialed Michael and filled him in.

"We're boarding now, so I'm turning off the cell," he said.

"Talk to you when you land."

Anne arrived back in Glastonbury in the late afternoon. She dropped the keys on the front hall table and walked back to the kitchen. Sheep grazed close to the fence. One ram kept trying to mount one of the females, whose only response was to move a few steps away from him and continue grazing. So much for her own romantic tryst in England. She picked at the leftovers from yesterday's breakfast extravaganza. Michael's grief wasn't personal to her. She'd never met Robert, but this death, following so quickly on the heels of Thomas's, brought the feelings rushing back. Not to mention the others who'd been killed in the underground temple in Egypt. And Cynthia. She pushed the food away after a few bites.

Shaking off her growing despondency, Anne stood up to explore the rest of the house. If they were going to pack it up and sell it, she needed to take an informal inventory. She already felt a growing attachment to the place. Even if she kept it though, she still wanted to know what was here. They'd only glanced at the rooms on the bottom floor and there was a whole basement to explore as well. She'd start there. It matched her mood.

A white paneled door opened off the kitchen to the basement stairs. She ran her hand along the wall, but found no light switch. She turned back and rummaged through the kitchen drawers for a flashlight. A small one hid at the bottom of a utility drawer. She switched it on and turned back to the steps.

Anne walked down the wood planks, resting her hand lightly on the railing to avoid splinters. The concrete floor was fairly dry, which surprised her considering their proximity to the springs. A cobweb brushed against her face and she reached up to push it out of her face, but it turned out to be a string hanging from the ceiling. With one quick tug, the harsh light of a bare bulb illuminated the basement. An ancient furnace stood in the front corner. Next to it several filters, still in their package from the store, leaned against the wall. She wouldn't have to worry about the heat for now. It was spring after all, but if they kept the house, she'd have to replace it.

Boxes loomed in the opposite corner. She pried open the first one and found strings of colored lights neatly coiled and several tin boxes. Inside, ornaments for a tree nestled in tissue paper. Cynthia had decorated the mantelpiece, but hadn't gotten around to putting up a tree. The next box contained more prosaic items, extension cords and light bulbs. A third old knickknacks. Maybe she'd find a few antiques in this one when she had time to unpack it. She closed the boxes and restacked them.

Gardening tools hung on the opposite wall. Several terra cotta pots nestled into each other like Russian dolls. An unopened bag of potting soil leaned against the wall. Next to this, two steps led down to a dirt packed floor. Wooden bins ran along both sides of the alcove. A root cellar, but the bins were empty.

Anne turned toward the back of the basement. Here another couple of steps led to a dark hallway with a low ceiling. Ducking her head, Anne made her way down the passage. The clean cinder block walls of the basement gave way to rough hewn rock. At the end of the passageway stood an old wooden door with a round top straight out of Tolkien. The gold handle turned out to be an elaborately carved dragon's head. Anne tried the door, but it didn't budge. She rattled the handle, pushed on the door, but it seemed to be locked.

Stepping back, she shone the flashlight around the passageway, but found no key. She ran her hands around the frame of the door, searching for a hiding place. Finding nothing, she crept back down the passageway to the cinder blocks and looked for a nook or a nail, something to hold a key to the mysterious door. No luck. She'd look in the kitchen. The key was probably floating around inside the large utility drawer in the kitchen. If not, she'd ask Tessa. Anne switched off the light and climbed back up the stairs.

Outside, orange and red clouds streaked the sky. The sun had already set. Anne walked to the front of the house and discovered an office across the hall from the front parlor. Maybe she'd get to know her aunt better if she looked over her books and papers. She heated a spinach and feta pasty in the microwave, made a pot of African rooibos tea and settled into a sleek, but comfortable grey leather chair with a low table beside it. After polishing off her pocket, she switched on her aunt's computer and brought up British Airway's website. She typed in the flight number, then clicked on the map. Michael's flight was over the Atlantic. A pile of papers sat next to the leather chair. On top lay a note in Cynthia's handwriting.

Dear Garth:

I've decided the best approach is to publish the material as a novel. I hesitate to join the throng of channelers. The family would die of embarrassment. But seriously, this way the material will be readily available. True sensitives will recognize the veracity of the story. Let me know what you think. Let's just hope we can discover how it all ends.

All my love,
Cynthia

"All my love," Anne read aloud. So there had been something between Cynthia and Garth after all. Curious, Anne picked up a handful of pages and started to read.

3

Prologue

"The time has come to tell you the whole story." Megan studied the face of the young woman before her. "And afterward, you will go into the hill and find the stones that I tell you about."

She pulled the red wool blanket tight around her shoulders, resisting the urge to move her chair even closer to the fire. The shears of the weaver goddess hovered just out of sight. So quickly, it had all happened so quickly, and she must leave this one to carry on. Already a mother, true, but not ready to become the elder. Now life rushed by, a tumbled race from infancy to parenthood and people became elders before they'd lived long enough to truly know themselves.

"I wish I could tell you what it was like then. So much has changed, my stories sound like make believe, but I tell you, it's all true, every word of it."

The woman across from her murmured acquiescence.

Megan closed her eyes, but felt Caitir studying her. She knew her skin had grown paper-thin, almost transparent, the dark smudges beneath her eyes the only color in her face. She listened to the crackle of the fire, willing it to fill the marrow of her bones and warm her. Where to begin, but her thoughts scattered with the wind blowing through the trees outside. Her chest, fragile as a small bird's, rose and fell as if she'd just climbed the Tor.

A rustle from Caitir made Megan open her eyes again. Caitir pulled her hands back from the herbs on the table—crocks of yarrow, feverfew and yellow dock. No need for these now. Megan's fever had abated, leaving behind the chill of November rain, so different from unfurling spring outside. Caitir pushed the black kettle out of the fire and sat back, waiting.

Megan's blue eyes gleamed with unshed tears. "He was such a glorious man—Govannan. Noble, gifted with the Sight. But this is ridiculous. Everyone had the vision then. We were all awake. Fully awake—"

A frown flitted over Caitir's face, a cloud darkening the sun captured in her strawberry-blond hair. Megan could no longer read her thoughts or feelings. Was it impatience, doubt? She hardly blamed her. How could Megan explain how they had lived in Eden, that gleaming city on the shores of the isle of Atlantis? Her lost home. If only she could reach through the veil of years, perhaps she would wake and find herself sitting on her terrace watching the waves, the buzz of the hummingbirds at the riotous bougainvillea loud in her ear. Or in the temple awash in the intricate harmonies of their chant, feeling the giant crystal come to life and open to the heavens.

But the disaster—she winced away from the memory of the wall of water rushing to the bare shore—the disaster had cut them off so unconditionally that Atlantis might have been just a story. They called them the immortals now, the fae. Megan had fallen into time, but the fae still lived, golden and glorious, beneath the Hallowed Hill.

Her twisted fingers clutched the wool. Irritated with herself, Megan squared her shoulders, rallying her strength for the task ahead. "There was a time when people did not age as quickly as they do now, when we lived hundreds of years and traveled to the stars through great crystals almost as tall as these trees." She pointed to the grove of yew up the slope. "When I was only a girl, I received my own calling, just like you."

SOMETHING SCRATCHED near the back door. Anne raised her head and listened. Maybe a tree branch blowing in the wind. She turned to the next page. Then came another scratch followed by a whining sound. She put down the manuscript and got up to investigate. As she neared the kitchen, she heard a low bark. Anne switched on the light. On the back porch stood a hound, white head cocked to the side, red ears perked. The pattern continued with red stockings on each leg and a red splotch on the rear.

Anne opened the door a crack and the dog's tail wagged tentatively. "Well, hello. Are you lost?"

The dog scratched the door again and stuck its nose into the crack. Anne blocked the dog with her body and stepped out the door. She bent over the hound but found no collar. It was female. She sat and regarded Anne carefully through eerie ice-blue eyes. She looked prepared to speak.

"Hungry?"

The dog woofed once.

"I hope you like eggs." Anne opened the door. The dog brushed past her, but instead of waiting in the kitchen, she trotted down the hall and disappeared into the office. Anne followed and found the hound curled up on a small rug next to the hearth, completely at home. If this was Cynthia's pet, where had she been? Perhaps with Garth? Maybe he'd let the dog out and she'd seen lights in her old house. Thinking her mistress had returned, she'd come home.

Anne went to the desk and hit refresh. Michael's plane would land in about an hour. The dog's eyes followed her every move. Anne settled back into her chair and picked up the manuscript. The hound lowered her head onto her paws, signed mightily and closed those haunting eyes.

The next page announced the first chapter.

MEGAN, are you ready?" Pleione called from the terrace below. "Really, child, we must hurry."

"You can't call me that anymore after today," Megan answered. "Besides, I turned thirteen two months ago." She smoothed the flowing white silk of her dedication robe, pushed her feet into the silver slippers, and started toward the stairs. A sudden pang hit her at the door and she turned to survey her childhood room. The translucent aquamarine curtain surrounding her bed billowed in the breeze, bright colors from the array of silk pillows flashing out, then muting again as the curtain stilled. Scarlet fuchsia outlined the window seat that looked out over the house to the bay. She'd spent so many nights sitting here watching the stars fill the sky, listening to the roll of the distant surf.

Eden was all abustle. In the spring when the peach trees bloomed, the newest adults of Atlantis celebrated their own blossoming, leaving behind fundamental education and their nurture pods, and presenting themselves to the oracle to confirm their role in society. Megan's intuition told her she would remain in the capital city, but the oracle could choose her for training far away. She might even transport right after the celebration. Most had a presentiment of their future role since they were close to full consciousness at this age, but surprises did happen. Her favorite shells and rocks covered a rosewood side table, and clothes lay scattered across the cool tile floor. Just as suddenly she was sure again. She would stay at home and study in the Healing Temple, taking her place beside her mother as she'd always imagined. She turned again and clattered down the stairs.

"There you are." Pleione held her at arm's length. Pursing her lips, she smoothed out the kohl darkening Megan's deep blue eyes, then stood back. "So beautiful. How did you grow up so quickly?"

Megan shifted under her mother's ministrations. "Is Diaprepes coming?"

"He should be here any minute. Nervous?"

"No," Megan shook her head and her brown curls danced around her face. "Well, maybe a little."

"I wonder what the oracle will say."

Megan looked up at her mother, surprised she didn't know already. Or maybe she was testing Megan's precognition. "I have a hunch," she said.

"What?" Pleione reached a hand out, but Megan bounded through the door.

"Come on," she called over her shoulder. "We'll be late." She ran past the fountain in the interior courtyard through the heavy scent of gardenias.

"Wait for me, young lady."

Megan lingered in the cool tiled foyer on the other side of the central garden of the family compound waiting for her mother to catch up. Each of her mother's sisters had an apartment as large as their own, and the elders of the sprawling maternal clan had rooms in the large house. Most of them still slept or perhaps they had kept to their rooms to honor the solemnity of the coming ceremony. They'd be at the party tonight. She looked up and saw one of her grandmothers peeking from a third story window. Megan waved, but the elder woman flicked the curtain closed.

Megan wondered if her friend Erythe would go with her to learn healing. She imagined Erythe's strong, square hands, her steady manner. Probably not. Her talents lay in working with plants, or maybe she'd join the government. Megan hoped someone from her group would accompany her. There were nine going through the Emergence Ceremony today. An auspicious number the teacher had said. A larger class than usual. The long-lived Atlanteans planned their families carefully.

Her mother caught up to her. "Now, let's have a little decorum, shall we?" She wrapped the train of her shimmering, ocean blue robe over her arm, then took Megan's hand.

Megan glanced back at the garden she'd played in ever since she could remember.

"You can come home any time you're free from your training." Her mother's voice was quiet in her ear.

"I'm ready." Megan squeezed her mother's hand. They stepped out just as a sleek, silver craft set down on the landing lawn in front of the house. The bubble top opened and her father climbed out. Tall and commanding, he shook out the folds of his deep purple robes. Diaprepes looked up and caught sight of the two. A smile broke out on his fair face, and Megan felt like the sun had just come out. He held his arms out to embrace her, but she was suddenly shy of him.

"You're alone," Megan said.

"No need for a retinue. This is your day." He studied her face for a moment. "Nervous?" He repeated the question of the day.

"Only if you two keep asking."

Her parents laughed, and Diaprepes took Pleione under his arm. There they stood, the Prince of Atlantis, golden haired and regal even here standing beside his personal conveyance on this ordinary landing spot, a thin gold band set with a simple crystal over the brow the only sign of his office, and the High Priestess of the healing temple, an elegant lily, exuding a power that sharpened the air around her. Today Megan would break from her orbit around these two powerful figures and find her own place in the world.

"We're going to be late," Megan said and slid into the back of the craft. Her parents settled themselves in front. Diaprepes closed the top, and Megan pressed her face against the window to watch the craft clear the trees. The square of the inner courtyard shrank, and the neighboring homes and gardens became a series of doll houses tucked away in the green folds of the hills.

Diaprepes skirted the verdant plain, its canals silver veins in the neat rows of crops and stretches of meadow. He veered south and they flew past the three rings of stone walls and round canals surrounding the main Temple of Poseidon. The harbor unfolded beneath them, dotted with sleek ships that cruised the ocean or dove beneath her depths with equal ease. Diaprepes avoided the southern shopping district and headed west over the first row of olive foothills toward the deep blue peaks. The rounded cone of one of the volcanoes rose in the distance.

Minutes later, the Temple of the Oracle appeared, a diminutive jewel on the edge of grey cliffs, the early morning sunrise reflecting in its faceted windows. The walls, built of the indigenous stone, blended with the mountain. Diaprepes landed his craft deftly beside three similar vehicles. They disembarked and headed toward the semicircle of stones in front of the entrance, careful not to step inside yet. A group of candidates and their parents waited just outside the semicircle like a flock of variously colored sheep. The parents' robes reflected their guild: blue for healing, purple for high government officials, green for the agronomists, and so on. Everyone wore their colors because today their children would discover their own future guilds. Although children were raised in their mother's clan, both parents usually came for the Emergence Ceremony.

"Diaprepes." A stocky man with a curly beard called to Megan's father as they approached. The two men hugged, then the women, then all of them together, and they began the usual banter of parents losing their children to the world, a predictable series of congratulations, speculations and condolences. Megan drifted around looking for Erythe, but it seemed she hadn't arrived, so Megan leaned against a stone at a distance from the group and closed her eyes, trying to quiet her mind in preparation for the ritual ahead. She let the buzz of voices wash over her. A gull's raucous cry carried from afar. The scent of vanilla wafted from the pines lining the mountain slope as the sun warmed their bark. Something rustled in the grass nearby. Just as she focused to send her consciousness into that form to explore, the stones spoke.

She has come at last. The voice came from the slim granite point she was leaning against.

A murmur of agreement vibrated through the semi-circle. *This is the one.*

What do you mean? Megan sent, but the stones only hummed a low note of contentment to themselves.

Before she could ask again, footsteps approached. She opened her eyes to Erythe, the white emergence robe setting off the soft brown of her face. "Nervous?" Erythe asked.

"Not you, too."

"What?"

"My parents keep asking me if I'm nervous."

"Well, are you?"

"Curious, I guess." Megan shrugged. "And you?"

Erythe paused, then said in a rush of warm breath. "What if they get it wrong?"

"Do they get anything wrong?" At Erythe's frown, she added. "You can change if you're not happy."

"Of course," but before she could say more, a single, resonant bell sounded from the temple. The heavy oak doors, a gift from the north where the trees were sacred, parted and two acolytes stepped out. The distinctive robes of the Crystal Guild shimmered in the light, showing now violet, now silver-white, always giving the feeling that if you concentrated, you could see whatever glimmered in the air around them just out of human sight. The acolytes walked toward the knot of people just outside the semi-circle of stones.

Without another word, Megan and Erythe hurried back to the group. As soon as they arrived, the young man nodded. "Welcome to the Temple of the Oracle. We are honored to serve you today. Please, those who are consulting the oracle line up behind this stone."

"The families will come with me," the woman said.

Megan glanced at her parents, but they had already fallen into ritual protocol and avoided her eyes. The young man gestured for the initiates to follow. He walked to the edge of the stones and paused, tuning to the circle, then moved forward. Megan felt a familiar tingle in her limbs when she passed the first stone, as if she'd penetrated a thin membrane. It closed itself behind her. They went through the ponderous oak doors, and here there was a slight pop in the air as the group moved through the second layer of energy surrounding the temple.

The initiates proceeded down a hallway lined with stained glass windows alive in the morning light. The first depicted Atlas, the axis of the universe, the Titan founder of their land. The window directly across from it showed the arrival of Pleione, whom her mother was named after, sailing across the heavens to mate with him. Next came the birth of their seven daughters, then the division of the land into the ten realms, and finally the gift of the Sacred Stone from the dragon Makara—all the central stories of the founding of Atlantis. Nothing secret here.

The hallway opened into a circular room with adobe walls and onion-skin marble columns. The ceiling flung the room up into the sky, soaring away in a triumph of selenite and thin, metal beams. A low bench ran the entire circumference, as if to attach the room to the earth so it would not float away. The blue tiled floor added the color of the ocean, but showed no design. A single flame burned in the brass brazier in the very center.

The acolyte paused just a few steps inside the circle, but before the group moved to sit, an older priestess stepped out from behind one of the columns, her violet tinged aura clearly visible around her. The first initiate was lead to her, a question whispered, then he disappeared through a doorway into the darkness from which she'd come. After about fifteen minutes, another initiate repeated the ceremony. The group settled on the benches and waited in tense silence. Finally, the acolyte nodded at Erythe, who squeezed Megan's hand before she walked to the priestess, answered her murmured question, then disappeared without so much as a glance back. At last, the acolyte nodded at Megan.

Her mouth filled. She swallowed and stood up. Why did she feel like she was stepping off a precipice, diving from a high cliff into the black depths of deep waters? This was Atlantis, she a well-loved daughter of gifted people, destined to take her place with them, to serve and grow into full consciousness as her body matured. But before she could rebalance herself, the priestess was leaning toward her. "What do you seek?" The sonorous tones tightened the knot in Megan's throat.

Well, what did she seek? Confirmation of what she already knew, that she would go to the Healing Temple and learn with Pleione, that she would take her place one day as High Priestess, that she would live long and ascend to the stars. But instead she whispered the ritualized response, "To ask the oracle for guidance."

This seemed sufficient, for the priestess nodded and with a slight gesture of her right hand sent Megan into the darkness behind the pillar. Megan had to push slightly to move through the invisible shield of energy, like crowning at birth, but she was delivered into darkness instead of light. The floor slanted downward at a gentle angle. Megan put out her hand to steady herself against the stone wall, smooth and cool to the touch. The solidity of earth reassured her somehow. The tunnel curved to the left and the angle of descent grew steeper. The darkness deepened and the tunnel turned again.

Megan made her slow and steady way down, but at the next curve, the darkness swallowed everything. The weight of the earth threatened to smother her. She stopped and groped around with her hand, but felt only the wall beside her. What if she took a wrong turn, what if the earth shook as it had in the past, and she was buried alive here, her life cut off before it could flower? What if she was found unworthy of the temple, sent to a simple shop in an anonymous town somewhere? But everyone's place was important, at least she'd been told that. Megan forced herself to take a deep breath, then a second, amazed by these fears. She followed her training. She surrendered to the black void that was consuming her and walked toward the womb of her remaking.

After the next turn, the darkness began to grey, and Megan forced herself not to rush toward the returning light. She continued in her deliberate way, allowing the temple to do its work of opening her awareness into the full receptivity of a newborn. The angle of the floor eased and, after another turn, straightened out. A soft glow from the low passage at the end of the tunnel beckoned her, promising solace and understanding. She stepped through.

The light came from a clear crystal ball in the hands of another priestess, whose face Megan never saw, for she could not take her eyes from the orb. Her eyes teared, as much from the sudden light as from the harmony it radiated. Lights swam in slow undulating spirals inside the crystal, alive and intelligent, like celestial dolphin. Incredibly, the priestess handed the orb to Megan and directed her to sit on the smooth stone in the very middle of the cavern. Megan nestled the ball in her lap as if it were a precious matrix holding the seed of all life. She sat, lost in the swirling light, bathing in the waves of energy coming from the stone as it took the measure of her soul.

Then she noticed there were other lights around the circumference of the room, more orbs sitting on slender pedestals. Most of them were muted, but one brightened and beckoned to her. The priestess was suddenly beside her, taking the orb, helping her up. Megan walked to the welcoming crystal sphere. But it was not a sphere after all. It had a face. It was a crystal skull.

I am in the Chamber of the Crystal Skulls, she realized, *the Chamber of the Thirteen*. She glanced back where she'd been, at the very center of the chamber. But where was the Master Skull? She had been sitting where it should have been. There should be twelve around the periphery. She started to count them.

Megan. The bright skull on the pedestal called to her. And the sweetness in that voice made her forget all her superficial questions and remember the deep one sitting in her heart. *What is my life's work?* Just as suddenly, she shed all her preconceptions and certainties.

Now she was right in front of the skull. His face, for the voice had been male, smiled at her from the center of several deep cracks inside the crystal. One divided his eyes, leaving one side frosty, the other with gold flecks floating in the clear depths like tiny stars. His nose resembled the entrance to a temple, and on the top of his head, full of rainbows and the hints of many forms, sat a milky white circle that looked like a cap. Long, long ago, this stone had been fractured by volcanic eruptions, incredible pressures of tectonic plates shifting in the earth, and then somehow had repaired itself. It was ancient beyond her imagination.

All this she saw at a glance, and then she felt a wave of self-consciousness, as if she'd been caught staring at someone in a crowd and they'd turned around and looked back. The skull chuckled. He certainly was cheerful for such a cracked up piece, and this time the skull laughed fully. *I have seen many ages of the earth, my dearest, as will you.* But before she could ask what he meant, he sent out a powerful beam of energy that struck her forehead.

She stood in a circular chamber resembling the one she'd just left. A simple bench hugged the golden adobe walls, running the entire circumference of the large room. Wide steps led to a blue tiled floor where intricate in-laid designs curved elegantly. Farther in they formed interlapping triangles and squares. In the center of the room stood the largest crystal she had ever seen. It soared high above her head, two, maybe three stories, and the domed glass roof had been pulled back, leaving the enormous crystal pointing at the stars. Then the stone noticed her and hummed a welcome, a sound that vibrated the bones in her head, making her vision blur. With a snap, she returned. She stood before the crystal skull.

You will apprentice in the Crystal Matrix Chamber, the skull told her, and she knew this was right.

CRYSTAL SKULLS. Anne wondered if such things really existed. Michael would probably know. But Cynthia's note suggested this material was more than some fantasy. She put down the manuscript. The dog, who had been sleeping peacefully, got to her feet and padded to the back door where she sat down and looked back over her shoulder. Anne followed, slipped on Cynthia's clogs and cloak, then opened the door. The hound streaked out, jumped the fence in one graceful bound, and swept up the side of the Tor, disappearing in the night.

"Wait." Anne ran to the back gate and whistled, but the dog was gone. Should she go look for her? She took a tentative step out the gate, then stopped. The dog probably belonged to someone else, lived over the hill on one of the farms edging up to the Tor. Perhaps she'd befriended Cynthia and just come for a visit. The faint ringing of the phone came from the house. Michael's plane must have landed. She ran back inside. If the dog got hungry, she'd come back. Anne had enough to worry about.

4

Michael wondered why Anne was taking so long to answer the phone. He checked his watch. She should still be awake. The phone switched over to voice mail, so he hung up and redialed. If he talked to her, he could stave off the reality he was about to face. The phone rang a few more times.

"Hello," Anne sounded out of breath.

"Where were you?" Michael asked. "Climbing the Tor again?"

"Outside chasing some dog."

"Dog?"

"Yeah, she showed up. Acted like she's lived here before, but now she's run off."

"Did she look like a stray?"

"Not really. She seemed well fed."

"I'm sure she has a home."

"You're probably right. And you?"

The baggage conveyor beeped and with a rumble jerked into motion. Michael turned to watch for his luggage. "Dr. Abernathy sent a car. I'm going to meet with the group, then have dinner with him."

"Let me know what happens."

"I will. What have you been doing besides chasing the local canines?"

Anne laughed. "Exploring the house. I found a manuscript in Cynthia's office, a novel. Well, she claims it's factual."

"She claims?" Michael repeated.

"I found a note she wrote to Garth. Seems they were close. She signed it 'all my love'."

"Glastonbury is good for romance." He tried to smile, but Anne must have heard the catch in his voice.

"I'm so sorry about this," she said. "I didn't even get to meet him."

Michael tightened his eyes against tears. "I miss you."

"Then I'll come. We can sort out the house later."

"No, I don't want you in danger again."

"But—"

"You don't know that."

"What did you think I was going to say?" she asked.

"That this has nothing to do with you or your family."

"Well?" Anne asked, a challenge in her voice.

"But we can't be certain, can we? Our common enemy knows we're together now."

She hesitated. "I suppose you're right."

"I'll be back as soon as I can."

"Do what you have to do. I understand."

A couple crowded up to the conveyor belt right in front of him. He moved over so he could still watch for his bag. "The service should be in a couple of days."

"Then you can come home—I mean, back here."

"Home?" The cold pit in his stomach warmed at her words. "Thinking of keeping the place?"

"Maybe. I kind of like it here."

"Here's my bag. I'll talk to you later."

"Love you," Anne said.

"You, too." Michael clicked the phone off and grabbed his luggage, then followed Lawrence, the family driver, to the waiting car. It turned out to be a limousine. He hoped the lodge members wouldn't notice. He disliked conspicuous displays of money, but after their adventures in Egypt, he had to admit it was safer than public transportation. He gave the address to Lawrence and settled into the comfortable seat, thinking back to his last meeting with his old friend. It had been late February.

They'd sat in Robert's study before a roaring fire drinking some of his special Jamaican Rum to celebrate their success in Egypt. Michael took his time narrating the story. Robert sat back in his chair with his feet up on a matching ottoman, interrupting occasionally to ask questions and offer additional insights. When Michael reached the end, he turned to his mentor. "We all knew that there was no physical Hall of Records, that the energy of the sites themselves triggers our collective memory. What do you make of it? Rosicrucian tradition has long held this hall exists."

Robert contemplated the question, rhythmically tapping the arm of his chair with his long index finger. Michael waited, watching the refractions of the firelight in the cut crystal glass. Finally Robert looked at him. "I still think there are Atlantean artifacts. Clearly, your group's mission involved opening the earth's main etheric temple. You've reconnected us to some galactic energy grid." His grey eyes sparkled. "I've felt a difference in the lodge rituals and my own meditations. Let's hope these more positive trends in the world situation continue."

Michael nodded. "But?"

Robert's mouth twisted in an ironic smile. "I know our ancient enemy too well. They will not let this stop them. Cagliostro survived. Not to mention Miriam." A former member of their lodge, she had betrayed them to the Illuminati. Robert shook his head. "I still can't believe she slipped by our security. Much less the group's psychic senses. Ritual creates a certain level of intimacy. I never guessed."

"Don't blame yourself."

"Who else? I'm the Grand Master."

"Her disguise was perfect. What do you think they'll do now?"

Robert set down his empty glass. "Keep searching the Giza Plateau. You described a maze of tunnels. There still might be a treasure trove somewhere."

"Perhaps." Michael still felt the certainty that he'd experienced that fateful night. He doubted there was a physical Hall of Records.

"There are artifacts in museums and private collections that date from Atlantis. They'll keep trying to gain control of everything they can lay their hands on. Speaking of, I've gotten some interesting results on those crystals you loaned the group."

"The ones from Frank in California?" Michael looked up expectantly.

"Yes, but it's late." Robert covered a yawn with his hand. "I'll send you a copy of the findings in England."

But he never got the chance, Michael thought as the limo drew near the Manhattan address. *And now he's gone.*

Lawrence pulled up in the loading zone, got out and walked around to open Michael's door. Michael slid across the leather seat and fumbled for the door handle, but Lawrence beat him to it. Michael reached for his bag.

"You can leave that, sir. I'll wait for you." He handed Michael a card. "My cell number."

"I may be a long time. I hate to make you just hang around. I can make my own way to dinner with Abernathy."

Lawrence pointed to the front seat where a thick book lay. "I'm used to it, sir."

Michael hesitated, then asked. "Do you have my cell? You can call if it's too late."

Lawrence smiled. "It's really no problem. This is my job, and it's a good one."

Michael blushed, realizing his reticence at accepting Lawrence's help might be condescending. The man must be well paid, not to mention imminently qualified. The Le Clair's had a tough security screening. "Thank you," he mumbled. "I'll just take my briefcase, then."

Michael hesitated before the steps of the group's headquarters, a neat brownstone on a quiet residential street mixed with a few businesses. When he went inside, somehow Robert's death would be final. After a minute, he squared his shoulders, took the steps slowly and opened the door to the familiar hallway with its polished wood floor and old umbrella stand, an antique from India. A portrait of their founder hung in a gold leaf frame over a French mahogany console. Harold Simon Llewellyn looked down at Michael with mild brown eyes above a full white beard. Footsteps sounded from the back of the hall. He turned to find Stephen walking toward him.

"It's good to see you—" Stephen put a hand on his shoulder "—although I'm sorry for the occasion."

"I still can't believe it," Michael said.

"You knew him so much better than I."

Michael nodded, his throat suddenly too constricted to speak.

Stephen spoke to cover the silence. "You made good time. Let me take your coat. The others are here already."

The front room usually resembled the lobby of a small hotel with comfortable groups of chairs clustered here and there separated by discreetly placed plants. Tonight, the chairs had been pulled into a rough semi-circle in the middle of the room. Guy spotted Michael first. He held out his arms, his eyes red. Somehow the hug solidified the reality and the tears Michael had held back fell. He pulled back and wiped his eyes, nodding at everyone. The rest of the group welcomed him and he sank into an armchair. Stephen pulled the sliding doors closed and took a seat.

Michael looked around expectantly, then realized he was waiting for Robert to begin the meeting. All eyes were on him, so he cleared his throat. "I'm sure we're all deeply shocked and saddened by this news."

Murmurs and nods answered his statement.

"What do we know?" he continued.

Guy spoke up. "The police have been cooperative in sharing their investigation with Jacob. He's an attorney."

A compact, energetic man with a head of springy brown hair spoke up. "Robert was shot with a 9mm. Probably a semi-automatic, a popular weapon with professionals."

Michael flinched.

"He died instantly," Jacob said in a more subdued voice. "There was no suffering."

Diane, a younger member, blew her nose loudly.

Jacob continued. "The killer probably used a silencer. None of the neighbors on the street reported hearing anything. One old lady heard tires squealing and looked out her window to see a black Mercedes speeding away. She didn't catch the number, but remembers the license plate colors and thinks it was from New York. I was frank with the lieutenant about Robert's esoteric interests; I think we'll make much better progress this way." He paused and looked around, then his eyes settled on Michael. "I'll keep you informed."

"Thank you," Michael said. "The services?"

Adeline, the group's secretary, answered. "Wednesday at 11:00. The reading of the will is on the following Friday, and the family has asked that we send a representative."

Michael nodded. "I would like us to spend some time meditating together before we leave."

"That's an excellent idea," Guy said, "but we do have one other piece of business."

Michael frowned in confusion. "Business?"

"We need to elect someone to lead our group."

"But surely that can wait," Michael objected. "Robert has just been——" He closed his eyes, unable to finish the sentence.

"Our charter requires that we replace the Grand Master as soon as possible," Guy said in an undertone.

"I think it's important, especially at a time like this," Adeline added. "We may all be in danger. It's urgent that we discover who's behind this and what they have planned."

She nodded to Michael, so he asked, "Are there nominations?" He looked around the circle of faces until he reached Guy, who smiled rather sheepishly. "We sort of already took an informal poll."

"Good." Michael nodded, relieved this would be a short process. "Who volunteered?"

"We all agreed it should be you," Guy said.

"Me?" This knocked Michael back in his chair. "But—I'm in transition. I've just left the museum. I'm getting married in May." He looked around in appeal.

Adeline smiled. "You were his star pupil."

Michael shook his head.

She pressed on. "And for several years now, you've been his peer."

"Never that," Michael objected.

"He said as much to me after you left for Egypt," Guy said. "You have the talent and the wisdom."

Michael looked around the group expecting support for his objections, but found only earnest expressions and nods. "You all agree?"

"Yes," Adeline said.

"There's no question," Guy added.

Michael wiped his hand across his forehead, then closed his eyes for a minute. He didn't feel ready to lead this group. How could he without the quiet strength of Robert? He'd always known what to do, what to say to bring out the best in everyone. The old saying sprang unbidden into his mind, "If not me, who?" No name came. He asked silently for guidance and heard a quiet chuckle in his mind.

Robert? Is that you? He felt a presence behind him that radiated a warm strength. Calm assurance washed over him. Michael opened his eyes and looked around the group again. "I'll never be able to replace him, but if you feel I could serve in this capacity, then I accept."

"Thank you," several people said at once.

"Excellent," Adeline said.

Guy sat forward, his face relieved but still somber. "Now, let's meditate together in honor of our friend and mentor, Robert Rhodes."

Michael closed his eyes, grateful for the quiet. His head swirled with the changes he was facing. He sent up a silent prayer for guidance. After a moment he caught the faint scent of sandalwood, the essential oil Robert had always worn. Perhaps he was not lost altogether.

The chime that ended meditation reached Michael from a long distance. He stretched his fingers, willing himself back. Conversations started around him. He opened his eyes and stood. A wave of dizziness washed over him. He steadied himself on the back of the chair, then turned to the lodge. No one seemed to have noticed.

Adeline already had on her coat. Michael quickly made the rounds to say goodbye, asking who would be at the service, thanking them for their vote of confidence, but assuring them he would need help. He wished another couple goodnight, then turned to look for the next person. Only the circle of empty chairs remained. Someone would return them to their proper places. He'd have to find out who cleaned the place now that he had accepted the responsibility of leading the group. Who held keys? But all the mundane details would have to wait. He didn't want to keep Dr. Abernathy waiting. It was almost eight o'clock.

He walked into the hallway and found Guy standing by the door. "I suppose business can wait until next week," Guy commented, as he helped Michael into his coat.

"That would be best. You'll be at the service?"

"Of course."

"Where can I meet you?"

"I live here," Guy said with a wry smile. "I'm the caretaker."

Michael tapped his forehead. "I forgot."

Guy simply shrugged.

Michael caught a glimpse of himself in the hall mirror. Red, blurry eyes. His tie askew. He ran a hand through his hair, vaguely wondering how long he'd been awake. "Think they'll let me into St. Anthony's Club looking like this?"

Guy straightened his tie for him, then patted him on the shoulder. "Everything will be all right."

Michael looked into his friend's steady eyes. "I can never replace him, Guy."

"No one is asking you to. Go get some sleep."

Michael walked down the steps. Lawrence had pulled the limo up next to the brownstone. He opened the back door with a nod. As soon as he slid behind the wheel, he put up the privacy window, perhaps sensing that Michael needed the quiet. Michael sank into the seat, deciding to meditate so he'd be somewhat alert for his next meeting. He woke with a start when Lawrence opened the door again, announcing their arrival.

Michael straightened out his jacket and walked up the marble steps of the club, moving from the familiar comfort of his group's headquarters into the elegance of the Le Clair family's club in town. An enormous chandelier dominated the front entrance. He approached the concierge who stepped out from behind the desk. "This way, sir."

Michael followed down carpeted hallways, passing the portraits of famous members, tall potted palms and orange trees marking out quiet nooks, to an elevator that swooshed silently upward. They emerged into another long hallway and walked halfway down to a set of double doors. The concierge knocked and the door opened from within. Arnold's large frame blocked the entrance.

An unexpected wave of relief washed through Michael. "It's good to see you."

The head of Le Clair family security waved Michael inside a surprisingly modern suite. The sleek wooden floors gleamed beneath Turkish rugs, but the expanse of windows overlooking the city drew his eye. Ice clicked in a glass, and Michael turn to find a chrome bar in one corner. Dr. Abernathy held out a glass of some burnt amber liquid. "I expect you need some fortification."

Michael accepted the drink, then looked around for a seat.

"Over here." Dr. Abernathy indicated a table near the windows. "Hungry?"

Michael shrugged. He hadn't eaten the night before and had only nibbled on the plane. He should be hungry, but only felt empty and cold.

"Soup?"

"I guess I should eat something."

"I'm sorry for your loss, son."

Michael sank into the chair and loosened his tie. "I was just in Glastonbury," he said almost at random.

"How did you find things?"

"I hardly had time to see the house, but everything seemed fine. We were at the Well when I got the news."

"What do you know so far?"

Michael told him what Jacob had shared with the group. He took a sip of what turned out to be cognac. It burned its way down his throat, then spread a fine fire through his torso.

"We've done a bit of poking around ourselves," Dr. Abernathy said.

"The group is grateful for any help."

"Nonsense. You're family now."

Another knock interrupted them. Arnold opened the door, and a white clad waiter brought a tray to the table and lifted the cover from the dish as if he were unveiling a masterpiece. The smell of French onion soup wafted up and Michael's stomach answered with a gurgle. "That was fast. Thank you."

Dr. Abernathy waited until Arnold had shown the man out, then talked while Michael ate. "We cross referenced the New York and New Jersey DMV with the names we know and found a black Mercedes owned by one James Smith. His fingerprints match Karl Mueller's. He's working for Cagliostro now. We suspect we've found our killer."

"And that the police never will." Arnold turned a chair around and sat straddling it.

"But you found it so easily," Michael said.

"Only because I have access to certain files," Arnold answered.

Michael had seen enough of his methods not to doubt him. He mopped the last of the soup up with a scrap of roll, then pushed the tray away.

"What did they steal?" Arnold asked.

"Crystals. Robert did some psychic research for us on a collection that was willed to the order by a member from the Bay Area. Robert was on his way to our headquarters to return them."

"You're certain they were with him?" Arnold asked.

"Yes, he thought they'd been programmed in Atlantis. That one of them was a sentinel for the Tuaoi Stone."

Dr. Abernathy let out a low whistle. "Do you concur?"

"Robert is—" Michael lowered his head "—was the best psychic I've ever known. I trust his judgment. He wrote a report, but we didn't have time to discuss his findings."

"Have you read it?" Dr. Abernathy asked.

Michael shook his head.

Arnold leaned forward. "Can you access it?"

"I don't want to rush the family."

Dr. Abernathy looked at Arnold, who nodded. "A private collector in Austria reported some items missing yesterday. One was a large crystal thought to be an important Atlantean artifact," Dr. Abernathy said.

Michael hit the table in frustration. "Damn."

"What is this Tuaoi Stone?" Arnold asked.

"Metaphysical tradition holds that the whole of Atlantis ran off the energy of an enormous crystal, several stories tall," Michael explained. "Cayce saw it in a temple with a retractable roof. It provided the power for ships, houses—the whole shebang. I'll bet there was more than one, though."

Dr. Abernathy nodded. "If Cagliostro is gathering Atlantean crystals, perhaps he's located some important artifact. Or even found the Tuaoi Stone."

"That crystal would be very large," Michael said. "I doubt any museum or private collector has it; I'd know about it. It must still be buried at the bottom of the Atlantic."

Arnold leaned his chair forward. "Let's stick to the facts. We know that he's stealing crystals. Are there others he's likely to target?"

Michael closed his eyes and tried to visualize the names of museums and private collectors holding such artifacts. "The organization keeps a list. My own files are in storage."

"Where?"

"At Grandmother Elizabeth's." He'd boxed up his apartment rather quickly after Anne was ready to travel. Difficult to get to now. Robert had a duplicate. Even harder to reach.

Arnold got up, opened his cell phone, and pushed a button. After a few seconds, he said, "I need the plane." His voice grew muffled as he walked back into the living room.

"We're going somewhere?" Michael tried to mask his dismay.

Dr. Abernathy chuckled. "No, Arnold is following up a lead about the whereabouts of Cagliostro. You have a funeral to attend and—"

"Some research to do," Michael finished for him. He started to stand up.

Dr. Abernathy held up a hand. "But first, you need to sleep."

Michael sank back into the chair. "I gave up my apartment before we left for England."

"We have room here."

5

Anne woke when the celestial tides stir the earth awake before the dawn. The birds had begun tentative chirpings just outside the window and by the time she'd finished her morning shower, they were in full song. She rummaged through her suitcase and found some clothes. Downstairs, she threw on Cynthia's cloak and began the climb up the Tor. Her calves started to burn half way up, but she soon reached the top. She sat against the stone tower and turned her face to the glowing horizon. Today, there was no voice from the long past, no vision of a standing stone. But the present was enough. The grey mists gradually gave way to the soft greens of spring as the sun peeked over the edge of the world.

A lamb ambled over and sniffed around her, then took a tentative nip at her cloak. Laughing, she pushed the youngster away. It scampered over to its waiting mother, nudged its nose under her belly and nursed, its black tail swishing back and forth. Anne leaned her head back, enjoying the warmth of the sun on her face. After a few minutes, a shadow blocked the light. She opened her eyes to a grey, thick bank of clouds that had blown in from the ocean. A cold drizzle started up. Pulling up the hood on the cloak, she headed for the house. She'd hoped to visit Chalice Well today and walk over to Wearyall, to explore the sites Michael had mentioned. But not in this rain. She'd wait for sun. Or at least until she acclimated to the English weather.

After a quick breakfast of toast and tea, Anne found herself drawn to the front office. She opened a few drawers, but felt no inclination to get down to work. She lit a fire and took out the manuscript. As soon as she settled in the well-worn armchair, she heard a scratch at the back door. She jumped up and hurried to the back door, but the porch was empty. She looked around the back yard and up the slope of the Tor. Two lambs chased each other, but she saw no red and white hound. Now she was imagining things. She walked back, settled into the armchair again and opened the manuscript.

AFTER THE EMERGENCE CEREMONY, the new citizens of Atlantis went back to their families to share what the oracle had told them. In their honor, the Council threw a party at the palace that night. It usually ushered in the dawn. The tension the initiates all felt before the ceremony melted into a spring rush of enthusiasm. Steady Erythe, whose expectations to work in agriculture had been confirmed, danced into the night, flitting from partner to partner like a mayfly. Megan resembled her shy friend more than herself, slipping away into the shadows to savor the intricate fruit punch and consider her future. She'd heard stories about the Crystal Matrix Chamber, of course, but the exact nature of their responsibilities was a mystery to her.

Pleione and Diaprepes sat at a table near the doors that now stood open to the balcony. Snippets of their conversation with friends drifted to Megan's ears.

"The Crystal Matrix Chamber? Such an honor."

"The training is demanding. Do you think you'll see much of her?"

Then later. "What a surprise. When was the last apprentice chosen for that temple?"

"It's been years. The Guild Mistress was concerned."

Megan wandered into the gardens of the palace where the members of the High House, the house of her father's mother, lived and worked. They coordinated the functioning of all Atlantis, from the operation of the temples to the growth of crops and trade. All the guilds reported to them. Eden was the capital, the major city on the central island, and every ten years the leaders of the other islands met here. Megan belonged to her mother's family, the famous healers from the north, not her father's, who ruled over all Atlantis. Now she also belonged to the Crystal Guild.

She turned from the laughter and music, and walked up the slope of the sacred hill toward the Temple of Poseidon and Cleito. The gate in the golden wall that surrounded the temple opened with a swing. Inside, the silver walls glinted in the moonlight. The statue of Poseidon grazed the ceiling of the ivory roof inlaid with gold, silver and orichalc, the famed Atlantean metal. Six winged horses drew his golden chariot and one hundred Nereid surrounded him, all riding dolphins. They in turn were circled by the five sets of twins who had been the original founders of the land, her father's almost mythical ancestors.

A muffled cough echoed from behind one of the statues. Megan stepped into the shadow of the dolphins, then peeked around. A man and woman, heads bent together, talked quietly. Something about the man caught at Megan's breath. Of medium height, but as solid as a draft horse, his shoulders and chest filled his robe. The muscles of his forearms stood out like ropes. He threw back his head and laughed, setting small shells and beads braided into his smoky black hair dancing. She imagined his hair grazing her cheek, the arms reaching out. Megan shook her head, trying to place him, but the memory hovered at the edges of her mind, elusive as the ocean's horizon on a misty day. Their voices grew more distinct. The scrap of a sandal sounded close by. She slipped out before they discovered her.

She walked home instead of returning to the party. The sky was still dark. In her room, she slipped into bed and lay listening to the ocean breeze play in the palms, trying to quiet the flame that voice had ignited in her. Her memory of this man refused to come, and yet he was so familiar. She tried to think about the ceremony. Had it really been just this morning? Never lying here dreaming of her future had she imagined working with the giant crystals, although she'd always had a facility with the stones. Small tabbies lay scattered about her room. She reached out and cradled one in her palm. When the sky grew pale in the east, she finally fell asleep.

Late the next morning, Megan took her time gathering her clothes, her garnet earrings, her favorite shells, and a few brightly colored pillows from the large stack on her bed. After she moved into her new quarters, she'd see what else she needed. It wasn't like she was leaving home forever.

Downstairs, her aunt pressed a huge mug of orange and passion fruit juice into her hand. "For your head," she said and winked. But Megan had left the party before drinking enough wine to need this much juice. She thanked her aunt, took a few sips and slipped the mug beneath the low bench in the garden. The grand matriarch, the eldest grandmother of her clan, sat nearby. The rest of the family gathered round, their bronze and creamy faces smiling. The grand matriarch cleared her throat and the adults hushed. Children still ran through the garden, the smallest screeching in delight at being chased. A sharp look from her grandmother sent the child's mother running to quiet her.

"Today you leave our home to go study with the Guild Masters of the Crystal Matrix Chamber. You may not realize this, but you had an ancestor who helped to set the Great Stones. Now we have the honor of sending another member of our family to serve there." Her umber face reflected the sun like a small moon. "Study hard and play well, Megan. But remember we are still here for you. This place will always be your home."

Sudden tears filled Megan's eyes, a confusion of sorrow, exhilaration, fear and one emotion she still could not name, a warmth in her belly when she remembered the laugh she'd heard in the musky dark last night. But like a child, she flung herself into her great mother's arms. The matriarch pushed her hair from her face and kissed her forehead in blessing. The tears passed like quicksilver. Now full of the adventure, she surged to her feet and spread her arms, trying to hug everyone at once. She was sent off by congenial laughter, fond tussling of her hair, little pieces of advice: "Study hard, but have some fun." "Don't be afraid to ask questions." "Your second cousin is near that temple." "Come back to see us soon." The children ran around laughing, not understanding the fuss, but enjoying it nonetheless.

They walked her out to the lawn to her father's conveyance. Apparently, he'd stayed the night. Her uncles finished loading her trunk and her father opened the back door for her. "Ready?" Megan nodded and got in. He closed the bubble top, then started the vehicle. A few stray tears wet her cheeks as she watched the waving crowd grow smaller.

Diaprepes headed straight for the ocean and dove beneath the waves, treating Megan to a jaunt among the fish and waving kelp. He let the craft rest quietly for a few minutes so the schools of fish reformed. From a distance came the song of a whale. Megan twisted to see if she could spot the giant, but saw only the blue water lit by the filtered sun. Diaprepes watched her for a while, then said, "Wonders await you, my dear." He winked and turned to her mother. "Hungry?" Pleione nodded vigorously, and they shot up out of the water and headed toward the shore.

Her parents flew to a pleasant restaurant in one of the merchant districts, talking easily once they arrived, speculating about her eventual role in the guild after training. Megan half listened, giving herself over to the moment. Hummingbirds shot through the patio, their ruby throats and emerald green bodies glinting amongst the scarlet fuschia. People called to each other on the street below, laughing, lounging in the doorways of their shops. Eden seemed reluctant to stop celebrating.

Then the time came to drop Megan off at her home for the foreseeable future. She pushed her nose to the window when they drew close. The complex was laid out in careful proportions, the Grand Hall a golden mean rectangle, the Crystal Matrix Chamber itself in the center of a tightening spiral of standing stones, like a flower at the end of a curved stem.

Diaprepes sat his silver craft down on the landing pad away from the headquarters of the Crystal Guild and turned to Megan. "This is it, my little dolphin. Do you want us to come with you to the house or drop you off here?"

Megan glanced around. "Where am I going, exactly?"

Pleione pointed past the complex to a villa tucked into the hillside.

"I'll walk," she said. "But the trunk?"

"Someone will pick it up." Diaprepes spread his arms and Megan hugged him goodbye, then her mother, and shouldered her bag. With a quick wave, she turned and walked across the landing pad where she took a path that meandered past the large golden buildings. She resisted the urge to look back. That was always bad luck in stories. She climbed the hill, passing garden nooks brimming with color, a splashing fountain. The water drew her and she sat on a stone for a few minutes, letting the sound soothe her. A breeze played with a set of wind chimes for a moment. She walked on. The gardens gave way to an open field that then turned into a stand of almond trees filled with buds. Above the orchard stood the villa, tucked into the hill. Megan scrambled up three steps to the porch and knocked on the door of her new home.

The house matron, a crone with pillow breasts and grey hair, eight hundred years old if she was a day, led Megan to her room. She introduced herself as Thuya, an Egyptian name. "Here's the dining room," she announced as they passed a room set with two long tables. "A classroom." Megan caught a glimpse of a long row of pillows and all shades of quartz set at intervals against the wall. They turned down a corridor. "One of the kitchen gardens." Green vines climbed a white string lattice. One more turn. "And your apartment is the last one on the left." Thuya opened the door and stood aside. "Welcome, Megan. It's been a long time since we've had a new apprentice. I'm glad I have a novice to look after again." She smiled, her brown eyes warm. This woman was wide where Megan's mother was narrow, short where Pleione was tall, but Megan relaxed, comforted by her presence. She shouldered her bag with a word of thanks and closed the door of her new home.

She'd been assigned a suite, the first room a small sitting area with a desk on one side. The sleek chrome and glass console holding her communication screen contrasted with the homey furnishings of her sitting area, a low couch upholstered in a loose weave, teal fabric with a small pine table in front. She went to the desk and ran her finger over the top of the screen, thinking about the stories of how communication had been telepathic in the not too distant past, how children had grown into full consciousness much earlier than now.

In the back room she found a cozy bedroom with a chest of drawers and a narrow bed covered by a simple coral spread. Her trunk already sat next to it. An alcove held a low mahogany table for an altar, now empty. Megan spent the afternoon unpacking, spreading her shells and pillows, moving them from the front couch to her bed, then back again. She placed a crystal sphere that had been a gift from her father's family in the center of her altar and lay on the bed, where she promptly fell asleep.

When she woke, the room was dark. She went to her desk and turned on the silver console. Dinner was over. She also found her schedule and a map of the facility. "Nine o'clock—meet with Govannan." She checked the list of names and found he was the head of the Crystal Matrix Chamber. A second message referred her to the rules of the house, which she read twice. She delved into the archives of the order, rapidly shifting between files, trying to decide where to begin. But as she read, her eyes kept closing. So she pulled the light muslin curtains closed, hung up her clothes and lay down in the small bed, where she fell asleep.

A knock woke her. She propped up on her elbow and looked around, startled by the unfamiliar surroundings. Morning sun brightened the curtains cover the window. Then she remembered where she was. The knock came again. "Yes?"

Instead of answering, Thuya bustled in. "You missed dinner last night." She deposited a tray with fruit and yogurt on the table in the sitting room and put a hand on Megan's forehead. "No fever. I suspect all the excitement finally caught up with you."

Megan nodded.

"I'll see you tonight, though?"

"I'll be prompt."

"Good. Just leave the tray in the hallway," Thuya said and left as quickly as she'd come, leaving behind a stir in the air.

Megan washed up in a small basin, deciding to visit the bathhouse before the evening meal, and quickly ate her small breakfast. Then she reached into the armoire and pulled out the unfamiliar robe of her new guild. The fabric felt substantial between her fingers, but the shifting white-violet still gave Megan the uneasy feeling something hovered just out of the range of her vision. She slipped the robe over her head, gave her head a shake so her brown curls bounced back into place, and went in search of her instructor.

THE OFFICE of the head of the Crystal Matrix Chamber overlooked the dome of the temple, now gleaming in the early sunlight. Govannan sat reading through the morning message crystals. A proposal from the New Knowledge Guild had snagged his attention, something to slow down the mysterious new illnesses cropping up. It sounded reasonable enough, but something bothered him.

A soft knock on his door pulled his attention away. "Megan is waiting," his assistant announced.

"Please tell her I'll be there in a minute." His assistant nodded and left the room. He'd have to speak with them later, and when he did, handle it delicately. Eager to meet their new addition, Govannan took the message crystal out of the reader and placed it in the proper tray, then got to his feet. He hadn't seen Megan since she was a child of six, running around in her mother's garden. He tugged at his robe and ran a hand through his hair, then stopped himself and moved to the door.

He found her sitting bolt upright on one of the chaise lounges arranged around the comfortable antechamber where he received visitors. She rose when he entered, her face flushed. She was short for a central Atlantean, with lustrous brown hair, pale skin and startling blue eyes. She took after the branch of her mother's family that had recently come from the northern island. He did not find her beautiful, but this was trivial compared to the bond they shared. As guild members, they were family at the very least.

"Megan." He put his hand on her shoulder and felt a slight tremor. "An Alban name?" he asked to put her at ease.

"Yes. I'm named after my great aunt."

He introduced himself. "I know your parents, of course."

Megan's shoulders relaxed a notch.

"Welcome to our guild." He gestured toward a seat. "But you're not just joining the Crystal Guild. You've been chosen to work in the Matrix Chamber itself. A high and rare honor."

She blushed a deeper red. "Yes, sir."

"Please call me Govannan. I imagine you have many questions; our work is not well known outside the temple."

"Good. I mean, I thought I wasn't well informed."

"Not at all. Let me give you a brief introduction. And then, we're in luck.

58

A delegation from Sirius is beaming in. You can watch the crystal in action."

"Thank you." Megan sat forward, fire in her pale blue eyes.

"Our temple complex," he waved his hand in a circle, "sits on one of the major energy vortexes of the earth. The main task of the crystal in the Matrix Chamber is to keep this vortex clear and balanced. Only the most experienced and gifted work on this task. This crystal not only keeps the planet in equilibrium, it harmonizes the earth with the higher dimensions and other star systems. This allows us to use the crystal for its more ordinary tasks— communication and teleportation."

Megan watched him intently.

Govannan sensed a question. "Yes?"

"I realized other life forms came and went. I've met them at official events with my father, but I," she flushed again, "I thought they came in ships."

Govannan smiled. "A common misconception. But ask yourself, why were these aliens you met in humanoid form?"

"You mean—"

"The planet dictates the form the being takes. Here most intelligences coalesce as humanoids, with some differences, I grant you. When we travel to other star systems, we also take different forms—dolphins or crystalline beings on Sirius, for example. Of course, the Pleiadians look much like us. We're more closely related to them. But, you know this. Your father is from a Pleiadian line."

Megan nodded.

Govannan closed his eyes and sent his awareness to the Crystal Matrix Chamber, then opened them almost immediately. "Now is a good time to go down. The preparations for the transport are just beginning. We can watch most of the process."

They walked to the temple. Once inside, Govannan took Megan to the observation balcony and motioned for her to take a seat. The young woman could not take her eyes off the towering crystal. It had been so long since he'd worked with someone new, he'd forgotten what an awesome site it was. The crystal rose at least three stories from a wide base, narrowing a bit at about the first story, then soared away toward the glass dome where the six gleaming flanks met in a translucent point.

He cleared his throat to get her attention. "I want you to open all your senses and observe, but you must not engage the energies. This is very important. Remain passive and notice everything you feel. Later, we'll meet again and you can tell me what you picked up. This is the best way to begin. It will help us know where to start your training."

Megan settled herself for meditation.

"Good," Govannan smiled, approving her choice. "Just a few minutes, then observe."

Megan nodded again.

"After the transport, you are free until tomorrow morning."

"Yes, sir. I mean, Govannan."

"Welcome to our family. I'm glad to have you here."

MEGAN WATCHED Govannan leave the balcony. Her pulse beat in her throat. Here he was, the very man she'd seen in the Poseidon Temple last night. The head of her division in the Crystal Guild. Perhaps that explained the familiarity she'd felt when she first saw him. A premonition of what was to come. That must be it. She pushed the giddiness away. She had to pay attention.

But her eyes strayed to Govannan as he walked to the first layer of inlaid designs on the tiled floor below, his powerful frame contrasting with the slender crystal points outlining the perimeter of the circle. He reached the second layer of the ring, where he paused and seemed to gather himself. Megan closed her eyes, pushing away the recurring image of the shells in Govannan's hair dancing in the smoky black strands as he strode across the temple. She finally settled, her breath only a flutter. Then she opened her eyes slowly and looked for him. He'd taken his place in what looked like a circle, but Megan sensed more complex energies at work. Invisible lines zigzagged across the floor. The twelve workers began a low chant which was repeated three times. Then they started to interlace harmonies that built on each other, enlivening those invisible lines she sensed. The harmonies layered in complexity, and then sharp dissonant notes cut across the humming peace, sung by a short, round woman near Govannan. Several of the smaller crystals lit up in answer. The light brightened as a man echoed the dissonant notes an octave lower than the notes the woman had sung, and the stones shot out beams of white-violet light, the same color as the robes of the workers. Lights flickered inside the giant rock, then fractured into rainbows. The different frequencies of the colors called out to Megan, the reds confident and bold, the blues cool as water, the greens—an image of Erythe formed in her mind and she laughed.

Another woman in the circle took a small crystal from around her neck which she positioned in her right hand. The others did the same. They pointed these stones at the enormous crystal in the middle and amplified their chant. The tall crystal sang to life, lighting up and vibrating in a deep tone that shook Megan's teeth in their sockets. She swam in the currents. Light from the crystal flickered on the walls. She melted in an eddy of butter yellow, then surfaced to the sound of a new chant. One strand was a deep bass; a second rich baritone pulled at her consciousness and she flowed toward the sound. A pitch sounded in her head, the perfect match to the baritone, but she resisted humming it out loud. She looked around the circle, searching for that voice, and found him. Govannan. His head was thrown back, a look of ecstasy on his face. His skin glowed, saturated with light. Megan yearned to join him, to give voice to the sound that mated with his, to allow her voice to twine around his. But the success of this transmission depended on the precision of the sound emanating from the group. The sound in her head blended, felt like a necessary strand even, but she kept silent as instructed.

The chant rose to an almost painful pitch. Inside the stone, a cloud swirled golden, then grew dense. A form began to take shape. The chant continued unabated. Megan's head ached with the unreleased energy. The shape inside the crystal solidified. Somehow, she knew not how, the form stepped out and morphed into a human male, only taller with a conical, sloped skull. The glow formed again, and a woman followed. The process continued until six beings, human except for their elongated heads, emerged from the central crystal. The workers slowed the chant, and the main transport crystal subsided, the rainbows folding in on themselves. The lights in the small crystals all went out at the same instant and the room seemed to give out a long heavy exhale.

Megan sagged against the wall behind her, only now aware she'd been holding her body taut as if she were witnessing a difficult birth. She pushed herself to her feet and went down the stairs, perching on a bench away from the main door. The newly arrived Sirians chose robes, the electric blue associated with their world, and Govannan escorted them out. Her eyes followed him. The lesson was over for now and she was on her own. But the only thing she wondered was when she would see him next.

A small group of workers stood to the side of the enormous crystal that was still sending out echoes of energy. They began a slow crooning chant that lulled the eddies in the huge stone to sleep, like a boat rocking on small waves in the hot afternoon sun. Megan slipped out before they finished, overwhelmed with sensation. Outside, the angle of the sun told her it was still mid-morning, but she headed for the bathhouse, intending to soak until the aching swirls in her own body subsided. Then she'd go back to the villa and meet her housemates over lunch, hopefully grounded and more herself.

6

Govannan escorted the Sirian ambassador and his party down the path Megan had taken the day before, enjoying the silent touching of minds. The group walked in a golden harmony, still resonating with the energies of the transport. They shared his joy that Megan had at last arrived after all these years of waiting. That she'd found the right tone at once, swimming in the currents of sound and light. That he looked forward to teaching her to work with the giant crystal, to the years of slow and patient instruction, slowly building in complexity, in subtlety, until the culmination, a journey such as the one this group had just completed. He and Megan would stream through the universe together, bursting in showers of light.

The silver tinkle of laughter brought him back from his imaginings, and he looked up to see one of the women glancing at him, her long head cocked to the side, her emerald eyes amused. Govannan blushed, and she sent him a reassuring mental nudge, saying without words that she too had discovered a lover, had waited long for that moment of union, that the wait was almost as enjoyable as the first act of love. He nodded to her, and she turned away just as he brushed up against a wall in her mind. She'd closed a part of herself to him. He shook like a horse, throwing his hair back, the shells clicking musically, taking no offense that she kept parts of herself private. After all, the Sirians were an ancient and wise people, one of the elder star civilizations who had guided the growth of life on earth.

They arrived at the vehicle pad and he gestured toward their new escort, forcing himself to speak aloud. Crisp, discrete words did not carry the nuance of telepathy, the bursts of imagery, the swirls of emotion. "May your visit be fruitful, your honor."

The senior ambassador inclined his head in a slight bow. "We thank you for your service, Master Govannan." His voice held the tones of a reed flute. "I would speak more with you on another visit."

"I am ever at your service." Govannan returned his bow.

The group flowed into the glass domed vehicle, and Govannan strode off toward his office. But halfway there, he turned into a favorite alcove garden and sat by the fountain, watching sparrows peck between the flagstones. One hopped into the stone basin and, spreading her wings, lowered her small, brown body into the water where she shook vigorously, sprinkling him with tiny drops. Then the bird hopped out and sat in a beam of sunlight to dry. The wind chimes spoke in the breeze. Govannan stood and stepped around the bird, who sat unperturbed in her sunbeam, eyes closed, completely at peace. He, however, was late for a meeting.

Govannan reached his office and snatched up the relevant message crystal from his desk, then hurried to the main headquarters of the Crystal Guild. He snuck through a side door of the large meeting room and was engulfed in the general din of conversation. Representatives were still settling in, so he took his seat in the circle, nodding to Evenor, the representative from the Guild of Governors. Opaque blue selenite panels divided the chamber from the circular vestibule that connected to the outer hallways. Inside, three tiers of seats circled around a large round scrying crystal that sat in the middle, its surface frosty at present.

Evenor stood and the guilds sorted themselves out, finding their seats. Quiet replaced the cacophony of voices. The central crystal began to clear. Evenor looked around the table, meeting the eye of each delegate before he spoke. "Today we meet at the request of the New Knowledge Guild," he looked toward their senior representative, "the newest member of this body."

Govannan wondered if he'd imagined the emphasis on "newest," but doubted his musical ears would miss a tone of voice. He allowed his eyes to slide over the group from the New Knowledge Guild and noted that they had not missed the implication. Several shifted in their chairs, and one woman turned to a colleague to comment under her breath. Fresh from a transport, his own senses were stretched to their finest attunement, and he noticed a certain—what was it exactly—flatness. He stretched his senses further. After all, each guild carried a certain frequency of energy. People who were talented in the arts vibrated in a different way than members of Gaia's Guild. Perhaps the delegation from the New Knowledge Guild had merely subdued their understandable excitement and anxiety over their proposal, but still, there was something. He turned his attention back to Evenor.

". . . hear their ideas and deliberate on the best course of action." Evenor sat down and folded his hands on the table in front of him.

Surid, the head of the New Knowledge Guild, stood and cleared his throat, a little ostentatiously in Govannan's opinion. He gave himself a little shake. They deserved a fair hearing and here he was passing judgment before they'd even begun. Surid smiled at the gathering. "Thank you, Guild Masters, for your attendance today. We at the freshly formed," here he nodded toward Evenor, "New Knowledge Guild have made a momentous discovery. As you are well aware, new and mysterious illnesses have been cropping up amongst us." As he spoke, images of people suffering from these mysterious ailments appeared in the surface of the central crystal. "Aches and pains, general malaise, premature aging, physical symptoms of all kinds. This has been particularly dismaying considering we have prided ourselves on the health, vigor and intelligence of the Atlanteans."

Was 'prided' the right word? Govannan wondered.

"At first we imagined this a passing illness, or a series of viruses that were challenging our systems. But the Healers Guild," he nodded toward the group of blue-robed representatives, "seemed unable to stop the spread and indeed the proliferation of the maladies. Now, Atlantis seems to be at a crisis point."

Evenor straightened in his chair and several members of the audience shifted uncomfortably. The crystal went blank.

Surid pushed on. "We have a theory."

Theory? Govannan pressed his fingers together. *Guilds usually called a meeting such as this to announce information or prophecy, not guesses.*

"We are all aware of the history of manifestation on this planet Earth. The creators perfected their plans in the etheric dimension before manifesting physical forms." Exquisite pictures filled the sphere—seals dived into aquamarine water, deer ran across a green meadow, a flock of parakeets launched themselves into the sky. "The creators manifested those blueprints into the reality of physical being."

Govannan nodded. The origin of life on earth was a familiar story to all Atlanteans.

"We at the New Knowledge Guild believe that physicality is now taking its own course, developing in ways not anticipated."

Nagaitco, a man from the Music Guild, leaned toward him. "What did he say?"

"Not anticipated," Govannan answered in an undertone.

"But—" Nagaitco wrinkled brow mirrored Govannan's own bewilderment.

"Yes, not anticipated." Surid enunciated the words distinctly.

The room buzzed with voices. Evenor raised his hand and the voices subsided. "Let us hear the entire presentation," he said in a voice so mild he might have been commenting on the weather. The crystal in the middle showed images of tall, light beings.

Surid nodded to the Master of the Guild of Governors and waited for absolute silence. Govannan felt another stab of annoyance.

"Of course, the first response people have when they are introduced to this idea is to say that the creators were incapable of making mistakes. And yet, do we not have evidence to the contrary? The illnesses exist and our talented healers," here he bowed in the direction of that guild's representatives, "still struggle."

Govannan would have thought the man was enjoying the Healing Guild's failure if such a thing were possible.

Surid drew himself up to his full height. "We proposed to check actual developments against the original blueprints. Once we have determined if our physical development has gone off course, we can correct the problems on this dimension."

A vast silence as chilly as the deepest waters of the Atlantic hung about the room. But the cacophony of emotion beneath that silence plucked at

Govannan's empathic senses like a lyre buffeted by gale winds. The Guild Masters sat in various attitudes of disbelief, some openly stunned, others hiding their feelings behind polite smiles. Govannan filtered out the emotions of the room for a moment to check his own response. The creators were beings of cosmic intelligence, and he doubted their designs needed improvement. 'Doubted' was actually a polite mask for his certainty that anyone who thought the creators could have made a mistake was himself deluded.

"As a matter of fact, we've already begun to collect some samples," Surid announced.

The words struck Govannan like a blow to the chest. The room erupted in a cacophony of voices. "Already begun?" "Without our permission?" "Mistakes of the creators?" Evenor stood, holding his hands out like he was giving the group a blessing. The crystal in the center frosted over completely.

Govannan shielded himself from the chaos and focused on the head of the New Knowledge Guild, who was trying to speak over the din. Govannan closed his eyes and sent a deep probe into the man. The surface of his mind was filled with facts, anxiety about how his presentation would be received, catalogs of species to be checked. Beneath this were images of a little girl playing in a garden, a woman sitting in the shade of a mango tree laughing. Govannan sank deeper still, searching for the natural link all life shared, that basic connection to the One Source. It ran beneath the man's conscious awareness, like a secret underground stream, but Surid's mind seemed unaware of it. Instinctively, Govannan reached for the key crystal he carried with him at all times, his link to the Mother Stone, and directed a stream of energy to Surid to restore his connection. But the energy fell flat. Surid continued to talk, his mind separated from this deep inner stream of knowing. Govannan sat back heavily in his chair. How could this be? He'd never encountered such a case in an adult. Certainly young children needed nurturing to establish a firm connection with the One, but an adult? The head of a guild?

Evenor finally managed to restore order with the assistance of the Healers Guild, who chanted a quiet undertone that calmed and reassured. Evenor straightened his robes, nodding at a comment whispered in his ear. He looked around the room, again gathering the attention of each member of the group much as a shepherd gathers his flock. "The Elders will meet to seek balance in this matter."

Murmurs of agreement began, but Evenor held up his hand. He turned to Surid. "We will call for you to hear more testimony when we are ready."

Surid opened his mouth as if to protest, but must have thought better of it.

Evenor looked around again. "Let us be wise in what we say to others. There is some unrest in the city due to these illnesses. We do not wish to increase our fellow citizens' alarm, but to soothe it. Healing comes with calm."

Govannan hurried through the crowd without stopping to speak with anyone. He needed to find Rhea, the head of the Crystal Guild. She could help him understand what he'd felt from Surid.

MEGAN FLOATED like a piece of kelp in the middle of the hottest tub in the bathhouse. The waters had worked their magic. She took a deep breath and submerged, then tilted her face up and surfaced, a dolphin breaching, allowing the water to sluice off her body. Hurried footsteps approached and she reached for a wrap, still shy in her new surroundings. Thuya stopped at the edge of the pool, her face flushed, panting from her rush. "The Head Mistress has sent for you, child. You must come at once," she blurted out.

Megan clambered out of the pool. She toweled her hair while Thuya dried off her back. Megan grabbed her clothes and dressed quickly. Thuya held her at arm's length, as her mother had just yesterday, and straightened her hair and robe until Megan met her approval. "Now, come with me. I'll show you the way."

Megan followed, although privately she thought she could get there faster on her own.

"Of course you could, dear, but I want to tell you who you're going to see."

"Sorry," Megan said in an undertone.

Thuya chuckled. "No need to apologize. I know I'm an old woman. Now, pay attention. Rhea is the head of the Crystal Guild. Govannan leads the Crystal Matrix Chamber." She looked back at Megan, who nodded. "Rhea heard we have a new apprentice and wants to meet you."

Thuya led her to the Grand Hall, across from the building she'd met Govannan in this morning. "Let the Guild Mistress speak first, and only answer her questions. Don't introduce your own topic." She waited for an answer.

"I understand," Megan said.

"It is customary to bow in honor of the wisdom of the guild. Then stand and wait for her to invite you to sit."

"Yes, ma'am."

They made their way down a long hallway, Megan trying to silence the slap of her slippers on the wood floor. Thuya, with all her girth, made no noise at all. At the end of the hall, Thuya stopped, catching her breath again. She gave Megan a once over, straightened her hair again. "Such thick curls," she murmured. She gave Megan's robe one last proprietary tug, then nodded.

Glad she'd regained her composure in the bathhouse, Megan straightened her shoulders and knocked on the door. A young man her own age opened it and waved her in. He ushered her past a small reception room into a larger one, then closed the door behind her. A bank of windows commanded a view of the formal gardens of the complex. Columns of water from the tall fountain in the center spurted high into the air over the heads of circular beds of roses. An elegant desk with a slim communication screen atop it stood in one corner of the room. Shelves artfully arranged with scrolls, crystals and statues covered the wall behind. Megan looked around for the Guild Mistress and found her sitting on a low divan at the other end of the room, a tall palm arching over her head like the cobra that protected one of the Indian deities. Her hair haloed her face, a translucent cloud like a dandelion gone to seed. She gestured for Megan to come closer. She walked over and stood before the Guild Mistress. Green eyes looked deep into her, taking her full measure. Megan took a step back, a cub surprised by the power of the lioness. Then a smile lifted the corners of the Guild Mistress's delicate mouth, lighting up her face like the sun. Megan forgot all Thuya's careful instructions and introduced herself, then sat down in a chair opposite the Guild Mistress's divan. Remembering, she jumped back up. "I'm sorry."

"And I am Rhea." A smile flitted across her lips. "Please sit and make yourself comfortable. I wanted to welcome you to your new home."

Megan sat down and studied the rug.

"I understand you observed a transport today. Your arrival was well timed. Govannan will be here momentarily—"

Megan flushed a deep red that matched part of the rug's pattern.

"—and you can tell us what you experienced. This will help us decide what you should study first."

Before Megan could recover from this news, the door opened behind her and Govannan rushed into the room. "We have a problem. The New Knowledge Guild has already—"

Rhea cut him off with a gesture. He looked around, setting the shells in his braids jingling. "Megan," he said in surprise.

Her face flushed again and Megan cursed her fair skin. "Sir," she nodded at him, wishing she could disappear.

"Please have a seat." Rhea pointed to a chair with a potted palm between Megan and Govannan.

Megan moved back so the plant hid her face. A trickle of water ran down her neck from her damp hair, and she wiped it off on the sleeve of her robe.

Rhea rang a small silver bell by her side and the young man came in. "Bring us some juice, please." Govannan shifted in his chair, setting his shells off again. The assistant bowed slightly and left.

Rhea turned to Govannan. "The arrival of a new student in the Crystal Matrix Chamber is a momentous occasion, don't you agree Matrix Master?"

"Indeed, Guild Mistress."

Megan wondered at their sudden formality.

Govannan looked at her. "Please tell us what you experienced during the transport."

Megan looked at Rhea, who smiled encouragingly, so she began. "The people in the chamber formed a circle, but I felt energies running across the circle as well."

"Yes," Rhea said. "Were you able to figure out any of the formations?"

Megan shook her head. "It all happened so fast. When they started chanting, I saw colors and felt—" she groped for words.

"What colors did you see?" Rhea began to question her, and as she inquired about specific parts of the ceremony, Megan began to perceive a structure that she'd missed before. Rhea asked about the patterns in the circle, the preliminary chant, then the activation of the Sentinels.

The assistant arrived and handed out glasses of juice. Megan took a sip, and the combination of orange, mango and passion fruit reached a thirst left from her soak in the hot waters that she hadn't felt before. Refreshed, she relaxed under the Guild Mistress's guidance. "When the huge crystal lit up, it was hard to keep track. It shook my bones. I got lost in the swirls of colors."

Govannan nodded his head. "You'll get used to it."

"Did you hear any tones?" Rhea asked.

"I did." Megan sat forward in her chair eagerly. "A note that seemed to be a part of the chant that matched—" she looked down, suddenly remembering the aching intimacy of that song.

Rhea came to her rescue. "We in the guild become accustomed to the . . ." here the Guild Mistress paused, searching for the right word.

"Rapport?" Govannan offered.

"Yes," Rhea nodded at him, her eyes shining.

Megan looked from one to the other, briefly wondering about their relationship. Govannan had rushed into her office as if it were his own.

"The work we do brings our minds and hearts in close proximity," Rhea said.

Megan's heart sank. Of course they were lovers. Govannan was an accomplished man at the peak of his powers, the head of their division, Megan an untried beginner.

The Guild Mistress continued. "It can be uncomfortable to feel such familiarity with people you've just met, but the Thirteen chose you because your energy signature completes the circle."

"I heard it too, Megan." Govannan's husky voice reached into her and pebbled her flesh. She looked up at him and their eyes locked. "Welcome to the circle. We have been missing you."

Megan could hardly breathe. What was he saying to her? Had she misunderstood his relationship with Rhea?

"Welcome home." Rhea raised her juice, breaking the tension between them. Govannan reached for his drink, and they all touched the rim of their glasses together. "To the completion of the Crystal Matrix Circle," Rhea exclaimed.

"To the Circle," Govannan said.

"To the Circle," Megan murmured, her eyes on him.

"Now Govannan," Rhea took command again, "we need to decide where she should begin her education. I have an idea, but I'd like to hear your thoughts." Megan started to stand up, but Rhea stopped her. "This discussion is for your ears, too, my dear." Then she turned back to the Matrix Master.

He kept his eyes on Rhea. "She is sensitive, quite perceptive. Her responses are lightning fast."

"I agree," the Guild Mistress said, much to Megan's surprise.

"She needs to learn to hold her own in the midst of all the different energies. The power of the Crystal Matrix Chamber can overwhelm a new worker. She should start with less vital work—seasonal ceremonies." He glanced at Megan "I think she needs to tour the power spots and do ceremony to experience a wide range of people and places. After this, we can begin the special training of our own temple."

"Exactly so. We usually see eye to eye, my friend." She turned to Megan. "It is close to Beltane, the change of seasons in the northern isles. I'm going to send you to your mother's people first." She reached for her bell and gave it a slight shake. Her assistant came in and stood at attention. "Megan will be leaving for Avalon tomorrow. Please prepare transport."

"Yes, ma'am." He turned and left.

"Thuya will help you prepare." Govannan voice reached her in the midst of the swirl of emotions. She was going to the northern isles. It was a long-time dream. She'd finally get to visit her mother's homeland. But for Beltane. She'd be leaving the only man she wanted to explore those rites with here in Eden. And hadn't they said power spots, plural? Would she go elsewhere? When would she come back?

Rhea and Govannan sat beaming at her, looking as if they'd just given her the best present possible. Megan looked down at her hands and tried to steady herself. How could he smile at sending her away? She had arrived only yesterday. Hadn't he said—what had he said, really? She stood and looked at Rhea, avoiding Govannan's eyes. "Thank you. I guess I'll go get ready."

"Your time will pass quickly, my dear." Rhea's face showed she felt Megan's turmoil. "You will come home prepared for what awaits you here. You have a long life ahead of you."

7

On Wednesday morning, Michael sat in a pool of gold-tinted sunlight that fell through the stained glass window on the south side of the church. Circles and squares of sky blue, green and scarlet decorated the pews and walls. He'd waited outside until the casket was sealed, not because he was squeamish, but because that had been the tradition in his own family. Better to remember the person as they'd been in life. The body was a shell, and Robert was gone. Well, not gone exactly. He still hovered in the upper corner behind the choir, singing at the top of his—voice, he supposed, for he no longer possessed lungs in the strictest sense. How was it possible to properly mourn his beloved mentor when he was having such a good time at his own funeral? Michael shifted irritably, then scolded himself. Would he prefer Robert to be truly gone, simply a memory as someone had said at the wake?

In the family pew, Robert's wife, Laura, dabbed her eyes with a handkerchief. His son sat stiff and proper in his black suit, his own wife clutching his hand. Robert's daughter held her toddler on her lap. The child kept pointing to the corner that Robert hovered in and saying, "Ga Da," probably the closest she could come to "granddaddy." Michael hid a smile behind his hand, grateful for the confirmation.

Quite a bright light, isn't she? Robert sent.

A chip off the old block, Michael answered, then half-joked. *Now be quiet so I can hear the hymn.*

Robert snorted, or at least it sounded that way, and disappeared. He'd be back. He'd been popping in and out over the last three days, his mood growing more cheerful and his light brighter with every visit.

Guy had discussed it with Michael at the wake the night before. They'd sat in an outer room away from the family and business acquaintances. "He's between worlds, tying up loose ends here, connecting with lost friends and family there, preparing for his life review."

"How do you know?" Michael asked in a low tone.

Guy gave him a sharp glance. "All the books say so."

"The books," Michael repeated with mild distain. "I'd rather depend on direct experience."

Guy continued unperturbed, "But he'll go after the funeral. Conduct his life review. Move on to his next work."

Michael pushed his feet back and forth on the carpet, then asked, "So, why didn't I see Thomas?"

Guy shrugged. "Maybe you didn't know him well enough."

He remembered that Anne had seen her brother shortly after his death, but she hadn't said anything about it lately. Perhaps what Guy said was true.

Adeline bustled in and joined them. When Guy told her of Michael's experience, she leaned forward, eager to hear more. "Does he seem disturbed or confused?"

"On the contrary. He seems . . ." Michael hesitated, "happy." He shrugged in apology.

But Adeline nodded. "That's a relief. When someone's life is cut off like that, it can cause problems. The person has to reorient themselves if there's unfinished business."

"You've had experience with this?" Michael asked.

"Oh my, yes." Adeline looked around to be sure they weren't overheard. "I used to work with Frank, the man from the California lodge, exorcising houses."

"Really?" Guy leaned forward.

"Many of those spirits had met a violent end. We helped them reconcile and move on."

"But you haven't felt Robert?" Guy asked.

"Not yet. I expect I will tonight or during the funeral."

Other members arrived, and they began to reminisce. Michael joined in, savoring bitter sweet memories, relishing new tales. They had finished the evening late in an English pub, one of Robert's favorite places.

A sudden silence in the chapel brought Michael back to the present. The choir had finished their hymn. At a gesture from the director, they sat, scraping chairs and shuffling music sheets. A lone sniff sounded through the church. Michael rubbed his temples, hoping to unseat the dull headache that had been with him since he woke up this morning. Too much Queen's Blond Ale from last night, he supposed.

It's more than that. Robert's voice sounded in his ear. *But don't worry. You'll do just fine.*

What do you mean? Michael asked, but the minister had introduced Robert's wife, who was walking to the front to deliver part of the eulogy, and Robert gave her his full attention. She talked about how she'd met Robert, how it had been love at first sight. Michael thought it probably was a past life connection. Robert hovered in his corner, his light pulsing as she spoke.

One of Robert's long time business associates talked next. Then it was Michael's turn.

He walked quickly to the pulpit, note cards in his moist hands. Gulping water from the glass sitting next to the thin microphone, he looked out at the sea of faces—family, friends, business associates. Sprinkled among them was Michael's audience, the Lodge, a group most of the others had no idea existed. A few well-chosen words, nothing more, to soothe the hearts of those who'd stood by Robert as he led their ceremonies and come to him with their questions. He'd recruited them, trained them and finally conducted their initiations.

"I'm honored that the Rhodes family asked me to speak today," he began. "Robert was my dearest friend. I am an archaeologist," easier than Egyptologist, he thought. "Robert and I shared an interest in the past. Some of the most productive and pleasurable moments of my life have been spent in his company, delving into his extensive library. I want to thank Mrs. Rhodes for her indulgence in our pastime."

Laura waved her hand to dismiss this.

"His knowledge in our pursuits was profound, a fact that always amazed me considering how hard he worked," Michael nodded to the head of Robert's firm, "and how devoted a husband and father he was." The daughter wiped her eyes with a handkerchief.

The time will come soon when you no longer have to hide. Robert's voice sounded low in his mind.

"To those of you who shared our interest—" Here a few business associates looked around, surprised, but found no one in particular to focus on "—I say that Robert Rhodes was a great scholar, a great friend, and a luminous soul."

Robert's boss frowned at these last words, but Michael continued. "He will be missed more than my paltry words can say."

You shall do greater things than I, Robert quoted in his ear.

At this, Michael's throat closed and he squeezed his eyes shut, but the tears finally escaped, and he wept in front of the entire congregation. The minister came to him and escorted him to the edge of the platform, where Guy took him by the arm and led him back to his seat. He wiped his eyes. The headache was gone and he felt better than he had since getting the news of Robert's death.

Adeline patted his shoulder from the pew behind him. "Well spoken."

Michael nodded, now content in his silence. The minister announced the service would continue in Eternal Rest Cemetery. Somehow Michael couldn't imagine Robert resting for eternity. The family followed the pallbearers out with the congregation crowding behind.

Guy and Adeline hovered around him on the steps. "Are you going to the graveside?" Guy asked.

"I don't have my car," Adeline answered.

"Come with me," Michael said on impulse, and led them to the waiting limo.

His two friends looked at each other. Lawrence opened the door and, after a slight hesitation, they got in. Michael slid across the seat and faced them. The limo pulled out, and the police, mistaking them for family, waved them toward the front.

"At least we fit in," Michael observed.

Adeline laughed, then looked chagrined. Then, Michael and Guy burst out laughing.

"What?" Adeline asked.

"I think it's just tension," Guy said.

"I saw him, Michael," Adeline said. "I'm glad I finally saw him."

"Yes?"

"He looked proud of you."

Adeline looked at Guy, who shook his head. "I thought I felt a hand on my shoulder when I walked Michael back."

"Yes, he was with you," she said. "You know, I'm surprised Robert wasn't cremated."

"His family's tradition took precedence," Michael answered. "Robert said it wasn't worth upsetting Laura."

When they arrived, the crowd had thinned significantly. The family sat in a row of metal folding chairs before the casket and a heap of earth discreetly covered in a green tarp. The Lodge members gathered behind them. Stephen found them, then Diane, and they stood together in a tight knot. After the minister read from the liturgy and the group made the proper responses, he held up his hands in blessing. A sudden burst of light made Michael glance up to see if the sun had come out from behind a cloud, but the sky was a clear blue. He looked back, and standing beside the minister was Robert, radiant with light. A shimmering form waited behind him. Robert gazed at each of the lodge members in turn. Guy took a sharp breath. Michael felt an urge to salute him. Then Robert turned back to the form behind him and they disappeared.

Goodbye, old friend, Michael sent, but this time there was no answer.

THE DRIVE to Grandmother Elizabeth's house was a welcome respite from the surge of people at the wake and this morning's funeral. Michael had time to sit back and watch the scenery change from city to endless strip malls. He felt as empty as the repetitious display of chain stores. Finally they ended, giving way to rolling green hills, and peace of a kind settled over him.

Lawrence pulled up to the wrought-iron gate and the man in the booth pushed a button, nodding to them as they passed. They drove through the fenced pastures, dotted here and there with grazing horses. Around a bend, a new foal cavorted near its mother, legs wobbling.

"Two days old," Lawrence said. "The first one this year."

Michael watched the baby until the stand of oaks blocked the view. They pulled around the crescent driveway and stopped in front of the star-shaped reflecting pool. He made his way across the drive, gravel crunching underfoot. Inside, he climbed the sweeping stairway, and walked down the dark paneled hallway until he came to the library. The double doors stood open. Dr. Abernathy sat at the large desk, Arnold in a chair in front.

Dr. Abernathy waved him in. "Arnold has just returned."

Michael sat and Arnold continued. "He rented a house on the island and a yacht, but the locals say he comes and goes by plane."

"This is Cagliostro?" Michael asked.

"Yes," Arnold nodded. "He arrived yesterday. I couldn't dig up any information about his plans. Looks like he's put the fear of God into the people at the marina."

"Not quite God," Michael said in a low voice.

Arnold snorted at this. "I couldn't get a word out of them. I'm sure they'll report back that someone was snooping around. I did manage to get some cooperation, so I'll hear about his movements."

"Who?" Dr. Abernathy asked.

"One of the housekeeping staff."

Dr. Abernathy nodded.

"What island is he on?" Michael asked.

"Bimini," Arnold said.

"Of course," Michael said, "The Bimini Road. That's where they found the underwater stones back in the sixties. Evenly cut rocks that look like the top of a wall or road. People think it's a remnant of Atlantis."

"Go find those records of yours," Dr. Abernathy said to Michael. "We need to get ahead of Cagliostro this time."

Michael strode down to a building near the stables that looked like another barn, but served as an environmentally controlled storage facility for the family. Rows of file cabinets filled one wall. Michael found his cardboard boxes, scruffy beside the neat crates that stood in the middle of the room on raised wooden platforms. He rummaged for a while before he found the box with his Atlantis research, then stooped to pick it up.

"I'll get that for you, sir."

A young handyman stood behind him.

"I don't mind," Michael said.

"Dr. Abernathy's orders, sir."

Michael was learning not to argue with the staff. He followed the man back to the library where he placed the box on the coffee table between the two sofas as if it were fine china. "Will there be anything else?"

"No, thank you."

The handyman left. Dr. Abernathy sat behind the desk absorbed in paperwork. Arnold worked on his laptop on the opposite sofa. Michael set the box on the floor and shuffled through the files until he found one marked "Crystals and Other Stones." He pulled it out and sorted through articles he'd cut out, a bibliography, photos. Then he found it, a report he'd done for Robert on all known Atlantean crystal or stone artifacts.

It was two years old. He'd have to do a little updating, but probably wouldn't find much new material. Archaeology usually didn't change that quickly. He skimmed the list. The first page and a half listed crystals in museums around the world. Beneath each, the owner was noted, the provenance, a short description, then a report if any psychics had worked with the stone. Next were stone artifacts. A longer list of private collectors followed, similarly divided. He'd put the artifacts that had a confirmed existence, but whose present location was unknown at the end of the list.

"Holy shit," Michael looked up at both of them. "The Chintamani Stone."

Dr. Abernathy let out a long sigh. Arnold looked from one to the other, a frown on his face.

"The Chintamani Stone has a long history," Michael read his report. "The main stone is said to reside in Shambhala, high in the Himalayas. The Sanskrit translation is something like 'magical stone from another world'. Legend holds it was given to the Atlantean Emperor Tazlavoo by a visitor 'from the heavens'. Some say Orion, others Sirius. In Asia, the crystal is known as 'the jewel that grants all desires'. In the west, 'the Stone of Heaven'. Good esoteric sources claim the stone tunes the earth to the rhythm of the universe."

"Well, if it's in Shambhala," Arnold said, "we don't have to worry about that one."

"Actually, Helena Roerich, Nicholas's wife, was given a fragment of the Chintamani to wear when they traveled in Asia." He turned to Arnold. "The Roerichs were artists and mystics. They studied eastern philosophy and the Theosophical Society's teachings. In fact, they translated Blavatsky into Russian. In the 1930s, they traveled in the east, studying and searching for Shambhala."

"Did they find it?" Arnold asked.

Michael shrugged. "The expedition was harassed by the authorities. I doubt it. I'm sure they met with spiritual leaders who had contact themselves, but it's possible that they went there themselves."

He looked back at Dr. Abernathy. "Their biographer claims that Helena was chosen to represent 'the Mother of the World'. She was instructed to use the stone fragment to set the energies for the new age. The bad news is that this piece is connected to the main body of the stone in Shambhala."

"So where is this necklace?" Arnold asked.

"No one knows, really." Michael rubbed at his eyes. "Some say the Roerichs left it in Shigatse, where the Tashilumpo Monastery is located. It's supposed to be connected to Shambhala by underground tunnels. Other sources claim it's in . . ." he squinted, trying to remember, ". . . Agartha."

"And where is that?"

"The middle of the earth." Michael couldn't help but laugh.

Arnold favored him with a look.

"Or it could be in the American Museum of Natural History right here in Manhattan."

"I vote for that," Arnold said.

"You'll like this one. Others claim it is with the Kaaba in the great mosque in Mecca."

"Kaaba?" Arnold looked first at Michael, then Dr. Abernathy, who took a breath to explain. "It's a large black meteorite sacred to Islam."

"No, a large scarab from ancient Egypt," Michael argued.

"Whichever." Arnold cut him off. "If it's there, it's safe from both me and Cagliostro."

"Or," Michael held up a finger, "it could be in the Moscow Museum or the Roerich Museum in Moscow. His paintings are in several museums, but I think we can count those out."

"It seems one of our tasks will be to find this fragment." Dr. Abernathy's tone was mild.

Michael eyed him. "Only a lifetime's work."

MICHAEL SPENT the next day back in the city. His first stop was the American Museum of Natural History—an unlikely place for the Chintamani Stone, but perhaps that was a good reason to hide it amongst dinosaur skeletons, human skulls and neckties for the museum shop. He waved at the clerk behind the information desk, who recognized him from his old job at the Metropolitan Museum, and took the stairs to the curators' offices two at a time. He arrived at Dr. Nancy Langton's door and knocked. At his second knock came a grumpy "Yes?"

He pushed the door open, but didn't enter.

Nancy looked up, a scowl on her face until she saw him. "Michael." She popped up from her desk, arms open.

He gave her a quick hug, "It's good to see you," he said and plopped down in one of the chairs facing her desk.

She sat down and glanced at her computer. "Let me just save this." She pushed a few buttons on her computer, then turned back with a broad smile. "Now, to what do I owe the pleasure?"

"I've got a question for the best esoteric geologist in the business," he said. At the word 'esoteric', Nancy's eyes darted to the door. Michael reached around and swung it shut. "Still in the closet, I see."

"Not all of us have been taken into the bosom of a wealthy family," she scolded, but her smile belied the harsh words. "When's the big day? Do I get an invitation?"

"Middle of May," he said. "The family's secretary is handling all the arrangements."

"Family secretary," she repeated, lifting an eyebrow.

"Your name is on the list," Michael said before she could tease him anymore. "Speaking of families, how's yours?"

"Great. The kids are shooting up like weeds, as they say. Tom's good. So, what's up?" Her eyes shone in anticipation.

Nancy spent most of her days planning programs to interest children in rocks. Michael imagined he brought her juicier fare. He told her the story of the missing crystals, leaving out the grisly detail of Robert's murder. Better not to dip into those waters today. "So, I'm trying to get ahead of this thief and imagine what other crystals he would target."

"He?" Nancy tapped a pencil on her desk. "Women steal, too, you know."

"We know who it is."

"Then why don't the police go arrest him?"

Michael couldn't very well tell her that the police didn't know or how he'd come by this information, so he said, "Lack of hard evidence, money, political influence—the usual."

"So," she sat back in her chair, hands clasped behind her back, "you must be wondering if this fine establishment is housing the Chintamani Stone in secret."

Michael blinked. "That was quick."

Nancy laughed with the glee of a sprite who's just tweaked someone's nose. "What else could it be?"

Michael grinned in spite of his heavy heart. "Well?"

"I'll have to check the records."

"Surely they wouldn't be available for just anybody to see," Michael said.

Nancy cocked an eyebrow. "I'm not just anybody."

Michael blurted "I didn't mean to suggest—" then pulled up short when he saw her smile.

"No offense taken," she said. "Any other artifacts I should look for?"

"I can't think of any that might be here."

"Consult with Robert. He knows his rocks," she said. At the look on his face, she stopped short. "What?"

Michael took a breath to explain, but it caught in his chest.

"What is it?" Her voice carried the experience of a mother comforting a fractious child.

"Robert was killed during one of the robberies," he said.

"I hadn't heard." She moved to his side and put her hand on his shoulder. "I'm so sorry, Michael."

He struggled with himself. This was not the time or the place.

"You should be at home, or with your lodge. Not out here conducting business."

He shook his head. "The funeral was yesterday. It's time to get back to work."

"That's the worst time," Nancy said, "when things are supposed to be normal again. That's when it hit me with my father."

Michael nodded, mastering himself. "I have to find out what they're planning and stop them."

He left Nancy with her condolences and a promise to think of all the likely stones these thieves would target. He moved on to his next appointment with the director of the Roerich Museum on Broadway and 107th Street, near the river. Since they were running a bit early, Lawrence drove up Central Park West, filled with budding trees and late afternoon joggers, Michael tried to decide how he should approach this meeting. He didn't have a personal relationship with anyone at this museum. He'd checked with both Guy and Stephen last night, but they weren't friendly with anyone there either. Guy had promised to check with Adeline, but Michael hadn't heard anything from her. He pushed Guy's speed dial number and waited, but there was no answer. It looked like he was on his own.

He asked Lawrence to drop him around the corner so he wouldn't be spotted getting out of such a luxurious car. That would lead to speculation, special treatment, and subtle requests for a donation, all of which he wanted to avoid. Around the corner, the Roerich peace banner blew in the March wind, a white flag with three red dots in the middle circled in red. Inside the grey stone building, the receptionist notified the director he was there, then escorted him to the office. They passed paintings of the soaring Himalayas. Michael paused before a striking orange and red angel carrying a sphere. The receptionist hovered politely.

"Sorry," he said, "I can visit another day."

"The paintings are inspirational. Have you been here before?" she asked.

"Not recently. I get so busy with my own specialty," he said.

They entered another hallway and she knocked on the first door. A youngish man opened the door and stuck out his hand. "John Schmidt."

Michael introduced himself in turn and shook hands.

The man's office was small, but several more paintings hung there. A woman veiled in white sat on a rocky island. Behind her the three dots of Roerich's Peace Banner were rendered as white circles with blue interiors. "Beautiful," Michael said.

"One of the few privileges of the position." Mr. Schmidt gazed at the painting reverently. Another painting hung next to it, a comet streaked across a brilliant teal blue sky filled with stars.

"I'll have to come back when I can spend an afternoon," Michael said.

"We have an excellent collection."

They sat at a small round table in one corner. "Thank you for seeing me," Michael began.

Mr. Schmidt leaned forward, an earnest look on his face. "How can I help you?"

"I'm doing some research for a book on spiritual artifacts. Now, I'm researching crystals and special stones."

"Ah," the director said with satisfaction. "I can guess the reason for your visit."

"I wanted to hear more about the legend surrounding the Chintamani Stone," Michael said.

Mr. Schmidt nodded vigorously. "The famous necklace."

"First of all, is it myth or reality?" Michael tried to adopt a look of mild academic skepticism.

The man laughed. "The necklace itself is real enough. The true question would be is the stone in Shambhala real?"

"Or is Shambhala itself a myth?" Michael added.

"Oh, Shambhala is real in some way, Mr. Levy. It is the pinnacle of human civilization, our reminder of the level of consciousness we can all attain with proper work."

"I agree," Michael said. "This is one of the reasons for this book, to inspire people to reach for enlightenment."

With this encouragement, Mr. Schmidt talked about the Roerichs' own search for Shambhala. Then he spoke at length about their commitment to moving beyond religious sects and embracing the truth behind all faiths.

"I couldn't agree more," Michael said.

"In fact, Helena served as the model for this painting." Mr. Schmidt pointed to the woman sitting on her rocky island. "She was given the fragment because she represented the Mother of the World, which is the title of this piece."

Michael looked thoughtful, as if the idea had just occurred to him. "In the book we've included psychic impressions from some of the best respected sensitives we have. Would it be possible to conduct such a session with the Roerich fragment?"

Mr. Schmidt's eyes narrowed. "That would be most difficult to arrange. The exact location of the necklace is known only to a select few."

"Of course," Michael murmured. He wondered if Schmidt was amongst those 'select few'. "How about Helena's own impressions? Are there diaries or letters I might be permitted to read?"

But Mr. Schmidt's loquaciousness seemed to have dried up. He tilted his head, as if searching his memory. "I'd have to check our records. Such personal items tend to be kept by the family." His tone of voice offered an apology, but his tight jaw suggested he was hiding something.

"I see," Michael said. He bowed his shoulders a bit. "I apologize for asking." He stood up and extended his hand. "Thank you for taking the time to see me."

Mr. Schmidt shook his hand and escorted him to the door. "Our shop has many books that might be of interest. And posters, of course."

Michael thanked him again and turned to leave. Mr. Schmidt knew something and would bear watching.

8

That same day, Alexander Cagliostro stood on the deck of the yacht staring at the GPS. His excitement did not match the calm, slate blue ocean that lay empty all around him in the late afternoon sun. This dive would be the culmination of his lifetimes of work.

"Stop," he called to Karl over the sound of the engine. "These are the coordinates."

Karl cut the motor and dropped anchor. The boat rocked gently in the sudden silence. A gull swooped down hoping for fish, then flew away disappointed.

Cagliostro gathered the rest of his gear, then sat on a low bench. Two assistants removed the two new crystals from their packing crate with meticulous care. Once secured in separate mesh bags, Cagliostro helped Miriam strap one on her back. As much as he hated giving up control of one of the new stones, he'd decided against carrying them both. He couldn't risk banging them together and wrapping them wouldn't work. The material would soak up the water, quickly becoming too heavy and difficult to handle. What could Miriam do with the stone he'd given her? They were five miles out, he carried a dart gun in case of sharks, and Karl now sat absent mindedly stroking his Heckler-Koch semi-automatic.

Cagliostro wrapped the straps of the mesh bag around his shoulders securing the crystal snug against his back. He pulled on her straps, tightening one. Satisfied, he walked to the edge of the boat. "OK, let's go."

The men helped Miriam lowered herself into the water. The crystal strapped to her back stuck up over her head. Cagliostro followed right behind her. Once in the ocean, they adjusted their special face masks, tested their oxygen and headsets, then followed the line down through the turquoise water. Cagliostro willed himself to maintain a steady pace, relishing the weight of his treasure. They followed the contour of the ocean floor until they reached the small hill that marked the valley where the enormous Atlantean crystal had waited for him all these centuries.

The base was still buried, but the sides of the crystal lay bare, reflecting the grey water around them. Shortly after discovering the huge stone, he'd supervised a crew hand-picked by Mueller, and they'd cleared most of the sand away. After the crew had finished their work, Cagliostro had stayed behind to create a circle for ceremony in the surrounding sand. He'd placed the appropriate gem or mineral at various points to create a make-shift temple.

Now, he stroked the flank of the crystal like a man anticipating his first night with the most beautiful woman in the world. Miriam swam up beside him and hovered in the water. He glanced at her out of the side of his face mask, wishing that he didn't need any help, that he could explore this relic alone, but he didn't know how powerful it would prove to be. He couldn't risk becoming so absorbed in vision that he lost track of time or his surroundings. Miriam was a necessary evil.

He gave her a curt nod, then gestured for her to take her position. They'd gone over the plan until he was certain it was drilled into her head. Not that she needed such instruction. She was an expert ceremonial magician. That's why he'd chosen her, but this working was too important for any slip ups. Miriam took up her position at the base of the crystal. Cagliostro swam to the tip that had, fortuitously, fallen pointing due north.

"Ready?" Cagliostro spoke into the mike in his helmet.

"Yes," Miriam answered.

"Are you oriented to the directions?"

"I'm in the south," she answered.

"Good. Prepare the crystal," he ordered. Miriam took her stone out of its bag and placed it near the foot of the large crystal, twisting it into the sand until its base was deep enough for it to stand upright.

Cagliostro nodded his approval. He switched on the external speakers he'd had made for this occasion, hoping the amplified chant would not be too distorted to do its job. Next he took out a nylon rope and tied it around his waist, then threaded it through a hook he'd had the crew drill into a sizable rock at his feet. He floated up until his tether stopped him and folded his legs in lotus position, hovering like some apparition from another time or place. Once he was comfortable, he removed his own crystal, the larger one from the Austrian collection, and held it out in front of him. The water buoyed it up.

"Invoke the directions," he said and closed his eyes, mentally orienting himself to the directions on the horizon, then above and below. Once he felt the temple activate, he began a wordless chant, calling on his inner contacts. Power built in the circle until it pulsed with energy. Cagliostro opened his eyes and directed his attention to the sentinel stone in front of him. He'd already found this crystal's frequency, and he chanted the note, allowing all his attention to flow through his voice and awaken the sentinel. And awaken it did. The crystal instantly pulsed with light.

Satisfaction surged through him, but he took that energy and channeled it into his voice. The crystal shone brighter. Cagliostro spared a quick glance at Miriam and saw to his delight that she had also been successful, although her crystal merely glimmered. She looked up at his, then focused back on her own sentinel stone, and it brightened.

Now, Cagliostro turned his attention to the master crystal. Its gleaming facets lay submissive before him. Pointing the tip of his sentinel toward the large crystal, he redoubled his chant. Miriam followed suit. Pouring his passion into his voice, crooning to the silicon female before him, he reached deep into the heart of the stone to ignite her flame. He felt a rumble, almost a purr, then light shot up from the base, illuminating the enormous crystal, bouncing off the inner cracks and breaking into colors. He wondered if the crystal had fractured when she had fallen or during the earthquakes, or if the Atlanteans had wanted the rainbow effects.

He gave himself over to the powerful currents of energy running up the body of his crystalline lover, caressing his mind, awakening him deeper. He answered this caress with his voice, asking for more, begging for admittance into her secret places. He lost track of time, pouring his lifetimes of desire for this moment, for access to the power of Atlantis, the secrets of the adepts, into his chant. Finally, the crystal opened to him and he entered her, plunging deep, almost losing himself. With his next thrust, she opened wider and took him fully inside. He exploded in ecstasy.

He floated in a golden sphere, free of thought and time. Then the light cleared and he saw below him a group of people in a circle. No, it was a dodecahedron, a twelve-sided figure. He could see the star shape traced in light in the air around them. Their robes shifted colors from ultraviolet to white, then back again, in a dance with the energies around them. He floated inside the Tuaoi Stone, which now stood upright in the center of a chamber. He watched the group chanting, intensifying the energy. Then something began to form in the stone next to him, a shape like a fetus that grew in the blink of an eye into a humanoid. The being pushed through the crystal to the surface, as if she were gelatinous, then startled and turned, catching Cagliostro out of the corner of her eye. One of the workers ran toward the tall crystal.

No, Cagliostro thought, *you can't stop me.* He reached past the being and brushed against the man who'd left the circle.

The entity at the surface of the crystal said in an apologetic tone, *You are not a harmonic,* then pushed Cagliostro into blackness.

THE WATER from White Spring glowed in the night. Anne ran her hands under a gushing spout. The water felt like star light. She turned and walked through a small gate in the wall between the springs and made her way through the yews and flower beds to Red Spring. Careful on the flagstone steps, slippery in the dew, she knelt beside the wellhead, tracing the overlapping circles on the lid. She lifted it and stared down into the fern and moss of the well walls, wondering how deep it was. As if in answer, water began to brim up, filling the shaft, running over the edges onto the flagstone. A deep rumble sounded higher up on the Tor and the ground shook beneath her feet. The water thickened and turned a deep red. Anne reached out to cup it in her hands. It was slippery between her fingers. She sat back on her heels, startled by the texture. Red blood gushed from the spring. Anne jumped up to run and woke sitting up in her bed.

She stretched her hands out in front of her. In the moonlight, they appeared clean. She reached over and snapped on the light. No blood. She pushed back the covers and walked over to the window, looking down on Chalice Well Gardens. The oak blocked most of her view, but one flower bed lay peaceful under the glowing moon. She turned and walked down the hall to the back window. The Tor was a black outline, majestic and still. The dream had seemed real, like something happening on another dimension. She remembered how Grandmother Elizabeth had brought her to a ritual that had taken place on the astral plane. The next morning, her grandmother had known all the details of her so-called dream. Maybe she should go see what was happening outside. Hadn't that local man said White Spring was flowing erratically? In her dream, if that's what it was, White Spring had gushed, but Red Spring had actually bled.

Anne pushed her feet into some slippers, wrapped herself in a terry cloth robe, and walked outside. She looked over at Chalice Garden from her front porch. The wall and trees stood as quiet guardians. She carefully negotiated the wet steps that lead down to the street and inched her way toward White Spring. She should have brought the flashlight; it was pitch black under the trees. A few feet closer, she made out a huddled shape next to the dark building and stopped. The figure whirled and shined a flashlight in her face. She threw up her hand to block the light, turned to go back.

"Anne, wait," the man called. He pointed the light at the ground.

"Who is it?" she called.

"Garth, your neighbor."

Her eyes adjusted. His hair stuck out at angles and his eyes were puffy with sleep. "What are you doing out in the middle of the night?" she asked.

He hesitated. "I could ask you the same."

Anne hugged her robe tighter, glad she'd taken to sleeping in pajamas since Michael had gone to New York. "Something woke me."

"Me, too." He regarded her solemnly.

"A dream," she said.

At this, Garth shined his light on the spout of White Spring. Water trickled out. He shook his head, then looked at her as if he'd made a sudden decision. "Let's talk. I'll make a pot of coffee."

"All right." Anne followed him up the street, Garth limping slightly, pointing the way with his flashlight. Neither spoke. His house turned out to be a way up the hill. He opened the gate and they walked across the farm-like yard, waiting for the comfort of a well-lit room and something warm to drink before they unpacked their respective nightmares.

The floor plan was similar to her own, with the kitchen in the back. A nightlight shone amber from halfway up the stairs, faintly illuminating bulky furniture and paintings. Stacks of books and files cluttered the floor in the room to the right. Garth switched on the light in the kitchen and turned to her. "Please make yourself comfortable."

Anne sat down at a round, plain kitchen table and watched Garth as he put the kettle on, pulled two mismatched mugs from his cabinet, rummaged for spoons, all the while frowning. He seemed to be circling the topic like a dog sniffing out something new in his territory. He put the carton of milk on the table and glanced at her. "Just let me get this ready."

She nodded, wishing now she'd gone home to change clothes, but Garth was still dressed in his worn robe. Red plaid flannel pajamas stuck out from beneath. Once the coffee was made, he poured, then sat down at the table. But instead of speaking right away, he ran his finger around the rim of his mug, seemingly lost in thought. Finally he looked up. "Why don't you go first? I've lived here a while and have had a lot more experience with the antics of this place." He gestured out the window that should have revealed the Tor, but only reflected their faces back to them.

The coffee warmed Anne, bringing her back into this world more firmly. She stretched out her hands. The sticky feeling was gone. Garth's solid form helped. Cynthia had trusted him, based on the note Anne had found. She took a breath and plunged into her dream. Garth listened without interruption, his brown eyes watching her intently.

When she finished, he sipped coffee, his eyes distant with thought. She waited, tapping her foot on the linoleum. Finally he said, "Much of your dream is standard imagery. Have you read about Glastonbury?"

Again, he seemed to be circling the topic. But Dr. Abernathy was equally careful when dealing with psychic phenomenon, so she answered him. "No, we just got back from Egypt, so I've been studying those sites."

"That you picked things up so accurately speaks to your spiritual development." He filled his cup again. "Perhaps your lineage as well."

She hesitated. "I've only been studying metaphysics for four months. I guess that might seem strange to you—knowing my aunt."

"Cynthia explained your circumstances."

"I did keep doing the meditation she taught me as a child," she added.

"Good for you," he said. "But my comment stands. You've done a great deal of spiritual work in past lives."

"Perhaps," Anne said, thinking of her memories of lives with Michael in Egypt.

"Now, let me explain a bit about our site here. Red Spring flows from the bottom of the aquifer in the Tor and is rich in iron. Thus, the red color. It is the spring of the Goddess, and, of course, the color also connects it to the fertility of women and the menstrual cycle."

"Then White Spring must represent the male principle," Anne said.

Garth nodded, a bit surprised. "To many. It flows from the top of the Tor through the limestone where it picks up calcium. If we see this spring as the male complement, the white color represents the seed."

"But, aren't these ideas of the god and goddess just neo-Paganism?" Anne asked. "Do these beliefs really go back that far?"

"Oh my, yes," Garth said. "This imagery is the foundation of the English spiritual tradition. Glastonbury has been a site of pilgrimage for over 10,000 years."

"Really?" Anne gave a half-hearted attempt to recapture her former skepticism.

"Absolutely. There's archeological evidence of use back to 4000 BCE. Legends suggest a much longer use."

Anne gave up. "I'm sure you're right."

"We're a few weeks past Alban Eilir." At Anne's blank look, he said, "Ostara?"

"Are you talking about the spring equinox?" Anne asked.

"Exactly, the time of the Sacred Marriage. Yet, in your dream, the blood spring literally bleeds." He put his chin in his hand. After a minute he added, "The springs also represent the energies of the red and white dragons."

Anne frowned. "Is that some political thing?"

Garth laughed, then caught himself. "Sorry. That's an unusual interpretation. The dragons represent the primordial earth energies."

"I see." Anne could not suppress a huge yawn. She covered it with her hand.

Garth glanced at the clock on the stove. It was half past two. "The thing that concerns me about your dream is the earthquake. The land here is geologically stable. At least it has been since a quake destroyed the church at the top of the Tor in 1275." He paused to consider her. "Myself, I think that quake was the faeries objecting to the church." He watched her carefully to see how she would react.

He seemed to need a reaction, so Anne shrugged. After Egypt, she wasn't going to rule anything out.

This seemed to satisfy him. "How did you feel when the ground shook in your dream?"

"Frightened. Like something had been torn. The blood didn't feel natural, either. Not like a monthly cycle. It felt more like blood from a wound. I didn't sense any other beings, though."

"Right," Garth said. He sat stirring his coffee, lost in thought.

Anne watched him, annoyed he hadn't said anything about his own experience. After a few minutes, she broke the silence. "You said you also had a dream. Is it something you're willing to share?"

Garth pushed his mug to the middle of the table. "Mine is not so straightforward, and it puzzles me how it's connected to yours."

"Maybe we can figure it out together," Anne suggested.

Garth nodded. "I was standing with a group of people. We seemed to be doing some kind of ritual. I heard chanting. Saw an enormous shaft of light.

Then something grabbed me." He rubbed his thigh. "Like an iron vise. Hot."

"It still hurts?"

"To be perfectly honest, it's always bothered me."

Now it was Anne's turn to cross examine. "Did you notice anything else?"

Garth closed his eyes as if trying to return to the dream. "Long, blond hair, but male," he said. "Then a tearing, something wrenched from its right place." After another moment, he shrugged and opened his eyes again. "Nothing more."

"What do you think it means?" Anne asked.

"My dream is not specific enough to draw any conclusions. But it is quite significant that we both had a troubling dream at the same moment, that we felt something torn or wrenched out of place, that it disturbed us so deeply we investigated. And we were both drawn to White Spring."

"You know, when we first got here, a local man said White Spring has been running erratically, that people are afraid it may fail."

Garth slapped the table with his hand. "That can never be allowed to happen."

Anne flinched, then said, "I agree, but what can we do?"

Garth studied her. "I'm not certain, but I believe your arrival is fortuitous."

"But I know nothing about this place," Anne objected.

Garth dismissed this with a wave of his hand. "Your dream suggests otherwise. I propose we work together to solve this mystery. Is your fiancé metaphysically inclined?"

"Oh, yes. Michael has studied all his life. He's much more talented than I am."

Garth's mouth crooked in a small smile. "Somehow I doubt that."

Anne ignored this. "But he had to go back to New York suddenly."

"Nothing serious, I hope?"

Anne decided not to explain the details. It was very late. "He should be back in about a week."

"Then our little project will be a distraction for you."

"I'd like to work with you. Maybe you can tell me more about my aunt."

Garth's eyes clouded for a moment, then he gave his head a little shake.

"Now, if you're going to be doing magic on the Tor, I need to show you around. Explain a few things."

"No time like the present," Anne said.

He glanced at the clock on the wall. It was close to three. "I have an appointment in London today. What about tomorrow?"

"Tomorrow it is," Anne said.

"You can start today, though. I suggest you go to Red Spring and meditate. Attune yourself to the place. See what you pick up."

"I will."

"Excellent." Garth's eyes strayed to the clock again.

Anne got up. "I should let you get some sleep."

Garth snorted. "Not likely after all that coffee. I was thinking that if I leave now, I can run a few errands before my meeting."

"Then I'll let you go." Anne pushed her chair under the table.

Garth stood and escorted her to the front door, his limp still distinct. "We'll meet at a more convenient time. Say one o'clock Saturday afternoon?"

Anne laughed. "I don't know. This place keeps waking me up right about this time every morning."

Garth looked at her closely. "The sign of someone closely attuned to energy."

Anne shook her head. "That's what Michael said when I told him."

"I think I'll like this man of yours."

"Drive safely."

"I shall. I'll come to Cynthia's—" his eyes narrowed "—I mean, your house tomorrow morning."

"I'm sorry for your loss," Anne said in a soft voice.

Garth teared up. He set his jaw, saying nothing.

"See you tomorrow." Anne patted his shoulder, then left him to his grief. There was too much death in all this.

9

Caitir listened to the low murmur of her mother's voice in the darkening room. If she'd been standing on the Tor, she could watch the sun slide toward the ocean and light the path to the old lands. Megan shifted in her chair. Caitir watched her for a moment, then sat back herself, satisfied the Morgen was comfortable for now. That was how she thought of her—the Morgen first, mother second.

A beam of sunlight fell on the oak door, illuminating the intricate carving of the god and goddess at Midsummer. The rooks were gathering in the orchard up the slope to sing the sun down. They needed to tend to the younger trees. Mend the fence on the north side. Weed the garden plots. Her mother claimed these extremes of the seasons were new, that before the disaster, the changes during the year had been mild. Now, even the stars had moved in the heavens and the seasons created a struggle to survive.

Caitir shook herself slightly, trying to clear her mind of all these mundane things, no matter that the small settlement depended on her guidance already. She should be preparing herself for the ordeal—for ordeal it had become, walking between the worlds. Her mother slipped between dimensions so easily.

Megan's voice stopped. Her eyelids drooped. Caitir waited, and when her mother's breath lengthened, she slipped into the garden and walked the paths between the beds of feverfew, yarrow and chamomile. How long would Megan tell her stories of the days gone by? Regardless of what her mother thought, Caitir had her own memories of those golden times, two long lives before the island fell, the land she yearned for despite her best efforts. But now her task was to establish this stronghold, to teach the young ones and serve visitors to the shrine. She feared the goddess had blessed her with an abundance of common sense and little of the psychic sensitivity she'd need for this quest. Why not send Sorcha? She practically lived in the other realms, traipsing through her days, her long flaxen hair flowing behind her, forgetting what was at hand to do.

A quickening in the air announced the turning of the tides toward evening, so Caitir made her way back to the vigil hut. Deep in the night, she would make her pilgrimage. She found Megan stirring. Without a word, Caitir poured a cup of the hot herbal brew that cleared the lungs and mind. Her mother's hand, dotted with brown age spots, was steady after her short nap. She drank half, then rallied her strength and began her tale again.

"The trip to the northern isles was quite the adventure of my young life. We went by boat. It was a cargo ship going to pick up tin, delivering goddess knows what. I was too young to think of that. No beaming through the crystal for me yet; they were saving that for another time. The dolphins ran with us on the first day, leaping and twirling. I stood on deck and watched them, forgetting my sadness at leaving Govannan. At night, the sickle moon sat low in the heavens with the closest planets a line in the sky, Venus bright and close to the horns of the moon, Mercury then Mars fainter dots of light. Pure magic.

"Most of the day we sailed under crystal power, but toward late afternoon, when the winds picked up, the seamen turned off the engines and ran up the sails for the joy of it. They used my father as an excuse to hang the purples out with all the other colors. The wind belled out the sails, and the sun slanting across the water lit them up like lanterns at a festival. If there was no wind, the weather worker called a bit of breeze, nothing to cause an imbalance, mind you." Megan looked up at Caitir as if to admonish her.

Caitir frowned at a memory. She'd been seven or eight. The gang of children had gone up to Wearyall to fly kites, but the wind had not cooperated. Onchu had called it up, but not just a breeze. The wind had quickly turned into a gale, and three priestesses had been needed to quiet it.

But her mother remembered that Caitir had done it. She wished she had that kind of power.

Megan was lost in her past again and continued her story, although Caitir had heard this one many times before. "We danced on deck in pools of scarlet, emerald, gold and purple. On the fifth day, we arrived just as the sun began to dip back toward the sea."

THE SHIP SAILED from the open ocean into the estuary where the land and water intermingled and made peace with one another. Cranes flew overhead or sat in the trees, ghosts in the haze. Ducks floated, breaking the silence with the bell beat of their wings when the ship sailed too close. In places, the heads of reeds just cleared the water and swayed with the tides, a forest in miniature. In the distance, an island appeared from the mist. Alders skirted the shore and willows dipped their graceful boughs into the water. Above them, a green hill rose, then dipped back down again and almost submerged like the coils of a giant water serpent. Another undulation of the land ascended into a terraced hill, the coils tightening into a spiral. On the summit, a circle of low standing stones with a tall, graceful obelisk in the middle announced that she had come at last to Avalon.

Megan grasped her bag to her chest, trying to calm her pounding heart. She was here at last, in the land of her mother's ancestors. She would meet the Lady of Avalon, someone she'd heard stories of all her life. At night when the family had gathered in the scented garden, her mother had told tales about the magic of this place, of the energy of the twin springs, the majesty of the Tor and the entrance into the Underworld, of the Lady who held the keys to all these mysteries. As a child she had yearned to walk beneath the Tor and find the crystal cave, to call the faeries and be invited to join them in their court.

Beneath the canopy of trees on the shoreline, a figure appeared dressed in white with a blue shawl draped over her shoulder. Wheat blond hair hung down her back in a long braid. From the trees the caw of a raven sounded, and with a rustle of leaves, it took flight, rounding back to perch on a distant standing stone, sending a shock of recognition through Megan. She'd seen this scene before, and despite the warmth of the sun, a shiver ran the length of her spine.

The sailors dropped their easy jocularity when they dropped anchor at the base of Wearyall Hill. It was well named, the point of arrival after a journey, where weary travelers could find rest and sustenance. The crew stood at their posts almost at attention, stealing glances at the priestess and the Tor. Megan straightened up and smoothed the folds in her clothes, suddenly aware of her wind-tangled curls. A skiff pushed off from the shore poled by a tall figure in white, not the woman, for she still waited on the shore. As the skiff grew closer, a man's long hair and beard became visible beneath the shade of his cloak. He pulled up to the boat and stopped, nodding to the captain who now took Megan's arm. "I'll help you down."

"But," she turned to him, "I haven't said goodbye."

"They'll be missing you." The captain faced her, his eyes bright in his wind-wrinkled face. "Hope we see you on your return."

It sounded like a question, so Megan said, "I don't know how soon I'll be coming home." A bank of clouds covered the sun and suddenly she missed the bright light and cheerful colors of Eden.

"Now, now," the captain clucked to her like a hen to her chick, "you'll be fine. I expect the Lady will keep you too busy to miss us much."

She turned and raised her hand in stiff salute to the crew. They smiled or nodded from their places, still overawed by the place. The captain lowered a rope ladder over the side and climbed down first. He handed the bag over to the Druid, then returned for Megan. With a final wave to the sailors, she followed him down the ladder and settled on a narrow bench, retrieving her bag from the bottom. The Druid turned his small craft, delicate as a mosquito, and poled back to shore. Megan glanced over her shoulder as they drew close to shore, but the ship was already turning toward the open sea. She settled in the skiff and looked at the Tor, silent as her new captain.

After a few more expert pushes with the pole, her guide stepped into the shallow water, pulled the skiff onto the beach and held out a hand for Megan. For the first time in five days, she put her feet on firm ground that still seemed to Rob with the rhythm of the sea.

101

The woman who had been waiting stepped forward. "Welcome to Avalon. May you find peace here." It had the ring of a ritualized greeting.

"Thank you," Megan said. She introduced herself.

"My name is Thalana," the woman said.

"An Atlantean name."

"Yes, I was born in Authochthesa." The far northern coastal region of Atlantis, close to Iber. Megan had never visited it. Thalana took her bag. "Come, I will take you to your quarters."

Megan turned to thank the Druid boatman, but found he'd also slipped away, his boat already blurred in the mist. They climbed the first hill along a narrow path through tall trees, a mix of ash, hawthorn, and oak. The forest thinned, then gave way to a green expanse. At the summit, they walked along the spine of the hill. The settlement of the Sisters of Avalon nestled in the clearing at the foot of this knoll, below the ceremonial site. The thatched roofs of the cottages blended into Chalice Hill and the Tor that rose behind them. Clusters of woodland herbs nestled among the trees surrounding the village, if village you could call it.

Thalana stopped in front of the first cottage on the edge of the tiny settlement. "This is for visitors." She put Megan's bag down on the threshold. "Settle in and I'll come get you when the Lady can see you."

Megan's stomach gave a growl. She'd skipped breakfast, but she thanked Thalana, took up her bag and walked in, closing the rounded oak door behind her. Sudden tears blurred her surroundings. This was her third new home in the space of ten days. Before she had lived in the same house, the same room, surrounded by the same people, all dear. In that rambling dwelling there had always been someone to listen, someone to play with, someone to comfort any hurt. Not now. Now she was alone in a cold, grey land of stone and water and dark trees, away from that family, away from the man who'd awakened her budding womanhood. Sent by him in fact.

She shook her head, trying to master herself. Avalon was her mother's old home. She had family here. Soon she would meet them. And she would meet the Lady. Megan wiped the tears from her face and forced herself to explore the new cottage. She found a small nook for preparing food, and on the table sat a jug of water, a loaf of bread, a round of cheese and a few of last fall's apples, a bit withered, but giving off a wholesome scent. Her stomach growled again, as demanding as a younger sibling. Beside the kitchen was a private bath. Steam rose from the tub, prepared to welcome a traveler. Next to it was a bedroom with a view of the hill she'd just come from. Megan dropped her bag by the bed, stripped off her clothes and sank into the steaming water. She lathered up with rose-scented soap.

After putting on the last of her clean clothes, Megan helped herself to a late lunch. She opened the door to explore the group of cottages, but found she only had the energy to sit in a pool of sunlight and munch the cheese and fruit. Lore promised eternal life for those who ate the apples of Avalon. A black, long haired cat with wide yellow eyes and a splotch of white on his chest sauntered up, plopped down and turned on his back, offering his belly to be scratched. Megan obliged him and after a while, found her usual good mood restored.

While she sat with the cat, two women walked down toward the water, giving her a friendly wave on their way, where a small boat, much like the one the Druid had ferried her on, waited. The woman in the boat was small with dark hair and olive skin. She gave the women woven reed baskets brimming with fish and vegetables, then turned and poled away. This answered one mystery of Avalon.

When the sun had moved halfway down the sky, Thalana appeared. She pointed to the cat who now lay in Megan's lap. "I see Malcolm has befriended you."

"Oh," Megan scratched under the cat's chin, which caused him to knead the air with his tufted paws, "is that your name?"

"The Lady will see you now."

Megan put the cat down and stood, shaking out her skirts. In the last two weeks, she'd faced the Circle of Thirteen, the leader of the Crystal Matrix Chamber, the head of the Crystal Guild, and now the Lady of Avalon awaited her. This time she felt no anxiety. Was she getting used to this constant judging, this assessment of her abilities and flaws, or was it this place that made her drowsy and tranquil? She followed Thalana through the small cluster of huts and across a meadow full of early spring flowers whose names she did not know. Malcolm followed. They came to a stream splashing through rocks, then followed it up the hill to a stone-lined pool in front of a long hedge. At one end, a horse drank, then lifted its head to look at them, mussel dripping. A butterfly flitted by and Malcolm abandoned her to chase it.

Thalana opened a gate in the hedge and Megan followed her up a grassy slope to a flat area circled by yews. A tiny stone shelter huddled behind the circle in the midst of thicker yews. Behind it the hillside darkened, suggesting the mouth of a cave. Two streams ran on either side of this circle, murmuring amongst the roots of trees. An older woman sat on a mossy stone bench, a red shawl wrapped around her shoulders. Thalana stopped a few feet away from her and waited. The woman raised her hand and beckoned to Megan.

"The Lady of Avalon," Thalana said in a low voice.

Megan hesitated, a sudden knot in her stomach.

"Go on," Thalana whispered, "the Circle of Thirteen is much scarier than this."

Megan jerked her head up to see Thalana smiling. This place was not so foreign after all. Megan walked across the expanse of needled forest floor and kneeled before the Lady.

"Sit." The woman patted the stone bench beside her.

"Yes, my lady." Megan started to stand.

The woman chuckled. "I see my niece has raised you properly."

"What?" Megan gaped, forgetting those manners all together.

A silvery laugh escaped the Lady of Avalon, which sounded much younger than the wrinkles around her eyes suggested. "Probably great, great niece, but who can keep up?" She patted the bench again. She had the same curly brown hair and ocean blue eyes as Megan, only her hair was streaked with silver. "How is Pleione? I haven't seen her in some time."

"Good. Busy with healing. She says some new illnesses have appeared." Megan realized she'd never really listened to her mother's concerns about her work. She tucked her head. It wasn't the first time in the last two weeks she'd been made aware of how little she had paid attention to the affairs of the world when she'd been a child, not even three months ago.

The Lady took Megan's chin in her hands and tilted her face up. "So, you've been chosen for the Crystal Matrix Chamber."

Megan met those eyes, which took immediate and thorough stock of her. She blushed under their scrutiny. How would she ever get used to these people who could look to the bottom of her soul in one glance?

"And they've sent you to help with the Beltane ceremony."

Megan looked around for a message crystal, but she'd seen no sign of even this most natural technology on Avalon. They heated the water somehow, but the cabin had no computer or communication devices.

"We use very little technology here. This spot must be kept clear of any energetic interference."

"I see," Megan said. She was already used to her mother picking up her thoughts. Her aunt had the same gift.

"Tomorrow before dawn, we'll fly to Avebury for Beltane. We must help prepare the site. Thalana will look after you."

And so Megan found herself dismissed. Thalana met her outside the circle and led her through the trees to a small clearing with a circle of benches. Girls and one boy, all about her age, sat around. One priestess sat on a low stone in the middle, feet tucked under her. Once Thalana and Megan had settled down, the priestess began her instruction. "Of course all of you understand the outer mysteries of Beltane. It is the beginning of the warmer six months of the year, when fertility comes to all." She pointed at some flowering honeysuckle that had taken advantage of a tiny nook between two trees stretching up for a small patch of sunlight. "On Beltane, male and female join to create new life and encourage that fertility in the world around us. For some of you, this will be the first time you will witness the Great Rite, yes?" A few raised their hands.

The priestess nodded. "It is quite dramatic and will most certainly sweep us all up in a wave of sexual excitement." Two girls giggled.

Their instructor smiled. "This is good, as it should be. But we do more than bring together male and female in the outer world during this ritual. Our job will be to bring male and female together in the inner planes." The two gigglers frowned.

"Avebury Circle has stones that channel male energy and stones that channel female energy. The Lady will appoint you to stand with a stone—a female stone, obviously. You will keep the energy of that stone flowing evenly during the ceremony. During the Great Rite, we will all come forward to the central altar, but when the people break to do their own private rites, you will not follow them."

This stopped the gigglers. They frowned at each other, obviously disappointed.

"If this is your first Beltane," the priestess continued serenely, "your job will be to meld with the male energy on the subtle planes. Next year, you may partake completely." She smiled at Thalana, who brightened. "Allow your awareness to connect to the three worlds if you know how. If not, meditate for a few minutes—you've all been instructed in meditation?"

Everyone in the circle nodded.

"Then simply allow the power of the stone to fill you. As this happens, be sure the energy is flowing on all dimensions. During the ceremony tomorrow, the flow will become quite intense, so this may require all your attention. We will practice with the stones on the Tor this afternoon."

And so they climbed the Tor. Megan's calves burned as they neared the top, but she was too busy looking in all directions at the expanse of marsh, trees and water to mind. The priestess assigned each a stone, but Megan's squat one drowsed in the afternoon sun, showing her dim pictures of past ceremonies, a bonfire, glimpses of gleaming crystals sleeping beneath the earth, an expanse of still, clear water, then told her to be quiet. Satisfied they had mastered the basics, the priestess dismissed them, and Megan meandered around the coiling pathway to the springs, taking her time. She arrived at her cabin content and full of sleep. She napped until dinner.

The Lady did not appear for the evening meal, which was served in a communal dining hut next to the round kitchen. Malcolm appeared along with several other felines and demanded his share of fish. He turned his nose up at the fire-roasted vegetables and bread. Megan listened to the gossip of the priestesses and students, while she picked the bones out of Malcolm's fish and drank mead, which tasted somehow like trapped sunlight. They talked of their homes, of the stories they'd heard of this isle as children. Some told how they'd been chosen to serve. The students stayed a few months or a year and a day, depending on their need and what they wished to gain in their time here. Only a few were chosen to become Priestesses of Avalon.

"Does everyone come here?" Megan asked.

"Only the girls for any extended time," one of the priestesses answered. "And a few boys whose energy is distinctly feminine." She smiled at the boy Megan had noticed this afternoon. "Everyone comes for special ceremonies during their lifetimes."

"What do you study?"

The answers came from around the table. "Herbology."

"The ceremonial cycle."

"The basics of childbirth."

"But before that, how to handle the energies of our own bodies. Sacred sex."

At this, several girls raised their mugs. "To the God." The same two who had giggled through the lesson that afternoon started up again.

"Which brings us to tomorrow," one of the older priestesses said. "We leave way before the God has risen in the morning."

"He'll be rising tomorrow night," said a throaty voice.

"Yes, and you will want to be ready for him," the priestess answered. "To bed." She clapped her hands as if she were herding geese.

The group gathered their plates and cutlery and returned them to the kitchen on their way back to their cottages. Malcolm followed Megan to her cottage, hopped up onto the middle of the bed and proceeded to groom himself. She had to push him over to get enough room. "Goodnight, my lord." He regarded her out of his round, yellow eyes, then turned his attention back to his bushy tail.

"MEGAN, wake up." Thalana's voice reached her from her room in her mother's house, sitting in the window seat listening to the call of the sea. She opened her eyes, and the sound of the surf gave way to the gentle swoosh of water leaving the estuaries at low tide. "We're leaving soon." The black of night hid the hill outside Megan's window, but she remembered she was in Avalon. "There's porridge in the kitchen," Thalana said, "if you hurry."

Megan threw water on her face and finished her morning routine, then grabbed her bag. She didn't even know if she'd come back here. She looked around for Malcolm to say goodbye, but he had abandoned her in favor of hunting field mice, she imagined.

After a quick bite of breakfast, a group of priestesses and students set off across the meadow toward the east. They skirted the shoreline, then crossed a narrow neck of land. "We can walk across at low tide," Thalana explained. The group climbed through the alders up to another meadow. At the top of a gentle slope, they stopped. The Lady sat and closed her eyes. The group stood away from her, waiting.

"What's she doing?" Megan whispered.

"Now we're far enough away from the Tor," Thalana said, as if this should explain everything.

Megan frowned.

"We don't use crystal-driven technology close to the Tor. She's calling the flyers."

The Lady opened her eyes and stood.

"She mentioned something about not using much technology. Why is that?" Megan asked.

"The Tor is full of crystals, and crystal-driven machines tend to over amp the frequency," Thalana explained.

Megan frowned. "I've never heard of that before."

But before Thalana could say more, she pointed to the sky. "They're here."

Two sleek craft flew over the hill and set down close to the group of women. Megan felt a surge of relief when she saw the familiar conveyances. One of the pilots approached the Lady, shouldered her bag and escorted her toward the closest craft. The group followed. The first vehicle filled up, so Megan and Thalana headed for the second one.

"Megan," called a voice from inside the craft, "is that really you?"

The dome light shone on a familiar face. "Demos, what are you doing here?"

The young man smiled. "I could ask you the same. I'm helping with the henges, learning how to sail the stones."

"Surely they're already built," she said.

"I'm building a new henge, this one for the highest initiation."

"Are you?"

"I'm an assistant." A smile lit his angular face. He was almost as handsome as her father. Megan relented, holding out her arms for a hug. "It's good to see you."

Thalana stood to one side, watching them with a bemused look. "Oh, I'm sorry," Megan said. "This is Demos, a cousin from my father's family. This is Thalana. She's showing me the ropes at Avalon."

Demos kissed Thalana's hand and she glanced quickly at Megan, who mouthed *show-off*. "My pleasure to make your acquaintance," he murmured, looking into her face. Thalana blushed under his scrutiny. "To think such a beauty lives so close and I was not informed."

Thalana took her hand back slowly. Megan rolled her eyes.

Demos turned back to his cousin. "You're studying at Avalon?"

"Not really. They sent me up to help with Beltane. I don't know where I'll go after that."

"Your first Beltane?" He raised an eyebrow suggestively.

Govannan's powerful shoulders, the roped muscles of his forearms, the incongruously delicate chime of the shells in his hair when he turned his head all flashed into Megan's mind. "I don't expect to partake." Her tone was prim.

"And why not? Don't you want the crops to grow and the herds to multiply?"

"I have other work to do." Megan chuckled at his pretend indignation. "Besides, you'll probably participate," she put some emphasis on the word, "enough for both of us."

"I certainly hope I am that fortunate." He looked at Thalana, who blushed again. The older priestesses chuckled.

"Ladies," Demos bowed them into the craft with a flourish. The others settled into the back; Megan and Thalana got in next to him. He took off and Megan sat back, wishing the sun was up so she could get a proper glance of the

Isle of Avalon from the air. The horizon pinked as if in response to her thought, and in just a few minutes, the golden head of the sun began to crown in the east. But they were already gone from Avalon. The ship had been airborne about ten minutes when Megan spotted their destination. The chalk banks of Avebury dazzled white in the rays of the rising sun, visible for miles. Then the stones appeared, dots from the air. Two avenues curved out from the henge, also marked with Saracen stones, making Megan think of a womb with two fallopian tubes. As they drew closer, stone circles appeared within the enormous outer circle. Just as Megan put her face to the window for a better view, the world turned upside down, then righted itself before the women in the back could get out good screams. Demos had steered the craft in a tight roll.

"Demos." Megan clutched at a handlebar. "Honestly."

He made the craft wobble, which elicited more screams.

"Stop it!" Megan scolded, but she saw a wide smile on Thalana's face, so she doubted he would behave. But Demos set the craft down beside the first one without any more shenanigans, and they disembarked, the priestess half-heartedly scolding him, the girls undaunted. Thalana seemed to be taking a long time arranging her shawl, so Megan walked to the group gathered around the Lady who was giving instructions.

"Who is here for the first time?"

Megan and another girl raised their hands.

She nodded. "We will be using Avebury as a lunar temple during this ceremony. Although we celebrate the movement of the sun, it is the lunar world that governs the ongoing creation of life—the fertility of the land, the animals and the people. This, of course, is only one aspect of its function. Like all sacred spaces, it connects to all three worlds. The priests will prepare the fire. Our first task is to cleanse the henge and balance the energy for the ceremony."

"It's always balanced," Thalana whispered in her ear. Megan looked around for Demos, but saw the crafts had taken off again on another errand.

The Lady turned in their direction. "Of course the energy of this temple was set perfectly when it was built, but we mustn't become complacent." She fixed Thalana with a look.

And so they spent the better part of the morning walking the outer circle sunwise, tuning to each stone as they came to it. Swirls of energy rose from the earth or sluiced down from the sky, modulated by the great Saracens, which they then channeled out to the ring. When the sun stood straight above them, they reached the spot where they'd begun and walked outside the circle to a stand of beech trees whose roots wove together in an intricate net where a light lunch was served. Megan's whole body thrummed like a tuning fork and she only took a few bites. Thalana insisted she drink water.

In the afternoon, they visited the stones in the northern circle. The cove called out for her to curl up and leave her body safe inside, to journey in spirit. "Later," she whispered. Another stone showed her a hand fasting, the bride's head festooned with flowers. The wind blew against her stone body, the rain drenched her sides, the claws of ravens scratched when they landed on her top, a herd of deer nibbled at her base. When the priestesses had finished their work, Megan stood in the field, a clear channel of energy almost without thought.

Thalana found her near the last stone they'd cleared. "The Lady has withdrawn to prepare for the ceremony. She asked that we go down and accompany the local women when the time comes."

Megan tried to make sense of what Thalana was saying. One of the stones sent her an image of a great group of women gathered together, singing and celebrating. "Oh," she said, "Beltane."

Thalana's laugh was cautious. "Yes, are you with us?"

Megan nodded.

Thalana gathered more of the younger students and led them across the northern circle. A huge pile of wood had been stacked between the inner rings. A long altar stone, flat on top, lay in the exact center of the Great Circle, where the energies of the two inner rings swirled together forming a figure eight. The group walked across a long meadow toward the flat hill in the distance. People milled around the base, shouting greetings, setting up tents, bringing out food they'd cooked at home to share in the feast after the ceremony. The villagers nodded to the priestesses, one man tipping his cap and bowing with a flourish. The crowd bustled around Megan and the excitement woke her from her entrainment with the stone circle. Or perhaps the Saracen stones felt the people and were themselves waking up for Beltane.

A low drumbeat began, stirring the growing crowd. It seemed to emanate from the ground itself. "The hill," Thalana said, pointing to a mound some distance away. A group of priests sat on the flat top in a circle. Couples separated, calling that they'd find each other later. The women gathered at the end of one of the corridors, the men at the other, a full two miles away, the hill equidistant between them. Each group waited for a signal to begin the walk through the tall standing stones marking the avenues to the Great Circle. In the growing dark, bodies pressed together, voices dropped to whispers. The priestesses began to chant, slowly gathering the disparate energies of the crowd of women into one force. Megan melted into the sound.

Then they were moving down the avenue. Some joined hands. Others adjusted their crowns of flowers, carefully woven from gardens at home. All sang together, their energies merging. The stones welcomed them as they walked. When they arrived at the cove again, the women flowed into their circle. A stream of men entered the southern ring. Their deep voices wafted across the field, already mating with the bell tones of the women. Thalana found her in the crowd. "Come with me. The Lady wants us to stay with the stones on the east."

They took up their stations, Megan leaning against the giant, tuning her awareness to the three worlds. This she had learned from her mother. The Lady of Avalon entered the ring, and a hush fell over the expectant group. She raised her arms and began her invocation of the Goddess, speaking of her growth into a beautiful maiden. The priestesses kept up a low croon and the villagers added their voices softly. As the Lady spoke, the standing stone Megan leaned against seemed to take a deep breath, gathering an enormous load of energy from the underworld that it pushed out into the ring. Megan reached into the stone, modulating the flow at the last minute. It flowed through her body, awakening her cells, leaving her keenly aware of her own life force and desire. She remembered that moment in the Crystal Matrix Chamber when she could have melded with Govannan. If only he were here. Opening her eyes again, she glanced over at Thalana. Her stone pulsed with energy, lights like hydra heads dancing around it.

The Lady cried out, "We call you forth, Blodeuwedd, the flower maiden, intended bride of Merlin the stag." She held a huge circlet of flowers in her hand. A beautiful young priestess who had ridden with them this morning stepped forward and bowed before the Lady. She placed the May crown on the young woman's head. At a higher frequency, a being of radiant light slipped into the priestess as she received the crown. She stood, taller than before, and the Lady removed her robe, picked up a bottle of some precious oil and anointed her body with it.

The priestess who was now Blodeuwedd moved toward the cove again. The women followed her, their voices pulsing with energy, some shedding their own clothing. A deep, joyful power swelled with the group. It was the quickening of the egg, the power of summer, of growth, the celebration of fertility.

They walked toward the altar stone. A young priest led the men's procession as the Lord Merlin, the horns of the stag on his head the only clothing he wore. He pranced and chanted, waves of light pulsing around him, his muscular body sleek with precious oil. Megan's body responded like a young filly on her first tether trying to break free. Then Blodeuwedd found her mate and she began to tease him, to circle the altar, beckoning, then dipping away again.

The crowd merged together, pouring their joy, their desire into their voices, demanding a consummation. Blodeuwedd teased more, weaving around the altar. The stone blazed white hot as she danced. At last, Merlin grasped her, and Blodeuwedd melted into his arms. He lifted her up and laid her gently on the altar like a bouquet of flowers. A cheer burst from the crowd. Merlin jumped up on the altar and stood outlined against the moon, his phallus fully erect. Then he dropped to his knees. Blodeuwedd lifted her hips to meet him and they came together. A great shout split the cleft of night.

The priestess grasped the stone as she pushed against the priest, the circle pouring its full energy up into her. Megan couldn't imagine how the priestess could embody the energy, but she felt it pouring into her. Megan felt the strokes of the God as if he were mating with her too, and with each push came a wave of power from the sky and stones. The chanting of the crowd grew to a fever pitch as the couple sped up their thrusts. The stones were now pure light, pulsing with the rhythm of the God and Goddess, sending waves of light into the couple with each push. Then the world exploded in ecstasy, the couple crying out their climax, the stones eradiated against the dark night. With this shout, the pile of wood burst into flame and couples found each other, moving into the outer circle to answer the call of their bodies.

Megan found her sentinel stone in the northern circle and leaned into it. She yearned to go into the fields and answer the call of her body and Nature herself. What better place for her first mating than here, in the sacred ceremony of life? But the man she longed for was not with her, and the Lady had given her a job to do. She listened to the cries and moans of pleasure around her. Her stone offered an opinion. *He is worth the wait.* She rode the waves of energy, feeling it flow out into the three worlds, finally ebbing to quiet.

At last the celebrants were making their way back to the fire, some dressing again, others remaining nude. The light turned their bodies golden. As the fire burned down, couples joined hands and leaped across it. Others followed, sometimes whole families, occasionally just one person. Then people came with their pails and scooped up the hot coals to bring home a piece of the sacred fire. The crowd streamed down one of the avenues toward the feast they'd brought with them. The world had been made fertile again.

10

Friday morning, Michael sat listening to the Rhodes' family attorney read Robert's last will and testament. Embarrassed to hear the intricacies of Robert's finances, he hunched his shoulders, trying to take up less space. The attorney droned on about stock holdings and accounts and the family home. Next came works of art, keepsakes, memorabilia. Michael was a bit surprised at how well off he had been.

"To the Rosae Crucis Lodge, I bequeath—" Michael sat up straighter "—my esoteric library and files. Furthermore, I set aside an annual endowment in the amount of $350,000, said amount to be increased equal to the cost of living index as determined by . . ."

Michael glanced quickly at Laura, then at the adult children to gauge their reaction to this generosity. Laura smiled reassuringly. Others listened intently, but their expressions remained as they had been before this revelation. Michael knew both Robert's children had done well financially and had nothing to worry about, but when it came to money, you could never tell.

"To my beloved friend and colleague Michael Levy, I bequeath my lodge regalia and accoutrements . . ."

Michael's hand tightened on the arm of his chair. Robert had left him his most intimate magical instruments. He'd burn the cord Robert had used as soon as he could. Tradition dictated this be done. But his wand, the chalice, he wasn't sure of the whole list—all these could be passed on. Robert had been a powerful magician and this was no small gift.

"Furthermore, I leave a trust for Michael Levy to be paid quarterly in the amount of $100,000, said amount to be increased equal to the cost of living index . . ."

This did raise an eyebrow from Robert's son. Michael himself was speechless. What a difference this gift would have made to him only four months ago. He could have retired and given himself over completely to his metaphysical research. Now his circumstances had changed and his relationship with Anne had already made this possible. He made a decision. After the marriage, he would give this money back to the family. He'd mention this as soon as the attorney finished.

Next came siblings, nieces and nephews, and a few charitable organizations. Michael let these details wash over him. He sat back again and sent a thank you to Robert. True to Guy's prediction, he'd had no contact since the funeral. Robert seemed to have truly moved on. When the attorney appeared to be winding down, Michael peeked at his watch. Ten past eleven. Just enough time to get to his lunch meeting with Nancy Langton. She'd insisted they meet today.

"This will was last amended eighteen months ago, on the birth of the new grandchild." The attorney looked up at Robert's daughter, who nodded. "Are there any questions or concerns?"

The family looked at each other, the son gathering their nods of approval one by one before turning to Michael.

"I am deeply grateful for Robert's generosity both to the Lodge and to me, but since he last updated the will, my finances have changed," Michael began.

"He would want you to have something," Laura said. "You were a second son to him."

"As he was a second father to me," Michael met her gaze, "but his regalia are gift enough. Considering the wealth of the Le Clair family, I wouldn't feel right taking the money."

"You'll excuse me for asking," the son spoke, "but is there a pre-nuptial agreement?"

"No," Michael said. He hadn't even thought of that.

"Shall I draw up the paperwork?" the attorney asked.

All three of the Rhodes family looked at Michael. "I'll leave that decision to you," he answered.

"Add a clause that protects Michael in case of divorce," the son said.

"That's really not necessary," Michael said. "I don't anticipate—"

"We never anticipate such events," he answered. "That's why you should be protected."

Michael ducked his head. "If you insist, but—"

"I do. I never shared Father's interest in the metaphysical. You helped him let me be free."

Michael studied his face for a moment. "I never realized."

"You are always welcome in our family," he said.

The attorney nodded. "I can take care of this. The paperwork should be ready say next week?"

"Fine," Michael said. The family nodded their agreement.

"If you'll excuse us, then," Robert's son looked at Michael, "I do have a few more questions about some of the family arrangements. We'll keep you informed of the investigation," he said, almost as an afterthought.

Michael stood to go, guilty that he could not return the favor. His sources were anything but conventional.

Laura reached out and touched him on the arm. "Come by for Robert's things. We'll have lunch."

"I'd like that."

Michael took his leave of the family and made his way to the waiting car. He was grateful Arnold had decided to let his assistant Rob drive him in an ordinary car. Actually, it was one of Thomas' hot sports coupes. Not that ordinary, but less showy than the limo. At least, he hoped so. He didn't really know car makes. He got in the passenger's side. "We're meeting Dr. Langton at Mesa Grill at noon."

"Good choice." Rob tore off, tires squealing.

"Dr. Langton is a bit of a gourmand. I've never eaten there myself." Michael had to raise his voice to be heard above the engine.

"Flay's too well known for me." Rob slammed on the brakes, making Michael almost come to his feet. "I like to discover the up and coming chefs, when they're still hungry." He grinned at his joke. "Get the Spice Rubbed New York Strip Steak."

Michael decided it was useless to comment on Rob's driving. "Actually, I'm a vegetarian."

Rob blew the horn and swore gustily at a cab. "Maybe the Chile Relleno, then."

"You can have the steak."

Rob jerked the car around the cab, then leaned out the window and cursed again. "Thanks for the treat."

"My pleasure," Michael tried to relax his clinched jaw. At least there was no time to mope about Robert when his life was in Rob's hands.

Rob whirled around and pulled the car into a parking spot near the park, using some fancy maneuver to cut off another contender. The man flipped him off and drove away.

After his heart stopped pounding, Michael couldn't resist asking, "Did you ever do stunt driving for movies?"

"Too tame." Rob grinned.

"You must have enjoyed driving with Thomas," Michael said.

A shadow flitted across Rob's face. "I taught him. A born driver. He handled a plane just as well. I still can't believe it."

"We've had too many losses," Michael said.

"Way too many," Rob agreed. They walked together toward the restaurant. About half a block away, Rob stopped. "Let me go in first and look around."

"I'm sure everything—"

"Boss's orders."

Before Michael could feel funny just standing on the sidewalk, Rob was back. "Looks okay. I'll eat at the bar."

"Feel free to join us."

"There's a spot for me with a good view." He walked in ahead of Michael.

Michael hesitated a minute, then gave his name to the hostess. "Your party is waiting, sir." He followed her along the wall until he saw Nancy sitting at the last table right next to the dark wood bar. Rob sat a few chairs away, casually glancing around the room that was reflected in the large mirror that dominated the wall above the bar.

Nancy popped up from the table, her usual energetic self, and gave him a hug. "It's good to see you. I ordered for us." Michael drew a breath to protest, but she rushed on. "I remember you're a vegetarian. Besides, what you know about food could fill a thimble."

"I'm not that bad, surely." Michael laughed in spite of himself. He could never get annoyed with Nancy's pranks. She was too full of life, and he needed that right now.

He reached for a white roll, but Nancy batted his hand away. "Try the corn bread. And add some salsa. It's incredible."

He took her advice. She watched for a reaction. He raised his brows at the spiciness. "You must have gotten right on our research."

"I was between projects." Nancy took a bite of the corn bread and half closed her eyes to savor it. "The best. Now, down to business."

Michael glanced at the people at the table next to them, who were deep in conversation.

"We don't have it," Nancy said. "Never did. Apparently the rumor was put around as a decoy."

"Too bad." Michael reached for another piece of bread, then decided against it.

Nancy had no such compunction. "But I did discover something interesting." She scooped the rest of the salsa from the small bowl. "Apparently, Rigden Jyepo, who was the head of Shambhala—still could be for all I know. Those guys are rumored to live way past one hundred. Anyway, he is supposed to have given a ring to Nicholas Roerich. Of course, Helena had the necklace with the piece of—" Her eyes darted around, but the place was packed and the noise level high. "Well, you know."

Their lunches arrived. The waiter set down a cut of steak smothered with a barbeque sauce smelling of mango in front of Nancy and gave him the Chile Relleno. She pointed to Michael's plate. "I'm sure you'll like it. Here's my theory." She pointed her fork full of steak at him before putting it in her mouth. He had to wait for her to chew. "I think there was one stone, and the story has been embellished by followers. Or maybe they turned the necklace into a ring to camouflage it since so many people knew about the necklace."

"I suppose that's possible." Michael was skeptical, but willing to listen. He took a bite of his Relleno, which exploded in his mouth. His eyes watered.

"Too much?" Nancy took it personally if her friends didn't like her recommendations.

"It's fine." He resisted the urge to cough. He'd had hotter curry in India, but just by a nose. His next bite was tiny.

Nancy cut her steak, looking like a cat with a canary. Then she leaned across the table and whispered. "I know where the ring is."

"Where?"

"Roerich gave it to Harvey Spencer Lewis."

"The former Imperator of the Rosicrucian Order?" Michael blurted out.

Nancy nodded, delighted to have surprised him. "It's in their museum."

Michael sat back. If she'd discovered this so easily, Cagliostro probably already knew. He wondered if they'd had a robbery. Maybe they wouldn't report it to the police. It could be that Mueller was casing the museum right now. If they hadn't stolen it yet, it could only be a matter of days before they made an attempt. If this was the artifact they were looking for.

"Michael." Nancy's voice reached him from far away.

He looked up. "Thanks for this, Nancy."

"My pleasure." She sat back, smiling.

"Did you find anything else about the necklace?"

"Not a word."

"Do you know this guy John Schmidt at the Roerich Museum?"

"Quiet type. Keeps to himself." Nancy shrugged. "He's fairly new."

"How long has he been on this job?"

"Maybe a year? Should I look up his resume? See what I can find out?"

"I'll look it up. You can ask around if you don't mind, but be discreet. I don't want you to get hurt." He dabbed his forehead with his napkin, then it put beside his plate.

"I promise to be careful." Nancy grinned. "It was too hot?"

"It sort of sneaks up on you." He scanned for the waiter.

"You've got to try the Crème Brule," Nancy said.

"Thanks, but I need to get going."

"Oh, come on. I don't get here often." Nancy looked about to pout, then her expression shifted to a wise mother. "Besides, it will cool you off. And I can't eat it all myself."

Michael relented.

She ordered, then leaned forward. "You know, there's a collector in Austria who has a beautiful crystal that many people feel is from Atlantis."

Michael nodded. "In Linz, right?"

"You know about it already."

"It's been stolen."

Nancy sat back, surprised. "What other thefts do you know about?"

"Just these two."

The dessert arrived, and Michael took a bite to be polite, then had to resist scarfing the whole thing. After they'd polished off the Crème Brule, Nancy turned back to business. "Have you spoken with Franz Maier?"

Franz oversaw the German Rosicrucian archives. Michael knew Thomas had consulted with him about the six crystal keys before he'd flown to India. "Oddly enough, we've never met," Michael said.

"Maybe it's time to rectify that," Nancy suggested.

"Perhaps, but I need to go to San Jose first." He gestured for the waiter. "Check please."

THE NEXT DAY, Michael parked under the shade of a large elm in front of the English Tudor that had once been the home of the first modern Imperator of the Rosicrucian Order, Dr. Harvey Spencer Lewis. Immediately across the street stood a statue of Tutmosis III, Akhenaten's great, great grandfather. Once a statue of Augustus Caesar had been there, positioned so as to point to the house. It had been a gift from Mussolini, not because Dr. Lewis approved of his politics, but because he'd been close with the Italian order. Rumor had it a tunnel ran beneath Naglee Avenue connecting Lewis's house with his office in Rosicrucian Park, that he'd call his staff to say he'd be right over, ask his secretary to put something on his desk, and when she'd open the door, he'd already be sitting behind it. Stephen, who had told him this story, also said the tunnel had been crushed during some repaving during the 1950s.

Michael walked across the street and ambled down the path beside the Francis Bacon Auditorium, Rob following behind at a discreet distance. Dr. Abernathy had refused to allow him to fly to California on a commercial plane or travel alone. "Not with Cagliostro on the hunt," he'd said.

Michael walked to the brightly colored, tiled fountain, topped with a glorious winged Isis. The park rumor mill had it that the gold statue that used to stand there had been stolen in the 1930s and replaced with the current brass one. The RCU building behind the fountain was supposed to be the only building in the world to combine Tibetan and Egyptian architecture. At least here was some evidence of Lewis's connection to Asia.

Michael turned back, pushed open the wrought iron gate marked "Members Only," and entered the Akhenaten shrine. He sat on a marble bench. Someone had put a vase of scarlet roses in front of the rose granite pyramid containing the ashes of Harvey Spencer Lewis. His son's ashes were marked by an obelisk farther back. Michael closed his eyes to find his silence, then asked for help in thwarting Cagliostro this time. No answer came, but he felt a measure of peace.

He left the shrine and stopped again under the sprawling trunks of the banyan tree, its hollow center representing the One, source of all consciousness in Vedic philosophy. This place had always brought him peace, just as Robert had always helped him see his way forward. Michael wanted to hear his mentor's voice in his mind again, reassuring and guiding him. Rob took a few steps closer, then looked around to see what he was missing. Michael sighed, forced a smile and followed the sidewalk between the buildings to the front of the museum.

A statue of Tauart standing in the middle of the fountain made Michael's smile genuine. Something about the protruding belly and snout of the hippopotamus Neter who protected pregnant women always cheered him up. He clambered up the stairs, walked between the blue and white papyrus columns and entered. At the front desk, he told the attendant his name. "I have an appointment with the curator."

"You're a bit early. She'll be available in about fifteen minutes. Would you like to look around? I can send someone to find you."

"I'll be in the Akhenaten room." Michael had downloaded the audio tour. No rings or other jewelry currently on display matched what he was looking for.

A knowing smile lit the woman's face. "Of course."

When he reached the room, a hunched, blond man was talking with a group of what looked like college students. "The Rosicrucians trace their teachings back to Tutmosis III and the Pharaoh Akhenaten. This explains the Egyptian architecture and symbols they use, and their fascination with this particular dynasty. We know, of course, that the time lapse and culture changes are too great to make this connection credible. Western metaphysics also claims that the Greek philosophers were trained in what they call the Egyptian mystery schools. This is a prime example of what Edward Said would call Orientalism, how Europeans see Easterners as wise and inscrutable. But this museum does have some pieces worth viewing."

Definitely a college professor, Michael thought.

The group filed out of the room, much to his relief, and he stood before the replica of a bust from the Luxor Museum. Akhenaten's face stared back at him from the case, the full lips, the round eyes, the high brow filled with a peace he himself yearned for today. Michael sat on a low bench and followed his breath, letting his awareness float, then reached out to the image. He knew this bust had been cast recently, that it carried none of the resonance with the past the real one did, but his own connection to this master was great enough to overcome the limitation. After a minute, the face blurred. Michael was in a bright, hot room. He leaned toward someone seated in a gold chair to whisper something in his ear. The faint smell of wax and lotus oil rose up from the seated figure. A young, bronze boy fanned them with ostrich feathers.

"Dr. Levy?"

The scene disappeared with a snap and Michael opened his eyes to find a middle-aged woman standing in front of him.

"I finished earlier than expected. I'm Rhonda Dunn." She walked toward him extending a hand in greeting.

No awareness that she just interrupted a meditation, Michael thought. He took a deep breath to return himself to the here and now. After all, he'd come to see her. He shook off his irritation, then stood and shook her hand. "It's a pleasure to meet you. I'm sorry to make you come find me."

"No problem. I enjoy my little museum."

Michael chuckled. "Not so small, really."

"Compared to the Met?" The corners of her mouth quirked up.

"Ah, well," Michael glanced back at Akhenaten, "You have the advantage of serving the Rosicrucians, not the general public." Her eyes darted to his face in confusion. "Besides, I've left that position."

"So I heard." With a gesture for him to follow, she turned and walked back through the museum.

"I'm writing now. Pursuing some life-long interests." Michael kept his voice low.

"What a pleasure." They reached her office and she sat at a small, round conference table. Michael took a seat across from her. "What interests you here?" she asked.

"So many metaphysical artifacts have colorful histories. I want to retell some of those stories to entertain and—" he lifted his hand "—uplift people. We need to teach in many ways."

She nodded for him to continue.

"Right now, I'm writing about Atlantean artifacts."

Her forehead wrinkled. "I'm not sure we can help you there."

Michael held up a finger. "Actually, I'm tracking down a story about a ring given to Dr. H. Spencer Lewis from a Tibetan Rinpoche."

The blank look on her face seemed genuine, so he continued. "Supposedly the Roerichs gave Dr. Lewis a ring that they'd gotten in Shambhala. It was supposed to be from Rigden Jyepo."

She shook her head. "This is the first I'm hearing this story. If you don't mind me asking, what is this ring's connection to Atlantis?"

"The stone in the ring supposedly connected to the Chintamani Stone. The mythic origin of that piece is Atlantis. Well, actually it's supposed to be a gift from another star system—Orion, Sirius, the Pleiades."

"That's some story," she said with a slight smirk.

Could it be the Rosicrucians had hired an academic Egyptologist as their museum curator, one who knew very little about the esoteric knowledge surrounding her? Michael wondered.

"We do have a whole filing cabinet marked with this Lewis's name." She stood up. "You can check the archives."

They took the stairs into the basement. Rhonda unlocked a door marked "Employees Only" which opened into a room filled with file cabinets and shelves. She walked to one of the file cabinets marked "H. S. Lewis" and opened the top drawer. "Let's see now." Biting her lower lip, she riffled through the files, closed the drawer and started on the second one. Half way through, she lifted several out. "These might help." She laid the files on the long table in the middle of the room and they both sat down. The first file read 'Artifacts: Museum'.

"May I?"

Rhonda nodded.

Michael reached for the stack. The next ones were labeled 'Artifacts: Library' and 'Personal Collection'. From the first manila file, Rhonda pulled out a typed list. "Good, there's a duplicate." She handed one to Michael. He scanned the items. Coffin of Lady Mesehti, Middle Kingdom. Cleopatra VII, Ptolemaic. He turned a few pages, running his eyes down the page, looking for categories, but the items seemed to be listed at random. This was going to take a while. He hoped Rob liked museums.

Rhonda had apparently reached the same conclusion. She half rose. "Shall I leave you to it?"

"If I may." Michael tried to look eager. "Would the library have anything?"

"No, all the information about artifacts is in the museum. Let me know if you need any help," she said, then closed the door behind her.

Michael waited a few minutes before getting up and inspecting the other file cabinets. He riffled through shipping manifests, agreements with other museums, program plans—all the usual business of any such institution. Satisfied that Rhonda had indeed found the relevant files, he sat back down and, with the patience of an archaeologist, worked his way through the stack in front of him.

Two hours later, Michael had learned a great deal about the holdings of the Rosicrucian Egyptian Museum, the expeditions Lewis had participated in and various gifts the group had received. But nowhere had he found any mention of a ring, the Roerichs, or even Tibet. He returned the files to their drawer and walked out to find Rob. He'd send a thank you with a donation to Rhonda later. He found Rob in the bookstore leafing through his own recent book. "So they carry it," Michael commented.

"You should sign it for them." Rob closed the book and returned it to the shelf.

"Nah, let's go."

They walked out past the fountain and turned down the sidewalk. At the light, a sign reading 'Ram Metaphysical Books' caught his eye. Something about the place pulled at him. "I want to check out that store before we leave," he said.

Rob looked at the place, the end suite in an aging strip mall. He glanced at his watch. "OK, but it takes a while to file a flight plan, you know."

"Go ahead and do it. I'll be just a minute."

Rob took a seat at a bus stop, and Michael crossed the street and pushed open the door of the shop. Bells hanging from the handle announced his entrance. The place smelled of cat mixed with sandalwood. An older woman sat at an untidy desk just to the side of a jewelry case stuffed with Celtic and Egyptian designs. A blue-point Siamese lounged on the various piles of catalogs and papers on top of the desk. The two regarded him with remarkably similar blue eyes, but the woman distinguished herself from the cat by her friendly attitude. "Welcome to Ram Books. Let me know if I can help you." The remnants of a French accent still hung in her voice. She seemed to be in her sixties, with a round face and body, and hair the color of her youthful blond, nicely done. The cat regarded him haughtily.

"Thank you." Michael made his way to the Egypt section and quickly found his latest book. He pulled the three copies from the shelf and took them up to the desk. "May I sign them for you?" he asked with a smile.

"You're Michael Levy?" The woman pulled a stack of local weekly newspapers from a chair next to the desk and patted the seat.

"That's right. You remembered the name." He took the seat she'd indicated. A stripped tabby looked up at him from yet another stack of magazines behind the desk, then tucked his nose back under his front paw, returning to his nap.

"Oui, I love Egypt. I try to keep up with all the new books." Her smile was as generous as her round curves and colorful tunic. She rummaged in a drawer and took out a ball point pen. "If you'd called ahead, I would have arranged a reading."

He opened the first book to the title page. "Quick trip. Just doing a bit of research."

"At the library?" She pointed over her shoulder.

Michael followed her gesture and discovered two Himalayans lounging on the bookshelves immediately behind the jewelry case. "Museum, actually." He pointed to the pair. "Beautiful cats."

"Yes, but this one is jealous." She pointed to the queen on top of the desk. "I'm a worshiper of Bast."

"So I see." Michael signed the book in his lap with a flourish, then opened the next.

She lowered her voice. "Are you a member?"

"Yes," Michael said, and she nodded. "Has the store been here long?"

"Twenty years. First opened up in the old Imperator's house."

Michael looked up with a start. "No kidding?"

She laughed at his expression. "That's right. I lived upstairs and ran the store on the first floor. Rented out rooms. The kids called it 'Pauline's Boarding House and Home for Wayward Mystics'."

"Imagine that. So, you would know." Michael leaned forward and lowered his voice even though they were alone. "Was there really a tunnel?"

Her blue eyes lit with enthusiasm. "We looked for it. This red headed kid—well, he worked for the Order as a research scientist. He was in his late twenties. Not exactly a kid, I suppose. He was always knocking on the walls of the spiral staircase. He swore it was hollow." She smiled at a private memory. "We found a passageway in the basement, but it ended in rubble."

"So the repairs to the street probably collapsed it?"

She raised an eyebrow appraisingly. "You do know the story."

"A friend told me."

"We talked about doing some digging, but never got around to it." She stroked the Siamese, who took the attention as no more than her due. "You know how it is. So many projects."

"I know exactly what you mean." He finished signing and closed the cover of the last book. "Shall I put them back?"

"I can do that later. Tell me about your research. Unless it's top secret." She waggled her eyebrows to suggest this would be her preference.

"I thought I'd write about Atlantean artifacts."

"That's right up the Rosicrucians' alley," she tossed back.

Michael laughed in spite of himself. "Yes, but I'm looking for something specific. And they don't seem to have any record of it."

"That new lot—" she waved her hand dismissively "—you could fill two libraries with what they don't know."

"Well," Michael hesitated now that the revelation was at hand.

"Come on. Maybe I can help." She smiled encouragingly.

"Did you ever hear a story about Nicholas Roerich giving a ring to Dr. Lewis?"

"Roerich." She frowned in concentration, still stroking the Siamese who had moved into her lap. "I don't remember a ring, but the house and museum were picked clean back when the Church of the Moon tried to take over the Order."

"Who?" Michael was stunned. "How could that be?"

She held up her hands as if being held at gunpoint. "I'm not kidding."

"This I have to hear."

Her bell toned laugh sounded again. "After Dr. Lewis died, his son took over as Imperator. Nice enough, but not the mystic his father was. He watered down the monographs too much, in my humble opinion. Nobody's asking, mind you." She looked around the store to reassure herself they were alone.

"He was a good administrator, though. The order expanded under his leadership. You know San Jose became the world headquarters in the late 1940s. The war bankrupted the European orders. We stayed the World See until the son died in 1987. That's when the real trouble began. The next

Imperator had ties to who knows—" she waved her hands and the blue-point jumped down in protest. "He appointed one of his minions curator, and together they raided the museum and library. When he proposed we move the World See to Andorra, people started investigating. Guess who owned the property he'd chosen for the site?"

"Reverend Li Yang Sun?" Michael answered.

"Exactamundo." She slapped her thigh for emphasis. "What a fight that was, but in the end the Supreme Grand Lodge was dissolved altogether." The tabby jumped into her lap, thinking it was his turn. "You see, there was never supposed to be a World See. The leadership did that because of the emergency created by the war."

She stroked the cat for a minute in silence. Michael waited, amazed by the story. Finally she looked up. "I think the Nazis were trying to steal sacred artifacts during the war. I'm not sure they stopped after it was over, although the new political situation made it more difficult. Rumor has it they moved certain items here to keep them safe. But when the new Imperator—" she said the words with a roll of her eyes "—started stealing, people soon realized the same group of dark magicians had found the hiding place."

"The Illuminati?" Michael asked.

She shrugged. "That's the popular name. Somewhat misguided, in my humble opinion. I'm not sure what they call themselves. Anyway, when the dust settled, the World See had been disbanded. What remained of any international leadership moved to the south of France. San Jose found itself missing several valuable artifacts and—" she jabbed her finger in the air "—the records if they ever existed. So your ring might be in Rev. Sun's vault. Or in the hands of what you call the Illuminati."

"Let's hope not," Michael said.

She made a small questioning sound.

He shook his head. "It's just that the ring is rumored to be a part of the Chintamani Stone."

She wrinkled her brow, trying to remember, and he explained it to her.

"Well, surely the monks in Shambhala know how to keep malevolent influences away," she said.

"Of course," Michael said, but privately he thought Cagliostro could give them a run for their money. It was a mystery how Cagliostro could maintain his strength and effectiveness while doing such dark deeds. Usually such activity disturbed the balance of energy more and more until it snapped back, as a rule on the person who'd done the negative magic, leaving them wounded but wiser. Cagliostro seemed to have some sort of free pass.

He stood up to go. "Thank you for the information."

She handed him a card. "Let me know if I can be of any more help. And tell me next time you come to town. We'll have a workshop for you."

Michael walked across the street and joined Rob. "Good thing I know some people at the airport. We can leave as soon as we get there."

11

After leaving Garth's house, Anne walked down the narrow lane in the still-black night. She climbed the stairs by feel, regretting she hadn't borrowed a flashlight, then went back to bed. She fell into a heavy sleep despite the coffee and woke late in the morning. The night had left her shaken, so she decided to risk waking Michael. She dialed his number, but his phone seemed to be switched off. She left a quick message, then showered, standing under the brisk spray to drive the away the remnants of sleep. Once dressed, she went down to the kitchen. She ate yogurt and watched the sheep graze on the green slope. A bird rode on the back of one sheep after another, blissfully eating its own breakfast—fleas she imagined. After the make-shift breakfast, she walked around the corner to Chalice Well, remembering the last trip, how she'd looked forward to a blissful month in Glastonbury alone with Michael, slowly exploring the sites, looking through the house, spending uninterrupted time alone. But now she had an assignment, to try to discover more about the disturbing dream and the erratic flow of White Spring.

When she reached the red gatehouse, she realized that in the rush Michael had forgotten to leave his companion pass, so she bought one for herself, thinking this was a good way to support the place. She pushed open the wrought iron gate, decorated with the recurring two circles of the Vesica Piscis, and started down the stone steps to the two overlapping pools that repeated the pattern again. A clump of tourists walked on the green lawn, one snapping picture after picture. A couple sat on the same bench she and Michael had occupied just a few days ago, the woman's head resting on the man's shoulder. On another bench, a young mother watched her toddler playing. The baby kept splashing the smooth surface, delighting in the waves she created.

Smiling, Anne dipped her fingers in the water, then went back up the steps to the two ancient yew trees. Leaning against the sturdy trunk of one, she asked for guidance, letting the peace that was Chalice Well Garden, even as crowded as it was, begin to soak into her. It was hard to credit any problem here, even after last night's nightmare and the meeting with Garth. There was no immediate response, just a sense of the slow growth of green needles and new shoots, the ripening of cones, the long sweep of time.

Anne stepped away from the tree and headed across the lawn where a wooden gate stood open. In the brochure, she saw this place had been named "King Arthur's Court." Here the shade dominated. A bench ran the length of the ivy-covered wall. Across from it, a rectangular pool at the far end of the courtyard caught the water that flowed down the stones. Sunlight glinted between the tree branches and reflected off the waterfall, highlighting the red stained rock beneath. A fuzz of rust-colored algae covered the bottom of pilgrims' bath. Anne kicked off her shoes and sat on the edge. A sign warned of the slippery bottom, but she tried to stand anyway, and sure enough, her feet slid right out from under her. She plopped back down on the flagstone where she stayed, soaking her feet, enjoying the play of light and shadow, listening to the music of the water. As the quiet returned, so did the sparrows, flitting from branch to branch, dropping down to the ground to peck in the ivy. Time and worry faded.

After a time, she grew thirsty. There had to be a place to drink here. The main attraction was a spring and they sold bottles at the gatehouse. She got up, put on her shoes and climbed a set of flagstone steps where she found a path. She followed it around into a large rectangular lawn. Water spurted from a lion's head set in the grey stone wall at the far end. The water had stained the stones below the fountain the characteristic red of this place. Algae mossed the wall. An ordinary drinking glass sat on the wall above and another below caught the flow of water from the lion's mouth, overflowing onto the two round stones it balanced on. Anne picked up the full glass and drank.

The water left a faint taste of rust in her mouth, but satisfied something deep within her. She filled it several more times, drinking her fill, then walked amongst the flowers soaking in the noonday sun, as free of thought as the open faces of the impatiens lining the walk.

A wrought iron arch almost lost in a profusion of white roses marked a new part of the garden. Anne walked through and immediately to her right in the shade of a bay tree sat the well itself. The lid, latched open, repeated the Vesica Piscis pattern, but with variations. The brochure said that the cover was English oak decorated with a bleeding lance passing through the middle of the circles. Filigreed oak leaves decorated the sides. Frederick Bligh Bond had copied the medieval design and donated the cover in 1919. Several people sat on the stone seats built into the wall surrounding the well. Anne followed a tiny path between tall flowers and found a wooden chair set in the middle, but someone sat there, eyes closed. Anne crept back out and stood on the cobblestone path waiting her turn.

Finally the group wandered off. Anne walked to the top of the step and stopped, asking permission to enter. A gentle swirl of breeze seemed to welcome her, so she went down and knelt on the flagstones surrounding the well shaft. She peered through the grate. The walls looked much as they had in her dream, covered with moss and ferns, but the water was visible, clear and brimming just out of arm's reach. Anne settled on a stone seat beneath the thorn tree, tucked her legs beneath her tailor-style, and let her eyes float on the water. Her intention, spoken to the yew trees, remained the same.

People came and went, some silently, others chatting, one even conducting a loud conversation on her cell phone, but Anne did not pay them any mind. Signs around the garden encouraged meditation and quiet. She didn't stand out. Others sat with eyes closed or hung colorful ribbons in the trees, each tie a prayer or spell. After a while, the surface activity faded away. A silver mist rose from the well shaft and billowed out, filling the stone hollow. Shapes moved in the mist, but when Anne tried to focus on them, they faded away. Whispers slid by her, just out of the range of hearing. Two people took the bench across from her, nodded, and continued their quiet conversation, not seeming to notice the spreading fog. Anne focused back on the water, trying to still her mind so she could catch what was happening around her, but the mist dispersed as quickly as it had come.

Disappointed, she unfolded her legs, wincing as the blood returned to one that had fallen asleep. Once the tingling faded, Anne left the well hollow and walked to the back fence. On the other side of the wire mesh, more sheep grazed. She followed the path around the back end of the garden and found a meadow with a few low trees and benches sprinkled around. She sat in a swing and, on looking up, found the Tor framed between the trees, a perfect postcard, Michael's tower pointing into the clear, blue sky. Here she stayed while her mind made a list of tasks she should be working on, inventory of the house, pack up Aunt Cynthia's clothes, fix the step that squeaked. Then came a list of worries. She should be solving the mystery of her dream and White Spring, helping Michael find the crystals he was searching for. But instead, she sat on in the peace of that green meadow, as content as the sheep.

ANNE WOKE the next morning still wrapped in the peace of Chalice Well Gardens. Her visit yesterday had brought no new revelations nor had her dreams last night. In fact, she didn't remember dreaming at all. But this was her pattern. After a vivid psychic experience, things went silent, underground as it were. Dr. Abernathy had taught her that patience and persistence were the keys. If she kept moving forward, more guidance would appear exactly when she needed it.

Late morning, Michael gave her a call, his voice heavy with sleep. Her longing for him returned in a flood. They'd exchanged news, then she asked, "When do you come home? We're supposed to be honeymooning."

"You're still calling it home," he chuckled. "I like that."

"For now, anyway."

"I need to find out what happened to these pieces of the—" he paused "—you know."

"Do you really think they're important?" She lay across the bed upstairs, plaiting and unplaiting the fringe on a purple chenille throw.

"I can only imagine what I would do in his place," Michael said. "I'd look for them."

"Where are you going next?"

"Back to New York. Find out what Arnold and Dr. Abernathy have discovered about our friends." Somehow they'd stopped calling Cagliostro and Mueller by name.

"I miss you."

He was silent for a minute. "It wasn't supposed to turn out like this."

"I know. I'm sorry you've lost your mentor."

"You lost Thomas."

"I'm tired of all this death. I wish we could put an end to it."

His cold laugh felt like a cloud over the sun. "It seems we have no choice."

Chilled, she reached for the warmth of their passion. "I love you."

"Me, too. I'll call when I get to New York." And they hung up.

Garth arrived promptly at one dressed in jeans, corduroy shirt and stout boots. He leaned on a walking stick with subtle spiraling lines running the length. The knob had been carved into the head of a badger. "Ready?" His steady brown eyes glinted beneath his shaggy brows.

His earthiness and steady confidence comforted her. "Let's go," she said.

Garth favored his left leg, but the limp seemed to have improved since Friday morning. He stopped at White Spring and bent to the pipe. A tiny trickle of water dripped into the drain below. He shook his head, but made no comment. They walked to the corner.

"Tor or Red Spring?" Anne asked.

"Did you go to the Well yesterday?" he asked.

"Yes, but I didn't receive any answers."

"How did you feel there?"

"Wonderful. I haven't felt that peaceful in a long time." The heightened state of consciousness she'd experienced in the underground temple in Egypt had left her filled with wonder. Yesterday, she'd felt a peace that transcended any problems that might arise.

Garth studied her face for a moment, then smiled. "Yes, Glastonbury has that quality at times. Let's just walk through then, to pay our respects."

The person keeping the gate greeted Garth as visiting royalty. The place was flush with children, ending any hope of another meditation, but they walked through the garden anyway, Garth pointing out the places she'd visited yesterday. "This pool in King Arthur's Courtyard used to be deeper," he said. "Up to your chin at least."

When they got to the Well, she told him about the mist and the subliminal voices.

He narrowed his eyes, chin resting on his barrel chest. Seemed to listen to something, then nodded. "You understand the basics of how the springs work with the energy of the Tor. I don't want to fill your head with legends. I'd rather see what you pick up on your own."

Just like Dr. Abernathy, Anne thought.

"Let's walk over to Wearyall Hill. I want to take you into the Abbey after hours some time soon. Visit the Lady's Chapel."

"Are you sure?" Anne pointed to his leg.

"Much improved."

As they walked down Bere Lane past the houses that separated them from the Abbey grounds, Garth told her how Glastonbury Abbey had seen a succession of various clergy, first the Druids, then the Saxons, who continued to consult the Druid priestesses. "Next came the followers of Joseph of Arimethea. He was a tin merchant, you know, but some say that's a reference to the alchemical element associated with Jupiter."

Anne shook her head. "What does that mean?"

"That he was an alchemist, not a business man," Garth said, as if this explained everything.

"I thought alchemy came from Europe," Anne said.

"But isn't this man of yours an Egyptologist?" Garth smiled down at her.

"I remember now." Anne held up her forefinger. "Al Khem. The ancient name of Egypt with the Arabic prefix."

"Right." Garth stopped at the small roundabout and guided them to Hill Head. They walked along a row of houses. "The next spiritual tradition to join us in Glastonbury was the Kabbalists."

"So, they displaced the Druids?"

"Certainly not. They got on well together. Had a grand time swapping teachings, comparing their maps of the universe, which were similar.

Glastonbury and Jerusalem have always had a connection. Mary's mother came from here."

"What? How could that be?"

Garth smiled at her. "In the ancient past, people connected over much larger distances than our anthropologists currently believe."

"Now you sound like Michael."

The end of Hill Head turned into a foot path that followed the ridge of the hill. Instead of sheep, cows grazed, lifting their heavy heads and staring while they chewed, wisps of grass hanging from their rubbery lips. Calves nursed, then nosed at the grass, copying their mothers. They came to a tree surrounded by a short metal fence. "Did your man tell you about the Holy Thorn?"

"He started to, but we were interrupted." Anne shook her head against the sudden wave of sadness.

Garth politely did not notice. "When Joseph arrived in Avalon, he pushed his staff into the ground and rested here. When he woke the next morning, the staff had sprouted, so he left it and it grew into a tree. People have taken cuttings and there are several around Glastonbury now. The Holy Thorns aren't native to the British Isles. They come from Lebanon—Jerusalem according to the legend. They bloom when the Holy Thorns flower in the Middle East, at Christmas, and again at Easter."

Indeed, buds swelled, close to opening.

"The Christmas blossoming is considered a miracle."

Anne smiled at the story.

"They pick a Christmas blossom every year and send it to the queen." Garth stroked a thick leaf.

"Michael said the earliest form of Christianity started here." She kept probing his loss like a person tongues a sore tooth.

"I suppose you could say that. It happened in Israel at the same time. The early Jews who came here followed their ancient ways. That grew into Celtic Christianity." He waved behind them. "And the Abbey."

They settled on a bench. "Let's spend some time in silence here, then tell me what you feel."

Anne obliged him. She sat beside Garth, as solid as a hill himself, and opened her senses to their surroundings. After a short time, Garth whispered, "Come back."

Anne opened her eyes and was startled to see the sun had moved a good way toward the west. "That was just a minute."

"About forty."

"But . . ." Anne glanced at her watch in confusion.

"Time runs funny here."

"I guess."

"What did you feel?"

"Quiet, but not peaceful like Chalice Well. This hill feels more energetic. It's like a transition place, moving from the ordinary world into the magical."

"I agree." Garth nodded enthusiastically. "Did you see or hear anything?"

"Nothing specific, but I felt Joseph put his staff here to protect Avalon. To mark the place for travelers to wait before entering Avalon."

Garth slapped his knee in delight. "The ocean surrounded the Tor before they built the seawalls, making Wearyall a landing place. The male Druids today do much of their ceremony here."

"It has a more masculine feel," Anne said.

"Another day we'll go to Bride's Mound." He pointed over his shoulder. At Anne's look of confusion, he said, "Bridget. You know this goddess?"

"Not really," Anne said.

Garth stood. "Let's watch the sunset from the Tor. It's a town tradition." As they walked, he explained, "Bridget is one of the oldest goddesses. She has three aspects."

"Let me guess—maiden, mother, crone."

"A good bet usually, but not in this case. She rules over poetry, smithcraft and healing." A cow lifted her head and sent out a deep bellow. Garth laughed. "Thank you for the reminder. She's often depicted with a cow."

"Like Hathor."

Garth nodded. "She is a fire goddess. These three crafts are all expressions of fire. We light a fire to her at Imbolc, when she is honored especially. Our country is even named after her—Britain. Brigantia."

Anne remembered the ceremony she'd participated in on February first, Imbolc, and the spiritual fire they had rekindled in the earth. She wished Michael wasn't so far away.

They walked the rest of the way in silence, finally turning onto Wellhouse Lane where they took the pathway up the Tor. Anne wanted to broach the question of Garth's relationship with Cynthia, but felt she'd be prying. Instead she said, "I found a manuscript Cynthia was working on." His sudden sharp breath made her regret that she'd opened the topic.

Finally he said, "I'm glad it's safe."

"There was a note to you. I apologize for reading it—" she tried to see his face, but he'd turned his head toward the small apple orchard on their right "—it said she wanted to write the story as a novel. Didn't want to be identified publicly as a channeler."

"I must have left the note at the house. She said she didn't want her sister to try to have her committed."

Now it was Anne's turn to be surprised. "I don't think mother would have gone that far. Besides, Grandmother Elizabeth would never have allowed it."

Finally he turned to her. His face showed no sign of grief. "How is Elizabeth?"

"You've met?"

"Oh, yes," Garth said. "A formidable woman."

"No kidding. I was terrified of her as a child."

"Surely not." He even laughed.

"She always knew what we'd been up to. When I read Greek myth, I thought she must be a misplaced Sybil."

"But she is also strong," he said, "like a queen."

"So, feel sorry for us kids." Anne punched his arm playfully.

"I concede your point."

The steep slope of the Tor took their breath, so they climbed to the top in silence. Quite a few people milled about on the summit, some propped against the wall of the tower, others sitting on the slope, all watching the sun as it met the ocean. Several people greeted Garth with nods and raised hands, but they did not speak. Anne and Garth sat on the western slope and watched the sun paint the clouds orange and purple.

When the sun disappeared beneath the waves, they rose without a word and walked back down the same way they'd climbed up. The hares had come out, small mounds of darkness with large ears, ancient shapes that tugged at Anne's ancestral memory. The jackdaws cawed in the trees toward the bottom. Farther down, human voices added to the racket. A crowd of townies, vagrants and tourists had gathered at White Spring, and everyone seemed to be talking at once.

"I told the town council we'd have to undo this mess the Victorians created," said a man dressed in jeans and a neat Oxford shirt. "Something's fallen in. Plugged up the works."

"Armageddon is upon us," shouted another man dressed in ragged trousers and several moth eaten sweaters, his face red. "The end is near."

A knot of women, heads together, buzzed like a swarm of bees. "The Goddess must be recognized. As long as violence against women continues . . ." Anne noticed with a start that her housekeeper Tessa stood in the middle of this group.

Garth made his way to the middle of the crowd and raised his hand. To Anne's complete astonishment, silence fell. "Now, what seems to be the problem?" He turned to a woman who held a few plastic water jugs.

"There's no water." She pointed to the spring's outlet. "White Spring's dried up."

General lamentations and opinions filled the air again, but again Garth raised his arms and the mutterings fell into silence once more. "When?"

"About an hour ago."

"Before that," one of the women in the knot said. "There was no water when I came down."

"When was that?" he asked.

"About half past two."

"Then we must restore the flow," Garth's voice rang out like a trumpet and a chill ran the length of Anne's spine. He'd used the same phrase that had been passed down through the family with her crystal key. They were to be used to "restore the flow."

"Do we agree?" Garth seemed to be addressing one of the women in the buzzing group, an ethereal blond who considered him through narrowed eyes.

Anne wondered who she was. Obviously someone with clout. After a minute, the woman nodded, giving permission for something. Anne wasn't sure what.

"Let's get into a circle as much as we can." Garth's voice had softened.

The group shuffled into a make-shift ring. A few people walked away.

"If you can, take your neighbor's hand." He waited for the group to settle again. "Now, let's take a few deep breaths." And he demonstrated, breathing in, his chest visibly expanding, then blowing air through his nostrils.

He sounded like a cart horse. Anne bit her lips against an inappropriate giggle.

After a few minutes, the group more or less breathed together. Then low chanting started from several points in the circle. Garth nodded encouragement. Soprano voices matched the tone an octave higher. One vagrant pulled a reed flute from his pack and added its voice. In a matter of minutes, harmony had replaced the uproar. Even the jackdaws sat quietly in the trees, their hovering presence somehow a part of the circle.

The chanting deepened and Anne closed her eyes, leaning against the cement wall of the spring house. She sent a silence request to the Tor for water, then floated in the sound of the chant. After a minute, the crystal key she'd inherited from Aunt Cynthia woke up. Startled, she opened her eyes. The crystal seemed to take a breath, then sent out a stream of energy.

Garth looked over at her, his eyes questioning. She pointed to her chest, but he shook his head, not understanding. "Later," she mouthed, and closed her eyes.

The stream of energy spiraled around the circle, gathering all the voices together, all the desire of those hearts for their beloved White Spring to be healed. The chant grew louder and faster. People swayed, made gestures with their hands. One man squatted and began to draw spirals on the flagstone in front of him with chalk. The crystal modulated all the energies into one frequency, then flung it into the flank of the Tor. Anne grabbed at the wall behind her, but found no purchase. She slid to the ground.

A shout went up from the people standing next to the spout. "Water! There's water." The crowd broke ranks and surged forward, heads craning to see. Someone stuck a jar under the spout, then held it above her head. A great cheer when up. After a few minutes, Garth held up his arms again and the rejoicing quieted enough for him to shout. "We did it. Thank you." More cheers greeted his words, but he held up his arms for quiet. "But I think we need to do more. I call for a town meeting in the Assembly Halls. Do you agree?"

The crowd shouted yes. Even the blond nodded, but she watched Anne through narrowed eyes while Tessa whispered in her ear.

"I'll post a sign," Garth said.

12

Tall, golden orbs of light wavered in the darkness, pulling him forward, tickling some deep place in his brain, but try as he might, he couldn't reach them, though his whole being yearned for them. He gave a great heave and rammed his face against a wall, invisible but rough, that left him bleeding and alone. Just what he would do once he joined those shapes of light, what this place was, teased him like a word just on the tip of his tongue, out of memory's reach.

Cagliostro fought the jumbled sheets, turned over and found a memory he could access—riding in his first hunt at six, stirrups tied short to accommodate his legs, heart thumping when the hounds sounded they'd found a trail, jaw clinched, determined he would keep his seat and not embarrass his father. He'd managed to hang on, had crowded in when the hounds cornered the fox, a quivering female, skinny, madly snapping, but the master of the hunt had called them off, pointing to her swollen teats. "She's got kits," he said. The man lured the hounds with meat he carried in his saddle bags. Once they crowded around, the master handed a few pieces to him, and he proudly fed the snarling pack, holding the meat like he'd been instructed to save his fingers. But his father didn't notice. He was been busy talking with some visiting dignitary.

Then a face, the one that haunted his dreams, deep blue eyes lit by an inner fire, a profusion of red curls snaking around finely chiseled features, laughing, that mouth a mixture of soft promise and cruelty. His whole being yearned for her. He'd searched for her his whole life, longer, and here she was.

She looked at him, then turned, throwing that wild mane over her shoulder, slipping down a path of . . . were those solid dark shapes the trunks of trees? Was she lost in some ancient forest? He opened his mouth to call her, but her name slid away into the shadows.

A hand was laid on his forehead, then something cool, and he slept quietly again.

DR. ABERNATHY POURED HIMSELF A DRINK, then looked over at Michael, who had settled back on the sofa and leaned his head back to admire the upper balcony. Abernathy's home library extended to a second story of books surrounded by a banister that looked like a crow's nest on a ship.

"Sherry?" Dr. Abernathy held the decanter up.

"None for me, thanks."

Abernathy put the hand blown glass top back on the decanter, then sat down in his armchair. Stacks of magazines and books bristling with yellow stickies lay scattered around his favorite spot.

"Heard from Arnold?" Michael looked over at him.

"Cagliostro seems to have disappeared. Left in the middle of the night. Nobody would talk. The flight plan registered London as their destination. The plane landed in a private hanger and a car took the party to his country house in Somerset, but there's been no activity that we can see."

"Playing with his newly acquired toys, no doubt."

Abernathy cocked his head at Michael's bitter tone. "Giving up already?"

"We're always three steps behind him." Michael crossed his arms.

"That's our Cagliostro." He lifted his delicate glass as if to toast him.

Michael's eyes lit up. "Know thine enemy."

"What do you mean?"

"You know him."

"Knew," Abernathy corrected. He took another sip of his sherry. "It was a long time ago."

"Tell me about him," Michael said.

Abernathy shook his head. "We need to find these artifacts. Keep them out of his hands."

"Indulge me. I can't see Franz Maier until Wednesday." Michael settled in as if he expected a long story.

Abernathy sipped his sherry, enjoying its sweet bite, then set the glass down and stared into the flames of the fire they'd lit, to stay warm in the unseasonal chill or as a talisman against Cagliostro, he couldn't really say. Perhaps Michael was right. With an effort, he broke the silence. "We were the same year at Oxford."

Michael looked up sharply. "I thought you said he was your teacher."

"Oh, yes. He became my teacher." Abernathy's eyes tightened. "Alexander Cagliostro outshined us all." He stared into the flames again, hesitating. What would Michael think once he knew the truth? Finally, he waded into the swamp of his memories.

"We became fast friends after we discovered our common interests. Shared rooms our second year. You see, old man Le Clair sent me to Oxford, and he made certain arrangements for my extracurricular education." The scene of their first meeting played across his mind.

They walked across campus, chatting companionably about classes, sports—Abernathy had won a place on the rowing team. But they seemed to be following the same path, taking the same turns, and Abernathy had been admonished to tell no one about this clandestine meeting. As they approached his destination, Cagliostro stopped. "Good talking with you."

"You, too," Abernathy waved his hand and continued. But when Cagliostro took the same turn he'd just taken and began following him again, Abernathy looked back, trying to decide what to do.

"I say, where are you going, then?" the white blond ponytail Cagliostro affected shown under the street lamp.

"Got to see one of the dons. Bloody inconvenient." Abernathy affected the favorite British slang. "And you?"

They walked a few more steps to the door of the chapel, and Cagliostro stopped, smiling like a Cheshire cat. "Could we both have an appointment here tonight?"

"You mean—"

He opened the door. "After you."

They laughed together, their comradery turning a dark, lonely walk to a mysterious meeting into a daring adventure. They made their way down an aisle in the quiet of the dusky church and headed to a door in the back. "I knew there was something about you I liked, Abernathy."

That night they'd been initiated into a secret group within the Masons, one with a long history. Two nights a week, the new crop of initiates attended hush-hush classes together, taking separate, circuitous routes to the don's quarters, where they sat in a tight circle listening to instruction, followed by putting that night's lesson to work in meditation or ritual. Cagliostro grasped the lessons as if he were just reviewing them. His visions stunned the class, but the professor remained aloof. They took to calling Professor Forrester names to make up for his snubs. "Dr. Dolt's jealous. He plods along. Magic by numbers," Cagliostro sneered.

Abernathy wondered about Forrester's attitude. Whenever Cagliostro had a particularly spectacular experience, Forrester lectured them about how colorful experiences, as he called them, were not in and of themselves proof of advanced ability. "These must be tempered by wisdom." He'd fixed Cagliostro with a look. "Sometimes it is better if this type of clarity comes later in life."

Cagliostro had a way of looking down his aristocratic nose at him that made Forrester's mouth tighten. He collected a group of admirers that practiced and studied together. With the classes came access to the special metaphysical collection in a private room in one of the libraries. All Cagliostro had to do was wonder about something aloud, and someone would stay up all night pouring over arcane texts to find the answer. He'd appear bleary eyed at breakfast, elbowing people away so he could sit by Cagliostro and brag about what he'd found. Abernathy became Cagliostro's right hand man, a position coveted by all the others.

In their second year, the group was ushered with due ceremony into a closet in their chemistry lab. The front part was indeed a closet, but behind the brooms and mops, another door opened to a spacious and well stocked alchemical laboratory. Here they worked among boiling beakers and test tubes full of oddly colored liquids. Abernathy preferred mental workings, but

Cagliostro excelled here as well, once making a temperamental potion that took an entire lunar cycle to complete. He'd won grudging praise. All the Masons who taught them seemed to resent Cagliostro except one, Cornelius Waldman, a man who inspired fear in everyone except his chosen apprentice.

Over the summer before their third year, Waldman invited Cagliostro to his home. When Cagliostro returned, he moved to the front of the class, then started studying with a more advanced group, even passing them. The Masonic teachers grew hesitant to criticize him. He won initiation into the secret order that next summer.

Abernathy stopped his narrative and sat staring into the fire in the library. After a long pause, he continued. "That's when Cagliostro became a teacher. He helped with the first year classes. In our free time, he hand-picked three others—I was one—for what he called special instruction." The words were bitter in his mouth. He remembered his pride, how he'd rubbed a friend's face in it. "We read Crowley, replicated some of his more daring experiments. But Cagliostro had to outshine even him." Abernathy groped for his glass of sherry, took two gulps, then set it down again. A log on the fire sizzled. The tick of the grandfather clock downstairs reached them in the quiet.

"What do you know about his life before Oxford?" Michael's voice seemed to come from far away. "Did you ever meet his family? I mean, he changed his name, didn't he?"

Grateful Michael had spared him a walk down the entire path of his regrettable association with Alexander Cagliostro, Abernathy gave himself a slight shake. "Yes, the family name is Ravenscroft. At least they took that name when they moved to England. Probably in the late eighteenth century. Cagliostro reclaimed his lineage and took the last name again when he declared his independence from his father."

"They were in conflict?" Michael asked.

"Oh, indeed." Abernathy's laugh was bitter. "He hated the old man. Not a shred of magic in his body, he used to say. Spent all his time doing business. He rebuilt the family fortune, though."

"Doing what?" Michael asked.

He narrowed his eyes, trying to remember. "Oil and gas. Gold. Diamonds during the war. The second one."

"I figured. Sounds like he was involved in some pretty shady business."

Abernathy nodded. "They had it out his senior year. He moved in with Waldman, changed his name." The fire had died down. He looked over at Michael who was only an outline in the darkness. He reached up to switch on the light, but changed his mind. The dark suited his mood.

"Were they lovers?"

"Who?"

"Waldman and Cagliostro?"

He snorted. "Probably, but Cagliostro devoured women as fast as he went through his basic studies. And with the same relish. He never fell in love. He seemed to be looking for someone special. An equal. Never found one, though. Slept with his share of men, but he seemed to do that for form. Maybe out of his devotion to Crowley."

"Did he ever meet him?"

"Crowley died in 1947. Sixty years ago."

"And his mother?"

"Beautiful woman. Wore the family jewels well, he used to say. They were never close."

"Poor little rich boy."

Abernathy yanked his head around at Michael's tone. "I've often wondered what turned him. I'm not sure it was his parents, although he certainly had a lonely childhood on that huge country manor. No brothers or sisters. Father off on business. Mother in London. No, Cagliostro damned himself."

Michael sat forward. "How do you mean?"

Now they had come to it. "Cagliostro took a trip to San Francisco. He had to experience the summer of love for himself. Then he and Waldman traveled to South America. He came home with some ayahuasca. Said it put acid to shame."

"Dr. Abernathy!" Michael sounded scandalized.

Abernathy smiled at Michael's tone. "We took the drug and waited for it to come on, then cast a circle. Cagliostro said he was going to conjure up some demon he'd read about. One that had been bound long ago. I didn't take him very seriously. I didn't believe in demons, not in the way people think of them nowadays."

"Neither do I," Michael added.

"Yes, well," he paused. "Let's just say I was surprised."

HE SURFACED from restful sleep to another memory. The drug rushed through his system, opening his vision to what hung in the air around him. Faces pushed up against the circle they'd just cast. Again, he dipped the athame into the chalice filled with sheep's blood and drew another backwards pentagram in the east. "I conjure you, Semiazas, chief of the fallen angels, to appear before us." He heard Abernathy shift his feet and briefly wondered if he'd hold up the north, but he didn't have time to worry. More faces pushed against their sphere, demanding entrance. Cagliostro sent a stream of energy to strengthen the circle behind him, then called again. "Semiazas. Appear."

A great roaring, then something flung him to the ground. He groped to get up, pushed his hair out of his eyes and saw hooves—no feet—but standing in fire. The smell overwhelmed him. Was it burnt tires? He coughed, trying to clear his lungs. His eyes streamed. Dimly aware of running feet, Cagliostro felt the circle sag. "No," he croaked, and sent another blast of energy into the now empty north. The ritual space held.

Thank God, he thought.

"You invoke God now?" the being asked, then spat at Cagliostro. The spittle smoldered, burning into the wood parquet floor, then turned into a snake that slithered back to the demon, leaving a trail of smoke.

Cagliostro staggered to his feet. "Semiazas?" He shook his head against the question in his voice. Cornelius said never to show weakness.

"He sent me because I know you. I know what you are."

The voice caressed him, leaving behind a wave of revulsion. He took a shaking breath. If the true name controlled the being, then he was in trouble. "How do you know me?"

"We started it, you and I."

"Started what?" *Damn, Cornelius said never to ask, always to command.*

The demon lifted up his sharp, red face and wailed.

Cagliostro covered his ears, blind terror replacing thought for a full minute. Then he realized it was laughing.

"How could you forget, Alexander?"

His mind raced. He'd seen a list. He'd had to memorize it. Then it came. "Thamuz," he said. "The Inquisition."

The demon laughed again and somehow he withstood the sound. Then it asked, "What do you want?" The question somehow contained the suggestion that he was an insect in the great hierarchy of beings, not worthy of any boon. And yet, the being had appeared.

He forced himself to look into Thamuz's face. It roiled like a furnace. Images floated to the top of men pleading, burning, stretched on racks, screaming as their entrails were torn from their body. Cagliostro looked into the demon's eyes and his bowels turned to water. He panted for a minute, then said, "I bind you—"

"You bind me? What comic book have you been reading?"

"—to serve me—"

"You inconsequential—"

A blast of fire burned Cagliostro's eyelashes. "—in this life," he gasped out.

A blast of rage, then Cagliostro came back to consciousness and found himself lying flat on the floor. Had it left? He sighed in relief, but then he heard something ponderous shift its weight.

"Look at me when I talk to you."

The voice alone picked him up off the floor. He looked again into those fathomless eyes.

"My master bids me remind you of your task. When the time comes, I will aid you, but only because He commands it." A burst of flames and the sound of gale force winds, and Thamuz was gone.

"No," Cagliostro screamed as if his lungs were raw. Footsteps sounded from the hall. The door opened. "No." He held his hands in front of his face.

He didn't want to see him again. Someone grabbed his arm. A sharp prick, then another drug, cool in his vein, seeped through his system, sending him into dreamless sleep again.

But the morning nurse found him sitting in bed, lucid, self-contained, as dangerous as a King cobra. She stopped short, then quickly gathered her wits. "Sir, how are you feeling?"

"How many days?" he asked.

But what he really wondered was how many days, how many lifetimes, he'd wasted serving the power hungry world elite, using his talents to conduct rituals to control the masses, to influence world events, to find and activate ancient technology. He had thought this was his own desire as well. But now the time had come to turn the tables, to use the shadow government for his own ends. Now, Cagliostro knew what he truly wanted.

13

Govannan sat in an undignified heap holding his thigh, trying not to groan. The sharp, stabbing pain gradually receded, and he nodded to Herasto, one of the pod members, who helped him to his feet, holding onto his shoulder. Govannan took a tentative step. Pain stabbed deep into his thigh. He stood, a thin line of sweat on his lip. The Pleiadian ambassador, still fastening her deep rose jumpsuit, ran over to him, her piercing blue eyes wrinkled in concern. "Are you injured?"

He nodded. "Something brushed against me. It was only a light touch, but it seems to have torn a muscle. What did you see?"

She looked him up and down, then said something in a low voice.

Govannan leaned closer. "Excuse me?"

She shook her head. "Someone out of his proper time."

Govannan stepped toward her in alarm and his leg buckled. Herasto grabbed him before he fell. Govannan spoke through tight lips, "Someone else was in there with you?"

She nodded.

"But, how could that be? I've never heard of such a thing." He looked around at his pod of workers who stood in a tight knot, some whispering, others listening intently to their conversation.

"It happens from time to time."

This comment reminded Govannan of the lengthy life spans of the Pleiadians, as she had probably meant it to. "What should we do? I've never had a slip up like this. We could have endangered your life."

She waved a hand in dismissal. "I was in no danger."

"If it would not be too much of an imposition," his head was clearing enough to remember that one had to treat the Pleiadian matriarchy with utmost respect, "I would appreciate hearing about any other times you've experienced this."

She studied him for a moment, her head cocked to one side.

"I would learn from you." He bowed his head slightly.

"The time to talk is approaching." Then she looked around the group.

One of the pod members stepped forward. "I will escort you."

The ambassador nodded and followed the pod member out of the chamber.

Govannan looked around at the group. "Let's get this crystal settled, then we'll meet." Ianara, a leader of one of the pod, stepped forward, a frown on her face. "What?" he snapped.

"You need to go to the healers." She ignored his tone.

"First we need to figure out what happened."

"Once you've seen the healer."

Govannan took a breath to object, and she raised an eyebrow.

"Oh, all right." He tried to take another step. Pain shot up his leg into his hip. He bit his lip to stop an involuntary gasp. "Perhaps you're right," he said in a subdued voice. He looked around at the group, then back to Ianara. "Will you lead the debriefing?"

She nodded.

"Please come report to me in the healer's temple as soon as you can."

"Of course." She turned to the pod. "Daphyll, go get a transport. Herasto, help him outside. Accompany him to the temple and report back when you know something."

Govannan frowned. The group, usually one mind for some time after a transport, seemed scattered, scraps of paper in the wind. But his next step wrenched his mind back to his injury. Leaning heavily on Herasto, he waited by the door for the transport. Once aboard, the vehicle lifted quickly and they flew toward the temple.

Situated near a long, quiet strip of beach, the healing temple sat on two acres dotted with gardens, streams and a lake populated by migrating ducks and geese, and their own resident flock of swans. The stone and selenite temple rested in the middle. From above, its blue dome suggested another lake.

Daphyll brought the vehicle down close to the main entrance. She got out and swung around. "I'll go get someone." She jogged toward the building. Two people had already spotted their approach and were running from the building with a floating stretcher between them. "It's not life threatening," she called, and the group slowed. She explained the accident as they walked back to the transport.

Govannan pasted an apologetic smile on his face. The healers each had two stars attached to the blue robes of their guild, indicating their rank as apprentices. "I'm sorry to trouble you," he began.

"It's your leg?" one asked.

"Yes, the left one." Govannan shifted as the healer reached out and began to probe his thigh with a practiced touch. He tried not to grunt when she reached the injured spot.

"Uh hum," she repeated with each poke. "Uh hum. And how did this happen?"

Govannan told the story again. The looks of the healers' faces grew more incredulous as he spoke. "Excuse me, sir, but we haven't been trained for such an accident."

"Neither have I, but the ambassador assures me the event is not unprecedented."

The group lifted Govannan onto the stretcher, ignoring his protests that he was capable of walking, and whisked him off to one of the treatment areas. Once they arrived, one apprentice went for a more advanced healer and the other covered him with a blanket, which he tolerated. "Go back to the meeting," he said to his two pod members. After a few objections, they left, and he lay back and examined the room. It had been some time since he'd been a patient. He rested in a private alcove awash with soft light. In one corner, water trickled down a sheet of limestone and dropped into an alabaster basin lit from within, a sound that soothed him. Above, a tinted skylight let in a bit of sunlight.

The swish of a robe made him turn his head. Megan's mother stood there looking at him. "Pleione," he started to get up, "but surely you're too busy to waste your time on a simple muscle strain."

"How could I miss the opportunity to visit with you?" she said lightly, but Govannan had not missed the flash of concern on her face before she'd put on her professional mask.

"Heck of an accident," he commented.

"But you say the Pleiadian ambassador has experienced such an intrusion before?"

"That's what she said, and you don't question that royal family."

They both laughed.

"Just relax now." Her hands spread warmth with their touch, and he closed his eyes. Even when she probed his injury, deeper than her apprentices had, there was no pain, only comfort. She brought a few stones from a cabinet he hadn't noticed before and arranged them on his body. Next she set a large crystal bowl between his legs next to the injury and began to run the wooden mallet around the rim. The bowl sat silent for a moment, then hummed, giving off a deep, aching tone. The sound intensified, and it set off the throb in his leg again. Pleione added her voice, and just as the pain became too much to bear, his leg seemed to lose its solidity for a moment and dissolved into nothing but vibration. He gripped the table. Strands of energy separated and lifted off. She allowed the bowl to quiet, then passed her hands over him as if she were dousing. "Better?"

Coolness and relief had replaced the throbbing pain. "Much." He started to get up, but one gentle hand pushed him back.

"Not yet. There's still some residue. I want you to rest here, and we'll put you in with the dolphins in a bit."

"But surely that isn't necessary. I feel almost normal."

"I don't question your professional opinions, do I, Govannan?"

"But, the pod is meeting. I need—"

"You need to be treated by the dolphins." Her tone sounded like she was chiding a fractious child.

He heaved a sigh. "If you insist."

Her laugh sounded like silver bells. "I do. Now, I'll just go check the schedule. Close your eyes and sleep."

Once she left the room, he hoisted himself up on his elbow and looked around the room. He considered sending for a messenger to find out what the pod members had reported about their mishap, but he couldn't bring himself to get up. Lethargy stole through his body, and soon he drifted off.

The next thing he heard was Pleione's quiet voice. "Good nap?"

He rubbed his eyes and stretched. "Time for my swim?"

"Come along now. I think you can walk to the beach. We'll go slowly."

His eyes widened. "As much as I appreciate it, I don't feel I can claim the sole attention of the mistress of the Healer's Guild for so long."

"Arguing again?" Her smile belied her stern tone of voice.

Obediently, Govannan slid off the table and tested his leg. It felt wobbly, like a freshly washed up jellyfish. Although he had a distinct limp, it supported his weight adequately. After a step or two, he got used to the sensation. "The beach?"

"Yes, our resident group of dolphins is busy all afternoon. We'll go to the shore and see who volunteers."

"I get to see you call the dolphins?" He realized that he must sound like a child anticipating a carnival, but didn't care.

"I'll even teach you how." Her smile was indulgent. Once outside, they walked through a series of colorful gardens, Pleione matching the pace he set. After a while, she asked, "How is Megan?"

Relieved to take the focus away from himself, he took to this subject with relish. "Excellent. She has the sensitivity to energy of her mother, but she needs to learn to hold her own frequency in a group."

Pleione nodded. "I remember having that trouble myself."

"So, we sent her to Avalon for Beltane. She'll participate in seasonal ceremonies at various temples until it becomes second nature."

"How long will that take?"

Govannan shrugged. "It's hard to say. Perhaps a few months. Could be up to a year or two."

The yearning must have come through in his voice, because Pleione looked at him closely. He blushed, then shook his head, annoyed with himself. The injury and treatment had shaken his usual reserve. She stopped and put a hand on his shoulder, turning him toward her. "What is this I see?"

He ducked his head. "She's a promising apprentice."

The silver tinkle of her laugh flew up like a small bird. "Govannan, you've fallen in love with my daughter."

He looked up and found a copy of Megan's blue eyes regarding him from her mother's face, but these eyes had dark smudges beneath them and fine lines in the corners. "But you're exhausted," he blurted.

She turned away from him and walked down a path between jutting sea grasses toward the beach. He followed close behind. "Just tired. We've been busy," she said.

"You're more than tired." Now it was his turn to be firm.

Pleione looked at him in surprise. "Come to think of it, I don't think I've slept for a few days." They reached the shore and Pleione stopped, kicking her sandals off and digging her toes into the fine, white sand. "It's these new illnesses. I'm not sure how to treat them all. The viruses are fairly simple. Just stimulate the immune system, use certain sounds. Then herbs if the organism is resistant. But the other problems." She shook her head and gazed out to sea. "It's like people are getting forgetful—" she struggled for words "—like parts of their awareness are shutting down. We stimulate them with the usual treatments, but some don't regain full consciousness. Others have to keep coming back."

He nodded, excited by this validation. "I know what you mean."

"How could you?"

"When the New Knowledge Guild called us all to the conference—"

"What did you think of their proposal?"

He frowned. "Not promising. But, when all the chaos broke out after Surid made his presentation, I tried to rebalance the group with my crystal." He paused, wondering for the first time if this had been a breach of courtesy. After all, one never treated another without their permission. But that was his job, he told himself, to help maintain balance.

"And?" Pleione's voice brought him back.

"Surid seemed disconnected from his deepest self."

She nodded slowly.

"I tried to reconnect him—" He stopped at her expression. "I know, but I just reacted. I couldn't do it. He was oblivious."

"Something is happening to Eden," she said.

"To all of Atlantis," he replied. "I've heard stories from other cities."

She walked to the edge of the water and he followed. A wave ran up the beach and licked their feet, sending a chill up his calves. She turned to him, all brisk competence again. "Well, let's get you fixed up at least. Perhaps the dolphins will have some insight."

He braced himself against the cold, and they walked deeper into the sea, jumping through the low waves. They reached the line of breakers and dove through, emerging in the relative calm of deeper water.

"Ready?" Pleione treaded water. Her blond hair, now dark with the wet, clung to her head.

"Sure." He wondered what would happen now.

Pleione flipped onto her back, closed her eyes and floated like a piece of driftwood. A few minutes passed. Govannan dog paddled around her, scanning the surface for fins. And then they came, two spinners, leaping above the water, corkscrewing through the air as if the world were made simply for play. His heart leapt with them.

Pleione opened her eyes and swam toward them, gesturing for him to follow. A sleek, grey head surfaced next to her. The dolphin nudged her with its snout. She put her hands on either side of its head and bent her forehead down to it. After their communion, both dolphins swam over to Govannan. Slick, rubbery skin slid past his leg. Then the strange clicking sonar of their call filled the water, and his leg buzzed with the vibration. Another nudge against his thigh made him stick his face into the water to see what they were doing. Both had their snouts pointed at his leg. They gave their call again. This time even his lips buzzed. He laughed and sea water ran up his nose, the salt burning his sinuses. He surfaced, sputtering.

Pleione slapped him on the back. "You can't breathe the water, Govannan."

He nodded, his eyes still streaming, but before he could say anything, one of the dolphins scooted halfway between his legs, then shot off along the surface, taking him along for a ride. He clung to the fin, then relaxed his grip, worried he'd hurt the animal. The turquoise blue water parted in white foam. The smooth muscle flexed beneath him. Then, the dolphin stopped suddenly, sending Govannan head first into the water, and it dove. Govannan came up coughing again, then scanned for his mount. Nothing but quiet until he thought it had swum away, then boom, it barreled out of the water nose first and spun once, twice, three times before diving down again.

Pleione arrived at his side. "I think she likes you."

"It's a she?"

"So she says."

"You can talk to them?"

"Of course. I wouldn't be much of a healer if I couldn't."

At this, the pair surfaced again, their heads bobbing in unison. Pleione swam to them and put a hand on each head. After a few minutes, both nudged her with their snouts, then they swam away, leaping and cavorting.

Govannan was disappointed to see them leave. "What did they say?"

"They say to relax, that it's a part of the natural turn of the tides." She shook her head. "I don't know exactly what they meant, but when I asked again, they said 'you need to play more' and then they left."

On impulse, he said, "Let's play hooky."

"What?"

"Let's stay on the beach for a while."

"I have a temple full of patients—overflowing in fact." A wave slapped her in the face and she spit water. "You've just had an accident in your temple, and you want to play on the beach?"

"Dolphins' orders."

She opened her mouth to protest, then closed it again.

"I'm too old for Megan," he said.

"What?"

"Are you upset?"

She reached out and pushed him under the water. He resurfaced and tried to push her under, but she was too quick for him. She swam for the breakers and rode one in, as supple as a seal.

Govannan followed and they walked from the sea, water sluicing off their bodies. Pleione plopped down in the sand and squinted up at him. "You're still limping."

He shrugged. "I guess so."

"Is there any pain?"

He put his weight on his left leg, testing it. "It's a little tender."

"You'll have to come back, then."

"Fine, but you never answered my question."

"What question?"

"Are you upset with me?"

Pleione turned up her palms. "About what?"

"I'm too old for her."

"You're not even through your first century," she said, dismissing his objection.

"I'm fifty-two."

Pleione tilted her beautiful face, so much more elegant than Megan's, and laughed. "She'll catch up with you soon enough."

Govannan threw himself down beside her and stretched luxuriously on the warm sand. "I can't wait."

"Then why did you send her off if you're so eager?" She sat up and squeezed water out of her hair.

"Because I need her to grow into her own before we work together. She's a powerhouse. Do you know that?"

Pleione's smile was full of maternal pride. "Really?"

"Absolutely." He looked out at the horizon. "We're going to make a great pair."

"She feels the same?"

He frowned. "I don't know."

Pleione patted his shoulder. "I have a good feeling about it. Welcome to the family."

"Thanks." And they sat on for some time, looking out to sea, relaxed and easy in their companionship, the weight of their responsibilities shed for the moment.

MEGAN SAT in the growing dark of the vigil hut, gathering her strength for the coming initiation. Although it was her daughter who would undergo the test, Megan wondered if she would survive the night herself. She drank the tea Caitir handed her, no longer able to taste the different herbs the honey was so thick, but it opened her lungs a bit. Whether the weaver cut her cord tonight or not, she must finish this story. She took a long, ragged breath and plunged in again.

"After my first Beltane celebration at Avebury, the priestesses herded the first timers back onto the transport just after the formal ceremony ended, but the revelry continued until dawn. Most of them hadn't made it back until mid-morning. It was a quiet day, with most people sleeping. The next morning, Thalana found me at breakfast."

"The Lady wants to see you."

"But," Megan looked at the full bowl of fruit and cooked grain sitting in front of her, "can I eat?"

"She said now." Thalana handed Megan's breakfast to another apprentice who'd just walked into the dining hut. "Come on."

Swallowing her complaint instead of food, Megan followed Thalana, who climbed the hill with a heavy step. She yawned several times in a row.

"How was my cousin?" Megan asked in a casual voice.

The corners of Thalana's mouth twitched. "I enjoyed all my partners." But they had arrived at the gate, so Megan couldn't pry any more details out of her. They walked in silent reverence until Megan's gurgling stomach protested the imposed fast. They both burst into laughter, but once they reached the edge of the grove of yew trees, Thalana pulled a serious face and pointed. "She's waiting."

The Lady of Avalon sat on her stone bench wrapped in a red shawl. Megan stifled her mirth, then walked up to the Lady and dipped a knee in respect.

"Sit. Tell me about the ceremony." Instead of the bench, Megan settled cross-legged on the needle covered ground and told the story of her first Beltane. The Lady asked a few clarifying questions, then stood up. "It is as I thought. Come with me." She walked to the small vigil hut, then turned back to her. "Wait here until I call you."

Megan stood outside the small stone structure, listening to the rustle of birds in the yews and the trickle of water from the springs. She wondered what would happen next, if she'd be sent to another temple halfway across the world, or if she'd be allowed to go home to Eden and learn to work with the giant crystal portal. And see Govannan again. The sun rose higher, burning off the chill in the air. After what seemed a long time, the oak door opened and the Lady stood in the threshold. "You may come in now."

Curious, Megan took two steps into the dim hut and looked around, willing her eyes to adjust. The Lady touched her arm and led her to a long, low table that stretched across the middle of the room. "Sit."

Feeling her way, Megan lowered herself onto a large pillow. She heard the Lady sit somewhere behind her. Finally, her eyes adapted. Across the table from her sat the oldest woman she'd ever seen. White hair hung in a long braid down her back. Milky eyes looked out of a wrinkled face.

"Megan, daughter of Pleione, daughter of Cordelia." The woman seemed to be speaking to herself, rolling the names around on her tongue as if to extract their deepest flavor. "You have come back to the home of your mothers."

This seemed to be more of a proclamation than a question, so Megan sat quietly and waited.

The old woman tilted her head as if she were listening to something, then she answered with a low, indistinct murmur. She listened again. "Too bad, too bad," she said, shaking her head, her forehead wrinkling even more.

Megan looked over her shoulder at the Lady, who shook her head sharply and gestured for Megan to turn back around. The ache in her stomach was no longer hunger.

"Hum." This sound seemed more hopeful. "A good choice." The old woman dug into her pocket and came out with something cupped in her palm. She focused on Megan, her eyes now inexplicably clear, her gaze sharp and steady. She stretched out a withered hand, her gaze holding Megan's. Light flickered as the twisted fingers opened, and the old woman dropped a slender crystal point into Megan's hand.

Before Megan could examine this gift, the old woman said in a firm voice, "Yours is a special talent, but a difficult path. You will stay with us a year and a day, then we will release you to your fate. The Morgen has spoken."

Megan's gasp seemed too loud in the sudden quiet. So this was the famous oracle. The old woman's eyes had clouded again. To Megan's relief, she closed them and sagged back in her seat, pulling her shawl tight. Then the Lady was at Megan's side, pulling her up, sheparding her out the door. Megan looked over her shoulder. "Thank you," she said, but the Morgen did not respond.

Once outside, the Lady continued down the path until they reached the stone bench. She sat and soothed her skirts. Only then did she speak. "Now we know that you will be a student here for the next year. We may send you to other temples to assist in ceremony, as your guild has requested, but you will live and study with us. Thalana will move you in with the first year apprentices."

Megan would miss her delightful cottage. At least at the Crystal Matrix Chamber, she'd had her own room. But that wasn't what was bothering her. She gathered her courage like the strands of a fraying shawl. After all, this woman was her aunt. Before the Lady dismissed her, Megan asked, "But, what did she mean about turning me over to my fate? Does she know what that is?"

The Lady shrugged. "Who can say? She sees so much, I don't know if she remembers it all. Much of the time she is in the other worlds."

Megan sat abruptly on the bench beside the Lady. She pushed her curls behind her ears, then opened her palm to look at the crystal. "What is this? Don't I even get to ask her?"

"I'm afraid not, dear. It is for you to discover the power of this stone."

Megan turned it over in her hand. The stone was clear and cleanly formed, coming to a perfect point. She held it up in a beam of sunlight that had found its way through the yew branches. Small cracks inside broke the light into rainbows.

"Put it on your altar. Meditate with it. The knowledge will come in the right time."

Megan nodded, then brushed away a tear. Another followed, and she rubbed her eyes, annoyed. The Lady put her hand around her shoulder, and this opened the dam. "I'm sorry," she managed between sobs. "I don't know what's wrong with me."

"Too many changes in too short a time," the Lady said. "But now you can settle down. At least for a time."

14

Anne put down Cynthia's manuscript. Could it be? She fished beneath her collar and pulled the silver chain holding the crystal over her head. The stone gleamed in her palm. She'd grown accustomed to thinking of Cynthia's story as just that, fantasy read at odd moments during the day, filling the lonely evenings of what was supposed to have been her romantic interlude with Michael. But perhaps Cynthia's note to Garth should be taken at face value. Maybe this wasn't fiction at all, but a vision of history Cynthia had received, the true story of the crystal, perhaps their own family.

She held the now familiar stone up to the lamp and let it dangle there. The light refracted off the cracks and spread rainbows on the opposite wall of the study. She'd come to think of it as the key to that underground temple near the heart of the Sphinx—one of six keys. But the crystal had sent a pulse of energy into the Tor to restart White Spring, and now it had appeared in the far past, not in Egypt where Tahir had said it came from, but in Avalon, passed from the mythological Morgen to a woman from the fabled land of Atlantis.

The ring of the phone made her jump. Laughing at herself, she followed the sound and found it inside her purse.

"Anne?" Michael's voice sent a rush of warmth through her.

"Oh, good. I have so much to talk to you about."

"Where are you?"

"I'm in Glastonbury, silly, in Cynthia's house."

"Look out the window."

"Why?"

"Just look out the window."

Anne pushed the blue curtains aside and peered out at the empty porch. "What?"

"Keep looking."

Her eyes scanned the dark yard. Just as she was about to close the curtain, she saw movement.

"What do you see?" His voice sounded through the phone and from the front yard at the same time.

"Michael!" Anne threw the phone onto the desk and ran outside into his arms. His kiss burned through the damp chill of the English spring and the lonely nights. Entwined, they somehow made it up the steps of the porch and through the front door. Anne pushed the door shut behind her and leaned against it, savoring the kisses Michael deposited down her neck. Buttons flew and she started to protest, but his mouth continued down the front of her body, pausing to worship each breast. He unzipped her jeans and pulled them off, gave a grunt of satisfaction when he found nothing beneath, then went down on his knees, finding her tender pearl with his tongue. She draped one leg over his shoulder and gave herself over to the sensations. She climaxed almost immediately, grabbing the door handle for support.

Michael picked her up and carried her up the stairs, where he deposited her on the bed. She lay, languid, watching his smooth body emerge as he pulled off his clothes, his phallus spring loose from his briefs. He pulled her closer and she melted around him. They spent the rest of the night exploring variations on this theme.

In the morning, they took a shower together. Soaping up led to more love making. Then they slept again, finally waking late morning, content.

Anne traced his nose and brow with her forefinger. "You didn't call."

"I wanted to surprise you."

"You did. It's good to have you back." She lifted her head and looked at him. "I do have you back, don't I? Is everything in New York settled?"

"We still need to ship Robert's library. I have some papers to sign." He rubbed his forehead.

"How are you feeling?"

Michael's eyes darkened. "I still expect to be able to call him. It's not like Cagliostro has given me any time to grieve."

"Now you'll have some time with me."

"I promised his wife I'd drop by to talk. And pick up the ceremonial tools he left me. But I told her it would have to wait a couple of weeks because of business."

"I imagine she'll appreciate the time. Grandmother Elizabeth won't allow Thomas' room to be touched yet."

"Then there's the lodge. Guy wants to show me the ropes, but the first priority is getting ahead of Cagliostro."

Anne raised herself on her elbow. "You haven't answered my first question."

He sighed. "I'm leaving for Germany tomorrow morning."

She sat up. "Then I'm coming with you."

He drew her back down. "I'd love to have you, but I'm on Cagliostro's trail. I don't want him anywhere near you."

"Where is he now?"

Michael blushed. "Actually, he's in England. At his country house."

"So," Anne smiled in triumph, "Germany is safer than here."

Michael's eyes narrowed. "Arnold hasn't seen hide or hair of Cagliostro since he came back from the Caribbean. So come with me."

She turned over and spooned against him. "Good."

"What about White Spring?"

"We fixed it." She told him about the impromptu ceremony.

"You're getting to be quite the adept."

"Hardly, those stones seem to have a mind of their own." She looked at their two crystal keys lying on the bed table.

"Which is why we need to keep Cagliostro from getting any more of the Atlantean crystals. Imagine what stones that size could do."

"Size matters?" she asked, trying to sound innocent.

He ignored her. "OK, Germany it is. Want some coffee?"

"Tea."

He started to get up, but she held onto his arm. "You're warm."

Michael settled down against her. Anne nestled closer, content, then chuckled when she felt him stiffen. She moved her hips and they came together yet again. Michael's thrust built in intensity and just as she felt him tremble inside her, the front door of the house opened.

"Hello?" A woman's voice called from downstairs.

Past the point of no return, Michael stifled his moan in the pillow.

Anne recognized the housekeeper's voice. "Goddamn that woman," she said in a fierce whisper.

Michael pulled the duvet over his head. "I knew I was pressing my luck."

Anne grabbed a robe and hurried to the head of the stairs. "Actually, this isn't a good time, Tessa."

The stolid woman stood at the foot of the stairs. She looked down at her bucket and plastic container full of spray bottles and rags, then frowned up at Anne. "When do you suggest I come back, then?"

"I apologize for the inconvenience." Anne bit back the desire to tell the woman just how inconvenient she was. "Perhaps tomorrow?"

Tessa put a hand on her hip. "My schedule is tight. I'll have to check."

"Today really is impossible. I'm sorry." Anne started to turn back, but then stopped. "When you come back, please bring the key to that cellar door."

Tessa frowned. "It's always open."

"Not the one in the kitchen, but the one in the back of the basement. The old one."

Tessa looked at her for a moment. "It's always been locked as long as I've worked here. I know nothing of a key."

"Could you just double check your key ring? I've looked in all the drawers."

"Certainly." Tessa picked up her supplies in one hand and awkwardly yanked opened the front door. "I'll call before I come again."

"I appreciate it," Anne said to her retreating back.

She went back to the bedroom, but Michael was pulling on his clothes. "What was that about?"

"She came to clean. Of all times."

"At least she didn't come last night," he said.

Anne softened and leaned against him.

"Where do you want to go?" His voice was muffled in her hair. "Shall we start where we left off?"

"Actually, Garth showed me both springs and Wearyall Hill. We didn't get to Bridget's Well, though."

"But I wanted to show you Glastonbury," Michael protested. "Just what does this Garth look like, anyway?"

"Tall, dark, handsome." Anne smiled up at Michael. "And he really knows his stuff."

"Worse and worse."

Anne laughed. "He was Cynthia's lover. I'm sure of it."

"Well, I have an idea for today's adventure."

Anne took another quick shower and dressed, accompanied by the sounds of Michael banging around in the kitchen. She came downstairs to toast and tea.

"What was all that about a key?" he asked while she spread marmalade on a wedge of bread.

"Oh, there's a door in the back of the basement that's locked. I haven't been able to find the key."

"Call a locksmith."

Anne tapped her forehead. "They have those in England?"

Michael laughed. "I'm glad I'm still good for something."

"He asked us to dinner, you know."

"Who?"

"Garth." She wiped marmalade off her lip. "Cynthia dedicated her book to him."

"Still reading it?"

"Yes, but I think it really is her vision. She mentions the crystal in it."

"But she already had it, so that doesn't prove anything."

"You should take a look at it."

"You can tell me all about it in the car."

"Where are we going?"

"It's a surprise."

Anne settled in the passenger seat of Michael's Peugeot and they headed off. She narrated the story in Cynthia's manuscript while she watched the green fields and small villages of Somerset pass by.

After she'd finished, he said, "It matches stories of Atlantis, and some of Cayce's information. The note says the story is real?"

"Yes, but she wanted to publish it as fiction. She didn't want the family to be embarrassed by her claiming that she channeled it. Garth said that my mother might try to have her committed."

"Garth again."

She punched his arm. "Stop it."

They fell into silence. Anne had lost track of where they were. Michael took yet another roundabout, then slowed down on a strip of road that looked to Anne just like any other. Suddenly to her right loomed a row of standing stones. She sat up. "What's this?"

Michael pointed ahead, where the road came to a T. An enormous stone stood in the field just on the other side of a fence surrounded by other stones almost as large.

"Oh, my God. Michael?"

"Welcome to Avebury, love."

"This is Avebury? The place where Megan did her first Beltane ceremony."

He negotiated the S curve in the road that ran through the stones. All the while, Anne turned her head back and forth, trying to see everything at once. The road straightened out again. More stones rose from the fields on both sides of the road. "How big is it?"

"The largest megalithic circle in the world." He pulled the car into a driveway, then put it in reverse and backed onto the road. "Let's go park and you can see for yourself." They drove through the tiny village again and left the Peugeot in the car park, forking over five pounds, then followed the path to a row of giants. Anne pushed open a small gate and walked past a couple of broken stones, then down a line of plinths, small concrete pyramids. "What happened here?"

"The work of zealots, from the middle ages on. But mostly the 1700s. Keiller bought it before they'd finished their handiwork. That wasn't until the 1930s, though."

"Too bad. Imagine what it must have looked like." She reached the first original Saracen in the line. "Can you touch them?"

"Of course."

She placed both hands flat on the stone and closed her eyes. Nothing. After a minute, she moved to the next one and did the same, but she felt only the rough granite beneath her hands. Anne continued down the line, pausing at each stone, spending a few minutes with each one. Some were round with curves and small cavities. Others tall, pointing to the sky. In a few, tiny round openings made spy holes. About half way down, a raucous caw startled her. A fat, shiny raven sat atop the long, lean stone. The bird tilted its head and regarded her with a beady black eye, then swiveled its head and looked at her out of the other.

"What?" she asked.

The bird squawked and flew down the line of Saracens, landed on an enormous stone across the street, then looked back at her and cawed again. On the ground lay a crisp, black feather. Anne picked it up and pushed it into her button hole. "Thanks," she called, then turned to Michael.

A wry smile lifted the corners of his mouth. "Maybe he's suggesting you could skip a few stones."

Anne walked over and took his arm. "Lead on. They're not talking to me, anyway."

"We'll try the Devil's Chair."

"The what?"

"That's what the old farmers called it. The later Christians taught that all the sacred Druid sites had something to do with Satan. Who came from their own religion, of course, not the Druid's."

"Show me." Anne tugged at his arm.

"It's the one the raven flew to." He sped up his pace. "The story is if you walk around it three times counter clockwise, the devil will appear."

"Why would anybody want to see the devil?"

"Indeed." Michael thought of the young Cagliostro. He was somehow hesitant to tell Anne about Dr. Abernathy's youthful indiscretions. They crossed the road and walked up to the same stone the raven had flown to.

Anne slowed down, picking her way through the sheep dung.

"Here we are." The massive stone hunkered near the road, rising at least three times Michael's height. Seven or eight people standing side by side might have been able to embrace it. Michael patted a natural ledge in the stone at a convenient height. "Have a seat."

Anne hopped up and leaned against the stone. It sent a wave of welcome to her. "Ah, this one says hello." She closed her eyes.

After a minute, Michael asked, "Does it say anything else?"

She opened her eyes. "Nope."

Michael snapped a picture and Anne got down. "Just like real tourists."

"This stone marked the entrance to the southern circle. Up a ways is the entrance to the northern circle. The ancients placed the largest Saracens in these openings, but there's another big one farther north."

"Do you think Cynthia's right? That this is where the men gathered?"

Michael shrugged. "It makes sense. Fire in the south. A masculine element. Earth in the north. Feminine. No one knows for sure." He looked around. "Now it seems to belong to the sheep."

And so they walked the circle at Avebury, pausing to lean against the stones, to touch them, to listen for whispers from the past. With the sun just past his zenith, they made their way to the Cove stones again, then on to the Red Lion, situated smack in the middle of the circle. Anne chose a table outside overlooking the southern circle and Michael went in to order. Sheep grazed, people drank their pints, and cars drove by. The bus to Salisbury stopped and picked up a couple of passengers.

Michael returned with beer and water. "Ever heard of Florrie?"

"Who?" Anne put her hand up to block the sun.

"The resident ghost." He sat across from her.

"Tell me." Anne took a long drink.

"Florrie was the landlady here—seventeenth century, I think. Anyway, her husband went off to war. When he came home, he discovered her with her lover."

"He found out she'd been disloyal, see," a male voice called out.

Anne looked down the long picnic table to a couple in motorcycle riding leathers.

"That's right. Killed her, he did. Tossed her down the well," the woman added.

"She still walks at night. Then there's the man as was stabbed in the cellar," the man added quite cheerfully.

"That's right. On the tellie, it was."

"Most Haunted is the show. Ever see it?"

"Never have." Anne shook her head.

"Staying here?" the woman asked.

"Just down for the day," Michael said.

"American, are you?"

"Yes," Anne answered, "And you? Do you live around here?"

"Just out riding. Live down near Kingston."

Their food arrived, rescuing them from more ghost stories. They ate Italian Cheese and Spinach Risotto and a jacket potato stuffed with goat cheese and onion marmalade, stealing from each other's plates, then topped it all off with French fries. Anne said no to the sticky toffee pudding.

"Let's go into the Henge Shop and check the crop circle board," Michael suggested.

"A bit early for those," the man down the table commented.

"I suppose it is. I want to show it to my wife, though."

Something in Michael's tone made the woman look up. "On your honeymoon, then?"

Michael nodded.

"Ah, that's lovely."

"Thanks for the stories." Anne gave a small wave, and she and Michael walked down the road toward the shop. "Honeymoon?"

Michael put his arm around her. "The Sphinx married us."

In the Henge Shop, Michael showed her the crop circle bulletin board with a detailed map of the area. Stick pins marked last summer's crop of earth art. Below, picture books of each year's best filled one shelf. Anne wandered off to look at the jewelry, while Michael stayed to check out the books. She decided on a puzzle ring, with two slender silver bands tied together into a Celtic knot.

"Ready for more?"

"Stone circles?"

"I want to save Stonehenge for a private viewing. It's always crowded." He pointed a finger at her. "Don't let Garth take you."

She smiled.

"There's lots more to see around here."

They drove by the flat-topped Silbury Hill and walked down to West Kennet Long Barrow, where Michael gave a long discourse on prehistoric burial practices in Britain. She lay in the spring grass and watched the clouds. When he realized she wasn't listening, he lay down beside her and the fire between them rekindled.

"Let's go back," Anne whispered in his ear, then nibbled the lobe.

"No one's around." Michael reached for her zipper.

"Are you out of your mind?" Anne laughed and pushed his hand away. "There's nowhere to hide."

"We could go into the tomb."

Anne shuttered and got to her feet. "Come on."

They drove home in the sultry air of anticipation, but when they pulled onto Wellhouse Lane, a crowd blocked their way. Michael leaned out of the window. "Excuse us." No one paid him the least mind.

Anne rolled down her window. "What's happening?" A couple standing on the sidewalk shrugged. She got out and slipped through the people until she could see the patio around White Spring. Tessa stood with the tall woman she'd been with before, her hands on her broad hips, complaining to Garth. Anne edged closer.

". . . and now some strange woman is there. Do you know what she—" Tessa stopped dead when Anne walked up.

Garth turned with a frown to see what Tessa was staring at and his face lit up. "There you are. I was looking for you."

Tessa colored a deeper red.

"I'm afraid we haven't met." The tall woman's upper crust accent matched the elegant hand she offered to Anne.

Garth took on the burden of introductions. "This is Joanne Katter, the well known writer."

Anne searched her memory, but came up with nothing.

"Joanne, meet Anne Le Clair, Cynthia's niece."

"A pleasure. I'm so sorry to hear about your aunt. Her presence in Glastonbury was an asset."

Anne wondered if she'd imagined the slight emphasis on the word "her."

"And this is?" Garth's hearty voice made her look around.

"Michael." Anne reached out for his arm. "My fiancé."

Tessa smirked.

"I was finally able to park," he said to Anne, then looked at the others. "Joanne Katter, is it?"

The woman thin lips curved up.

"I'm Michael Levy."

Her eyebrow arched. "Indeed? Another luminary come to Glastonbury?"

"You're too kind," he dissembled. "And you must be the infamous Garth."

"So, this is your man." Garth winked at Anne. "Pleased to make your acquaintance." His large hand swallowed Michael's.

"Tessa." Michael acknowledged her with a nod, then turned back to Garth. "What's all the fuss?"

Garth rocked back on his heels. "It seems our impromptu ceremony the other day didn't quite do the trick." He walked over to White Spring's water duct. The crowd parted for him. Water dripped at long intervals.

"We were trying to explain to Garth," Joanne said from Anne's elbow, "that a women's ceremony is what's needed. Bridget will answer to our call."

"Bridget?" Anne turned to her with a frown.

"Yes, this is her well. The white maiden."

"I thought—"

"Yes, well," Joanne brushed by Anne's opinion without stopping to pay attention to it and fixed Garth with a look, "we can straighten this out."

"I'm glad to hear it. Let me know if I can be of any assistance."

"We have the situation well in hand."

"Then, if you'll excuse me?" Garth looked at Anne and jerked his head toward her house. He turned back to the crowd. "Our good Joanne here will be doing some work to restore the spring. Your prayers are welcome, of course." He looked at her and she preened.

A few voices rose in protest, but Garth turned and started to climb back up the slope of Wellhouse Lane. Anne took Michael's hand and followed. A short man with a ruddy complexion and wild, brown beard hurried up to Garth. "You're leaving it to them, then?"

Garth glanced back to see if anyone was in hearing range, then said, "I'll be in touch, Bran. Tonight."

The man gave a curt nod, then walked back down the hill. From her front steps, Anne could see a small knot of people around Bran, their heads together.

She followed Michael and Garth inside where they arranged themselves in the front room. Garth studied them both for a long minute, then addressed himself to Michael. "I assume I don't have to explain to you just how grave the situation is."

Michael shook his head. "This is one of the major power spots on the earth grid. It keeps the planet in balance. Links the worlds. People have come here since—" he searched for the right phrase "—well, forever."

Garth's face softened. "I'm glad you understand."

"But what was all that about Bridget?" Anne looked at Michael, then Garth. "I thought this well belonged to the male side of the, uh—force."

"That's been my own experience," Michael said.

"It's never that simple, of course," Garth added. "Water is a female element, and springs and wells traditionally are kept by women. Many think of White Spring as belonging to the goddess Bridget, especially in her maiden form. Calling on Bridie should help."

"Who is that woman, anyway?" she asked.

"Joanne Katter wrote about the return of the goddess in the early eighties," Michael explained.

"She doesn't look that old," Anne said.

"True. Her face and her views haven't changed much since then," Michael said. "Good work for the time."

Anne sat back in her chair and folded her arms. "So men are the problem."

Garth barked a short laugh and looked at Michael. "It's a lucky thing to be in love with a Le Clair woman."

This melted the last of Michael's reserve. "I couldn't agree more. I am sorry for your loss."

Garth bit his lip, then shook his head in a gesture growing familiar to Anne. "She told me this might happen."

Anne leaned forward. "Her murder or White Spring drying up?"

"She felt that something was building to a crisis, something begun a long time ago." Garth looked across the hall to the study. "That's why she started looking into the past. She said she was searching for the other end."

"Of what?"

Garth shook his head. "When she left for New York, she wanted to try more trance work with Elizabeth and her group." His eyes filled. "They got to her before she could finish it."

Anne reached for Michael. The room filled with shadows as the sun sank. Garth took a breath to speak, then shook his head and closed his eyes again. "How could I not have known?" he whispered.

"Maybe because she never fully left you. She must still be with you spiritually and so you never felt an absence." Anne switched on a lamp. Amber light from the stained glass shade lit Garth's rugged face, which was wet with tears.

"I'll go make some tea." Michael walked into the kitchen.

Anne spoke in a soft voice. "We've all lost someone. First Cynthia, then my brother Thomas. Last week, Michael's spiritual mentor was shot in New York. He's just home from the funeral."

Garth opened his eyes and looked at her, the soft look in his brown eyes hardening. "And did they all die at the hands of the same man?"

Anne shuttered at the memory of her first meeting with Cagliostro. "At his orders."

"I should have killed him when I had the chance." Garth stared at his large, rough hands.

"You know him, too?"

He nodded, not looking up. "Everyone in the magical world knows Cagliostro. We just can't figure out why his deeds haven't caught up with him yet."

Michael came back with a tray laden with mugs, glasses and a squat bottle of Irish whiskey. "I thought we needed something stronger than tea."

Garth wiped his face with the corner of his sleeve and nodded at Anne. "I told you I'd like this man of yours."

Michael poured a finger for each of them and held his glass in the air. "For the ones we have lost."

"Here, here." Garth knocked back his drink, then grimaced. "Ah. That's better. Where were we, then?"

"White Spring is failing." Anne ticked the problems off on her fingers. "Alexander Cagliostro is stealing Atlantean crystals for God knows what nefarious purpose. Cynthia was having visions of ancient Atlantis and passing them off as fiction."

"But what's the connection?" Michael asked.

Garth's eyes lit up. "Let's see that crystal."

Anne pulled off the necklace and offered it to Garth.

His eyes widened. "I can handle it?"

She hesitated. "Is there a reason you shouldn't?"

"Magical tools are often attuned to their user. It can muddy the energy to hand them around."

Anne looked at Michael questioningly, but he said, "These stones are strong. They seem to be immune to disruption."

Garth sat forward. "Did you say stones, as in more than one?"

"Well, yes." Michael reached for the chain holding his own crystal, but didn't find it. "I must have left it on the bedside table." He got up and headed upstairs.

"I'd be careful. I'm not sure I trust that housekeeper," Anne called after him.

Garth's eyes darted to her.

Michael returned and laid his own stone next to Anne's on the ottoman.

Garth bent to examine them, but still didn't touch or even breathe on them. "How can it be that you two hold such similar artifacts?"

"You know the history of the crystals?" Anne asked.

"Only Cynthia's. She said a group in America held another in trust."

"Mine," Michael confirmed.

"And mentioned a legend saying there were more. She went to look for one in Egypt before she flew to New York. But I never held out much hope she would find it."

"We found them all," Michael said.

"Or they found us, more like it," Anne murmured.

Garth sat back in his chair and stared at them. Then he gulped down more whiskey. "I must hear about this."

As succinctly as he could, Michael told him the story of their adventure in Egypt with Anne chiming in from time to time to add a few details. After they'd finished, Garth sat in silence for what seemed like a long time. Anne was beginning to realize this was his pattern. Finally he spoke. "You've brought a massive surge of stellar energy into the earth. White Spring's flow was strong for a few days afterward. Then it became erratic again. Now it's slowed to a drip."

Michael and Anne nodded their agreement.

"There are two parts to this. First, I'd say your ceremony in Egypt was not the only action needed to bring in the Awakening, as you call it. If indeed any human action can affect such large cycles. Granted, we've seen some improvements in the world situation, but . . ."

Anne opened her mouth to say something, but Michael squeezed her arm, so she waited.

Garth continued, his gaze fixed inward. "Something else must have disturbed the grid and it's showing up in White Spring."

"Hasn't it been erratic for a couple of years?"

"True." He ran his forefinger around the rim of his whiskey glass. After a moment, he surfaced from his thoughts. "There's one sure way to find out."

"How?" Anne asked.

He pointed at Anne's crystal. "This stone started the flow again."

"I didn't really do anything. It was the key's idea."

"Now we have two keys," Garth said. "I suggest we put them in the lock and turn them."

"Yes," Michael said. "We can try to pick up the exact nature of the disturbance."

Garth got up and retrieved his cell phone from his jacket. "Bran should have gathered the group by now. Let's just hope that dimwit isn't holding her ceremony down there."

Anne hid a smile. The pressure had eroded Garth's normally diplomatic nature.

"Even if there's a crowd now, surely they won't stay all night," Michael said. "Sometimes this type of ceremony is best done late. Much quieter."

Garth clapped Michael on the shoulder. "Good man." He went into the study across the hall. Anne and Michael only heard snippets of his conversation. Minutes later, he returned, his face determined. "She's down there with her group. We'll do our work at midnight. I'll come back for you."

"She'll take the credit," Anne said.

Garth nodded. "All the better to keep ourselves hidden."

CLOSE TO MIDNIGHT, Anne opened the front door to Garth's knock. He made an imposing figure dressed in ceremonial robes such a deep purple they were almost black. Anne had found a black robe with a red silk lining in Cynthia's meditation room which she decided to wear for the occasion. Garth bit his lip when he caught sight of her, then gave her a nod of approval. Michael wore all black. His magical accoutrements were at the lodge in New York.

They walked down the street to the squat building that housed White Spring. The wooden door stood open. A set of rickety old stairs that led to an upper level divided the concrete square in the middle. "We've cleaned out the remains of the restaurant, but that's all so far," Garth said in an undertone. They made their way toward the back right hand corner where a huddle of people stood, some in long ceremonial robes variously decorated with Masonic symbols, pentagrams, and Templar and Celtic crosses. Others wore corduroy pants or jeans with flannel shirts. All stood in stocking feet. Anne kicked off her own shoes.

Bran stepped forward. "Everyone who could make it has come."

"Excellent." Garth rubbed his hands together. "You want to use this corner, then?"

"The abbot's sacrifice will aid our work," Bran answered.

Garth nodded, then seemed to remember Anne and Michael, whom he introduced to the group. Nods and murmurs welcomed them. A couple of women from Joanne's group smiled at her rather conspiratorially, she thought. Garth took Bran aside to discuss the ritual.

"What did he mean by the abbot's sacrifice?" Anne asked.

"Ah, that'd be Richard Whyting, the last Abbot of Glastonbury," one man answered. "He was hung on top of the Tor by order of King Henry VIII. But," he smiled gleefully, revealing tobacco stained teeth, "they cut him down afore he died, ya see. Thought the Tor was too holy to commit murder on. Brung him down here and cut him into quarters right on this spot." He nodded as if the import of this fact was self evident.

"What a death," Michael said.

Their informant nodded, satisfied with his response.

"I don't get it," Anne whispered, but the acoustics of the room echoed her words back to everyone.

"He was a sacred sacrifice, ya see," the man explained, "just like in the old days when a king died for the good of all." He struck the back wall with the palm of his hand. "And right here at the opening of the cave."

"His life force was offered to the divine forces," Michael said. "When the fertility of the land and herds waned, the old King sacrificed himself in a sacred ceremony, and a young and virile man replaced him. At least, that's the popular understanding."

Several of the men nodded, looking as if they would offer themselves on the spot. Anne shuttered and reached for Michael's hand.

"Let's find ourselves a comfortable spot." Garth's voice rang out.

Anne settled between Michael and a woman she didn't know on a kind of concrete curb that ran around the room. She took her crystal key in her hand and waited.

Bran drew out a short dagger and flourished it in the air at each of the quadrants, reinforcing sacred space, much as Grandmother Elizabeth had during her first such ritual on winter solstice last year. He added a chant, singing vowel sounds for each direction. A female voice joined him at a descant. By the time he stopped, Anne was deep in trance. The walls of the concrete building melted, giving way to living earth veined with the roots of trees and bushes. Farther in, clustered crystals shone in the dark tunnel that had opened in the back. Wet rock reflected moonlight and ancient torches. She steadied herself, then surrendered to the crystal in her hand. It sat quiet, waiting.

Garth began to speak about the White Spring, about Merlin, about the sacred entrance to the Crystal Cave. Then his words turned into a croon and the key in her hand came to life. It reached out with a stream of energy and nudged Michael's, and the two entwined their life force. The small stone grew heavier and heavier until she had to lay her hands on the floor and let the earth support its weight. But the stones both wanted to touch the floor. Michael laid his down first, then Anne moved hers next to it. They touched and a burst of light blinded her.

She woke inside a small hut coughing from the wood fire in the hearth. Something stirred behind her. She turned. An old woman sat in the corner behind a low table. A milky film covered her open eyes. The woman groped in front of her with claw-like hands. "You have come at last." Her voice rasped. Her breath came in labored bursts. "The time grows short, Anne Morgan Le Clair."

Anne jerked violently at the sound of her name, but the crone shushed her. "Listen to me," she hissed. "You must return what Megan let loose."

Anne woke to water. She sputtered and coughed. Someone pulled her head up.

"Get the key." She recognized Michael's voice. "It's all right. You can pick it up."

Rough hands chaffed hers. Someone pulled her hair from her face, then kissed her. The warmth and urgency of those lips brought her all the way back. She looked around wildly. Water cascaded through the concrete conduits, then overflowed and spread across the floor in transparent sheets that sparkled in the torch light. No, it was a candle.

Anne stood in the midst of cheers for White Spring. Some lay in the water, splashing like children. Others sang their thanks to the Tor, to Bridget, to the gods and goddesses in general, to Gwyn ap Nudd, the King of the Fairies. Garth grabbed a large goblet from the altar, dipped it into the gushing flood and passed it around from mouth to mouth.

Michael still held her. "Are you okay?"

She nodded, pushed the rest of her wet hair behind her ears. "I guess it worked."

Bran arrived in front of her, holding the crystal key by its chain, and offered it to her as if he were giving her the Grail itself. He bowed low when she took it, then bowed to Michael. "To the Lord and Lady, who have given us back our spring."

"Everyone did it." Anne took her crystal back and put it around her neck. "And there's more to do."

"Yes," Garth was there suddenly, "but for now this is enough." He offered her the goblet. The sacred water of White Spring never tasted so sweet.

15

The next morning, Anne woke to the smell of coffee and the sound of male voices downstairs. A bit groggy, she stood in the hot shower, letting the water wash over her, remembering the wealth of wet she'd awoken to last night. Michael had taken her home to recover more fully, while Garth stayed behind to talk with the group. A bit more awake now, she dressed quickly and went downstairs, the squeaky step protesting her weight. Michael and Garth sat at the kitchen table, heads together. Just like Egypt, where she'd arrive for breakfast to find Michael and Tahir deep in conversation.

"Queen Anne." Garth lifted his cup to salute her. His eyes were red and puffy. "How are you this fine morning?"

"Good, thank you." She squinted, unaccustomed to the bright sun. "Why do I keep passing out? I'm just like that woman in the *Perils of Pauline*, tied to the railroad tracks, eternally needing to be rescued."

"Quite the contrary." Garth slammed his mug down with such force that it slopped coffee all over the table. "It is you who have rescued us. Twice now."

Anne grabbed a kitchen towel and tossed it to Michael, who mopped up the spill. She poured herself some coffee and sat down at the table. The Tor rose in the sun outside the window. "Tell me everything."

"It is you who must tell us what you experienced," Garth said. He sounded a bit tipsy, probably from being up all night.

"But—" she started to protest.

"Yours is the missing piece. Then we'll repeat everything, I promise." Michael's voice was soft.

"Oh, all right." She took a big gulp, then told them about waking up in the Morgen's hut and her message.

"Who is this Megan?" Garth asked.

"A character from Cynthia's book." Anne tucked her damp hair behind her ears. "I guess she's not just a character."

"So it would seem," Garth said.

"Do you know what she meant?" Michael asked.

Anne shook her head. "There's really nothing in the story so far that matches this. She went to her initiation, got sent to work in the Crystal Matrix Chamber, then on to Avalon."

"Let's look at the manuscript." Michael started to get up.

"Wait a minute," Anne protested. "You promised to tell me what else happened."

"Fair enough." Garth chuckled. "Even though we flooded the spring house last night, I've set a watch on the well. I'm not sure we're done with this by a long shot."

"I'm surprised," Anne said. "Our results seemed pretty spectacular. I thought we'd float away.

Garth's eyebrows drew together. "Exactly. I don't trust these extremes. Michael, my man?"

"Want a pasty? Garth went by Burns the Bread this morning."

Anne shook her head. Her stomach didn't seem to have joined her in this dimension yet.

"Speak up," Garth said. He seemed accustomed to command. Anne wondered if he'd been in the military.

"I saw Robert." Michael's eyes shone.

"Why didn't you tell me last night?"

"You were asleep on your feet. I let you be."

She reached a hand across the table. "What did he say?"

"No words. He radiated light. He looked so happy." Michael squeezed her hand. "He handed me a Tarot card—the Wheel of Fortune. The wheel on the card spun in my hand and turned to gold."

Garth nodded, a satisfied smile on his face.

"Meaning?" Anne asked.

"That our task is fated, but more that we are turning the wheel, moving into a new era. Human society will be rearranged."

"What about you, Mr. Buddha?" Anne addressed herself to Garth, then winked at Michael. "He never talks."

"My gift is not the visions of the Le Clairs," Garth said. "I'm more tactile. I experience energy through touch." He paused until Anne got antsy.

"And?" she urged.

He chuckled. "The energy of the Tor was fractured, as if the dimensions were bleeding into each other. We've almost got it realigned."

"Almost," Anne repeated.

He nodded, an abstracted look on his face. "I find it difficult to put into words."

"At least we've made progress." Anne took a bite of her pasty.

"A door is still ajar," he said.

"Let's take a look at that book of Cynthia's. See if we can figure out what the Morgen meant."

Michael got up.

"It's in the study on the floor under the reading lamp," Anne said. She turned to Garth. "Did you get any sleep?"

He tried to cover an enormous yawn with his equally large hand. "There will be plenty of time for that."

Michael came back into the kitchen, a frown on his face. "Where did you say it was?"

"Right next to the chair, on the floor."

"Well, it's not there now."

"What?" Anne stood up. Her chair scraped across the floor. "Of course it is. That's where I always read it."

"Show me."

They walked to the front room together. Anne plopped into the chair and reached down for the manuscript, but found only the grey and purple pattern of the Persian rug. "Where is it?"

Garth stood with his hands on either side of the door frame. "Think now."

Anne stood and looked around the room, then beside the desk and all around the floor. She lifted up a stack of newspapers and looked under them, then shuffled through them. Michael opened the drawers of the desk and riffled through their contents.

"What does it look like?" Garth asked.

"Just regular paper. A big stack." She pushed down a rush of panic. "You both search the house. Look everywhere. I'll see if I can find the file in her computer." She went to the desk, already knowing what she'd find. Or wouldn't find. The dark wood grain of the desk stared up at her, but no computer.

They turned the house upside down, even the basement, but found nothing. Cynthia's manuscript was missing. They reconvened in the front study.

Anne turned on Michael. "I told you to be careful of that housekeeper."

Michael held up his hands. "We don't know who took it."

"Well, who else could have? She has the key. Why are you defending her?"

Michael's brow furrowed. He looked to Garth for help, who again stood leaning in the doorframe watching Anne through narrowed eyes.

"What?" she asked.

"I've known Tessa a very long time. I've always found her to be trustworthy."

"Not you, too." Anne flopped down in the armchair.

"Why do you think it was her?" Garth asked.

"She has a key. Besides, I've never trusted her. Not since the first time I laid eyes on her."

Garth nodded slowly. "Perhaps some past life experience."

"Oh, for God's sake. Both of you . . ." Anne sputtered to a stop.

Garth held up a placating hand. "Your intuition is something to attend to. I have a way to investigate her."

"Good."

"But we should consider other options." Garth looked at Michael. "You say Cagliostro is in the country?"

"Yes," Michael said, "at his country house."

"I won't ask how you know that." Garth's mouth crooked in a smile.

Anne softened a bit. "Our family's security man has remarkable abilities."

"Cagliostro could have sent someone for it," Garth suggested.

"He could have sent Tessa for it," Anne mumbled.

"Or someone we don't know about," Garth said in an even voice. "Or it could be another person here in Glastonbury, someone who knew Cynthia. Even a stranger, someone who felt what was happening and slipped into the house. It's not your Fort Knox, after all."

Anne nodded, conceding his point.

Michael looked at his watch. "I'm going to miss my flight unless I leave now." He turned to Garth. "Do you think it's worth pursuing the whereabouts of the other Atlantean crystals?"

"Absolutely. We've seen what these two little tabbies can do."

Michael studied Anne as if she were a temperamental cat.

"I have an idea," Garth said. "We can do some trance work while you're in Germany. See if Anne can reconnect to Megan."

"But—" Anne reached her hand out to Michael, then let it drop on the arm of the chair. "Oh, go. Just go."

"Anne," Michael knelt at her feet. "Sweetheart." He took her face in his hands. "You know I have to do my duty."

She nodded, a tear falling down her cheek. "I'm sorry. I can't seem to stop acting like a baby."

"It's the ceremony. Your nerves are raw, emotions all at the surface," Garth said. He turned to Michael. "Come back as soon as you know something."

"I will." Michael stood. "I'll go get my bag."

"No, old chap, I'll fetch it for you." Garth climbed the stairs, the squeaky one at the top protesting his bulk.

Michael sat next to Anne and pulled her into his lap. "One day we'll have finished with the Illuminati. We'll have put the world back as it should be. We'll lie in the sun, we'll have babies." She laughed into his chest. "We'll grow old together in peace." More tears fell and Michael kissed them from her cheeks.

"What's wrong with me?"

"It's what Garth said. You go so deep."

Garth arrived carrying Michael's suitcase.

"I'll call you from the airport," Michael said.

"Actually, it would be best if we worked right away. We can use her emotional state to our benefit."

Anne looked at Michael. "I'll call you, then."

"I'll take your case out to the car," Garth said.

They kissed goodbye, then Anne watched him leave, her hot forehead pressed to the cool glass of the front door. The white and red roses shone in the bright sunlight.

"BE AWARE OF THE DIRECTIONS." Garth's strong voice surrounded her like warm water. "East, south, west and north." They'd decided to do the working in the study where Anne usually read the book. "What is above you. What is below." Already she was slipping into an altered state, but he helped her relax deeply, starting with her feet in the earth and working their way up to her head in the stars, then he built a visualization of the crossroads, where all the worlds meet.

She saw a beautiful city, golden in the sunlight, spires of colored glass reaching into the blue sky, domes of crystal. People in colorful tunics walked the streets. The markets, full of vegetables, fruits and fish, bolts of brilliant cloth, pottery decorated with spirals and diamonds, did a brisk business.

"Direct your awareness to those whose actions affect us still, whose work we must complete."

A compact, muscular man appeared in her inner vision, his hair braided and decorated with sea shells. He walked across green grass toward a silver vehicle with a bubble top.

Megan, she thought, *show me Megan.*

The scene flickered. The craft was aloft. Below her lay the city nestled against the blue ocean.

Megan, she repeated, but something stirred deep in her consciousness.

Hush, child came a voice.

GOVANNAN GUIDED his personal craft down to the landing field near the headquarters of Gaia's Guild, even though his ultimate destination was the research facility of the New Knowledge Guild. He'd decided to surprise them with an impromptu visit. His quarterly appointment with Gaia's Guild, the group that kept them all fed and clothed, served as perfect camouflage. A young apprentice greeted him from a long desk at the front of the building and directed him to the top floor. He climbed the stairs, hoping continued exercise would help heal his new limp. The persistent lameness puzzled Pleione. She kept insisting he come for more treatments, but he simply didn't have the time. He felt well enough. And the leg gave him no pain. It simply didn't work like it had before the accident. He arrived on the seventh floor winded and still limping.

He spent a pleasant hour talking with Oria, the head of the guild, a woman as round as the Earth Mother herself. They sipped a delicious tea from Asia blended with rose petals from her personal garden, while she listed their crystal technology needs. As head of the Matrix Chamber, Govannan often assisted the larger Crystal Guild in simple business matters when the chamber did not demand his attention. It kept him grounded and in touch with those who ruled Atlantis. Once she'd finished her list, he asked for another cup of tea, then pointed toward the rectangular building across from her facility. "How are your new neighbors?"

She glanced after his finger, then hunched her shoulders. "Nice enough, really." She paused. "It's unfortunate they didn't follow our geometrical recommendations for their building. We find it's best to blend with the land, but that box over there . . ." she hesitated to continue.

Govannan nodded. "As one sensitive to energy flows, I must say it seems stagnant."

Oria relaxed. "Thank you for that phrase. Exactly my experience. The building seems to cut off the natural circulation of energy."

"May I ask, what is your impression of their research proposal?"

Again, the gentle woman looked uneasy. She picked up the tea pot, then realized it was empty.

"No more for me." Govannan anticipated her again. "What a delicate flavor."

"Yes, isn't it?" Oria smiled, then her eyes slid away from his face.

He waited.

She signed. "Of course, our work depends on the cycles of day and night, heat and cool. One of our elders speaks of an old legend about human cycles. Cycles of . . ." she searched for the exact word like a woman transplanting a delicate orchid, "growth and harvest, then dormancy before the next cycle." She glanced at Govannan to see if he understood.

He sat forward. "Do you think this explains the new illnesses?"

"Oh, I'm sure that is a matter for Pleione," Oria demurred. "But delving into the energetic makeup, our very blueprint . . ." she shuttered, leaving the rest unsaid.

Ever the diplomat, Govannan thought, then asked. "But you've heard nothing specific?"

Oria shook her head. "I try not to listen to gossip."

"Of course." He paused, but it seemed she really meant what she said. "I will see to your needs, Guild Mistress."

She rose and bowed slightly. "We are indebted to your guild, as always."

"And we to yours." He matched her bow. "May I meditate privately in your gardens before taking my leave?"

She gave a little pleased murmur. "I can send an apprentice . . ." She trailed off again.

"Oh, no thank you. I need the peace of Gaia and do not wish to interrupt anyone's duties."

She inclined her head. "Our guild is your guild," came the ritual saying.

Govannan took the stairs down to the ground floor and walked down a hallway that separated a long line of greenhouses from kitchen-like prep rooms. He ducked into one filled with bins of small grape plants, then found a back door into a vineyard. He followed a long trellis that hugged the side of the hill, making his way up the rows until he arrived at a rather nasty metal fence. On the other side squatted the red brick square of a building.

Govannan walked the fence looking for an entrance. He briefly wondered at himself, so recently turned to attuning people's energy fields without their knowledge. Now here he was slipping into a facility unannounced. In secret.

He checked his inner compass, his sense that told him if his actions were in harmony with the greater cosmos.

Continue, his deep mind whispered. Then came a small map, a sense of weakness farther down. He came to a part of the fence that was frayed and made short work of enlarging the small hole that some animal had begun. He promptly crawled through.

Now the challenge was to find a way in. The brick outer wall extended for several blocks in a monotonous and oppressive sameness. He consulted his inner compass again and saw in his mind two workers standing outside an open door talking. Govannan pulled off his guild robe, folded it into a tight square and stuffed it into the overalls he'd pulled on this morning for just this purpose. He felt for the location of the workers, sensed a tug and walked to the edge of the building, then turned left and continued down the ominous sameness of the brick wall. After what would have been two city blocks, he spotted a man and woman dressed in the same sort of outfit he now wore about to go back inside. He raised his hand and hurried toward them. Showing little curiosity, they held the door for him, then turned and went into what looked like a warehouse.

Govannan found a small nook between two locked doors. He leaned against the wall and stretched his finely tuned senses through the facility. The cacophony of energy flows repulsed him. He recomposed himself, tuned his sense to a higher frequency and tried again. A high whine, almost a scream, tore through him. He winced and pulled back. He'd have to explore the place physically.

Hoping his intuition would lead him to what he needed to see, he began to walk down the first hall. But they all looked alike. How would he find his way out? Then he noticed numbers. Not glyphs that communicated a concept, but numbers. In sequence. He was in hallway 8, junction 22. Eight suggested a complete cycle, the balance of four seasons and their mid points. Twenty-two, the master builder, brought the archetype into reality. Surely here was the location of their research into gene manipulation. Govannan put his hand to a door, but again could not bear to extend his senses. He tried the door and it opened. Stepping inside, he found a store room of supplies.

Behind another door he found stacks of metal cages of all sizes, behind another vats of liquids sealed by metal lids. They gave off an odd odor. Nothing he could identify.

Puzzled, he walked to another junction and went to his right. He passed two more turns without taking them, then took the third left at random. Section 11, junction 21. Not trusting these numbers held any meaning, he tried another door. These were locked. Down two more halls, he opened another door. The pungent smell of urine and straw made him cough. He stepped in and closed the door, forcing himself to take shallow breaths. Darkness permeated more deeply than the smell. Something rustled. He pulled out a small crystal tabby and held it up, asking for light. After a long moment, much longer than it should have taken, the crystal gave off a tepid glow.

A sharp movement caught his attention. Inside a series of wire cages, shapes lay in the straw. He stepped closer, trying to pierce the shadows, but couldn't make out what he was looking at. A whine came from the creature on the floor, something between a plea for mercy and a moan of fear. He called for more light, and his crystal reluctantly brightened. On the floor, its dull eyes looking anxiously up at this new human, lay a tapir whose stomach had been carved open, then clamped back around tubes running a sluggish green liquid. The animal's limbs, bloated and useless, moved in a gross semblance of flight, like someone caught in a nightmare. Govannan took an involuntary step forward, and the animal whined in panic, thrashing about, dislodging one tube that seeped green onto the straw. He stretched his hands out to the poor creature, which screamed in terror. Govannan took his crystal and sent a hard stream of energy toward it, stopping its heart and its agony. He retched into the straw.

But there was more. He couldn't look, but he must. In the next cage, a small monkey sat, its hands bound. Wires protruded from a metal cap where the top of its head should be. In another cage, a large mountain lion lay motionless, its eyes focused inward in pain. Halfway down its back, the tan fur suddenly gave way to long, coarse hair, what should have been soft, padded paws now the close toed pads of a wolf. Govannan's stomach turned itself inside out again, but he could not clear the smell from his nostrils, the anguish of these tortured creatures from his heart. He looked down the row of cages. His courage failed. He did not have the strength to bring peace to them all. He must escape and report to Evenor. The Governor's Guild would help him. They would bring justice, end this suffering, return the land of Atlantis to sanity.

Govannan fled, his mind dark, his heart torn and bleeding. Instinct led him down the passageways toward sunlight and fresh air. He found a door to the outside and pushed through it, thinking himself unnoticed.

ANNE FOLLOWED Garth's voice back from Atlantis, through the streets of the city, back to the strong magnetic pull of the Tor. She opened her eyes in the chair in Cynthia's study where she'd begun. She groped for his hand. "Oh, my God."

"What?"

"Horrible experiments. Animals, half one thing and half another."

"Oh, my dear, I am so sorry." He reached into his pocket and brought out a small brown apothecary bottle. He percussed it against his hand, then took out the dropper. "Open up."

Anne obeyed him. The alcohol from the tincture made her cough, but the flowers and herbs spread reassuring warmth. "How long?"

"It should work immediately."

"No, how long was I gone?"

"About twenty minutes."

"That can't be."

Garth just watched her.

"But . . ."

"Time runs differently here in Glastonbury, and of course, in such a deep trance."

She rubbed at her eyes, looked around the room. The grandfather clock ticked mechanically in the hall.

"Tell me everything you saw," he said.

And she did, all about Govannan and his grisly discovery. "But no Megan. I tried. I kept thinking about her, but it was like I was trapped with him. Then something told me to stop struggling."

"I am very sorry you had to witness such atrocities. Keep the tincture and take it at two hour intervals until tomorrow at this time."

Anne put the bottle on the table beside her. "Govannan seemed determined to stop it, though. It was like being behind his eyes. I could feel his reactions." She folded her arms around herself. "He's a good man."

Garth studied her, sitting in his customary long silence. Just when she was about to ask what he thought, he spoke. "We must accept the visions we receive. Somehow this is important to our work."

She nodded.

"How are you feeling?"

"I'm all right, now."

He nodded and watched her for a moment longer. "In that case, I'll go home. I need to talk to some people about the spring, then see about Tessa, of course." He ran his hand through his brown curls. "We need a town meeting. Call the groups together."

"I'm going to call Michael, then sit in the sun. I need light after those visions." Anne wrapped the shawl that decorated the back of this chair around herself.

"Red Spring will soothe you. Go sit by it. Drink the water."

"Let me know what else I can do to help you."

"You have done more than enough. Check in with me this evening."

"I will. Thank you."

"Of course." Garth turned and let himself out.

The first thing she did was call a locksmith. She'd get all new locks and see about that door in the basement. The man said he could run round tomorrow.

16

Cagliostro ran along the path through the woods on his country home, his heart thudding against his ribs. One of the Akitas paused to wait for him, but Cagliostro forced himself to keep going. Satisfied, the dog turned and loped ahead. Cagliostro despised this weakness that the last dive had left him with. The only way to deal with it was to push past it, to train harder. He ran on, the trees a blur, and emerged in the formal garden on the east side of the house. One of the grounds keepers stepped forward and called the dogs, who ran to her, their tails waging. Cagliostro walked into the front entrance, shoes squeaking on the Italian marble, where the butler handed him a towel. He wiped the sweat from his face, threw the towel on the cork floor of the dining room, and made his way to the gymnasium in the back of the house. He banged the door open, and Karl Mueller snapped to attention from a quad stretch.

"Kajukenbo," he snapped out. Mueller walked to the large mat in one corner of the room. In the mirrors surrounding the workout area, Cagliostro glimpsed the shadows beneath his eyes and his flushed skin. He turned his back on the reflection and gave his attention to his opponent. "Full force."

Mueller's eyebrow twitched up.

"Nonlethal," Cagliostro said.

Mueller bowed, enclosing one fist in his palm, then took a stance, a deadly concentration of muscle and reflexes. But Cagliostro knew his own spiritual power added an edge Mueller would never gain in this lifetime. He returned the bow, then attacked.

Mueller stepped back, avoiding the first flurry of fists, then surged forward, sweeping his left leg around, knocking Cagliostro off balance. Cagliostro rolled with the force, then came up in perfect form. Mueller stalked him, found an opening and struck as fast as a jaguar, stinging his boss on the jaw. He followed with a kidney punch that sent him sprawling.

Cagliostro struggled to his feet and took his stance, wobbling a bit. Something flickered in Mueller's eyes. "What?"

Mueller came out of a crouch. "Permission to speak freely, sir?"

"Granted." Cagliostro maintained his fighting stance.

"You are not well, sir. It is not rational to push yourself—"

Cagliostro's foot cracked against Mueller's temple, followed by a punch beneath the chin, bouncing Mueller's head around. Then Cagliostro danced back. "You were saying?"

Mueller's eyes darkened. He circled his boss, whose breath came now in ragged gasps. Mueller feigned an attack, then dropped down and delivered a solid punch to his opponent's solar plexus. Cagliostro collapsed in a heap, trying desperately to get his breath. Mueller stood over him. "I rest my case. Ordinarily, I wouldn't be able to get that close to you." He turned on his heel and went into the shower room, not waiting to be dismissed.

Goddamn his arrogance. Cagliostro ground his nails into his palms. He lay on the mat until his breath returned to normal, a process that took entirely too long. He had to admit he was not fit for another round with the enormous crystal that lay waiting beneath the waters of the Caribbean, calling to him in his dreams. It was agony to wait when all he'd ever yearned for was in his reach. Cagliostro forced himself to his feet, not wanting his overheated muscles to grow cold and stiff, and climbed the stairs to his suite. He ran a hot bath and soaked. What exactly had happened during that last dive? He'd been over and over it, but was sure a piece of it was missing from his memory. He'd seen a ceremony, people arranged in a circle, but with complex lines of energy running everywhere. And chanting. He'd seen it all through a golden haze. Then—he'd woken up three days later a continent away.

He got out of the bath and called his physical therapist. Healing was like training. After a massage, he called Miriam and Mueller to report to his office.

Cagliostro sat at his desk and checked his emails before the two arrived. A gold statue of the Egyptian god Amen that had once decorated the Holy of Holies at Luxor stood behind him. An original draft of *Abra-Mellin, the Mage*, the magical grimoire by S. L. MacGregor Mathers, sat under glass on one side of the room. Above it hung a painting he'd commissioned himself depicting the city he dreamt of often, its airy domes awash in the slanted rays of the sun, its spires leaping into the sky like flames. A round stone omphalos of deepest black sat in the middle of a pool of water. A face framed in wild curls looked from behind a pillar, the sensual mouth drawn back in a smile like a leopard. It was how he remembered it. Atlantis, the land he longed for.

Miriam arrived first. She nodded, started to speak, but apparently thought better of it. He gestured for her to sit. Then Mueller walked in, looking annoyingly fresh.

"Thank you for deigning to join us, Mr. Mueller," Cagliostro said, although the implied criticism was unjustified. "I would like your reports. First, the crystal?"

"Undisturbed," Mueller said, his face placid. "No boats have come near the site. It seems that no one else knows of its discovery."

Cagliostro nodded. "The other sentinels?"

"We've learned of one more possibility," Miriam said. A stone held by a private collector in India. An old Sufi family."

"How secure is the artifact?"

"The family relies on a small security force picked from the military. Privately trained. Their technology is not up to date, however. Medium threat."

Mueller sniffed as if he disagreed, but when Cagliostro looked at him, he said nothing.

"Fine. Let's collect it. I want to have more crystal power before we make our next attempt, which needs to be soon. We can't rely on that crystal remaining undetected." He fixed Mueller with a look. He would not admit to them that what he really needed was more time to heal. Maybe he'd call on his old mentor, Cornelius Waldman. Even at eighty-two, the old man was still sharp. He might make up a potion for him, but then he might pick up more information than Cagliostro wanted to share. Better not.

"There's one more thing." Miriam sat straight in her chair.

A dry stick, that one, Cagliostro thought. Maybe he needed someone fresh for his bed, someone whose virginity he could take along with her vitality.

"The Le Clairs are on our trail," Miriam said.

"This is news?" Cagliostro asked with a snort.

"They know we're looking for Atlantean crystals."

"Of course they do. That's what we took from Mr. Rhodes, your old Grand Master." He watched her for any signs of regret. Finding none, he continued. "Is there anything specific?"

"They seem to think you're looking for a fragment of the Chintamani Stone."

Cagliostro steepled his fingers and stared into the painting. An interesting idea, he had to admit. "Do we know the location of this fragment?"

"No, sir."

"Do they?"

"Michael Levy is searching for it."

"Find it before he does. But after we've secured the sentinel."

Miriam hesitated.

"Is there a problem?"

"That last could prove difficult." She looked at the statue behind him, avoiding meeting his gaze directly.

He stared at her until she lowered her eyes to his. "Do not disappoint me again, Miriam." Really, he was ready to be done with her. He wouldn't mind if she failed.

ANNE STRETCHED out in bed and pulled the duvet up to her chin. The clock downstairs chimed eight, but it felt more like midnight. Her calves ached from her sunset hike up the Tor, and now her head had started to throb. Her stomach was still uneasy. Sleep would fix it all.

Michael had called from the Rosicrucian headquarters in Freiburg, Germany soon after he'd arrived. Franz had extended him the same courtesies he'd always given Thomas—carte blanche to explore their records, along with free room and board for as long as it took. She missed her brother. Not only had he been one of the world's foremost metaphysical scholar, he'd brought her the security only an older brother could. Thomas had always been there to try something first, to take the blame when something went wrong, to tell her what to expect when she was entering a new phase of life. She switched off the light and lay listening to the faint sounds of people at White Spring. A new vagrant had shown up and seemed to be camping there. Someone had a flute. The town seemed to take turns caring for them, and really they posed no threat to her. If he was really a vagrant, not some black ops agent. Besides, Rob was still staying at Berachah on the corner. He'd stayed in Glastonbury rather than follow Michael to Germany, saying Cagliostro was the one to pay attention to, not his security force. She wondered if he was right.

She turned on her back, annoyed with the thought, and began to build a sacred circle around the room. Just before she sealed it, a scratch came from the back porch, then a whine. Anne ran down the stairs and opened the back door. The hound stood there, her red ears perked forward, looking at Anne with those ice blue eyes.

She filled a bowl with water, which the dog ignored. "Hungry?"

In answer, the dog trotted through the hallway, up the stairs and sat on the rug at the foot of the bed. Anne watched her for a moment from the doorway. The dog lay down and studied Anne in turn. "You want to sleep here?" she asked.

The dog lay her head down on her front paws and sighed.

"I'm glad of the company," Anne said. She climbed in bed and switched off the lamp again. The dog's eyes reflected some stray light from the street. She'd thought only cats' eyes did that. She rebuilt the sacred circle, including her new companion, then fell asleep.

The dream came immediately.

MEGAN LOOKED around the stone vigil hut she sat in now, remembering the youthful tears she'd shed the afternoon she'd received the crystal key from the

Morgen. She'd wept to learn that she would not see Govannan for another year, afraid he'd forget his insignificant new apprentice. If only she'd known then, but wasn't this the universal lament of the aged? To think she'd grown as old as the ancient Morgen before even a hundred years had passed. She took a few raggedy breaths in a vain attempt to fill her lungs fully, then pushed on with her story.

"My year in Avalon went smoothly. They put me to work with the other girls doing the daily gardening, tending the sheep, spinning the wool, doing all the tasks that keep people fed and clothed. At first I rebelled. After all, I was the daughter of Diaprepes, the High Prince of Atlantis. But my mother had been born here, daughter of a priestess of Avalon, conceived of the High Rite I'd just witnessed. Avalon was a center in its own right, but everything was interconnected in those days, the earth balanced by the great stone monuments, gently shaped to reflect the stars above in precise harmonic resonance.

"So I settled into this routine, trusting the Lady, if not the Morgen, and every so often the Lady would send me to another temple to help with a ceremony. I grew accustomed to blending my energy with others in rituals—strangers, people I'd probably never see again. That year, I traveled to Crete, Greece, Egypt, Palenque, even Tibet."

Caitir's look of wonder broke Megan's heart all over again. Caitir's options had been curtailed. She had never seen the wide world, and probably never would. She would remain within a few hundred miles of this place her whole life. And that life would be short, if the trends continued. Megan forced herself to continue.

"Soon I could feel the intricate weaves of energies around me, yet stay grounded in my own strand. Sometimes the Lady gave me a lesson separate from the other girls. I'll never forget the first time she took me into the hill. There were three of us, but we went on separate nights."

MEGAN FOLLOWED the Lady of Avalon up the hill, staying beside the stream. She had prepared for the coming rite, spending the night in the ritual hut alone, fasting, listening to the whispering of the waters, feeling the hands of the spirit women who attended Red Spring reach into her body and adjust her own streams of energy. She'd watched the sun move across the sky as she sat among the hectic reds, yellows and orange leaves of the season. The Lady had come for her at dusk.

Acorns crunched beneath their feet, then moss softened their steps, the sibilant whispering of the water ever present. Where the two streams parted, they followed the clear, white one until they came to the cave that held the source of White Spring. A quarter moon stood in the darkening sky, just visible between the branches of the forest. The Lady motioned for her to sit. "The Seven Sisters will rise, followed by the Hunter and his Dog Star, and stand at the apex of the sky at midnight. This marks the beginning of the winter half of the year. The Wild Hunt rides."

A shiver ran the length of Megan's spine.

The Lady put a comforting hand on her shoulder, warm in the cooling night. "You have nothing to fear from the High Ones, regardless of the stories the village girls tell. It is safe to eat and drink with them, to accept any gifts. Show proper respect."

Megan frowned up at her, but the Lady offered no further comfort. "Gather your intention as you sit here. Once you have clear in your mind what you wish to know, walk into the Crystal Cave and follow your inner urgings. There may be outward signs as well." In the fading light, her face, shadowed by the red shawl, was unreadable.

"I don't know what to ask," Megan said. "What do you recommend?"

The Lady stood suddenly and loomed over her. "It is time to stop asking childish questions and claim your life for yourself. Look deep into your heart." She pushed her forefinger into Megan's chest. "That is where you will find what you need to know. We will watch for your return. If you do." And with that, she turned her back on Megan and walked away.

Megan's heart lurched. "Wait," she shouted, but she knew the Lady of Avalon would not look back. Soon the mists swallowed her tall figure, and she was gone.

Megan sat at the entrance to the Crystal Cave, listening to the flow of water around rocks, letting her breath slow. The images of the Wild Hunt that the girls whispered about in the dark of their dormitory filled her mind— the huge hooves of the horses, the sharp teeth of the hounds, the exquisite, terrible beauty of the fae themselves. She shivered again and tried to remember Govannan, the music of the shells in his hair, the thrill his laugh called into her heart, but his image was fading. How could she believe in the warm sun and bright colors of Eden surrounded as she was by mists and shadow? Had the enormous crystal in the Matrix Chamber even been real? And her connection to Govannan. Had it been just a girl's infatuation?

She realized with a start that now she thought of the Megan who'd been taken to the Crystal Matrix Chamber as a child. She pulled the crystal the old Morgen had given her six months earlier out of her pocket and put the stone into her palm. It winked at her, seemed to ask her to take courage. She'd grown accustomed to it, learned to scry in its slender sides, but why had the Morgen given it to her? Perhaps this was her question. Perhaps they all were. They added up to one question—what is the purpose of this life? Megan blew these thoughts across her palm into the crystal key, then stood and walked into the cave behind her.

The way was ordinary enough at first. Water ran beside a well-worn path, trickling through water-smoothed pebbles. A pool gathered between large rocks that jutted out on one side of the hill. She climbed up and looked into the water, but saw only herself, her blue eyes wide, her hair a mess of curls in the humidity. Stilling herself, she let her focus rest just past the surface of the pool and waited. Nothing came, only an urge to move on.

The path forked and Megan stopped, waiting for some indication of which way she should follow. Nothing came, so she picked the smaller one and walked on. Soon it narrowed. White calcite points hung from the ceiling. Whiter quartz veined the walls. A large boulder loomed before her, blocking the path. She scrambled around it and, on the other side, heard a faint sound of drumming. The faeries were dancing, preparing for the Wild Hunt. She crouched beside the boulder, but no one came. The sound remained constant. Gathering her courage, she crept forward. The drums grew stronger.

Suddenly, the passageway opened out. A lake stretched before her, its surface velvet black. Mist filled the air, dampening her hair and face. She ran her tongue over her lips. White Spring water.

Breathe onto the key, came a voice. *Ask for light.*

Megan did as she was instructed, and the crystal became a torch in her hand, burning with a cool light. She held it aloft and stood, overpowered by the sight before her. Light reflected from the ceiling and walls, stars within the earth. Crystals and gem stones sparkled from every direction. Long and graceful clear crystal points reached for the water. Amethyst geodes glinted in the black rock. Streaks of blue dusted with gold gave way to ruby reds and clear yellow stones. Chunks of rose quartz and deeper rhodocrocite blossomed from the walls like a field of wild flowers.

The drumming sound came from the back of the cave. Megan took a few steps along the edge of the lake, careful of her footing on the damp rock, then held her crystal up. A clear sheet of water flowed from a dark cleft high in the wall into the lake where it foamed white, then gradually stilled. She should wait here for her vision, find a comfortable spot perched on a rock, but something pushed her toward the waterfall. The slippery, wet rock demanded her attention. Lodged in crevices and scattered along the shore in places lay pebbles, and among the ordinary grey and black stones gleamed amethyst and quartz, citrine and rubies. Megan stopped and listened, thinking perhaps she'd stumbled into a dragon's lair after all, regardless that the Lady taught her the dragon forces were the energy streams that made up the universe itself. But she heard no scrape of claw on rock, felt no fiery breath on the nape of her neck, so she walked on, ever drawn toward the veil of water.

A flat rock protruded from the cave wall close enough to the waterfall to watch it, but far enough away not to get drenched. Megan groped around on the rock, and found small indentions, toe and finger holds. She climbed up and found a flat spot. She sat and leaned her back against the cave wall, tucking her legs beneath her, and gathered herself for a vigil. The light from the crystal had tapered down to the size of a candle flame. She laid it beside her and discovered a hollow in the rock that had gathered a pool of water. She watched for images in the water, but none came.

The urge to move toward the waterfall grew stronger, so she took up her crystal and climbed down the other side, where she found neat steps cut into the wall. Once down, she picked her way across the wet rock to the booming water. The shower drenched her and she expanded like a wilted flower

Walk through, the same voice whispered.

Megan looked around, but found no one. She closed her eyes and saw nothing.

Come through the water, the voice repeated.

Megan held her breath and stepped through the silver stream, emerging on the other side on a green strip of grass lit by an even light, bone dry. She stood stock still, looking around for the source of the light, but found none. The sky above thinned to a haze, like an even bank of fine clouds that did not part to reveal the sun or moon, but the ambient light revealed a meadow dotted with flowers. Beyond lay a forest of ancient oak and rowan. At the edge of the trees stood a stag, his head heavy with a large rack. He stepped forward, pawed the ground, then turned, flicking a white tail. Megan followed.

The stag bounded through the trees, making no sound. Megan ran hard to keep up with the hart, but he darted down a slope, jumped a stream, and she lost sight of him. The stream ran cold on her feet, which she noticed were now bare. How had she lost her shoes? The moss on the other side cushioned her steps. Through the trees, she saw a sphere of golden light which she walked toward. Music filled the air, and laughter, the sounds of cutlery on plates. At the edge of the trees, an old man in a cloak waited for her. He took her hand and they walked into the court of the fae.

Lords and ladies sat at tables filled with mounds of globed grapes, ruby apples, golden squash. The smell of roasting nuts and vegetables filled the air. Bowls of ripe strawberries and heavy cream spread in abundance. A tiny brown gnome tottered by carrying a pile of steaming tubers three times its height. One tall, impossibly elegant woman held up a goblet that gleamed gold beneath encrusted jewels, her gown diaphanous folds revealing curves of milk thistle skin. Others leaned against trees, dressed in velvets and silks of scarlet, peacock blue, peach and rose, and green, every imaginable shade of green. Some gossiped and flirted, while others sang a complex harmony tune accompanied by a group of musicians strolling along playing hand harps and golden horns with lithe fingers.

Beneath low bowers on beds of soft moss and mounds of flowers, a group lay together in various states of dress. One man raised his head, his hair a mass of burnished curls, his lips the color of wine, his bronze skin radiant with some fragrant oil that flushed Megan's skin, and reached a graceful hand out for her, his phallus a graceful stamen rising from the petal folds of his robes. It seemed more Beltane than Samhein in faery.

The king—at least he looked like on—sat at the high table, dressed in fine red and gold threaded with gems and glimmering lights. He looked down at them and smiled. Megan felt that the sun had just risen.

"And who has our friend Merlin brought to our table?"

The host of faeries quieted at the sound of their king's voice. Heads turned and necks craned as they tried to get a look at her.

"Megan, one who studies in Avalon, but serves the Crystal Matrix." Merlin's voice was like sitting in front of a roaring fire. It warmed every part of her. But how did he know so much?

"Welcome, friend Megan." And a plate laden with food appeared on a low table near the dais along with a golden chalice. Megan was suddenly sitting before it. The mead tasted of honey and magic. The food filled the secret hollows in her soul and soothed her heart.

"We celebrate the betrothal of my brother," spoke the King. To his side sat a tall being, his hair as blond as the King's, his eyes as blue, his fine brow and chin haughtier. But he could not tear his gaze from the vision beside him. Her skin was alabaster, her lips mulberries, her hair fine, curling flame. "This night he will endure his trial for her hand."

At this the whole host surged to their feet and raised their chalices of silver and gold, bedecked with sparking jewels. The faeries sang their blessing, a sound that made Megan forget why she herself had come.

The King's brother stood receiving their good wishes, and at the end of the song, quaffed the rest of his mead and threw the golden cup behind him. He went down on his knees before the beauty still sitting beside him. "I pledge my troth to you, my beloved. This night I will do great deeds in your name and will return in the morning to claim you for all eternity."

She rested her fine white hands on his head for a moment. He rose, and behind him appeared a host of horses ridden by men and women with golden, red and coal black hair variously combed and braided, hung with gems and feathers, flying behind them in an imagined wind. Megan wondered if Govannan had copied their hair style. And hounds, their teeth bared, their sky blue eyes eerie with magic. One great stallion stood riderless. The King's brother leapt onto the horse's bare back and blew a great horn. The horde of riders shouted their blood lust, chilling Megan to the core. She set down her chalice and looked for Merlin, who stood at the edge of the forest, his eyes on her.

"We ride for glory and the souls of men," the King's brother cried. He looked at the woman with flaming curls, waiting for her tribute, but she had turned to the King, her head bent. The King leaned over to speak to her, so close to her ear. They laughed together. The brother frowned and called to her, but the Hunt was off in a churning of hooves and braying of hounds. His horse whinnied to follow.

Merlin called for Megan, and she ran to him. He stepped into the shadow of the trees and Megan followed right behind him, but already he was lost. Farther in, she saw the stag standing next to an ancient oak waiting for her. She went after him through the forest to the edge of the waterfall. She hesitated, then turned to the stag. "But my question."

That is all for now, said the voice.

Megan stepped through the veil of water and found herself once again beside the lake with the jeweled vaulted ceiling. She retraced her steps, pausing at the rock shelf, wondering if she should seek more answers, but she knew her quest, at least on this night, was over. She passed the lake and followed the stream of White Spring down its path. The rock turned to dirt laced with roots again, and soon the lighter black of the cave mouth showed the hard, crystal stars.

Megan walked out of the cave into the night air. The Seven Sisters crowned the midnight sky. But something was different. The cry of a pack of hunting hounds sounded from a distance. A deep shiver pebbled her flesh. She pulled her cloak tight around her and sat, waiting for the Lady to come for her at dawn.

THE OLD MEGAN brushed her tears away—no time to mourn the losses now—and dug into the pocket of her smock. She reached her hand out to Caitir, who startled as if from a doze. Had she slept through the story, she wondered, a spike of irritation starting her pulse racing again. Caitir cupped her palm and Megan let it go, her sacred charge, her lifeline to the past. And the future. The crystal lay in Caitir's palm, gleaming softly in the firelight. Megan sat back and let out a long breath. She'd passed the key. Her purpose had been fulfilled, and yet she still felt the inner pressure, sense of urgency. She looked up at her daughter, who sat with the crystal in her hand, but with her eyes on her mother's face, eyes full of questions and worry.

"Tonight," she glanced out the one window in the hut. She'd had it put in herself after she had become Lady in her own right. "In just a few hours, you will go into the Hallowed Hill and find your own fate. This stone will guide you."

ANNE WOKE in the predawn grey. She sat up and looked for the dog in her place at the bottom of the bed, but she was gone. Somehow. Anne had not opened the door for her, she knew that. The dog had the same eyes, the same markings, as the hounds of the Wild Hunt. Had her mind just reached for that familiar image to represent the dogs in her dream, or was it something more? Shivering, Anne lay back down and pulled the duvet over her head. She would call Garth when the sun was up.

17

Garth arrived at Anne's house late the next morning and suggested they go up to the meditation room in case more hypnosis was called for. Anne hoped they wouldn't have to resort to that. She needed to spend some time in this world. Once upstairs and settled on cushions, she told him her dream.

"So," Garth said, then sat in his customary silence until she thought he'd never respond. Just as she took a breath to speak, he continued. "Megan saw the Wild Hunt ride out, but that doesn't match what the Morgen said to you. What were her exact words?"

"*You must return what Megan let loose.*"

Garth shook his head. "Are you certain she took nothing with her?"

Anne nodded. "Except what she ate and drank."

"A foolhardy stunt, that."

"I remember the stories caution against eating or drinking anything in faeryland, but the Lady of Avalon seemed to think that was—" she stopped. She'd been about to say *ignorant superstition*, which was exactly the impression she'd picked up, but clearly Garth believed it.

He pressed on, "I've always been taught not to accept gifts, eat or drink in faery, although I've been sorely tempted at times. It seems—" he scratched his beard and looked out the window at the Tor, today dotted with cattle "—unsociable. Taking in faery food or drink is supposed to attune you to their world too closely or even trap you there."

"Like Persephone eating the pomegranate seed," Anne said.

"Something like that." Garth glanced at her, then turned his gaze back to the slope of the Tor. "One is likely to lose touch with our time there; they could come back months, even years later. There are some reports of centuries passing." The yearning in his voice was unmistakable.

"You've been in faeryland?" Anne asked. "I thought they were just—"

"Faery tales?" His eyes sparkled.

Anne laughed. "So, what are they then?"

"Ancestral legends. Wisdom teachings. Stories of humans going into faeryland have been told for centuries. And the other way around. Lancelot came from faery."

"No, France," Anne said.

Now it was Garth's turn to laugh. "If you look carefully at the various versions, you'll see that in the early Arthurian romances, Lancelot is said to have come from the land of faery. It's the old triangle—a man and a faery vying for the love of a female." He studied her a moment. "I think it's time you learn your own tradition. Egypt is fine and all, but you are a Celt, after all."

"According to my family, we're originally from Israel. And the family went into Egypt when—" She stopped and looked at him carefully. "Did Cynthia tell you?"

"All that bunk about the bloodline?" Garth dismissed this idea with a wave of his broad hand.

"Bunk? But, Thomas showed me the research." At the scowl on his face, she hurried on. "I didn't believe it at first either. I thought they were all nuts, but Thomas showed me ancient scrolls. And all those books."

"Plantard forged those records of the Priory of Sion. It's well documented. He duped Baigent, Leigh and Lincoln. He renewed some old medieval scam for money." He pointed a huge index finger at her. "You, my dear, are a descendant of the Le Clairs, who came here with William the Conqueror. But your branch of the family married into the Brythonic tribes. You carry the old blood."

Anne wished for the thousandth time that she could talk to Thomas. "What did Cynthia believe?"

"We agreed to disagree." Garth smiled at a private memory, then focused on her. "The point is you don't understand the cosmology of your own people."

"So, would you teach me?"

He reached out to the coaster on the low table, but found no mug.

"Want some tea?"

"That would be lovely."

Anne smiled at the incongruity of that delicate word coming from the mountain of a man lounging on Cynthia's silk cushions. She ran down to the kitchen and put the kettle on. She rustled up some egg salad sandwiches while she waited for the water to boil, then poured it into the pot, and took everything upstairs.

"Excellent." Garth consumed two sandwich wedges in one bite and washed them down with half a mug of tea. "Now, the Celtic cosmos." He rubbed his hands together and looked around, then pulled out a sketch pad wedged between the table and the wall.

Anne let out a little exclamation of surprise. "I still haven't found everything. Do you know where the key to the cellar door is?"

"You have them all."

"Except for—" Anne began, but Garth shushed her.

He drew a diagram with three circles connected by the trunk of a tree. "I'll forgo the branches and leaves. Basically, there are four worlds—earth, moon, sun and stars. You could say the lunar world includes the moon and the earth. It's where we humans live with the animals and plants. The solar world includes the planets, but also spiritual beings, those the Christians call angels, and humans who have perfected themselves. In the stellar world, we find the stars, obviously. And the divine beings."

Anne pointed to his drawing. "This looks like the tree of life in Kabbala."

Garth snorted. "You don't think Odin hung on a Jewish tree, do you?"

"But he's from the Norse tradition," Anne said. "He's not Celtic."

"Ever notice the Green Man has a vine through his mouth?" He didn't wait for an answer. "He hangs on the tree as well. You'll find this same diagram in most traditions because this is an accurate depiction of the created universe."

"Created?"

Garth gave her a sharp look. "The highest plane of existence might be called uncreated. It's the unmanifest pure consciousness. What we'd call God now—*Ceugant* in Welsh. At least after the Romans. What those people who taught that meditation in the sixties called the transcendent."

Anne pointed to the drawing. "I don't see any faeries."

He gave her an approving nod. "That's because the lunar realm is divided into three levels. The moon, of course, then the surface of the earth, where we live now—Tolkien's Middle Earth or *Abred* in Welsh. Then there's the underworld, which is the home of the faeries, elementals and underworld deities. The Welsh word is *Annwn*. The Christians say this world is evil, but that's nonsense, of course."

He ate another sandwich, licked his large fingers, then stopped and looked at Anne like a little boy. "Excuse me."

"I forgot to bring the –" she stopped herself from saying 'napkins', remembering that meant something quite different here in England, but she couldn't find the right word. "I don't stand on ceremony."

His laugh was as hearty as Merlin's had been in her dream. "So, when your Megan walked through the waterfall, she went into faeryland, into the underworld."

Anne nodded. "And you're saying this is a real place?"

"Yes. And this spot—" he thumped the floor with his index finger "—is a place where the worlds are close together. Because of the energy of the Tor and the twin springs, it is easy to slip through."

"So, now what? We don't know what Megan let loose, but we've balanced White Spring."

"Not quite," he said.

"What do you mean?"

"Last night I sensed something—like a door ajar between dimensions. The alignment still needs work."

"And the spring? How's the water?"

"An excellent question. Let's go see." He jumped to his feet, graceful for all his bulk.

They walked down to White Spring. Besides the vagrant Anne had noticed earlier, a small knot of people milled around. Joanne stood with a circle of women holding hands in the middle of the flagstone patio. "Blessed be," they chanted in unison, then broke up the circle.

Joanne approached Garth. "Bridget has heard our prayers." She pointed to the pipe, which gushed water. One man filled his gallon jugs. Several waited in line behind him.

"Congratulations." Garth seemed entirely genuine, although Anne knew he'd led the ceremony that had freed the water. Perhaps it had been the combination. "Tell me—" he leaned his head down to her, one adept to another "—do you feel the spring is healed entirely? Did you pick up anything during your ceremony?"

"The goddess had withdrawn her abundance because of the violence against women in the world. We pledged to redouble our efforts. Our group is taking up a collection to send to the rape victims in the Congo. And we want to help with shelters for battered women in the UK. How much can we put you down for?"

Garth nodded his approval. "I'll write you a cheque when I get home."

Joanne glared at Anne, who said, "I'd be happy to contribute to such a worthy cause."

Garth continued. "You think White Spring has been healed, then?"

"If we continue to be vigilant, yes."

"Excellent." He clapped her on the shoulder. "Good work."

Bran sat next to the door, inconspicuous in his well worn trousers and flannel shirt, but his brown eyes held such a bright spark that Anne marveled no one deferred to him. With a twist of his head, Garth invited him to walk with them. They turned up the path to the Tor. "And what is your assessment, Master Bran?"

He waited until they'd passed the houses to their left before answering. "That one's a wee bit daft is my assessment, Master Garth."

The two guffawed shamelessly.

"You two." Anne shook her head. "The situation in the Congo is horrible, you know."

"And has nothing to do with White Spring," Garth said. "Nevertheless, I'll make my donation to stop that atrocity. She's quite right that the goddess needs proper honoring in this world and that women should be treated with more respect."

Bran nodded his agreement, then answered Garth's initial question. "The spring seems happy enough this morning, but I'm still not easy about it."

"Nor am I," Garth said. They reached the gate at the end of the meadow and walked up to the bench on the lower slope of the Tor, where they sat down. Bran chose the ground. Below them, the cows nosed around in the spring grass. Garth sat in silence, which didn't seem to bother Bran. Finally, he spoke. "I'd like to set a watch. Discreet, of course. Any change in the water should be reported directly to the both of us."

"I'll see to it." Bran stood and brushed off his trousers. "Anne," he doffed an imaginary hat at her.

"Nice to see you again. Let me know what I can do to help."

"You and your man have helped more than we could have hoped for. And where is he this fine morning?"

"Gone to do some research."

"We'll keep an eye out for you, then." He jerked his head toward a man lingering in the meadow below.

Anne looked down and saw Rob. "Oh, he works for my family. Security."

Bran nodded. "Good, but we'll keep an eye out regardless."

Anne's eyes filled and she shook her head, annoyed with the strong and unexpected tides of emotion she was experiencing. She said simply, "I appreciate your kindness."

Bran walked down the hill and Garth stood up. "I have business as well. Let me know about any dreams or visions. I'll be in touch."

"Thanks for everything," she said.

He left her sitting on the bench. Rob wandered past her, and she turned and climbed the Tor after him, enjoying the burn in her calves. At the top, the green of England stretched out to every horizon. Tourists stood in the tower, looking up, one narrating the Christian history of Glastonbury. Anne took the path down the other side of the Tor, then walked down the road to her house.

A small truck pulled up just as she reached the steps. A workman got out of the truck and pulled his tool box out after him. He started up the stairs.

"Hello," Anne called. "Did you come about the locks?"

"I did." He turned and waited for her.

"I'm Anne Le Clair, the current owner." He shook her hand. "I'd like to change all the locks. We had a burglary recently."

"Indeed? Unusual in Glastonbury."

"Yes, well," Anne said. "And there's a door in the basement that I haven't found a key for."

Once inside, the man set to work. Anne went to check her cell phone to see if Michael had called, but found no messages. She went to the desk to check her email, but the empty wood grain surface stopped her short. The computer had been stolen along with the manuscript. She touched the crystal hanging between her breasts, grateful the thief had not taken the most important artifacts in the house. The workman stood in the hallway, waiting for her attention. "Yes?"

"I've replaced the locks on the outer doors. Here you are." He handed her two shiny new keys on a circular ring. "You said something about a locked door in the cellar?" He bent down to pick up his tools and a pentagram on a black leather cord fell out from his shirt.

Pagans are everywhere, Anne thought.

She turned off the email program and led him to the kitchen. "Just leave the door open until I switch on the light." She made her way down the steps in the semi-dark and found the string hanging from the ceiling. With a sharp pull, harsh light invaded the corners of the basement. The man climbed down the steps, his heavy boots setting the boards vibrating. "It's just back here." She walked to the low passage, ducking slightly, and walked to the rounded oak door. The man had to hunch over. "See this old door?"

His forehead wrinkled, then he shook his head. "That's quite old, madam."

"Yes, but surely you have the tools to open it."

He stood looking at the door for a while. He glanced surreptitiously at her, then back at the door, and mumbled something about needing different tools. The stairs vibrated with his footsteps. Anne waited by the heavy oak door, tracing the engraved dragon head on the handle with her finger. He seemed to be taking an inordinate amount of time. Finally, she went upstairs and walked to the front door. His truck was no where to be seen. Anne walked through the yard. She looked up and down the street, but the truck was gone. Perhaps he hadn't had the right tools with him. He'd probably gone to get them. She hadn't even paid him, for heaven's sake. He was a trusting sort.

Anne went inside and looked up the phone number. It rang through to his voice mail. She hung up and tried again. This time he answered.

"This is Anne Le Clair. You just left my house. Have you gone for special tools?"

After a pause, he answered in a stiff voice. "I'm afraid I won't be able to help you with that door, madam."

"What's the problem?"

Another pause. "I just can't help you."

Anne frowned. "Could you recommend a specialist perhaps?"

"I'm afraid not."

"Well, uh, what's the problem?"

No answer came.

"We may be selling the house, and I need to pack up everything."

"Selling that house?" He sounded scandalized.

She didn't see what business it was of his. "But I haven't paid you for the new locks."

"I'll send a bill," he said and hung up.

Anne stared at the phone in her hand. *What in the world was his problem?*

MICHAEL SAT ALONE in the Rosicrucian Order's large library in Freiburg, Germany in front of a thin computer monitor. Shelves of books and manuscripts stretched to the far wall, with chairs, sofas and computer desks closer to the enormous stone fireplace. The place brought Robert strongly to mind. They'd shared research in a library like this one in England. Most of the German collection had been scanned into an electronic database. His first search term, "Chintamani Stone," resulted in a blinking message: "*Bitte Wartezeit für Abstand.*"

Franz Maier arrived in the library moments later and glanced around, only slightly ruffled by the unusual event. Michael stood and waved at him. "I didn't mean to disturb you, Frater Maier." He introduced himself and extended his hand.

"A pleasure to meet you." He shook Michael's hand. "Please call me Franz." Thomas spoke about you. And of course, I know your work. No one told me you had arrived."

"Your secretary assured me you were in the middle of something important."

Franz went to Michael's computer, typed in a password, then offered him the chair. "Now you may continue with your search." Seeing Michael's questioning look, he continued, "The computer is programmed to alert me to certain types of inquiries."

"I see."

Franz smiled. "I believe we have a conference scheduled for this afternoon?"

"Yes," Michael said.

"I am in the middle of another matter, but look forward to talking with you then." Franz turned to go, then hesitated. "How is the Le Clair family? You are almost a member now, yes?"

"So I'm told." Michael smiled wryly.

"They've sustained such losses recently."

"Two death, but they're doing all right. You know the Le Clairs." He smiled weakly. "Adversity has toughened them."

Franz nodded, but still hesitated. "There's something else?"

Michael shook his head, but a wave of grief made him tighten his jaw.

Franz sat in a chair near the fire. "Tell me."

"It's nothing that can't wait."

"Please, what is it?"

Michael stood up again and went over to the fireplace that was almost big enough to walk into. He turned his back to the fire, letting the warmth sink into him. Freiburg hadn't lived up to its reputation for being the warmest city in Germany with this wet spring. "The head of my lodge, Robert Rhodes, was killed on the equinox."

"Killed? I heard of his passing. Was it an accident?"

"Murder. The Le Clairs tried to keep that out of the papers. No need to draw unwanted attention."

Franz's face hardened. "Was it the Illuminati?"

Michael nodded. The fire grew uncomfortably hot, so he walked a few steps away.

Franz shook his head. "And you think the Chintamani Stone is somehow a part of this?"

"Maybe. They stole an ancient crystal he was transporting."

Franz stood up. "I'll finish up this other business as quickly as I can. The archives won't tell you where it is, but they will give you a thorough background on the stone. I'll come back as soon as I can."

"Thank you." Michael sat in front of the computer, opened the first document, and started to read. The piece gave him a summary of the Roerich's adventures in the East, most of which he already knew. Then came the various claims about where the stone was currently located. One author maintained that the stone had been donated to the Moscow Museum, another that it was held by the Museum of Natural History in Manhattan. He'd already checked at these places and found the stories to be false. Maybe deliberately circulated to mislead. He clicked on a link about legends and read again how the stone had been a gift from an extraterrestrial civilization to the Atlantean Emperor Tazlavoo. Several abstracts promised an in depth discussion of the exact star system they'd come from. Orion, Sirius and the Pleiades had the most links, but Draconis, Ursa Major and Orphiuchus were among the contenders. Enjoyable reading, but of no consequence to his current problem.

An Asian legend claimed the stone had belonged to a dragon named Makara who lived in a palace in the bottom of the sea. The dragon, of course, must refer to the telluric forces of earth. One version of the myth claimed the creature had been a dolphin lord. Perhaps a reference to Atlantis, but Asian myths usually favored Mu.

Another link led to the Tuaoi Stone, the fabled Fire Stone of Atlantean technology. Michael poked through the references to see why these two stones were linked, but found nothing more specific than the fact that they were both legendary crystals with connections to Atlantis. The Tuaoi Stone seemed to have no contemporary stories connected to it. He reread the Australian aboriginal tales of Lemuria's sunken towers of crystal, marveling at how closely these descriptions matched the European and Latin American ones. Then he found a reference to "the Turoe Stone" in Ireland, a white granite omphalos with spiraling patterns. The report said it had been carved from 150 to 250 BC. The spirals and animals heads were beautiful, but the name seemed to come from the Gaelic, meaning "Stone of the Red Pasture." This might refer to the ritual sacrifice of kings. Or the red dragon. Either way, there was nothing of relevance here, either.

Michael made his way through a summary of Cayce's readings about the Tuaoi Stone, which had tapped into the basic energy of the universe and been used to power that ancient civilization and to uplift consciousness, some thought even to heal. At least until the very end. Several complicated dissertations speculated on the sacred geometry likely involved in the crystal's function. These would demand very close reading and some review of quantum mechanics. He'd come back to them if need be.

Another link led to a claim that the Chintamani Stone was the true Grail in Wolfram von Eschenbach's *Parsifal*. The article linked the Chintamani Stone with the Philosopher's Stone and various meteorites of Moldevite. It then made many complicated connections showing how the Johannites, those who held that John the Baptist had been the true Messiah, traced their spiritual lineage all the way back to Sanat Kumara. The two brothers Sanat and Sananda Kumara were reputed to have arrived in Lemuria from Venus where they revealed the sacred teachings of the temples on their home world. They were now venerated in Sri Lanka and other sites in Asia. Interesting, to be sure, but not immediately applicable.

After two hours, Franz reappeared and Michael closed down all his links with a sense of relief. While these legends would ordinarily keep him reading for weeks at a time teasing out all the various permutations of the original folk tale, then the convoluted interpretations and wild speculations offered by centuries of metaphysicians, nothing here pointed him in a direction that would solve his current problem: to identify Cagliostro's next target and stop him from gaining control of whatever remained of the Atlantean technology lying beneath the waters of the Atlantic or tucked away in hidden chambers in the ancient sacred sites of the world.

"Let's walk," Franz said. "I find it clears my head."

Michael followed him out to the formal gardens. The sun had won out and shown from behind nimbus clouds rapidly moving away into the east. Leopard's bane, wood anemone, primrose—he lost track of the varieties—already crowded out the hyacinths and daffodils. They turned into the herb garden where each square sported varying shades of green. Finally, Franz broke the silence. "Tell me what you know so far."

Michael recounted the details of Robert's murder, what they knew about the theft of the Austrian crystal, and Cagliostro's activities.

"So this Austrian stone was thought to be a sentinel for the Tuaoi Stone?"

"Perhaps," Michael said.

"What makes you so certain Cagliostro is after that other stone?"

Michael smiled at Franz's veiled reference to the Tibetan crystal. They both greeted a gardener pushing a wheelbarrow full of weeds passed them toward what appeared to be a compost pile. "I thought he'd go after the most powerful artifacts."

"And you say your man tracked Cagliostro from Bimini to his country home in England? That he'd taken out his yacht with diving equipment?"

Again, Michael nodded.

"Perhaps he has found it."

Michael's frown. "The Chintamani—oh." He stopped in the middle of the path. "The Tuaoi Stone," they said in unison.

"Could it possibly be?" Michael asked. "I can't believe I've been so dense."

Franz shook his head. "Who could imagine it, really?"

"You did," Michael said. "But this could be disastrous. He could set off more earth quakes."

"Surely not," Franz said.

"What's to stop him? He's got one sentinel, perhaps two."

"Are there others?"

They took off toward the library at a run. They burst in, their breath loud, the door banging. Thankfully, the room was still empty. The fireplace radiated heat. Michael threw off his coat. Franz typed something into the database and waited, his finger tapping on the desk. Michael walked up behind him. One response to Franz's enquiry blinked on the blue screen. He clicked it and they both read the entry:

Crystal, Atlantean. Most likely a sentinel stone. Psychometry done by Frederick von Greter on 4 July 1913. Held by the Chishty family in Chandigarh, capitol of Punjab and Haryana Districts.

They stared at the screen, then Franz turned to Michael. "We must combine our efforts."

Michael grabbed his cell phone and dialed New York. He didn't even check the time. They were probably days behind Cagliostro.

18

Once Govannan reached the metal fence outside the New Knowledge Guild's building, he dove through the weak spot he'd found before, catching his arm on a torn bit of wire that left a line of red on his skin. Not feeling the sting, he followed the trellis along the curve of the hill, some part of his brain registering the green of the grape leaves, the brown of the wood. But he couldn't stop to feel his return to natural surroundings and regain his balance. Could he ever? He had to make it to Rhea, to tell her.

He reached the greenhouses, but instead of ducking inside, he ran outside toward his hover craft, heedless of the impression he made. It wasn't until he clipped a worker, sending tray of seedlings flying, that he came to himself. Apologizing profusely, he stooped to pick up the mess until she shooed him off for breaking more stems. "I've had bad news. An emergency," he mumbled.

"Then perhaps you should attend to this business," the woman suggested, her tone of voice at once compassionate and chiding.

"Yes, thank you," he said and hurried to his craft. He willed his hands to steady, then lifted off and flew as fast as he could to the Crystal Guild Headquarters.

Once aloft, the images flood him again, the terrified eyes of the tapir, the eyes of the monkey that begged for death. Dry heaves shook his body. He forced his mind back to the song of the Crystal Matrix Chamber, the golden laughter of the woman from Sirius when she realized he was in love. But these memories seemed pale and removed—locked behind a glass wall. He flew across the jeweled city beneath him oblivious to its beauty, forcing himself to scan the airspace around him for other crafts and birds.

How could he not have known? How could he not have sensed such a breach in the balance of things? He shook his head against the horror of it.

Finally, he saw the glass dome of his home faithfully reflecting the afternoon sun in streaks of pink and mauve. He pushed everything from his mind and brought the craft down. Once the bubble top rose, he leapt from the seat and ran headlong toward the Guild Headquarters, his steps pounding. The door to the Guild Mistress's office stood open and he dashed inside, ignoring the growing pain in his leg. The startled attendant jumped to his feet, knocking small message tabbies on the floor.

"I must see her," he said, and turned the knob of her inner office door.

"But, she's—"

He walked in.

"Govannan." Rhea's voice scolded him from a world of propriety and good sense, a world he had lost.

The familiar halo of her hair around her head like a dandelion gone to seed reassured him. Not everything had changed. Then he realized another woman stood in the room, younger, a clear beacon of light, pure and untouched by the evil he'd seen, that he carried with him. "Megan," he exclaimed and tried to smile, to show how pleased he was to see her.

"Govannan." Rhea's hand touched his shoulder, steadying him, reading the riot of emotion inside him.

Megan stood there, her brow clear starlight, her blue eyes a haven of peace. But confusion and a touch of fear were already replacing it.

"I'm sorry," he started to say, but Rhea interrupted. "She's passed her lessons with flying colors, and the Lady of Avalon has sent her home for a celebration." Rhea turned to Megan. "It would seem the Master of the Crystal Matrix Chamber—" the words seemed to realign the shattered pieces of his mind and heart "—has some news of import for me."

He nodded. "I apologize—"

"He'll want to hear your news later. And celebrate your return." She walked Megan to the door of her office where her assistant stood, his mouth agape. Megan stared over her shoulder at Govannan, her brow furrowed. "Go and settle into your room, dear. I will tend to him," Rhea whispered, then closed the door on them both.

"What has happened?" She ushered Govannan to a chair and, with a gentle push, made him sit. She reached into her desk drawer and brought out a small glass vial. She squeezed out three drops into a glass of water and handed it to him. He drank it without thought. It steadied him more. "Tell me immediately."

Govannan obeyed her command like a child reporting to his mother. Oh, for that innocence again. The sordid tale poured from his mouth, the words corroding his tongue like acid.

When he finished, Rhea sat staring at him, her nostrils flared like an animal testing the wind for a predator. She poured a glass of water, an action so normal it made Govannan question her sanity, then reached for the small vial of medicine she'd dosed him with, and let three drops of the tincture fall into the water. She drank it herself, then sat for a moment, soothing the silk of her robe with her hands. She pushed a button on the desk and the door flew open. Her anxious attendant stood there, his eyes darting from her face to Govannan's.

"Please call Evenor and Pleione." Her voice wavered slightly. "Tell them to drop whatever they are doing and come here immediately. Cancel all my appointments for the day."

"Yes, ma'am," he murmured.

They sat in silence for a minute longer. "I can't imagine the shock, Govannan."

"But those creatures. We must stop their suffering."

"Of course," she murmured. "We'll set this right."

But Govannan only shook his head. How could anything be set right when the unimaginable had happened?

She asked him simple questions. "Where is this room?"

"In the new building near the Guild of Gaia.

"What hallway?"

He tried to remember. "Section 13, I think."

224

"Did anyone see you?"

He shook his head. "Only on my way in."

"You were dressed like this?"

He looked down and remembered he had put on clothing suitable for gardening. He nodded.

"I doubt they would have recognized you, then."

The door opened and Pleione rushed in carrying her healing bag. She came to him. "Is it your leg?"

He frowned. "Leg?"

She touched his thigh where the wound had been, then pulled back her hand as if from a fire. "Govannan, what has happened?"

Evenor, the Governor of all the guilds, walked into the room. "What is it, Rhea?" Behind him came the Sirian ambassador who stood in the doorway, his elongated head almost touching the lintel. Rhea saw him and took a step back.

"He insisted on coming," Evenor explained.

"If you'll pardon us, Ambassador, I'm afraid we have some internal business to attend to."

"I can be of assistance," he said.

Rhea studied him for a minute, then nodded. "Please have a seat." Once they'd all settled, she looked at Govannan. "Should I tell them?"

He shook his head. How could such words come from her throat? Sitting up, he told them the story in a flat monotone at first. But the revulsion returned, then anger. "We must stop this atrocity at once." He reached his hand out to Evenor, who stood up and strode to Rhea's desk.

He sent a message through the com system, then returned. "I've called for the head of our security forces."

"Thank, God." Govannan leaned his head back against the cushions.

"You do not seem as surprised as we are," Rhea said to the Governor.

He shook his head, his eyes full of storm clouds, his brow promising thunder. He looked at the ambassador, who sat, a pillar of light and calm. He nodded, giving Evenor permission to continue. "I have just come from a briefing from the Sirians. They were warning me about a—" he wiped his forehead with his hand "—decline in consciousness." He looked at Pleione. "They claim the illnesses are a part of this. That this loss of connection is . . ." he closed his eyes for a moment.

"What?" Pleione looked at the ambassador, then back at Evenor.

He continued. "Normal. They say it's a normal part of the cycle."

The Sirian ambassador nodded.

"Normal?" Rhea burst out. "How could it be normal to lose one's connection to the great source?" She appealed to Pleione and Govannan.

But before either could answer, a knock on the door made them all look up expectantly. Xandaros, the leader of the warriors, walked in. "You called, sir?"

"Thank you for coming so quickly," Evenor said.

"It is my duty, sir." With a quick look around the room, the soldier took in the distraught guild leaders and the calm ambassador.

"Govannan has discovered a crime which must be set right immediately." In cold, colorless terms, Evenor explained the situation. The man concealed his reaction except for a growing tension in the hand that gripped his staff. When Evenor finished, Govannan described where the room was.

"I'll take a platoon over immediately."

"Stop the experiments," Evenor ordered. "Put the place under quarantine. Allow no one to come or go."

"Take healers with you. Tell them what to expect," Pleione said. "They may be able to save a few, but they can bring peace in the end." A silver tear ran down her cheek.

"I'm afraid we'll need a few troops for the city," Evenor said. "Who knows what will happen if word gets out."

Pleione walked over to the computer and sent a message. Then she looked up at Xandaros. "My people will be expecting you."

With a clipped nod, the man marched out, Evenor on his heels.

Pleione came over to Govannan and held out a hand to him. "Come with me. I'll take you to someone who will soothe your heart."

"No, I have work to do." He glanced at Rhea.

"You've had a bad shock. We'll need you at your best."

"If I may?" The ambassador stood up, towering over them again.

Pleione frowned at him. "I assure you we can take care of him."

"Of course you can." He smiled at her. "I am merely offering assistance. We would like to help our friends here in such a time." Pleione stepped back, and the ambassador kneeled down in front of Govannan.

The sight of this beatific being kneeling before him made Govannan try to scramble to his feet, but the ambassador put out a hand to stop him. "Please allow me this honor." He moved his hand to Govannan's heart and placed the other on top of his head. Then he tilted back his long head, closed his eyes and let out a sound that would have stopped the planets from rotating around the sun and turn to him as their source of life, a sound that would have made the sun melt into the firmament, that held the knowledge of loss and corruption, but brought the sure knowledge that the One encompassed even this, that there was no place or action that could separate any part of creation from another, that all would be reconciled. Peace flooded Govannan and a sort of acceptance even of what he had seen.

The ambassador opened his eyes and smiled at him. "Good." He stood and addressed himself to Rhea. "I would ask your permission to take the Crystal Matrix Master to our home world so we might explain what is to come, to fortify him. We would also ask for his beloved to accompany him."

"Megan?" Pleione's eyes widened.

"Your beautiful and talented daughter," the ambassador said, "for she has a part to play."

The three Guild Masters looked at each other, the realization showing on their faces that the sound healing of the ambassador had restored them to a state of clarity they hadn't felt in quite some time. "Even we have slipped into this . . ." Rhea groped for a word.

"Dullness?" Pleione offered. "We've accepted the growing army without remembering that conflict on this scale used to be . . ."

"Unheard of?" Govannan finished for her.

"Yes," Rhea turned to the Sirian. "Ambassador, what can we do?"

"Allow me to take these two with me. We shall return them with knowledge and sound codes to aid in the turn of the cycle. Think of it as, what do you call it, a honeymoon." He smiled rakishly at Govannan, a change so swift it made them all burst out laughing.

"If Megan agrees," Rhea said, pausing to get a nod from Pleione, "then we accept."

The ambassador nodded, clearly satisfied.

"Thank you for your assistance, Honorable Elder." Rhea used the old term for the Star Elders.

"It is our pleasure to help our relations." He inclined his long head.

AFTER FINISHING the first six months of her training, Megan was sent home from Avalon to visit her family and friends. Her homework, for the Lady could not resist setting her a task even on vacation, had been to test her new attunement skills with the other Crystal Matrix workers. Neither of them had dreamed that she would be making a jump through the towering crystal, and with such illustrious company. That the Sirians wanted to meet with Govannan she could understand, but why had they invited her, a neophyte compared with all the others in her group?

When the Guild Mistress had called her to a meeting, Rhea only repeated the ambassador's invitation. Megan was too shy to ask her for more information. The Lady of Avalon never answered her questions. She expected Megan to figure it all out on her own. Her mother had come in at the end of the meeting with word from the Prince, her father, that he would be honored if she would undertake this journey for Earth.

So formal, Megan thought.

Afterwards, her mother suggested they eat dinner at the Crystal Guild complex. "We can catch up a bit."

"But I thought we'd go home. I want to see everyone," Megan protested.

"It's best to keep things simple tonight. You can see the rest of the family when you return," Pleione said.

Megan chose one of the restaurants in the main Guild Hall rather than the more intimate setting of the Crystal Matrix living quarters. That place was intimate for everyone but her. She barely knew the other people she was going to be working with. She'd been looking forward to spending a few days getting to know them and their routine, but here she was set to go off on yet another journey. At least this time she'd be traveling with Govannan. She tried to hide her thoughts from her mother, but this hardly seemed necessary.

After they picked a table, Megan answered her mother's questions about Avalon, her training, and who still lived there. Pleione listened to the answers with a distracted air. Once the food came, Megan changed the subject. "Why me? I'm just a beginner."

Her mother blinked, then realized what Megan was talking about. "They've invited Govannan."

"That doesn't answer my question." Megan looked up from her plate to find Pleione smiling. "What?"

"Aren't you his complement in the circle? His polarity?" She raised an eyebrow, trying to look innocent, but failing.

Megan blushed furiously, remembering the first transport she had witnessed, how she'd felt the pull of his baritone voice, how she'd practically swooned at his feet. Now that she had experienced group ritual so many times, she realized her feelings must have been painfully obvious to everyone involved.

Her mother's hand patted hers. "Never be embarrassed by such feelings, dear one. They are a gift."

She looked up at her. "Does everybody know?"

"I'm your mother." Pleione took another bite.

Which doesn't really answer the question, Megan thought. Then she asked aloud, "What happened today? Is Govannan all right?"

Pleione tucked a strand of her hair behind an ear before answering. "We had some disturbing news. Apparently we're in for a—" her eyes closed for a second "—shift, you could say. The Sirians want to help prepare us for it."

"How?"

"By giving you two some instruction—" she smiled, but Megan still felt uneasy "—and new sound codes. It's an honor."

"So, I'm needed because I will eventually compliment Govannan in the circle?"

Pleione nodded and pushed her plate away.

"But when can I talk with him? We'll be constantly surrounded." Even Megan realized she sounded like a child. She gave herself a little shake.

Pleione gave her an appraising look. "You've grown."

"Only a little. All my clothes still fit."

"No." Pleione laughed. "You can handle your energy much better. You're coming into your own."

Megan squared her shoulders. Her mother wouldn't say this if it weren't true.

"Well," Pleione stood up. "I have a good deal of work to do before I can sleep tonight."

Megan grabbed her hand. "Come to the transport."

"I would only distract you."

"Please." She allowed herself to be a child for one more minute.

Pleione ruffled her hair. "Oh, all right."

After her mother left, Megan decided to walk off her restlessness and discovered the alcove that she'd found on her first day at the Crystal Matrix Chamber house. She sat looking up at the stars. A fountain splashed in the dark, keeping her company. The birds that had bathed here that first day now slept in the thick branches of the wisteria or farther away in the orchard. Even though her fellow Atlanteans went about huddled in their woolen cloaks, she was enjoying the warmth. The scuff of a sandal in the dark made her draw into the shadow. A man walked up to the fountain. He leaned down to the water, and the sea shells braided into his hair clinked together.

Megan's breath caught. She sat as quiet as the birds in their nests, taking in his broad back, his muscled arms, his long fingers as he filled his palm with water, then let it drip into the pool again.

He tensed. "Is someone there?"

She sat forward. "It's me."

He turned. "Megan?"

"I'm sorry. I should have told you I was here."

"No, I'm glad to run into you. I had hoped to speak with you before we left."

"My mother tells me I'm traveling with you because I'll sing opposite you in the Matrix Circle one day. That the Sirians want to teach you something for the new times. I'm sorry I'm just a beginner." She forced herself to stop talking.

He took a step toward her. "Is that what you think?"

"Isn't it true?" She blushed, then stood and shook out her skirt. "I'm sorry to bother you, sir. I'm sure you need to gather your thoughts before we leave tomorrow." She turned to go.

"Please stay." His whisper was husky.

His voice reverberated through her body, pulling her back to him. She stopped and turned back, but didn't dare look up at him.

He walked toward her—his vitality radiated across the space and warmed her flesh—and sat on the bench, then patted the seat next to him. She perched on the very opposite edge, far away from him.

"It's just that, well," he paused for a long moment, time enough for her to catch her breath. He chuckled, but it was a sad laugh, ironic. "Let's just say I've had quite a day."

She stirred. "Then you need your sleep."

"No, I need—" he stopped himself from saying something "—I'd appreciate it if you'd stay and talk with me. Your company is soothing."

"Oh," she said. His, on the other hand, disturbed her in deep and delightful ways.

He sighed. "How much did Rhea tell you?"

She schooled her voice to neutrality. The Lady would be proud. "Just what I said. That we'd be leaving tomorrow for Sirius to receive special training. Is there something more?"

He shook his head and the sea shells shifted against each other, making their intimate music. "It would seem Atlantis is falling out of full consciousness. That we are in for a time of—" He didn't finish, but sat silent studying his hands. Lines etched the corners of his eyes.

"My mother said it was a shift." Megan wanted him to talk so she could sit here in the dark and feel the sensations his voice arose in her.

"Yes," he sighed.

Disturbed by his sadness, she said what she thought her father would say. "But the Sirians are one of our father civilizations. Surely they'll teach us what we need to know to restore people to health."

He didn't answer immediately. Megan searched for a way to comfort him

He sighed, "I've always liked this garden."

"Me, too. I found it the first day I was here."

"Really?" He chuckled. "We are a matched set, you and I."

Startled, she asked, "Why do you say that?"

He hesitated.

She cursed herself for blurting things out without thinking.

"For one, we love this little alcove." He seemed to be smiling, but his face was in shadow. Should she say anything? "Surely you've felt it, Megan." The words seemed to have escaped against his will.

"That first day, I heard a song that matched yours, which means I'll work opposite you in the circle." She waited. "Is that what you mean?"

He reached out and touched her hand.

She shivered at his touch.

"Are you cold?"

"No," she whispered, not trusting her voice.

He stroked her arm. "That day . . . it felt like I'd been waiting for you a long time."

She tried to see his expression in the dark. "But you sent me away," she whispered.

He stroked her cheek. "One of the most difficult thing I've ever done. At least before today. But I thought we had time then, time to get to know each other properly." And he bent down and kissed her, a chaste peck on the cheek he'd just stroked.

Megan turned her face to him and their breath mingled.

"We mustn't—" then he brushed her lips with his own, tentatively, asking permission.

She captured his mouth before he could pull away. The kiss lit a spark that blazed up into a bonfire. He took her into his arms and kissed her deeply, then he jumped up. "I'm sorry."

She surged up into his arms, finding his lips again. She had waited too long, watched too many others satisfy their desire under the blessings of the Goddess, thinking of him, trying to remember his face, the curve of his jaw, to feel his strong arms around her, always hearing his voice. Wondering how he felt, if he remembered her, if they could ever be lovers. And now a miracle had happened. Now she knew that he wanted her.

He swelled hard against her, and her own body answered in a flood of desire, but he took her elbows and pulled her back. "Megan?" Her name was a question.

"The first time I heard your voice, that night in the dark. I knew then." At his questioning look, she said, "In the Poseidon Temple, at the party after our Emergence Ceremony. I was there, hiding behind a column. I've been thinking of you ever since."

"Thank the Mother." He looked down at her, his face tore between tenderness and passion. She moved closer. "We must wait, dearest. Tomorrow is your first real transport. Your energy must be clear."

She leaned into him, inhaling his natural deep musk laced with sandalwood oil. "But I will be longing for you all night," she murmured.

"Yes, but it's best this way," he whispered into her ear, then nuzzled her neck. He took a deep breath and broke contact. "I am not in control of myself tonight."

"But—" her stomach lurched. "I thought—"

He took her hand and pulled her into a pool of moonlight. "I've wanted you since I first heard your voice in my mind. Then when I first say you— you were only a child—I sensed you might be the one. I've waited longer than you." He shook his head. "I want to do this right. To watch you learn. To wait until you'd grown into a priestess. To show you all of Eden—my favorite restaurants, gardens—" he gestured to the fountain "—to hear the best concerts, swim with the dolphins. Finally to take you up into the stars."

"We are going to do that," she said.

"This damn mess has me off balance, and I've blurted out what should have slowly come up to the surface." He shook his head again, the clinking shells singing to her.

"We've both waited long enough." She stroked his face.

He laughed and kissed the top of her head. "Trust me, dearest. Tonight I cannot properly modulate my energy. The transport must be right for you."

"How can I sleep?" she asked.

"Ask our Thuya for one of her magic potions. Come, I'll walk you home."

⟳

AFTER WALKING Megan to the villa that served as the home of all the Crystal Matrix pod, Govannan turned away from his own bed and headed over to Evenor's office. He wanted to know how things had gone.

"I have to tell you this. Some of the—" Evenor hesitated "—experiments were moved before the soldiers reached the facility." He rubbed his hand through his hair. "You know what that means."

"That one of us warned them? That I know to be impossible." Govannan's jaw clinched.

"That you were seen, dear friend." Evenor straightened his already tidy desk. "We're searching every nook and cranny of the New Knowledge Guild's buildings."

"Search their members' private compounds as well," Govannan suggested.

Evenor shuttered. "Surely not."

"Anyone who would do what I saw—" he left the sentence unfinished. At least since the ambassador's healing he could think of the atrocities calmly.

"We have arrested the—" Evenor bit back some other word "—Guild Master, along with his staff. We've taken them to the Temple of the Oracle." At Govannan's double take, he explained. "We want the best sensitives to question them. I'm sure they will attempt to dissemble."

Govannan shook his head at Evenor's delicate word. Too bad he hadn't seen what Govannan had. Maybe the others wouldn't be able to truly grasp the situation until they saw for themselves. "What do they say?"

"They deny any wrong doing, of course."

Govannan shook his head. "That could mean they don't think the experiments were immoral." He realized he'd used Evenor's euphemism. "I mean the torture."

"We'll get to the bottom of it."

Govannan stood up. "It's time for me to go. I don't know when I'll return."

"Surely the Sirians won't keep you long."

"They experience time differently than we do, but I'll remind them of our need." Govannan left the Governor sitting behind his ponderous, neat desk. Evenor's stooped shoulders and his hesitancy to send the soldiers into the New Knowledge Guild homes worried him, as did the predicted fall in consciousness. If that had led to the abuse of other creatures in the beginning, who knew what might develop. But try as he might, his mind kept turning back to Megan. They would finally have some time together. His step quickened.

19

The next morning, Megan waited in the large foyer of the Crystal Matrix Chamber fidgeting with the unfamiliar robe of the guild. She kept reaching for her travel bag, then remembering she didn't have one. Thuya had told her the night before that she couldn't take anything inert through the transport.

"Only living beings. Stones and plants can go through since they're conscious. On Sirius you won't need anything. Except the ambassador sent word you should bring the crystal from the Lady of Avalon."

"But—" Megan looked down at herself "—I won't have any hands."

Thuya chuckled. "The ambassador also sent this." She held up what looked like an ordinary gold chain. "He said it will transport. It adjusts to the shape of the body no matter how it coalesces on the other side."

Megan turned the chain over in her hand. "Neat trick."

"Let's get the crystal smith to put a hook on your little tabby."

"But will that transport?"

"Don't tell the ambassador—"Thuya winked at Megan "—but we have the same material in Eden."

Megan had gone to her unfamiliar room and lay in her unfamiliar bed. She crawled under a shawl she'd brought from her room at her mother's house, but that didn't help. Her body was alive with Govannan's kiss, her mind busy imagining more—and her coming journey. After tossing and turning for a couple of hours, she took Govannan's advice and asked Thuya for a sleeping potion. She woke the next morning from a night of deep rest and clear dreams, but none of the grogginess the herbs she knew about would have left. Her new necklace lay on the desk in the outer room. She slipped it on under her robe, then walked to the Crystal Matrix Chamber, deciding not to risk breakfast.

The workers finally began arriving in twos and threes, greeting her cheerfully, introducing themselves. A priestess named Daphyll invited her to come watch the preparations.

"Is it all right?"

"You'll have to learn eventually," she said.

Megan followed her into the chamber, but when she caught sight of the gigantic crystal, she stopped in her tracks. It soared up toward the selenite dome where the six gleaming flanks met in a translucent point.

Daphyll waited for her. "Sort of takes your breath away, doesn't it?"

Megan nodded. "I thought maybe I just imagined it was this big."

"Wait until you work with it. The power is even more amazing. We're the luckiest people in Atlantis." She smiled, her brown eyes dancing in her coppery face. "Come on."

Megan followed Daphyll to the far wall where she flipped a switch. A sharp metallic clang answered her, then the selenite petals of the ceiling began to pull back with a smooth whirring sound. A wisp of wind flowed into the chamber, lifting Megan's hair.

"The crystal operates at a harmonic of the earth's basic frequency. As you've probably noticed flying in, the Chamber itself is at the end point of a long logarithmic spiral. It starts at the Pyramid of the Sun in Teotihuacán. Various temples are built on the vital spots, of course. You'll learn all about them. They're used more when we balance the grids."

Daphyll walked the perimeter of the circle checking the outer ring of comparatively smaller stones, each about six feet tall. "These sentinels vibrate at different frequencies to create a spherical container in all levels of manifestation. It's more complicated, of course." She put her palms on one sentinel, seemed to listen, then nodded.

Megan was reminded of the Lady of Avalon teaching them to clear the stones at Avebury.

Daphyll continued around the circle. "Now, the stargate we create is a circumscribed tetrahedron, but we need a runway for the energy to flow down." She jutted her chin toward the long aisle of the temple. "Once the energy enters here, it flows down to those three points, which amplify the frequency until it enters the heart of the Fire Stone. Then, boom—" she threw her hands up "—the vortex opens." She nodded as if this should all be perfectly clear.

"Confusing our new apprentice?" Govannan's voice brought Megan out of the swirl of words.

"Just explaining a few basics. Don't worry," Daphyll winked. "I'll leave the rest to you."

Oh God, Megan thought, *they all know.*

Govannan waited until Daphyll was out of ear shot. "Fortunately, you don't have to do the math to make the jump."

"But to operate the stargate?" she asked.

"If you take it in increments, it becomes quite clear." Seeing her wrinkled brow, he added, "That's why Daphyll doesn't teach. She can never resist explaining the whole thing at once."

Megan followed Govannan back to a waiting room. He closed the door behind them. "I need to clarify a few things before we go." Megan smiled into his face, but he was all business this morning. "Here's what's going to happen. Once the stargate engages, we connect with its complement on Sirius simply through our intention to travel there. Attune to your particular color within the crystal matrix."

Megan's eyes widened.

"Don't worry." He pushed a strand of her hair away from her face. "It will happen quite naturally. As the vibrations increase, the physical body will dissolve into its etheric component. Your natural affinity will show in the color of your energy."

"But—" Megan held out her hand and looked at it, remembering what she'd said to Thuya.

Govannan took her hand. "It's a blissful experience, like a hard knot dissolving into an effervescent sea. But you won't lose your identify. In fact, your consciousness will expand. There are certain levels of awareness that we can't embody in this form. Just keep your destination in mind and find the color that matches your own."

"But—"

"The very first time can be startling, but I'll be right beside you." His voice deepened, making her shiver. "You don't think I'd let anything happen to you, do you?"

She tried to smile.

"Besides, the Ambassador is a renowned adept. He'll be with us, too. Any questions?"

"You're sure this is safe?" Megan asked.

Govannan threw back his head and laughed, setting his shells tinkling. Then he kissed the top of her head. "Just wait here. I'll come get you when we're ready."

Megan looked back to find her mother standing by the door. On his way out, Govannan greeted her rather formally. Once he left, Pleione held her arms out and Megan ran to her.

"You two must have talked," her mother said.

Megan pulled back and looked at her.

"He kissed you, silly."

"Oh, right. Last night." Megan beamed.

"And this morning," her mother said.

"That was just a peck."

"I see." Pleione chuckled. "How do you feel?" She looked her up and down. "As if I need to ask."

"But now we're going to leave our bodies here and go flying through the universe."

"Not exactly leave them. They sort of tuck into your higher energy." Pleione said. "It's a wonderful experience. Better than sex."

Megan looked at her mother sharply. "And how would I know?"

But before Pleione could come up with a retort, Daphyll appeared in the door. "We're ready for you."

Megan turned to her mother, who said, "I'll watch from here."

Megan followed Daphyll into the Crystal Matrix Chamber, already alive with currents of voices and energy. Daphyll asked her to wait at the first ring of crystals. Before she could even look around, Govannan and the ambassador came in and took their place beside her. Megan's gaze darted over to Govannan's ordinary spot in the circle. Another man stood there. Directly across from him was Rhea. She gave Megan a reassuring smile.

"Ready?" Daphyll asked.

Govannan and the ambassador slipped out of their robes and handed them to her. Megan tried to keep her eyes off his muscled form, but failed. Family life and group ritual had accustomed her to nudity, but why did she have to share this moment?

Daphyll cleared her throat. Megan blushed. Govannan grinned, then reached out and unhooked the top catch of her garment. She shrugged it off, and goose bumps spread up her arms. She told herself it was the cool breeze blowing in from the ocean.

With a nod from Rhea, the pod workers began the chant she'd heard the first time, three short repetitions of vowel sounds, a common beginning to ritual work she now realized. Then they built complex harmonies, and the chamber shifted from an open room to an enclosed ball of energy that grew more palpable as the chant built. The same round woman she'd noticed before lifted her head and sang short dissonant notes, and just as before, half the sentinels lit up. Her male compliment woke the others with his deep bass voice, and the giant Fire Stone whooshed to life. Megan's ears popped as the pressure in the sphere built.

Govannan took her elbow and guided her up to the towering crystal. He placed his hand against the firm sides and waited. The chant intensified again. His hand sank into the body of the crystal. After a minute, he pushed more and walked inside. His muscled form took on a glow.

Megan gulped a breath and followed him. The closest sensation she'd ever experienced was walking through water, but the crystal felt more viscous. She wondered how she was still breathing, but forgot about that when her body began to glow. She held up a transparent arm, then stared, amazed, as her vision widened and the colors of the ambassador's energy field swirled in front of her, purple and violet resolving to a diamond-clear white.

Remembering Govannan's instructions, she looked down at herself again and found she'd turned to silver blue light deepening to sky blue. Above her, an arch of blue stretched up and with a whoosh, she flowed into the corridor. Just that easy. Once inside the column of light, her being expanded. She was free, free of those limitations she hadn't even realized she felt. She could know anything, go anywhere in a thick stream of stellar light, manifest wherever a portal stood. And there were many. She saw them in her mind as points of light.

A stream of deeper blue flecked with gold flowed by her—Govannan. A series of lives flashed before her—Earth, the Pleiades, and Sirius. Always he returned to Sirius. The genetic code she now carried as a seed, her body in this life, resonated more with the Seven Sisters, but she had borne strands of the other worlds in the past—Sirius also, and Vega, Orion, Ursa Major. They left subtler impressions, swirls of possibilities.

Where are we going? she thought to him, and a picture of an even larger receiver crystal than the one in Atlantis came to her. It stood in the middle of a water temple. The best form for this world floated to the surface of her consciousness—a long, sleek grey body highly sensitive to touch, the nose long, the forehead receptive like a satellite dish. With the thought, she felt her energy coalesce inside the giant stone. Then she pushed out of the crystal and landed in the cool, blue water of Sirius and swam around the circular pool in the temple, leaping into the air in her exhilaration. Around her stood tall, crystalline beings, their silicone limbs transparent and stiff, their faces difficult to focus on. She sent out a sonar greeting, then thrilled with sensation as another sleek body brushed against her. He sang a lower note. She turned back to him, entwining with his muscled wet skin, then remembered they were guests.

The ambassador, his elongated head now changed into its native form swam down a tunnel at the end of the pool. A request for them to follow him appeared in Megan's mind. She followed behind Govannan, and they emerged into an open expanse of pure aqua. A group of dolphins waited there. They swam around the ambassador, stroking him with their bodies as they passed. The pod spiraled up to the surface where they conversed with clicks, whistles and sonar.

A plethora of questions swam in the water. Megan could follow it all. *How is Earth? Have you told them about the cycles? Do they understand? Last time we should have intervened.*

A female dolphin scolded the pod. *May I greet him first?*

The ambassador swam with her some distance away, their bodies brushing together. *You were gone too long,* she said. The ambassador's reply was too soft to hear.

After a minute, the two rejoined the others. *Here are the two workers from their Crystal Tower.* He introduced Megan and Govannan, then turned back to the group. *This time we will help them.*

The pod inspected them. One dolphin glided past, sending out a gentle sonar sweep of their bodies. Soon they were surrounded and images crowded Megan's mind: Eden long ago, the canals full of visitors from Sirius; breath taking crystal spires in a city she didn't recognize; swimming through space in a golden stream of energy.

The ambassador intervened. *This was her first jump. She should eat. And I am old and need to rest.*

A sonar burst tickled Megan, which she recognized as laughter.

The ambassador nosed a smaller dolphin. *Take our guests hunting, then tour the crystal city. When the tide has turned twice, we will meet again.* He swam lazily away with his mate.

The smaller dolphin introduced himself as the couple's descendant, a grandson six generations removed. He asked Megan what fish she preferred.

I've never been a dolphin before, she explained.

Delighted, he swam toward his favorite hunting ground. The water turned from turquoise to deep blue, with patches of almost purple. Odd creatures grew from rocks on the bottom, swaying in the current, fanning out delicate sails that filtered microscopic algae and crustaceans. Then she saw them, a huge pod of red-gilled fish, and her body's instincts took over. The three swam in spirals, herding the fish into a thicker cloud. Then they swam through, opening their mouths and gulping them down. After their meal, they drifted in spirals, first down to the dark, sandy bottom, then up again, dozing. They woke some time later, how long she no longer cared, for her life in the ocean was not bound by the sun in the same way it had been on land.

You must see the Crystal People's city. The nap had refreshed their guide's enthusiasm, and they raced through the water, leaping and twirling in the air, then diving back. The deeper blue water lightened to cerulean, then turquoise, and finally back to the almost transparent aqua that told Megan's dolphin brain they were close to land. Their guide followed a channel that tasted of leaves and rich sediment. At last, it opened into a large circular bay with more channels turning off at regular intervals.

They swam up a wide river, then into a smaller channel that circled an island. Above the water, tall, elegant fingers of crystal touched the clouds. The main sun was setting, the second star a distant golden ball in the sky. The rays of the first sun reflected in the crystal buildings as streaks of magenta, orchid and bruised plum, all glowing in the gold of the second. Megan kept spy hopping up, her small eyes just clearing the water, trying to see as much as possible. Tall crystalline beings walked along the shore, their heads leaning together, conversing. Trees with feather leaves blew in the breeze. Beneath them, flowers bloomed in hues whose spectrum could not have been seen on earth.

The taste of the water changed. The current had begun to run back toward the sea, so the three dolphins followed it. The water darkened to navy blue as the sun set, but their sonar guided them unerringly to the dolphin pod. When the tide reached its lowest ebb, families sorted themselves out, forming long spirals of bodies, floating down and gently swimming back up, resting one half of the brain, then the other. Megan swam close to Govannan, who nosed her. *Let's rest together.* And they spent a most curious time together, spiraling up and then back down in the dark, deep waters of the planet Sirius, half awake, half asleep, but always the One Consciousness supporting their minds, connecting them to each other, and all that is, was or would become.

When the tide was at full, the large pod woke and divided up to hunt for breakfast. The young dolphin took them to another of his favorite spots, and this time they feasted on small quicksilver fish that flashed in the water as one, waking more of Megan's dolphin instincts. When the tide had begun to turn again, they made their way back. The pod regrouped for a conference with those they called the humans, even though Megan could barely imagine having legs again.

The Sirian Council met in a round area of sand surrounded by hills. Some broke the surface, forming rocky islands. The rocks reflected the clicks of the dolphins back to them, keeping their meeting somewhat private, but also allowing leaders the Crystal People to take part. They stood on the hills, their tall, thin bodies oddly similar to the architecture of their cities, refracting the rays of the sun, breaking the light into rainbows.

After the greetings and introductions had been dispensed with, the ambassador addressed himself to Govannan. *You have probably remembered why you are on Earth at this time.*

Govannan bobbed his head up and down. *I remember now that I have sheparded Earth through these cycles twice before, but always I forget my mission. I forget what I know.*

This forgetting—it is a natural part of the cycle. Like sleep, the ambassador said. *The torture you discovered, though, is a sign the upcoming cycle may be more violent that others have been.*

Images spontaneously arose in Megan's mind—flying craft raining down white beams of destruction, adepts chanting mantra wars, children huddled alone in shattered buildings. More violent than the fall of Lemuria? she wondered.

Perhaps, the ambassador answered her thought.

But somehow, it didn't matter. Not here in the full flood of the One Consciousness, in the sure knowledge that all was that blissful fullness, that this forgetting the Earth was entering was nothing more than an illusion, that it would pass, then come again, like the tide.

But this loss—it isn't real. Nothing could exist in separation. Not really, Megan said.

Yes, it is true, though difficult to explain to one who has forgotten the Link, an elder dolphin said.

Still, the amplified sound of the crystal leader's voice seemed tinny compared to the dolphin's whistles and clicks, *the suffering is real to those who cannot find their connection. We have prepared a crystal with codes to help enliven the One during this cycle. We offer it to you, Govannan, son of Sirius.*

The woman leaned down and dangled a small crystal tabby remarkably similar to the one Megan carried. It, too, hung on a chain made of the same material that could transform and move through the portals.

I am honored by your gift. Govannan swam up to the chain and stuck his nose through. It automatically adjusted to fit over his head.

You must use them to step down the portals when the shift is complete. This will keep the Earth safe from those who might use the Fire Stones in ignorance.

The dolphins murmured their approval.

When the cycle ends and the tides of the One Consciousness flow back, use them to activate the portals. Then we will know you are ready to receive us again.

So we will be cut off? Megan asked.

If we visit you, we too will lose our memory, the ambassador said. *As you know, a few volunteers will stay through the low tide, taking up body after body, always guiding, always teaching.*

Yes, Megan remembered now. *How could she have forgotten?*

Govannan looked up at the crystal leader. *You say* them, *and yet you have given me one stone.*

Your mate carries another given at the beginning of the current cycle to one of her ancestors, the woman said. *Now, there are six on Earth. We think this will be enough. They are encoded so that the knowledge of when and how to use them will come to the mind of the bearer. Guard them well, son of Sirius*—she looked at Megan *—and daughter of the Pleiades.*

Everyone seemed to realize at once that Megan and Govannan were expected on the home world of the Seven Sisters. The knowledge simply appeared in their minds. The Crystal People sang a song of thanks and the dolphins joined in. Megan and Govannan said their goodbyes to the ambassador.

Megan knew it would be thousands of years before she could come here again, that the ambassador would be long gone, but in the high frequency of Sirius, in fullness of the One, she could not truly feel sad. She only felt love. Her mind floated in contented silence until an event occurred, then the knowledge she needed, the memory that was relevant, surfaced automatically.

She knew she would lose this connection again, yet she found this impossible to believe since the One Consciousness was the foundation of all life, shared by all minds, the very stuff the universe was made from. How could one lose what one was?

But only yesterday—had it been one day or two? She couldn't say—only yesterday, she'd been on Earth and had not be aware of the One. Oh, she'd been taught about it, been given meditation exercise to do, told she would grow into this state of consciousness. Now she knew they were falling. Falling from enlightenment, falling from grace, falling into darkness and violence. But she and Govannan carried a possible remedy. Not a remedy to stop the fall, for the elders all seemed to think it was a natural cycle, but to bolster consciousness, to raise the vibration of the planet, to bring some light into the coming darkness.

She broke from her reverie and sang her thanks to the Sirians. The dolphins bobbed in the water and the Crystal People bowed stiffly. With the goodbyes said, a few of the dolphins broke away from the pod and led them to the Temple for the jump.

THE MAIN WORLD of the Pleiadeans orbited Alcyone, the central star in the cluster. The form for most sentient beings there was humanoid, almost identical to earth humans since the Pleiadeans had contributed maternal genetic material often in the growth of humanity. Govannan stretched out his hand and found dusty red skin. Megan sported the same color and seemed taller. From the temple, they were escorted to Megan's matrilineal home, where she was received with fanfare worthy of an empress. She modeled her behavior on her father, humble, focusing on those around her, but the family was having none of it. She was a descendant of the Grand Matriarch of Alcyone, the leader of all the planets of the Seven Sisters, and her Pleiadean family was going to honor her. To them, it had only been a generation. On earth, it had been ten at least.

Once through the main doors of the compound, Megan and Govannan were greeted by rows of adults and children all carrying bouquets of what looked like roses and lilies, only purple and silver ones nestled amongst the more familiar reds, pinks and whites. After the briefest of introductions, the matron of the house said, quite firmly, "You must rest from your trip," and escorted them to a suite of rooms on the third floor. The windows overlooked fields with long rows of crops and another compound set on the top of a distant hill. "Refresh yourselves. We dine in three hours," she said, and closed the double doors behind her.

Indeed, the sun was heading toward the west. "It feels funny to walk again," Megan said, then looked around the room stuffed with things. "Different from the bare ocean."

"The dolphins live a simple life."

"Now all this." She spread her hands. "A state dinner. Humans are so formal."

Govannan threw back his head and laughed. "Already the jaded traveler."

She turned from the window and went to explore their suite. He followed her at a distance. Off the common sitting room was a water room with a large pool that continually refreshed itself. A dressing nook opened up from it. A variety of clothing filled the wardrobe—colorful robes, roomy pants, long tunics, scarves of a soft, silky fabric. Back across the sitting room, curtains of a soothing blue cocooned the bed. Robes lay across it. She went back to the windows in the sitting room and look out.

Govannan switched on the com unit, looking for messages from Evenor or Rhea.

"Any news?" she asked from the window.

"Nothing," he said. The screen flashed through a series of connections. "But I'm not surprised. The government will want to keep this quiet until they've fully investigated. And the ascended races don't take our troubles so much to heart, as you've noticed by now." He switched the machine off.

"It's true, and now that I've experienced full consciousness, I understand. It's like—" she searched for a word.

"Nothing can ever be a problem?" He smiled up at her.

"Right." She took a step toward him, then danced away again. "But why do they have computers if anything they need to know is in this—" she waved her hands in the air "—cosmic brain already?"

He gestured toward the farm that lay outside. "Why eat when you could live off pure prana?" He stood up and walked toward her. "Why talk when you can hear the thoughts of others? Why make love when you can—" he reached for her.

She stood in the circle of his arms. "Turn to pure energy and melt together?"

He reached down and brushed her lips with his. "I can't remember why, come to think of it. Let's see." He kissed her fully.

"I have no experience in the matter," she whispered.

He bent down and picked her up, cradling her in his arms, and walked to the bedroom.

"But, Govannan," she began.

He laid her on the blue coverlet worked with small flowers. "But. It's always but with you."

"We have dinner in three hours."

He chuckled. "And how long do you imagine this will take?"

Her new dusky red skin flushed a deep rose.

"Besides, this planet's rotation is slower than earth's. You know what that means, don't you?" He unhooked the tunic he'd been given when they arrived, deep purple in honor of his role as consort to the high house. He let it fall open.

Megan's eyes feasted on his broad chest.

"It means three hours is about four and a half earth time," he answered himself.

She reached up and stroked his chest. "If we make love here, will I be a virgin again when we return to our old bodies?" she asked.

A small moan escaped his lips. His body responded with a prodigious erection.

She rubbed her hand over the outside of the silky, flowing pants. He made a guttural sound and she laughed. "Are you this large at home, or is this a gift from the Pleiadean matriarch?"

Govannan fell onto the bed laughing, his member softening a bit. "Megan, you have changed from the blushing young girl who first came to my office."

"I did go to Beltane," she said.

"But did not partake?"

"The Lady forbade it the first time."

"Then I owe her a debt of gratitude." He took her head in his hands and looked into her eyes. "This is not how I imagined our first mating, my love."

"Tell me how you dreamed of it."

His eyes softened. She began to kiss his face, his chin, his cheeks, then kissed each eye closed. He sighed. "I thought to take you through the crystal, stream through the stars."

She kissed each ear, then the hollow of his neck. "We did that."

"Then come home and swim with the dolphins."

"Even better to be dolphins." She stroked his arm, kneading the ropes of muscle.

"Then, I'd take you to my bed and kiss every inch of your body."

"Like this?" She kissed his chest, ran her hand down his belly, over his phallus again, which strained against the fabric to follow her hand.

He pulled her back. "Slowly, my love. Let us go slowly this first time." And he began to take off the clothes they had given her, unfastening the exotic hooks one at a time, planting a kiss on each new area of exposed skin, licking and nibbling until he pulled off her pants and came back up the bed where he kissed her knees and thighs, until Megan opened to him, her Pleiadean body almost identical to a human female's. He licked and kissed and stroked her until she spilled over into the first orgasm, wetting his face with the primal salty liquid of the sea and of sex.

Once she stopped trembling, he turned her over and massaged her back, his touch lightening until she turned back and pushed against him, entwining with him almost too quickly, pushing under him, reaching for him, guiding him to meet her warm, wet, silky center.

"Now," she breathed, and he thrust into her. She gasped, her fingers tightening on his back, then threw her head back, eyes closed. He pulled back, almost coming out of her, then pushed in again, filling her to the hilt. He moved slowly at first, arranging her so he could stroke the larger Pleiadean clitoris at the same time. She groaned in animal abandon and convulsed, her silk muscled cave grabbing and releasing him in the rhythm of climax. But he held on, not wanting to end this.

He waited until she quieted, then began his stroke again. She pushed against him, then he lifted her and turned on his back, letting her ride him as she willed. He watched her straining face, so close to her earthly face, since these people were after all her relatives, her eyes closed, her mouth open, her hair damp with sweat. She began to tremble again, so he closed his own eyes and let himself go, coming with her.

They lay in silent contentment for a long while, then he lifted her pliant body and carried her to the bath, where they entwined yet again, the soft wet sounds their bodies made echoed in the waves their movements created.

Afterwards, Megan's mouth moved into a slow smile. "I think now I know why people make love."

"Just what I was hoping for."

Her eyes widened. "What time is it?"

He got up and looked out the window. "We've got about an earth hour to bathe and get dressed."

About half an hour before dinner, two attendants arrived to help them finish dressing. They laid out dress after tunic and pants after robe, until she could not chose. "Please, you know what is appropriate. They are all so beautiful." The two dressed Megan and Govannan in matching colors, green and blue.

"For Earth," they said. "Is it not right?" Then one swept up Megan's hair in dramatic loops. The other braided Govannan's and hung it with tiny chimes.

"Now I know where you got the fashion." She watched him from the sitting room.

He smiled, indolent from their lovemaking.

"Some Pleiadean lady arranged it that way after an afternoon spent much like this one, no doubt." Megan raised an eyebrow.

"There has never been an afternoon like this one in all history." He leaned over to kiss her, his braids jingling again just as they did at home. But here his skin glowed red.

She hadn't been trained to jealousy. Men lived with their mother's clan, staying with their lovers only when they both wished it. Much like this place. In fact, Megan felt right at home in this extended family compound. After their afternoon, she thought Govannan's previous experience was only to her benefit.

"Please come with us." One of the young women opened the double doors and tilted her head. The second followed behind them as they walked, arm in arm. They passed into the garden again, then into the main hall where the dining room had been set for a feast. Children ran shrieking, mothers yelled at them to behave, helpers fussed with table clothes and vases of breathtaking flowers. Cooks brought in platters of bean cakes, bowls of vegetables, pitchers of juice and wine.

"I see your cousins have made you festive," the matron called to them when they approached the main table.

"Cousins?" Megan turned to them, "but you didn't say."

"We are all family here," one said.

The matron nodded, her wheat gold hair falling in curls down her back. "Tomorrow, we take you to the Grand Matriarch, but tonight I want to hear of my earth family."

And so Megan sat with the matron of the house, who introduced her to the elder women of the family, and she spent the meal answering questions, straining to remember obscure great aunts, to sort which grandmother was the child these women remembered from just the other day, a century or two ago on Atlantis. The cousins had taken Govannan to another table where he lounged, sampling strange fruit, talking with everyone. His native grace had reasserted itself in his Pleiadean body, and she watched the long hands peel the rind of some red globed fruit. She kept glancing over at him to reassure herself their afternoon had not been another of her dreams. The pleasant throb in her center reassured her it had all been real. They had a long Pleiadean night before them, so Megan relaxed and told the family news.

"This season of darkness is a part of Earth," one of the elders reassured her. "The Grand Matriarch will help you. Now, how goes the Lady of Avalon?"

So Megan told them of her time there, what she had learned, how she'd gone into the Tor, what she'd seen there, and of the old Morgen. Well into her tale, she looked up and realized all the children had been taken off to bed, and that the eldest of her listeners snoozed. "I'm sorry. I've talked too long."

"Quite to the contrary. We enjoyed our evening immensely," the matron said, but she stood up and looked around. The same two young women appeared. "Take our guests to their suite. We'll leave mid-morning for court, so please help them prepare."

The two curtsied, then led Megan and Govannan back to their rooms, although they could have found them easily on their own. Once behind their doors again, Megan pushed against him.

"More?" he chuckled deep in his throat.

"Yes, please." She pushed her hands beneath his tunic, finding hard muscle. He swept her up again—she delighted in his strength—and walked into the bedroom. Halfway there, she slid down. "Govannan, you're not limping anymore."

He took a few steps. "It's true. So, it's healed." He looked at her appraisingly. She pulled off the flowing pants they'd given him again and pushed him onto the bed, where they made love until they fell asleep, sated.

THEIR RECEPTION at the high court of the Pleiadean Grand Matriarch was as ornate and baroque as the Sirian ambassador's had been simple and natural. Her two cousins dressed them in such elaborate robes that Megan could hardly bend over. Govannan looked primly official, but unruffled. They'd both been instructed to wear their crystals, which somehow fit in with all the finery.

When they arrived, the two women stayed with them, whispering where to step, what words to repeat, until finally it dawned on Megan that this was a ritual. At one point, Govannan went to the left, she to the right, and they made their way around the room, walking, saying the appropriate words at each stop, walking again. As she approached the throne with Govannan coming from the opposite direction, she realized the room was laid out as a labyrinth, with the white haired, surprisingly petite Matriarch in the very center. She stood ramrod straight before a gold throne encrusted with jewels. She carried a crystal rod that seemed to pulse with each movement of the gathered host. Megan arrived at her feet and looked up into startling violet eyes. A thin diadem graced her head, sparkling with tiny diamonds. The Matriarch held up her wand, topped with a stone that seemed to be pure light.

It came into Megan's mind that she should hold up her crystal. Govannan did exactly as she did, holding up his new gift from the Sirians with her gift from the Morgen. They touched the points together. The chant of those gathered here crescendoed at the exact moment, and the Matriarch chanted in an ancient tongue that sounded like the very language of the stars themselves, then brought her wand down to touch the two crystals. A stream of energy entered the crystals and flowed down into their bodies, so high and pure that Megan blanked out for a few seconds. She came back to herself to find her cousin discreetly supporting her, but Govannan stared into the Grand Matriarch's eyes, his whole countenance etched in light, a beatific look on his face. She would ask him later.

Again, the knowledge that it was time to go came into everyone's mind at once. The Matriarch turned and smiled at her. "I shall come with you." And they walked through the room and down a long hallway, then entered a temple set up much like the one at home. This crystal dwarfed the one on Atlantis. Still elevated from the ceremony, Megan flowed with the ritual, listening to the chant that opened the crystal. But then the Grand Matriarch took her forward alone. "The Morgen requests your immediate presence. We will send you back to her directly." And she barely had time to turn and wave to Govannan before she was in the crystal.

I will see you soon, my love, he said in her mind.

"Bless you, child," the Matriarch intoned.

But I'm a woman now, surely, Megan thought as her dusty red skin turned to silver blue light and she whooshed up the channel toward home.

20

The Chishty family had wanted to make all the arrangements in India for Michael and Franz, much to Arnold's irritation. "I couldn't very well tell them that the Illuminati wants to steal an Atlantean sentinel crystal from them," Michael said.

"I thought that was the purpose of this trip." Arnold made a sharp turn and pulled onto the main road.

"It's not something you just blurt out on the phone," Michael answered.

Arnold had insisted on renting their own car. He'd told Franz this was not negotiable. Michael hoped the family wasn't offended.

Chandigarh was the only city planned by French architect Le Corbusier that had actually been built. The city's edict laid out the ideas behind the plan, with admonitions for future generations to keep industry and traffic away from the parks and residential areas, not to replace landscaping haphazardly, even declaring no personal statues could be erected. The name Chandigarh came from Chandi, the supreme Mother Goddess. Michael was depending on her help. But they were driving out of the city. The Chishty's home turned out to be in the trendy Mohali Hills, a three-thousand-acre township with brand new villas and town homes a few miles north of the city. A guard at the gate checked with the family before letting them in.

Once inside, Franz turned to Michael. "Our order had a relationship with the elder Chishty. He was a well respected Sufi writer with a keen interest in the Vedas and Buddhism. In fact, all the world religions. But his son inherited and moved the family here."

Michael pointed at a golf cart driving across a green. "I'll hazard a guess the son is not interested in Sufi philosophy."

Franz said, "Most likely, but you can never tell."

The female voice of the GPS admonished them to turn right. Every time Arnold missed a turn, the prerecorded voice announced "Recalculating," sounding like an elementary school teacher scolding a rowdy class.

"Maybe he'll want to get rid of his father's collection," Michael suggested.

Franz hesitated. "Our order's funds are—"

"I'm sure Grandmother Elizabeth would cooperate," Michael assured him, hoping he wasn't speaking out of turn. If so, he'd use the money Robert had left him.

The GPS announced that they had arrived, and Arnold pulled into the drive of a house that looked like it belonged in Spain. The door opened and a man walked out, his stiff back and starched white uniform suggesting that he was an employee, which turned out to be the case. He opened the back door for the two men in the back, assuming Arnold was a servant like himself, gave the two a slight bow, then directed Arnold to park next to the garage. "Wait for me here," Arnold mouthed to Michael, but the servant led them inside.

The reigning Chishty received them in a large entertainment room replete with an enormous flat screen TV and attendant silver boxes for DVDs and MP3 players, all elegant and understated. The hardwood floors gleamed, unrelieved by carpets. Basir himself stood with his arms wide, a wide smile on his face. "Illustrious friends of my father, my home belongs to you." He kissed them on both cheeks. His cell phone rang, and he glanced at it, frowned, then turned back to his guests. "Refreshments. What can I offer you? Mineral water, wine, cola, fresh juice? We have the best oranges. Or have you developed a mania for chai like all Westerners?"

Michael introduced Arnold when he arrived, and Basir went through the same ritual. They agreed on mineral water, and Basir sent his man for it, then they settled in a seating area next to a wall of windows that looked out on a newly planted garden.

"You just moved, I take it?" Franz asked. "It must have been quite a job sorting through all the family belongings."

"Oh, my sister's family has stayed in the city. She's sentimental, so I left it all to her. Everything here is new—the latest." He sat in his new house like an old maharaja.

"I knew your father when I was a young student," Franz said. "I enjoyed a long evening discussing the fine points of Sufism with him on several occasions."

Basir nodded politely, clearly uninterested. Franz asked about the circumstances of his father's passing, and Basir told him it had been peaceful. Then, evidently counting on the man's worldly manner, Franz cut to the chase. "We have come about an artifact your father owned. A large crystal, as tall as a man. Are you familiar with it?"

Basir's eyes narrowed speculatively. "May I ask your interest in it?"

Franz glanced at Michael, who sat forward. "My grandmother is fond of such items. We thought we'd see if the family would be interested in parting with it, given the new circumstances."

"And you've come all this way for this?"

"We were in northern India on business. We wanted to pay our respects, naturally."

The man studied him for a moment, his head tilted. "Indulge me with the story of this crystal."

Michael called up his old museum persona. "This particular stone belongs to a set. We're not sure how many there were originally, but I know of three. They are supposed to hail from Atlantis." He smiled indulgently. "My grandmother is fond of such romantic stories. She has come into possession of two of them and would like to collect the entire set, if that would be possible. Would you be interested in selling the stone?"

"Perhaps I should put it to auction," Basir laughed.

Michael tried to stifle his reaction, but Franz stiffened. Basir glanced at him, then back at Michael, who asked, "Don't tell me another collector shares my grandmother's taste."

"This man claims his employer has two others as well." Basir's hard eyes undercut his smile. "Perhaps I should put you two in touch."

Arnold stood up. "We need to go now."

Basir frowned at his rudeness.

"I'm sorry, sir," Arnold said, "but you've put your sister at grave risk."

"What could you possibly mean by—" Basir's cell phone rang again. He looked at it, annoyed by the interruption, but his expression changed to incredulity. He frowned at Arnold. "It's the police." He answered the phone, speaking Hindi. His expression grew more disturbed with each exchange. Then he threw the phone down and ran across the room, shouting for his servant. He gave him orders, then turned to his guests. "My sister is in hospital. I must go at once. You'll have to excuse me."

"What happened?" Franz asked.

"Someone broke into the house. In the middle of the day. She was shot."

"Is there anything we can do?" Franz asked.

Basir turned sharply. "You have brought trouble to my house. Please."

Franz started to reply, but Arnold took his arm and headed toward the door. "This is what we came to prevent. I'm sorry we were too late."

Arnold drove while Michael tried to punch in the Chishty's address in the city into the GPS system. "Are we sure they had such a large crystal in their home?" he asked Franz, who hung on in the back seat.

"The last I knew, the elder Chishty had a temple of sorts in the back of his house. That's where the sentinel was last located, according to our records."

"If I hadn't gone off on a wild goose chase, maybe we could have saved this woman's life," Michael said.

"Basir said she'd been taken to hospital," Franz answered. "She's not dead."

They reached the city quickly and Arnold turned onto the residential streets, cursing at the slow traffic. Suddenly he took a tire-squealing turn down an alleyway.

"Recalculating," came the voice of the GPS.

"Turn that damn thing off," Arnold snapped. "I know where we're going." He drove another block through the alley, then stopped in a spray of gravel. He ran past two houses and stopped at the back of a large home. They followed more slowly. Arnold listened for a minute, then scaled the six foot fence.

Franz blinked. "Where did you get this guy?"

Michael burst out laughing, then clapped a hand over his mouth.

"Doesn't he know the police are here?"

Before Michael could answer, the gate swung open and Arnold stuck his head out. "Come on. What are you waiting for?" The two followed him around a jacaranda bush to the back door. Arnold tried the knob, but it didn't budge. He pulled out a tool and unlocked it.

"Why don't we just go to the front door?" Franz whispered.

"The police will ask too many questions," Arnold breathed to him. "Wait here."

They hid behind a large freezer on the back porch. The minutes crept by until Arnold reappeared. "They're upstairs. Probably checking the jewelry," he whispered, then gestured for them to follow him. He glided down a hallway, frowning at Michael when his shoe squeaked, then pushed a door open by increments. Brilliantly colored tapestries depicting a variety of deities came into view. Low tables were overturned, the floor scattered with small statues, incense burners, Shiva lingams, and other stones. A large black statue of Chandi lay on her side, one of her many arms broken off, the tray of fruit and rice before her trampled. A serene Buddha surveyed the mess.

"Look at this," Michael whispered. Franz joined him at an empty metal base with a raised edge around it. One side had been bent down. "Do you think this was the pedestal for the sentinel crystal?"

"Could be." Franz said. "Looks like they may have gotten it."

Arnold slipped away from the door. "The police are coming down," he said in an undertone. They back tracked through the house, sneaking out the back door just in time. Once they were in the car, Arnold said, "I'll find out what the family reports missing."

A FEW DAYS LATER, Cagliostro stood on the deck of his yacht putting on his diving equipment as if it was his ceremonial robe. He hung Paul Marchant's crystal key around his neck as an afterthought. He doubted it would be important now that he had the three sentinels, but why not bring it?

Yesterday, he'd supervised the team of divers bringing down the three crystals yesterday, forcing them all to move at a snail's pace, careful of every detail of the operation. They'd set up the stones to his exact specifications, which he'd triple checked.

He still had a dull headache from being down so long, but he wasn't willing to wait another day. And this time he was going down alone. No Miriam. No assistants at all, except Mueller up top scanning for intruders. He'd sent Miriam after the Roerich fragment. A wild goose chase, that. He didn't need it: it was just something to keep the Le Clairs confused. With a nod to Mueller, he secured his extra tanks, then lowered himself over the side of the boat. He followed the line from yesterday down to the bottom where his underwater temple awaited him.

He'd had the sentinels set in a triangle around the large Fire Stone which still lay on its side in the sand. The expert from Black Ops had said it would take a crane to lift it, that it could be done, but he decided against it. It wasn't the expense. He couldn't risk damaging the stone. Based on his last attempt, the crystal was working, although not perfectly. Maybe the distortion from the angle had kicked him out. He couldn't be sure there had actually been another being present. The whole experience had been a blur. The three sentinels should help stabilize the field.

Moving carefully and methodically, he positioned his body at the mid point of the triangle, about halfway up the body of Tuaoi Stone. Still tethered to the line, he closed his eyes and began. First he reinforced the directions and sealed his circle. At home in his laboratory, he'd been able to activate the sentinels by thought alone. He hoped the new environment would not change this. He began an inner chant. Sensing a shift after just a few minutes, he opened his eyes. All three crystals glowed with light.

He turned his focus to the larger crystal, switching on the prerecorded chant he'd made, hoping the water would not distort the sound. He reinforced the chant in his mind. Nothing happened for a while. Just when he wondered if he'd miscalculated, if he needed a second person, the atmosphere deepened, like the pressure of an approaching storm. Then the large crystal came to life, light streaking up through the stone, illuminating the cracks, sending out rainbow bursts. Cagliostro sank down to the flank of the stone. He pictured the chamber he'd glimpsed last time clearly in his mind. Then he reached out and touched the crystal.

Nothing. Schooling himself to patience yet again, he kept up the chant. After another minute, the stone warmed under his hand. Then it softened like a lover loosening beneath his attentions. His fingers sank beneath the surface. He started. Could it be? Could this be the way the transports had been accomplished? He couldn't remember what had happened last time. Maybe they'd wiped his memory. Steeling himself, he pushed against the flank of the crystal. It gave way. He was inside.

Cagliostro fought to control his excitement. What next? His destination. Again, he built the image of the chamber in his mind, and in answer, the crystal sent a surge of energy through him. His body became transparent. He forced down a wave of fear. Then, everything dissolved in light. When he could see again, the room he sought shimmered outside the wall of the crystal. The floor came into focus first, blue tile with gold symbols embossed in it. Around the wall stood crystals, twelve tall sentinels, all lit up.

Cagliostro moved toward the surface of the Fire Stone, pushing his now naked body forward through the congealing crystal as if walking through a strong current. He emerged, new born, falling to the tiles, gulping air. When he caught his breath, he stood on still shaky legs and looked around. The Tuaoi Stone towered above him, the clear base reflecting the dying light in small bursts. The flanks soared above his head, tapering to a translucent point. Above the tip, paper thin crystal panels in the shape of a flower the sun shone through. He'd made it at last. He was in Atlantis.

Names and explanations for the symbols on the floor began to come to him. Of course, the Platonic solids. Then the equations for balancing the energy of the crystal appeared in his mind. It was all so clear, simple really. How could he have forgotten? He moved toward the door of the temple. Beyond them, the city—his city—waited for him. Then he stopped, realizing he needed clothes. More doors led off the main chamber. He tried the first. It led to an observation lounge. Then a hallway with small rooms furnished with cots, then a central bath. The next door opened on a dressing room.

Robes hung of a series of pegs, various sizes and shapes. He chose green. It reminded him of something—he couldn't stop to remember what. Then he made his way back across the blue tile, past the row of sentinels to the door. He pushed it open.

The sun blinded him at first. Tropical sun, somehow different, whispering to him. He shook his head against it and kept walking across the flagstones. Soon the path forked, one leading up the hill to a pleasant villa tucked amongst the trees—he yearned for shade, for plants, for water—the other heading toward a larger building of yellow limestone blocks. This would lead to the city.

He walked through a series of gardens, nooks of brilliant flowers, a small tree filled with flowers—it must be spring here too—past a splashing fountain. A smaller building lay ahead. What looked like a car sat outside waiting. Two people got in and it lifted off. Cagliostro stopped in his tracks to watch the silver craft fly through the sky. Someone spotted him and waved him forward. The man asked him something—the language, he didn't speak the language—then gestured to a worker inside the building. Another silver craft pulled forward and the man opened the back door. Cagliostro stepped inside and sat down. The driver turned and said something. He nodded in reply, and—miracle of miracles—the craft lifted off.

Like a small boy, he pressed his face to the window and watched the beautiful temple complex grow smaller. The blue expanse of the ocean opened up beneath them, then the craft turned and the emerald green of the plain stretched away, turning to sage, then the blue and purple of mountains and a round cone of a volcano. The craft tilted once more and before him lay the city, the three circular canals that Plato told of gleaming blue, the buildings golden in the mid-morning sunlight, a riot of colorful gardens crisscrossed with small streets. Then the vehicle flew past it, toward the hills.

"No," Cagliostro said, his hand flying up to the window, "no."

The driver frowned, then hit a switch. "Have you forgotten your translation crystal, sir?"

Cagliostro stared. He hadn't thought of this, a foreign language spoken in his own home. "Yes, I'm sorry."

"No problem. It's understandable with all the excitement."

"Uh, yes."

"You don't want to go to your guild, sir?"

"My guild?"

The driver's eyes darted to his robe.

"No. The city."

"Of course." The craft banked at an alarming angle. "Anywhere in particular?"

"Uh, the market." Yes, that would put him in a crowd. He needed to look around, get the lay of the place, before searching for the artifacts the Shadow Government had always coveted. The man still frowned, so he said. "The main one." This seemed to satisfy him.

The craft set down minutes later at another garage-like building just off a series of crowded streets. Cagliostro got out, briefly wondering if payment was expected.

"Here, sir." The man handed him a small tabby connected to an even smaller silver box. At Cagliostro's frown. "A translation device."

"But—"

"Don't worry. The Crystal Guild keeps plenty on hand." He nodded. "Enjoy your stay in Eden."

Eden. Yes, it was paradise, wasn't it?

"Thank you," he said, nodding in turn. The man got back into the craft and Cagliostro walked to the street. *She must be here somewhere.*

The stalls and shops of the city of Eden enthralled him. He smelled essential oils from Egypt, sampled exotic spices and foods from the Americas, tried a horn from the mountains of the east. When the sun had passed its zenith and begun its journey toward the western mountains, he found a restaurant serving the most ingenious stew he'd ever tasted, made of some root vegetables, beans and spices. He drank a fruit drink of citrus and mangos—at least he thought that's what was in it. They expected no payment, just like the cab driver.

Satisfied, he strolled the streets, looking for a vantage point. The dome of the crystal temple had been beautiful, but nothing compared with his memories. First he'd find the area of the city he remembered. Then . . . but the desire to do the bidding of the Shadow Government was fading. They didn't know he'd succeeded in reaching Atlantis. He went in search of those airy domes, those spires of captured fire. He would find her there, then decide what to do next. He walked toward a large garden he'd seen from the air.

Everywhere the talk was of the trial. Shopkeepers and customers speculated on the crimes that had been committed. "I heard they were restructuring our genetic code."

"No, no, they've killed other creatures—changed them somehow."

Outside a crockery shop, someone said, "Have you heard about the attacks from the mountains?"

"Attacks? What are you talking about? Atlantis has been at peace—well, always."

"Right, that's why we have an army," a young man sneered.

"I heard the animals are retaliating," the girl on his arm added.

Cagliostro listened to the talk with growing alarm. Had he come at the wrong time? This did not match his memories of peaceful days spent dallying with his friends, drinking sweet mead, sailing the barge on the water, and always her—her smiling face, her laugh, her flame-red hair. Where was she? He hurried into the park and walked through the sheltering trees, searching. Then he came to the edge of the hill and a vista opened up before him—of houses built of golden stones nestled among trees, of streets that meandered up the small hills, then the city farther north. Yes, there were domes of glass and even one spire stretching to touch the ever-blue sky, but this was not it. This was not the city he remembered.

Agitated, he made his way back to the street and walked. He must get back. He must get back to the crystal. He must go home. Maybe he'd come to the wrong city. Perhaps the place he remembered was south of here. He didn't know. All he knew was he had to return. He had to find her. He'd go back to the portal. He'd hold the image in his mind. The Tuaoi Stone would return him. Finally realizing he was lost, he went to the nearest shop and asked for directions. The man frowned at his tone, but Cagliostro didn't care. He was close. Just around the corner. At the garage, he asked for a ride back to the Crystal Guild, yes, that's what it was called, and he rode in silence, hands clinched, eager to return, to go back and sink into the Fire Stone, to go home again.

The craft set him down outside the Crystal Guild complex and he made his way back up the hill to the temple. The sun was setting. He hurried in, relieved to find the place empty, closed the door and began the ritual of switching on the great Fire Stone. The chant, the sequence of tones, it all came to him. It was so much easier to think here, to remember. But it wasn't the right place. He'd come to his real self once he found home. Soon the towering crystal sang to life. He dropped his green robe, sang more, but there was an edge to his voice, an unfamiliar urgency in his soul, and the hum of the crystal was rough. It didn't matter. Nothing mattered but to open it up. He sang again, and the crystal answered him, softening under his touch. He forced his way inside, groaning against the pain, then he showed the stone where he wanted to go, the airy domes and towering spires of his home. The crystal waited, emitting a high pitched whine, vibrating alarmingly.

What is wrong with you? Don't you remember? Here—he pictured the city—*take me here.*

But something was wrong. He looked out and saw people running into the temple, a muscular man in the lead. They were shouting.

Take me home, he demanded, and the crystal swooshed to life, eradiating him with light, dissolving his body. In the blink of an eye, the scene shifted. He was back, back at the bottom of the ocean, back to the impotent triangle he'd set up of three, only three, sentinels.

No, he screamed, and something deep inside the earth rumbled, matching his rage. The world tilted. He tried to take a breath, but choked. It was water. He kicked toward the shimmering surface as fast as he could, his lungs burning, his head exploding. His head cleared the surface and he gulped air. An arm reached out from nowhere and pulled him onto a flat surface, began to push on his chest. Then he lost consciousness.

21

Govannan ran flat out toward the central crystal, but the form had already begun to fade and he bounced off the hardening surface of the stone. What in the name of the One was happening? How could only one being manage the energy of the Fire Stone? Then the floor tipped out from under him and he knew the answer. No one could, not safely. He landed hard, tried to scramble up, but another quake sent him sprawling. His head ached and his stomach threatened to turn itself inside out. This crazy person had unjointed the earth's balance, the delicate harmony of the dimensions. Would they be able to repair it in time? More members of the pod arrived, racing to their stations.

Ianara ran to him. "Are you hurt?"

"No, I don't think so," but his leg buckled with his first step. He grabbed her shoulder. "Just help me to my place." Already the chant was building around him, soothing but strong, like the voice of a mother separating squabbling children. With her help, he limped to his place, then looked around the circle to see who was missing.

"Herasto," he and Ianara said in unison. She moved off to find him.

"And Rhea, call Rhea since we don't have Megan," he shouted to her retreating back. Another tremor shook the ground. The Fire Stone groaned alarmingly. He looked around at the frightened faces of his pod. "If one person can do this much damage, nine of us can fix it," he shouted above the creaking of the stone.

A few nodded, and they began again, singing the notes that always opened their circle, then moved into the calming chant again, the one used to lull the eddies of energy to sleep after a transport. It seemed paltry against the enormous currents rushing through the crystal, like spikes of fever in a shivering patient. Herasto came running in followed by Ianara. They took their places, and the psychic connection they usually shared during a transport finally took hold. As leader of the pod, Govannan directed their awareness deep into the Fire Stone. A sharp pain stabbed through his head. Daphyll threw up, then clutching her stomach, began to chant again. Rhea rushed in, took a look around, and went to Megan's place. Finally the circle was complete.

They worked for hours, it seemed, knitting the boundaries of the worlds back together. They ran their awareness through each temple on the huge spiral, restoring their frequencies, shunting off the excesses of energy, enlivening places that were fading because no energy flowed at all. They sang to the great Tuaoi Stone, wrestling with the huge surges of energy, the sudden bursts of almost emotion. The images didn't make sense. The bottom of the ocean. A being with white-blond hair. Such anger. Such loneliness. Could anyone feel such things?

Once peace had been restored to the towering crystal and their spiral, they switched to Gaia herself, feeling deep into the solid plates that made up her shell over the red heat of her heart. The enormity of power dwarfed them. Their efforts seemed futile. Govannan opened his eyes and the outer world swam into view. The observation room was packed with people, most in silent meditation, channeling their strength to the workers. Oria, the head of the Gaia Guild, stood on the outskirts of the circle with a group of her people, their green robes somehow comforting among all the white violet. She waited for the Crystal Matrix workers to all open their eyes, then she held up her palms.

"Please don't move," she said, then she looked at Govannan. "The earth's mantle has been wounded. May we join you?"

Govannan glanced at Rhea, who nodded. The Gaia priests and priestesses took up places at even intervals between the Crystal Matrix workers. Once all were arranged, Oria guided them in meditation deep into the earth. This was different from their usual quicksilver work with the crystals. The steadiness, the careful plodding, of the Gaia Guild that had maddened Govannan in the past he now appreciated. It was the consciousness of granite and basalt, the pace of the earth itself, the patience of water winding through rock to create, eventually, a canyon. He slowed to that vibration, barely breathing, and followed Oria into the mantle beneath his feet. Then he saw it in their collective mind, the crack, a long line showing red, just like a cut on skin. But this was not blood welling up. It was fire, a fire that would consume them all. The volcanoes of Atlantis, their source of power, of heat, the temples of attunement—they would welcome this fire. They might open too far, consuming all life.

The two groups worked well into the night, slowly mending, cajoling, chanting until their voices grew rough and their throats threatened to close. Someone brought them water. Govannan drank greedily. Water, wet and cool, to quench the fires, to quiet the eruptions. Slowly, the earth settled. The aftershocks came to a halt. The cracks, still showing red, congealed. A hush fell over everything. Then the healers came on silent feet, leading them off to cots, some to the Healing Temple, others to their rooms in the villa. They were bathed, fed soup, put to bed. Govannan fought to stay awake.

"But we aren't finished." He moved his head back and forth on the pillow. "There's still a crack."

"Shh," a voice said, "hush now. We are safe for now. Sleep."

And he did.

GOVANNAN WOKE WITH A START, but when he tried to get up, he found every limb ached. He lifted his head, but put it down again when the room started spinning. Someone came to him—ancient Thuya, of all people. "Pleione sent over this remedy." She squeezed some drops in a glass of water, wrinkling her nose. "It smells vile. Now in Khem, we make our medicines tasty." She held the glass for him.

He lowered his mouth to the rim, then made a face.

"Drink up," came the order.

He gulped it down, then laughed, remembering how she'd been here when he'd first come, a young boy, fresh from the Emergence Ceremony, home sick already. She'd made him a dish from his home city, humming while she watched him eat. His head cleared from the medicine. "What time is it?"

"Late. The sun has almost set." He made a move to get up, but she pushed him back, and indeed, he was weak as a newborn. "Pleione says all of you must stay in bed until morning."

"But—"

"But nothing. The earth is quiet now. The Crystal Matrix Chamber is closed. You need your strength for the trial."

He got an elbow under himself and tried to push up. "I forgot about that. But we need to find out what happened."

She pushed him back down, gentle but insistent. "You need to get well. Everyone is resting. It will keep until morning."

Pleione must have slipped something into her concoction, because try as he might, he couldn't keep his eyes open. He drifted back to sleep.

The next morning he felt himself again, except the limp had returned. He arrived in the villa dining hall to a flurry of speculation.

"It couldn't have been a human," Herasto said. "No human has enough power."

"What are you saying then?" Daphyll frowned at him over her cup. "That one of the Star Elders did it? That's impossible."

"But it had to be one of the Elder Races," he insisted. "They're the only ones with that kind of power."

"He could have been helped by a group at another portal," another pod member pointed out.

Govannan sat with Ianara, and they surveyed the room. It was their responsibility to keep balance here. "I'm afraid the predication of the Star Elders is coming to pass," he said.

She nodded. "That's the only explanation. Evenor asked the Sirians to come help us straighten out the damage, but they said the portal is no longer safe."

Govannan looked at her sharply. "We're on our own, then?"

She started to speak, then stopped.

"Go ahead," Govannan said.

"That stone they gave you."

"Yes?"

"Why didn't you use it?

"What?" Govannan pushed his bowl away. "I didn't even think of it. Besides, you know as well as I do that I haven't had time to study it yet."

She put her hand over his. "Perhaps the time for such caution has passed. Try it, Govannan."

He shook his head. "The earth is stable now. And the Fire Stone?"

"For now," she said.

"Then there's still time to study it under controlled conditions."

She mumbled something about donkeys and stood up to go. Then she turned back. "I'm just worried."

"We're all frightened, Ianara, but that's no reason to take extra risks. We'll get through this together." He tried to sound confident.

She shrugged. "I've got to go check on things."

"I'm going to the trial."

"Yes, I suppose they'll need to hear from you."

After a small breakfast, Govannan walked to Rhea's office. He stopped for a moment in his favorite alcove, listening to the patter of the fountain, watching the sparrows jump into the water and splash about. But he didn't have time to linger, not now.

Rhea looked tired. "Didn't you rest?" he asked, after her assistant closed the door.

"You mean did I drink Pleione's medicine?" She snorted. "I didn't have time to sleep that long."

He watched her for a moment. "Maybe you should have."

She ran her hand through her hair, which sprang right back into its halo. "The city is going crazy. You heard about the rumors that animals are attacking, right?"

"What?"

"Apparently some citizens think large animals in the mountains are harassing the city at night, taking revenge for what has been done to them."

"Revenge? Animals?" He stared at her. "But how do people know about the experim—" he shook his head against this new euphemism "—torture?"

"Secrets always get out, Govannan, no matter what you do. But now, it's not that the information just comes to people, like it used to. It's all distortions, exaggerations." She put her head in her hands. "They want us to mount an attack of our own."

"Who?"

"Citizens. The guilds are flooded with demands. They want us to create a barrier to guard the city at night."

"How?"

"With the Tuaoi Stone."

"What? But that's . . . that would . . . that's an abomination." He stared at her.

"Yes, and that's not all. Another rumor has it that the Star Elders were behind the attack on the Crystal Matrix Chamber."

"Attack? But it was a misuse of the crystal. It wasn't malicious."

"Are you sure of that?"

He sat forward. "I'm certain the Star Elders would do nothing to harm us."

She frowned.

"For the sake of the One, Rhea, the Sirians and Pleiadeans are ascended races. Their enlightenment is certain. They could never do such a thing—never would."

"Perhaps these stories they're circulating about a fall—" she studied him for a moment "—how can you be sure they're not a cover?"

"Rhea." He blinked as if she'd thrown cold water in his face. "What's come over you?"

"I don't know. It's just—it's all happening so fast."

"You should have taken Pleione's medicine." He stood up. "I'm calling her right now. We can't have your judgment affected."

She looked at him from sad eyes. "But don't you see, Govannan? It's inevitable. Sooner or later, we will be affected. The leaders. Our wisest." She waved her hand in the direction of the Poseidon Temple where the High House was located. "Sooner or later, we too will lose our way."

He straightened to his full height. "But not today."

His voice reached her and her face cleared. After a moment, she smiled. "Thank you, old friend."

"Of course."

She smoothed her robe. "I guess we are due at the trial."

He nodded. "I wanted to go over with you."

They threaded their way through a large crowd outside the Governor's Guild. One man barred their access, accusing them of trying to hide things.

"Come hear for yourself," Govannan said.

"They're not letting us in," he said.

"What?"

"They say the room is full," a woman answered.

Rhea took Govannan's arm and whispered, "We're late. Let Evenor deal with them." They pushed past the protestor and made their way through the crowded hallway into the large public hall usually reserved for celebrations and award ceremonies. The room had been transformed for this unprecedented event. Three tiers of seats had been formed into a semi-circle, which were filling with the heads of the guilds. Surid sat on the floor facing them. Two guards stood on either side of him. He sat placidly, hands folded, looking as if he were here to accept congratulations. The tiers above him buzzed with people from the general public.

Govannan was surprised to see Diaprepes, Megan's father. He'd thought Evenor would preside, but perhaps the High Prince would conduct the proceedings. Then he glanced up to the next row and saw that Diaprepes' mother, Merope, the Grand Matriarch of all Atlantis, had come, her purple robes lapping around her feet, which were clad in golden sandals. She tilted her head to Evenor, who was whispering in her ear. Govannan and Rhea slipped into the seats reserved for the Crystal Guild. The other guild heads, resplendent in their colorful robes, watched. Their calm faces belied the taut atmosphere, like an overfilled balloon just about to burst.

Evenor finished his conversation with Grand Matriarch Merope and took his seat beside Diaprepes. The Prince cleared his throat and all conversation instantly ceased. He looked up to the top tier at Merope, who nodded to him. He looked around at the guild heads, then the public and said, "We are all gathered together for a most unusual event."

Murmurs of agreement came for around the room.

"Just a few days ago, the Master of the Crystal Matrix Chamber, our good friend Govannan—" the Prince inclined his head in his direction "—made a most grisly discovery."

Surid opened his mouth to object, but must have thought better of it.

"He found that our friends in the New Knowledge Guild had been conducting unauthorized experiments on our fellow creatures. I myself have seen some of the results—" he paused, seeming to gather himself, then continued "—and I must say I was shocked that any member of Atlantis would treat any living being in such a manner." His eyes flashed and Surid paled. The crowd stirred, but the Prince forestalled them. He turned to Govannan. "Would the Master of the Crystal Matrix Chamber—"

Govannan shifted uncomfortably. After yesterday's events, he wished Diaprepes wouldn't draw attention to his work.

"—please tell us what he found when he visited the facilities of the New Knowledge Guild?" Diaprepes took his seat again and sat with a slight frown on his face. The Matriarch's face remained serene.

Govannan stood up, leaning most of his weight on his right leg. He narrated the story of his discovery, of the tapir with tubes in his belly, the monkey with the metal cap and wires stuck in her brain. As he talked, the room became more and more agitated. "But then I found the most horrible torture of all." The room quieted once more. He pointed at Surid, whose jaw was clinched. "They cut a mountain lion in half and tried to sew on the hindquarters of a wolf."

The room erupted. "What?" "Who in their right minds—" People turned to each other, shaking their heads. "How horrible." "The poor creatures."

Diaprepes stood and held his arms up for silence. The room slowly returned to order. "Thank you for your information, Govannan." He then turned to Xandaros. "I believe the Governor sent you to investigate this report, Captain?"

The warrior stood, his muscled physique dwarfing even Govannan. "Yes, sir. I took a group of my people to the location." He waited.

"And what did you find there?" Diaprepes prompted. "Please tell us the whole story."

"We found several of their guild workers cleaning out the cages Govannan had told us about. There were a few animals there, but we did not find the ones the Matrix Master told us about. Only a few who seemed to be awaiting some kind of—" he glanced over at Govannan "—torture. But the smell and the mess confirmed that the cages had been occupied. We found very odd equipment—tubing, an assortment of knives and saws."

A few people broke down. One sobbed loudly, and she was ushered outside.

"The workers seemed agitated and refused to answer our questions." Xandaros stopped and looked at the Prince.

"Did you search any further?" Diaprepes asked.

"Yes, sir. We went through the whole facility, but we didn't find what had been reported." He hesitated.

"Is there more?"

"Some suggested we search the homes of the New Knowledge Guild members, but this was not allowed." He glanced quickly at Evenor, then away.

"Thank you, Captain Xandaros." The Prince looked over at Surid. "What do you have to say?" Diaprepes did not use his title.

Surid shook his head and stood up. He smiled, but his attempt at normalcy was undercut by his flushed face and odd laugh. Several people recoiled from him. "I have a question of my own, my Prince."

Diaprepes looked at him with distaste. "Then ask your question."

Surid turned on Govannan. "You accuse my guild of improper conduct, but then you yourself go off with foreigners."

Govannan's head jerked back. He had never heard the Star Elders referred to in such a derogatory fashion. The word 'foreigner' had never meant something negative before.

"And on the heels of your return, these same extra terrestrials—"

What did he mean by such an odd phrase, Govannan wondered.

"—attack our city through your portal." Surid shook his finger at Govannan.

The room erupted in shouts, and the Prince called for order. "We are not here to discuss the incident with the Tuaoi Stone."

"And why not?" another member of the New Knowledge Guild shouted from behind Surid. "They have put us more at risk than our experiments—"

Surid cut her off with words that made her shake her head angrily. No one else heard the exchange over the general din in the room. Surid turned back to face Diaprepes. "We have only been trying to cure these illnesses that the Healer's Guild—" he said the words with such contempt that Pleione flinched "—is incapable of dealing with."

"We already know the nature of these illnesses." Grand Matriarch Merope's calm voice cut through the mayhem. The room lulled to quiet. "Our friends from Sirius explained it to us on their last visit." She looked at Surid with the compassionate concern of a mother baffled by the bad behavior of one of her children. "Can you please explain to me, Guild Master, how cutting an animal in two could teach you something about these illnesses?"

Surid visibly pulled himself together before answering, "It is difficult to explain, madam. You would have needed to follow our theories." At her withering look, he stumbled on. "We were trying to understand the basic nature of the species. What exactly makes our structures incompatible? After all, we are made up of the same building blocks." He was warming to his subject.

"So you admit to this abomination?" Her quiet voice filled the chamber, reaching into the hearts of everyone there. Surid reached for his theories again, but they failed him. He could no longer meet her gaze. She turned to Govannan. "Master of the Chamber."

"Yes, madam?"

"Do you know what occurred in your temple yesterday?"

"We do not have the full story yet."

"Is the earth's mantle stable, Guild Mistress Oria?"

"For the present." Her voice shook.

"Then we will hear your reports as soon as possible."

They both agreed.

She turned back to Surid. "Sir, I hereby order your guild to cease all activities."

"But what about the animal attacks?" someone shouted from the balcony. "Aren't you going to protect us from them?"

"And those creatures from space who're trying to tear the earth apart?" another voice yelled.

Then the balconies exploded. People shouted, demanding protection. Others wanted more experiments. "The Healers want to keep us sick," came another voice.

Pleione, who had been chanting to calm people, fell back into her seat as if she'd been punched in the stomach. Such a thought had never been had before in Atlantis. That a healer could deliberately harm. That hurt and torture would lead to knowledge. That the Elder Races would attack their own children. The guild leaders boiled in chaos. Some wept openly. Others argued with their neighbors. Diaprepes shouted for the warriors to arrest whoever had accused the Healer's Guild. Merope sat in her royal robes and shook her head.

"Come with me." Rhea spoke into Govannan's ear, her warm breath somehow waking him from his stupor of amazement. "We need to figure out what happened yesterday. Clear answers will calm people. There's nothing we can do here."

They made their way out of the chaotic chamber, somehow escaped the shouting crowds outside, and ran to their guild, Govannan moving as fast as his limp allowed. Once they ran into the main building, she sent for the senior members who were still present. It took only moments for them to assemble in her office.

"We're shutting down the buildings to the general public. Lock the doors," she ordered. "Set a guard on the Crystal Matrix Chamber."

The Crystal Guild members stared at her in disbelief.

"Now," she shouted, "before any more damage is done."

They scrambled to obey her.

22

Cagliostro only allowed himself a day to heal. The doctor had told him that he was lucky he hadn't drowned and given him antibiotics to stop any infection in his lungs. He'd also said that if he dove within forty-eight hours, he'd be risking his life. But Cagliostro didn't have time for corporeal weakness now, not when he had the tool he needed to get back home. He no longer searched for artifacts or power. He was certain the crystal would take him to his city. He'd somehow gone to the wrong place. The first time the Fire Stone had been used in five thousand years, it had naturally taken him back to its own point of origin. His second attempt had been stopped by that man running into the temple shouting. It had distracted him. If he'd had time, he could have visualized his destination clearly and the portal would have taken him there. He was certain of it.

A sharp wind gave the sea some chop today, and the boat bounced with each swell, but he stood in the prow watching the GPS carefully. He knew he was being watched and wondered if the Le Clairs had brought a boat out yesterday. Mueller's men said no one had bothered the site, that Michael had gone from India straight back to Glastonbury. *Couldn't get enough of that Anne*, Cagliostro thought. *Presumptuous neophyte. I'd never let a woman deter me like that.*

The GPS clicked to the right coordinates. "This is it," he called over his shoulder. "Look for the buoy."

Mueller stopped the boat and took out his binoculars, searching the surface of the water. After a few minutes, he shouted that he'd found it and maneuvered the yacht over to the spot.

"Drop anchor," Cagliostro ordered. Mueller did as he was told, but kept glancing at him when he thought Cagliostro couldn't see. It was clear his body guard thought he was taking unnecessary risks, but wisely kept his mouth shut.

Mueller held the oxygen tanks while Cagliostro pulled on his gear, then helped lower him over the side. He followed the line down, forcing himself to pause at intervals, making that one concession to the doctor. About halfway down, a manta ray swam by, majestic as an eagle in the sky. He watched it until it disappeared, then began his descent again. At long last, he reached the sandy bottom.

To his relief, nothing had been disturbed. He went right to work, repeating his ritual exactly as he had before. Soon the sentinels purred to life, glowing in the dark water. But today it seemed to take longer to wake sleeping beauty, as he'd come to think of the Fire Stone. His lungs burned, but he ignored the pain. Soon he'd been transmuted into light, and they'd heal in a flash. The Tuoai Stone woke reluctantly under his persistent pressure, finally stirring to life. Cagliostro floated down to sit on the surface of the stone. When it softened, he took one last deep breath, then stripped off his tank and mask, laying them carefully within reach. Just in case he ever decided to come back. Then he pushed his way inside the crystal.

During the ritual, he'd built the picture—those airy domes, those spires of fire reaching into the sky—and as soon as he felt the gelatinous body of the stone close around him, he sent this image into its heart, his passion fueling the command. He held his hand before his face and watched it become transparent. His body turned a reddish light, like fire, then seemed to merge with all the red light in the rainbows, with all the fire in the universe. He could go anywhere, he realized with a rush, but pushed the thought away and pictured his city again. The crystal seemed to hesitate, then he dissolved in light and felt the whoosh, just like a fast elevator.

When vision returned, he saw the same room he'd been in before, twelve sentinels brightly shining, the blue tiled floor. But maybe all the temples were set up exactly this way. Of course they were. It was the geometry that made the transport possible. He pushed his way through the stone before it hardened, confident. And then he saw him. The man with the muscled shoulders, his hair a mass of braids, his face white with shock, his eyes staring. The man pointed at him, turned around and shouted.

"Where is it?" Cagliostro screamed. "Where's my city?"

The man frowned, trying to make sense of what he was hearing.

This man had prevented him from going home once again. Cagliostro launched himself at the culprit, grabbed his throat and squeezed. The man's eyes bulged, then his huge hands seized Cagliostro's forearms and pulled.

Cagliostro lost his grip on the man's throat. "Where is it?" he demanded.

"What do you want?" Cagliostro flinched when he realized he could suddenly understand.

"I want to go home," he spit out. "Why do you keep stopping me?"

The man's eyes lit in sympathy. "Where is your home?"

Cagliostro bellowed his rage, then he heard pounding feet, many feet, and the doors of the temple being thrown open. Before anyone even entered the chamber, he threw up a shield at the doorway, then put his opponent in a neck lock and dragged him to the Fire Stone.

"Are you crazy?" the man managed to choke out. "You'll kill us. You're going to bring down the whole city." A tremor snaked through the floor confirming his words.

"I want to go home," he panted in his ear, emphasizing every word.

The man sagged in his arms, surrendering. "Show me," he said.

Cagliostro drove the image of his city into his mind. The Tuaoi Stone seemed to sense his desperation, because it flared to life with a hum. The stone softened and Cagliostro dragged the man inside with him.

Home, Cagliostro demanded, and the two turned to light. The man glowed blue, which freed him from Cagliostro's control, but for some reason he cooperated. When they came through into his city, Cagliostro would teach him a lesson he'd not forget.

Vision returned. Cagliostro braced himself to see yet another room, but this one in the temple of his home city. But, no. It couldn't be. The tepid light of the three sentinels turned the Caribbean water a sickly green. *No*, his mind screamed, and he lurched as the crystal shifted.

Stop it. The man reached out to touch him. *You must calm down. I'll help you. I promise to help you.*

Cagliostro pulled him to the edge of the Fire Stone, then pushed out first, grabbed up the mask and oxygen tank he'd hoped never to see again, and took a breath. Then he held the mask to the man's face. His eyes darted around wildly. He started to thrash about, but Cagliostro tightened his grip on him. Then he took another breath from the tank and pushed the mask to his face again. Finally the man took a breath. Cagliostro swam with him to the line and slowly they ascended together, breathing in a slow rhythm, sharing the oxygen.

GOVANNAN HUDDLED in the cell the stranger had thrown him in, trying to clear his mind. But it was like breathing thin air. Something kept him from thinking straight. His captor must have set up some energy field to scramble his ectoplasmic field. Or somehow stopped him from shifting to the compatible life form for this system. He'd rematerialized exactly as he was in Eden, right down to the limp. His stomach growled and his body yearned for water, but nothing came. He'd spent the night on the stone floor, but this morning the one high window showed a tropical blue patch of sky. The color of the sky in Eden. Perhaps he was still on earth, since he'd had a vision of the Fire Stone lying on its side when he'd tried to calm it after the first dangerous transport. But where? Who would treat him so badly? The New Knowledge Guild? Had they sunk so low as to torture humans now?

When the man had grabbed him, he'd decided to go with him rather than risk bringing all of Eden down on their heads. He hoped he hadn't made a fatal mistake. The stranger had been a roil of contradictory emotions, but his power. Govannan had been shocked by his raw power. No wonder he'd created so much damage. But his captor hadn't visited him since he'd ordered the other man to lock him in this cell. Govannan had to be patient and wait. If he could clear his mind, he'd be able to figure out where he was and what his captor wanted. He straightened his back and chanted, but the stones poked into his buttocks and ankles making it hard to meditate. He kept it up, but his focus kept drifting. He felt like an apprentice. Worse.

He smelled it before he heard the footsteps. Water. He stood up to welcome his captor. But it wasn't the one who had dragged him up from the bottom of the ocean, making him breath through that artificial apparatus. Why not just shift to dolphin shape? The man hadn't seemed to know how, and Govannan had needed to stay with him to try to calm him, to stop him from popping in and out of the Fire Stone and unhinging the earth's mantle. He'd begun a terrible chain of events, and it seemed Govannan's fate to repair the damage. But first, he had to understand what was happening. The man who brought him the water was the one who'd been piloting the water craft, who had come close to panic when he'd seen not one person come out of the water, but two. He still smelled of fear, but an old, habitual fear, probably of the man he worked for.

"Thank you. I'm very thirsty." Govannan took the water from him. The man only shook his head with a frown, not understanding. What was wrong with these people? Where was their translation crystal? And the boat. It had only floated on the water, not been capable of diving below it or even rudimentary flight. Once they'd reached the shore, they'd stuffed him in the back of a conveyance with wheels that let out a trail of stinking exhaust.

As he drank, he tried to probe the man's thoughts, but came up with nothing. His telepathy seemed to be gone, although he could still read rudimentary emotions. He finished the bottle and held it out. "May I have more?" he asked. But the man frowned and tossed it into a circular metal can behind him, then clanged the door shut and locked it. Govannan watched him leave, then studied the padlock, wishing he possessed the skill with metal that he had with crystal. Feeling somewhat better, he sat back down and began a silent chant. Sometimes persistence worked. In this thick atmosphere, it seemed the only hope.

Some time later, a noise roused him. He stretched his legs, trying to get the blood flow back. He had never fallen asleep in meditation before. The blue patch of sky had been replaced by a patch of black. A lone star twinkled. He needed to see more stars to figure out his location. The sound of footsteps grew louder, and suddenly light flooded his cell—harsh, white light from a glass globe hanging down from the ceiling by a string. He shielded his eyes with his hand. The same man who'd brought him water stood outside pointing a dark metallic object at him. A woman came up behind him. She surveyed Govannan with an air of disbelief, then said, "Stand up."

Govannan blinked in surprised. "You found the crystal?"

She frowned. "What are you talking about?"

"I can understand you. You found the translator crystal."

"Hold out your hands."

"Why?"

"No more questions," the man said. "Do as she says."

Govannan held his hands out from his sides.

"No, in front," she said.

He held them straight in front of himself.

"Together," she snapped, clearly exasperated.

Govannan took a calming breath. "If you would demonstrate, I would be happy to do as you ask."

"No tricks." The man waved the metal object at him.

Govannan looked from one to the other, then put his hands closer together. Lightening quick, the woman snapped two metal rings around his wrists. He pulled his hands back and discovered a chain connected the two rings. "What is the purpose of this device?"

"Shut up. Now move it." The man waved the metal object again, this time suggesting a direction.

Govannan stepped out of his cell and stood looking at the two.

"You first," the man said. They walked up the stairs and down a hallway. At the back of the house, windows stood open, letting in a breeze that smelled of flowers, ocean, mold, and exhaust. They continued out the door toward a smaller building. Govannan paused to look up. Earth constellations. And spring ones at that, but not quite in the right positions. The smells suggested a warm ocean and tropical flowers. The woman touched a panel and bright lights drowned the stars. Why did they try to light up the night? Maybe they'd heard the rumors of animal attacks and thought the beasts would be frightened off.

"Keep going." The man poked him in the back with the metal thing. The woman opened the door of a long, black vehicle, another one with wheels sending out a plume of some kind of smoke that made him want to sneeze. "Get in," the man said.

Govannan stopped. "Where is my host?"

The two burst out laughing. "Host? Get in the car," the man said.

Govannan turned around. "I've complied with your requests only because I agreed to help the man who took me. He asked me to help him find his home. I will not go any farther until I speak with him."

The man reached out with his left arm, grabbed his throat and applied precise pressure. The sudden pain made Govannan gag. His eyes watered and he tried to catch his breath. The man held him up by his throat, stuck his face up to his, and said in a quiet, deadly voice, "You will do as I say or suffer the consequences. Do you—"

"Enough," came a weak voice from inside the vehicle. The man released Govannan. There was a sliding noise, then a familiar face appeared in the open door—the same sharp nose, pale blue eyes, and silver white hair of the man he'd seen in the crystal. "Please join me—I don't know your name."

Govannan stood as straight as he could and introduced himself.

His captor nodded his head and returned the favor. "I am Alexander Cagliostro."

But the vibration of this name did not match the man he was looking at.

"I've waited twenty-four hours and now I can fly again."

This made no sense at all, although he did look ill.

"I am taking you home."

Govannan's eyebrows lifted. "So you have found your home, then. I am happy for you."

Cagliostro turned a vivid red, then started to cough. When he recovered, he said, "Not my real home, idiot. Just the house I've been using."

The man holding the metal object gave Govannan a shove, so he got into the vehicle. "This craft can fly, then?"

Cagliostro's forehead wrinkled. "No, not this one. We're driving to the jet."

"You have different conveyances for water, land and air?"

"Of course." Cagliostro studied him a moment. "You don't in Atlantis?"

"You know the name of my home?" Govannan sat forward eagerly.

"Everyone knows about Atlantis," he said. "Most of them just don't believe in it."

Govannan took a breath to ask what he meant, but Cagliostro held up his hand. "Enough. We'll talk once we've arrived."

Govannan ducked his head. "As you wish. I am your guest."

The guard snorted. Cagliostro shot him a threatening look, and he subsided.

As it turned out, Govannan was glad his host had asked for silence, because truly, he would not have been able to hold a thought in his head while watching the amazing sights unfold outside the window. Cagliostro watched his reactions in a sort of exhausted fascination. Bright lights on tall poles pushed back the night. Outside the boxy buildings, other lights burned. These people must have developed a permanent dread of animals. Could the rumors of the attacks have been true?

The black streets divided the town in rectangles, not golden mean rectangles either. They'd abandoned geometrical symmetry as far as he could tell. Then, as soon as he'd gotten used to the pattern, it changed again, and they drove onto white streets with tiny lanes created by lines on the pavement. The long, black vehicle picked up speed, and the hum of the wheels filled the silent compartment. Other vehicles whizzed by. They didn't care much about safety, but his host had amply demonstrated that by the way he'd misused the Crystal Matrix Chamber. Then more bright lights, so many he knew they were not to keep the animals at bay. Could it be these people could no longer see in the dark?

Long strips of metal divided a field from the street. A man with an even longer metal object opened a gap in the metal, and they went through. The vehicle entered a squat metallic building and stopped. Didn't these people know that artificial material obstructed the proper flow of energy? The guard waved at him to get out. They walked toward a graceful, white vehicle with wings like a bird. They'd tried to imitate wings in order to fly. The Sirians had been right. Consciousness had fallen dramatically.

Once they were situated on what these people called the plane, his host explained that he was going to sleep. "I recommend you do the same." He closed the door of his tiny room, and the man who'd been guarding him showed Govannan into a similar compartment.

"I'm locking you in, but I'll be right outside. Don't try anything." He waved the metal object at him again. He seemed quite fond of it. Then he closed the door and Govannan heard a click. Another lock, he assumed. He lay down on the hard cot and closed his eyes, reminding himself he was here voluntarily, that there was no sense in escaping. The man would just return to the Tuaoi Stone and this time he might rip a hole in the world that could not be fixed. The enormous noise of the engines hurt his ears. Then the vehicle rolled off, gathered speed and seemed to launch itself into the air with an ungodly roar. The ride smoothed out. He sat up, expecting to arrive any moment, but they stayed in the air for such a long time that he did eventually drop off to sleep. He dreamed of Megan and the simple joys of swimming on Sirius, then the more delightful pleasures they'd experienced on the Pleiades.

MEGAN STREAMED THROUGH THE STARS, a blaze of blue light, reveling in the freedom, the infinite possibilities of the One. But she couldn't agree with her mother. She'd rather be making love with Govannan. Even so, the trip was over too quickly. Already she was thickening into corporeal form. But something new began to manifest along with her, a speck of light she hadn't noticed before. A nascent consciousness nestled within her womb. The Grand Matriarch's last words replayed in her memory. *Bless you, child.* She was pregnant.

Before she could take this in, she gasped air, felt damp rock beneath her feet. She hadn't come back through the body of a crystal; she had manifested directly into the world unmediated. How could that be possible?

"The Tor itself—"

Megan jumped, surprised by the voice filling the cavern.

"—is a portal, if handled properly." The Lady of Avalon stepped forward and handed Megan a robe. She spotted several other priestesses in the shadows of the cave. "You didn't think we'd let you transport alone, did you?" the Lady asked.

"I—I didn't even know . . ." she gestured to the cave around her, noticing small sentinels set at intervals around the wall. As her senses returned, she became aware of an underlying tension in the women, even fear. She tried to catch The Lady's eyes, but she looked away. "What's wrong?" Megan asked.

But the Lady Winifred only shook her head. She turned and the priestesses filed out of the cave on silent feet. There was no energetic residue to soothe after her transport, no Fire Stone to sing back to sleep. The earth simply swallowed the waves of energy, returning to balance. Megan gave the chamber one last glance. A rounded black stone stood in the darkness, pulsing with a deep note. It pulled at her to come back, but a hand slipped into hers, and she found Thalana by her side.

"It's good to have you back," her friend whispered.

"What's happened?" Megan kept her voice low, but the Lady shushed them. Ever obedient, Thalana fell back and they walked single file through a dark tunnel. The sound of water soon reached Megan's ears, and they came to a fork, the same one she'd found on Samhein, except from the direction she had not explored that night. Now she knew where it led—into the heart of the Tor and the black omphalos stone. The Lady took the path toward the outside, still leading the priestesses in single file. The tension seemed laced with grief.

Megan shivered in the damp night air. She wished the Lady had brought a wool cloak, but she'd find something once she returned to the dormitory. The Lady dismissed them and turned toward the vigil hut, and the rest broke into conversation as soon as her back was turned. Thalana told her all the news as they walked through the night. Inside the dormitory, the other apprentices joined in. Megan's head kept nodding. "I'm going to bed," she announced.

"But you haven't told us what happened in Atlantis," Thalana complained.

Megan smiled like a Sphinx. "Tomorrow."

The next morning at breakfast, Megan held everyone in awe as she narrated her trip to the Star Elders' worlds. She spoke about swimming as a dolphin, the tall crystal people, about meeting her distant relatives on the home world of the Seven Sisters. They seemed distant to her, although they'd said otherwise. She thought it was the difference in their life spans. She held back the news of her pregnancy. She wanted Govannan to be the first to know.

It surprised her how easily she fell into the routine once again—classes and chores. No rituals were scheduled for a time. She'd been back a few days when the Lady of Avalon asked to see her after the evening meal. Megan made her way up the meadow through the fence to the stand of yew trees where the Lady waited.

Without another word of explanation, the Lady of Avalon led her once again to the small vigil hut near Red Spring. They paused at the oak door and the Lady knocked softly, then pushed it open. Megan walked into the stifling hut. Her eyes, used to the growing darkness outside, found the low table, but not the Morgen sitting behind it. At the side of the room, the lead healer bent over a smoking fire, stirring something in the three legged cauldron. A bundle in the corner stirred. "Anne?"

The healer and the Lady exchanged a glance. "No, it's Megan," the Lady said.

The Morgen rose from her nest of blankets, her wrinkled face grim with pain. Her blue eyes looked on this world tonight, and she stretched her withered hand out. "Come closer, child."

"It's not catching," the healer whispered. Nodding, Megan stepped up to the bed.

"Sit," the old woman said, then turned to the Lady. "Can't you make it warmer?"

The healer poured some liquid into a mug and brought it to the old woman. "This will warm you." She held it for her as she drank.

So, she's human after all, Megan thought, *not fae.*

After her medicine, the Morgen caught her ragged breath and watched Megan for a long moment. Finally, she spoke. "I will be leaving this world soon. My era is passing."

"But—" Megan began. A tiny sob escaped the Lady.

The Morgen ignored them both. "It has come upon me suddenly, although I've felt it creeping up on us these last years." She stopped a moment to catch her breath, then pointed her bony finger at Megan's abdomen. "The child you've carried to us from the Pleiades, she will take my place. I have waited for her a long time."

Megan's hand moved to cover her stomach unbidden.

"But not before another." She gestured toward the Lady. "You—" she inclined her head toward Megan "—are not fated for this world." The Morgen closed her eyes again and stayed silent so long, Megan thought she'd fallen asleep—or left them. What did she mean 'not fated for this world'? Would she die giving birth? Return to the stars with Govannan? Live hundreds of years by his side enjoying the glories of the Seven Sisters? But she could never leave her child behind.

The healer crept up and passed her open palm over the front of the Morgen's body, then moved back, satisfied she still lived. At long last, the crone opened her eyes again and said in an eerily conversational tone, "How is our family in the stars? Do they still live in glorious homes, dress in the softest silks, eat the most delicious food? Or have I embellished my memories, embroidered imaginings while I sat here guarding this crossroad?"

Megan leaned forward and touched the Morgen's hand "It is as beautiful as you remember." It frightened her to see this legend's frailty.

The Morgen chuckled, which led to a cough. Once she caught her breath, she said, "I am truly flesh and blood, my dear. It is but the mantle of the office you saw before." As if the mere mention of this power were enough to summon it, the old woman suddenly straightened, her eyes clouded in a blink, and her strong voice filled the room. "Go to Eden and save the sentinels. Shut down the Tuaoi Stone so it may pass the coming darkness in safety." Her voice rose almost to a shout. "Hurry before it is too late." Then she sank back into the nest of blankets.

The Lady took Megan by the arm and pulled her up. They moved toward the door. "But," Megan hung back, "I've only just returned."

The Lady hurried down from the vigil hut toward the yews, Megan in tow. A figure separated itself from the shadows and approached them. The Lady whispered something in her ear and she took off at a run. Then the Lady turned back to Megan. "The priestesses will be here soon. Sit by the well. It will give you peace."

"But—" Megan thought she should say goodbye, that she should pack something for the trip, but this was ridiculous, of course. She sat by the well, trying to quiet the tumult in her heart.

Once the priestesses assembled, they formed a line and began to chant as they walked through the mist to the opening of the cave. As the line wound into the Tor, their lovely voices seemed to light the night, to soothe Megan's fear. When they entered the chamber, the Lady took Megan forward. No hint of grief or weariness hung about her now. "Do not fear. Your child will be safe."

"Thank you." Tears welled in Megan's eyes. She had only learned of the baby a few days before and already she felt the protectiveness of a mother.

"Now, take your place in the center of the chamber. The transport will be just as it is in any Crystal Matrix Temple. After all, this is the Crystal Cave."

Megan glanced around, but saw only dark stone, not the magnificent display of radiance and color in the ceiling over the lake, only a short distance through the rock. The glint from the sentinels was the only light in this chamber. Here she was tucked in the womb of the Dark Mother, just as her new child was tucked into hers.

The Lady took her robe, squeezed her hand, then stepped back to her place on the wall. The chant deepened and built in layers of intricate harmony. The energy grew intense, as if it was too large to contain, but the final surge did not come. Megan remained standing, naked and confused, in the middle of the cave. Then the chant quieted and finally stopped.

"What's wrong?" she asked. It seemed a question she kept asking.

The priestesses looked to their leader, waiting for her to speak. The Lady lifted her head. Silver tears reflected in the dim light. "The Tuaoi Stone is no longer safe. They cannot receive you."

Megan stepped forward, but the priestesses still stood silent, waiting.

The Lady took a long, shuttering breath, then proclaimed, "The Morgen is dead."

23

The old Megan stared into the fire, wondering what the Morgen had meant those many years ago. Not fated for this world? She'd been wrong about that. Megan had spent long years in Avalon tending the crossroads, so long that she too wondered if she'd imagined the glories of the worlds of the Star Elders or even the wonders of Atlantis. She drew a breath to continue her story, but it triggered another bout of coughing that shook her body like a tree in a wind storm. Old. She was the same age Govannan had been when they'd made their child, Caitir, who sat before her now on the verge of replacing her, trying to be brave. The cough died down and Megan waited for enough breath to finish the story. Not only had she shared the old Morgen's fate, she was dying of the same disease. The damp took its toll.

Megan took a breath and pressed on. "The Lady sent word that we needed a ship, but my cousin Demos came walking over the crest of the hill a day later saying that he needed to go home, too. So, we flew back in his silver craft, the work of only a few hours in those days, and he told me what he knew."

"Earthquakes. Someone misused the Crystal Matrix Chamber and set off a series of earthquakes."

"Misused? What do you mean? Who would do a thing like that?"

"They don't know."

"Can't they stop the quakes?" she asked.

"They've sent to Khem for help. The Great Pyramid is even more powerful than the Fire Stone. It should be able to stabilize the crust."

Megan pulled her wool cloak tight around her shoulders, even though the sun grew stronger as they flew south.

"And there's more. The New Knowledge Guild is on trial."

"Trial? What do you mean?"

"They're being questioned by the Prince himself. I heard Merope sat in."

"Questioned about what?"

Demos stared out at the empty sky.

"Tell me. I'm not a child anymore."

"No one can believe it." His voice lowered to a whisper. "Apparently they've experimented on some animals. It was torture, really."

"What?" Megan's heart gave a lurch. "But that's—"

"Impossible," he finished for her. "Seems this will be the age of the impossible."

Megan hugged herself, trying to push away the images that came unbidden to her mind. Then she watched Demos for a while. "So you've heard that, too?"

"What?" He glanced at her, then back at his gauges.

"That we're entering a new time."

He nodded. "That's why I'm going home. To be with my family."

Megan stared through the window down at the water below. Her hand moved to cover her abdomen again. "What will become of us?"

"Oh, now—" Demos put strength in his voice "—the world is still a beautiful place."

She gave him a weak smile.

This did not seem to satisfy him, so Demos pointed the craft down, a touch of the old scamp returning, and they plummeted toward the water. Megan screamed when they sliced through the surface, then let go of the arm rest when he straightened out.

"Honestly," she said, but didn't have the heart to scold him. They moved through the turquoise ocean lit with filtered sunlight. Soon their presence attracted a pod of curious dolphins who swam along beside them. Megan watched their grey, sleek bodies and remembered the sensation of gliding through the water, of rocketing upward, breeching the surface, and leaping through the air. She pressed her palm against the glass and smiled. "You're right. The world is still a beautiful place."

Demos dropped her off at the Crystal Guild Headquarters. "You're sure you don't want me to take you home?" he asked.

"No, but thank you for the ride." She picked up her bag from the back, one benefit of flying in a craft rather than popping through a portal, then stepped back. "Let me know what you hear," she called. He waved goodbye and lifted into the air.

That's when the next quake hit. The ground lurched and she fell, lucky to land on her bag full of clothes and not the hard pavement stones. People came running from the garage and the guild headquarters, all making toward the Crystal Matrix Chamber. She grabbed her bag and followed, but the earth did not cooperate. It bucked again. People fell, then picked themselves up and staggered across the shifting ground, all still heading in the same direction.

The temple was filled with knots of people milling around. She made her way through the crowd to the first circle of stones in the Matrix Chamber. Above the din of their raised voices, the Tuaoi Stone screeched. Megan stopped dead. All along the base, new cracks had appeared. Light bounced around at odd angles. The crystal still resonated from a transport, but its song made her head ache and her stomach threaten to turn over. She searched the throng for the Matrix pod workers and finally spotted Ianara, who stood on one side of the inner circle trying to get the crowd's attention. But no one was listening. The buzz of the towering crystal grew more dissonant, which seemed to fuel the chaos.

Daphyll ran in, her hair flying behind her, eyes wide. Herasto arrived on her heels. The floor shook, knocking many people down, but her two pod members made their way to Ianara, who pointed for them to take their places in the circle. Then she spotted Megan and elbowed her way through the crowd. "Take your station," she shouted above the din. "We have to calm the Fire Stone or it may break apart."

"But, I'm not trained."

Ianara took her by the shoulders and looked into her face. "Just trust your instincts. You'll know what to do."

"Where's Govannan?" Megan asked, but Ianara had turned back already and didn't hear.

Another quake hit, and the Fire Stone swayed. People screamed. Some ran, staggering, out of the temple. Ianara started a chant. Megan strained to hear, but she couldn't pick it out from the clamor of human voices and the ear-wrenching sounds coming from the crystals. She closed her eyes, trying to find her ground of silence, doing as the Lady of Avalon had taught her. Finally she succeeded. Then she stretched her senses toward the other pod workers, attempting to connect with them.

A new quiver ran through the floor, and the Fire Stone groaned. Megan's eyes flew open. The crystal rocked back and forth in its base, the tip coming within inches of crashing through the selenite ceiling. A new crack ran through the giant crystal, making a sickening popping sound. More people fled the chamber, screaming about an attack. The racket subsided enough for Megan to hear the calming chant rising from the three intrepid Matrix Chamber workers, as incongruous as a lullaby on a battle field. At first Megan matched Daphyll's part until the pattern began to sound in her head and she found her own harmonic. Rhea arrived, wild eyed, then she took another spot in the circle. More matrix workers found their way through the chaos into the temple. Then others came who Megan knew worked in different specialties. But they joined in, each matching the sounds of one of the pod workers, reinforcing the chant.

They sang and sang, shifting their tones to neutralize, to calm, to heal the earth and the wailing Tuoai Stone. As the group synergy built, Megan could see in her mind the temples along the spiraling grid that culminated at this spot. Some swayed and bucked. Others were empty of energy, like dried grass in autumn. The group worked to bring peace once more, but as the afternoon turned to night, it became clear that their efforts would only bring them a brief respite. The damage ran too deep. The red core of the earth ran fingers of molten rock up through the deepening cracks. The volcanoes of Atlantis began to leak fire. The city trembled. In parts of Eden, buildings with wood smoked, then caught fire and burned. The stone ones cracked and fell.

Megan swayed where she stood, chanting, yearning for water. And for

Govannan. Where was he? He had never come. Was he safe? Had he been injured in the quake somewhere? Then, her mind would merge into the ritual once more, and she'd lose track of her individual wants and needs for a while, the energy of the group feeding her, sustaining her. Some time late in the night, she became aware of Thuya whispering in her ear. "Come back, now. Come to my voice."

Megan looked at the old woman, her mind a blank, her every muscle aching, her heart broken. "Where is he, Thuya? Why has he abandoned us?"

"Rhea says you are to rest now. You mustn't risk your baby."

"But he doesn't even know." Tears ran down her face.

Thuya put her arm around her waist. "Lean on me, now." Another person slipped into her place and the chant continued.

The Egyptian woman led her up the hill to the villa, still safe from the quakes and fires, at least for the moment. She listened to Megan weep, singing little nonsense verses to her, reassuring her that all would be well, that Govannan would be found, against common sense, as if Megan were the baby instead of pregnant with one. Thuya took her into the water room, stripped off her clothes, and bathed her, holding her head above water, massaging her limbs, Megan passive beneath her nurturing hands. Then she wrapped her in a soft, warm blanket, led her down the hall and sat her on a bed. Megan recognized the pillows she'd brought from her childhood home an age ago— only half a year. Thuya put a cup up to her mouth, told her to drink. She sputtered when the bitter herbs hit her tongue.

"Drink it down," Thuya said.

The medicine stole into her battered heart and quieted it, like a root in the ground slowing at the approach of winter.

"Now sleep. In the morning, we will find the Matrix Master. Then you can tell him your news."

She did sleep. And finally, so did the earth. For a time.

MEGAN WOKE the next morning to a quiet earth, but no Govannan, so she started to search for him. Everyone in the villa slept except sturdy Thuya.

Megan found her in one of the classrooms putting the crystals right. "Has anyone found Govannan?" she asked.

"I haven't seen him or heard any news." Thuya straightened up, massaging her back. "The others came in just a couple of hours ago. We can ask them this afternoon. Let them sleep now."

"Have you rested?" Megan asked.

"Don't worry about me," Thuya said.

"Can I help you?" Megan asked out of guilt.

Thuya chuckled. "Go look for him. You won't be any good until you've found him."

Relieved, Megan went to an empty classroom and sat with a rather large rutilated smoky quartz in her lap to reinforce her vision. She stretched her senses over the city as far as she could, hunting for his energy signature. Then she went out on the streets where chaos reigned. Some areas of the city lay in rubble. Others were pristine. Shopkeepers shifted through debris, trying to assess the damage. Families moved rocks, lifted fallen beams, trying to set things right, some searching for lost loved ones. Maybe he'd been hurt and taken to be healed. She found her way to the Healing Temple. Crowds of people with crushed limbs, broken bones and shattered hearts filled the benches, then spilled over across the floor. Just inside a large room where patients lay waiting, Megan spotted Pleione.

Her mother ran and grabbed her up. "You're safe. Oh, thank the gods."

Megan returned the hug, trying not to cry.

"What are you doing here, anyway?"

"The Morgen sent me." Before she could explain, someone came up and asked Pleione a question. Megan saw another healer hovering, waiting for Pleione's attention. Before they were interrupted again, she asked, "Have you seen Govannan?"

"He's not at the Temple?"

"No, I haven't seen him since I arrived yesterday. I was out looking for him."

"See if you can contact his mother's house. Some of the communication screens are still working."

A healer came running up. "They're bringing in the survivors from the north market."

"I'll be right there." Pleione turned to Megan. "Go back to your temple; the city isn't safe. I'll come when I have time." She ran off to see about the new patients.

Megan made her way back to the Crystal Guild, realizing only later that she hadn't told her mother the one piece of good news. Back in her room, she found Govannan's family listed in the computer files. They lived in the mountains of the Evaemona district, but she wasn't able to get through nor could she find any news about the conditions in that region. It contained one of the largest volcanoes on Atlantis. Half the communications net was down, and the quakes had knocked out some of the energy stations, so flying was no longer safe. Suddenly, an emergency announcement flashed on the screen. Rhea had called a meeting.

People packed the room when Megan arrived, filling the seats and leaning against the walls, so she stood at the edge away from the other Crystal Matrix workers, her eyes scanning the crowd for Govannan. Maybe he'd come in with the Guild Mistress, but Rhea walked on stage without him. A line of area heads followed her slight figure. Govannan was not with them either.

"Where is he?" Megan whispered to herself.

"Missing someone?" a woman standing next to her asked.

She nodded.

"You're not the only one."

Rhea held her hand up for silence, which came quickly. "I'll come straight to the point. We must evacuate Atlantis."

Questions and lamentations erupted from all around, but Rhea stood her ground and waited for everything to die down again. "The Guild Masters met all morning. It's clear that the damage is too deep to repair."

A tremor shook the room, seeming to punctuate Rhea's words. The quakes had started again just after Megan had returned from the city.

Rhea waited for the shaking to stop, then continued. "We have lived in harmony with the volcanoes for thousands of years. For the last hundred years, the telluric pressure has been increasing. As you know, our temples and grid systems have worked to balance things, tapping that pressure and turning it into energy—among other things.

"But now it seems the earth is going through large changes. The accident in the Crystal Matrix Chamber only hastened the inevitable." She stressed this last word, looking around at everyone. "Soon, parts of Atlantis will sink."

A sickly silence followed this announcement, then people began talking at once, asking how this could be, assuring her that with enough help the earth could be stabilized. Another quake hit, and the earth shook long and hard. People grabbed onto whatever they could, most clinging to each other. Some just sat down, praying the ground would not open beneath them. After two full minutes, which seemed an eternity, it stopped. A small crack ran through the ceiling of the room. Everyone stared up at it, breathless. It stopped and the ceiling held.

"As you can see, our city is no longer safe," Rhea said. "Go to your division. Make your plans." Her voice broke, and silence fell. "Some of us may never see each other again. I want to thank you for the glorious life we have lived together."

Weeping broke out, but the earth trembled once more, cutting off anything but survival plans. People scrambled out of the hall toward their various division homes. Megan ran to the Matrix Chamber. Ianara came in on her heels. The pod workers arrived in clusters. Finally everyone was accounted for. Except Govannan. This was Ianara's first question.

"I may know what happened to him." Herasto stepped forward. "Before the accident, I was walking to the Temple. I heard voices. One man shouting, another trying to calm him. I didn't recognize the angry man, but the other voice was Govannan's. I called for help, and a group of us tried to get into the temple. But the angry man set up some kind of energy barrier. We couldn't get into the chamber in time."

He looked at Megan, his eyes begging her forgiveness, so Daphyll continued. "The first quake popped his shield. When we ran in, they were gone. The Fire Stone had just been used. It took all of us to keep it from splitting in two."

Herasto looked over at Megan, guilt written all over his face. "We couldn't follow them." Then he turned back to Ianara. "I would have told you earlier, but—" he tried to straighten his disheveled clothes "—I just never got the chance. I worked all night, then—"

Ianara held up her hands. "We all know what's been going on, Herasto. No one blames you."

Megan stood rooted to the floor. What was he saying? Govannan gone with some stranger? And no one knew where? "But there must be some way to find him," she blurted, then realized Ianara had been saying something.

"The Fire Stone is damaged, Megan. Our first task is to balance it. Then we can see if enough information is left to trace him."

Megan let out a wail and several people moved to comfort her.

"I thought you were in Avalon," Ianara said, then shook her head. "I'm sorry. We'll find him."

Megan nodded, her throat closed by hot tears.

"What happened?" Ianara asked more gently.

"The Morgen. She sent me back. She said I should bring the sentinels back to Avalon so they would be safe."

Ianara shook her head. "We need to speak with her about this."

"She's dead."

Gasps and shouts of dismay erupted from everywhere. Ianara raised her hands for quiet. "An era is passing, and we must survive. We have to heal the Fire Stone so people can transport out. Then we'll have to close it down so when—" she shuttered, then forced herself to continue "—when the island sinks, the crystal will not create space or time disruptions."

People were beginning to focus.

"But before this, everyone needs to seek guidance about where they are supposed to go. I propose we sit together for this." She looked around. "Is everyone here?" She winced. "That we know to be in Eden now?"

The pods grouped themselves together, each making a count. Megan sat on the floor, numb. Daphyll sat with her, but was barely aware of her. The missing people were accounted for, and Ianara seemed satisfied. "Now everyone find a comfortable place." The earth shivered again. "As comfortable as you can under the circumstances."

The pods settled down together. Herasto sat on Megan's other side. "I'm sorry we couldn't stop them," he said.

"We'll find him." Daphyll squeezed her arm.

Then Ianara began a chant to enhance awareness, and the group joined her. The complex harmonies worked their way into Megan's numb mind, gradually bringing relief and peace, finally even hope. Next, Ianara led them into contact with their inner world guides, and silence reigned, more powerful that the small tremors that ran through the room periodically.

The stag appeared in Megan inner vision. He walked toward her, then shifted into the tall man with dark hair and luminous eyes who had led her into faeryland. "You know already where you should go. I will keep you company until you find him again."

So she would find Govannan. Megan sat back, satisfied, and waited for the others. It was her first experience with the full power of the Crystal Matrix workers. She began to be aware of a group mind thinking in harmony, a beautiful, multifaceted sphere, like a crystal ball, but infinitely more beautiful.

"It is complete." Ianara stood up and waited for everyone to return from their experience. "Let us hear our destinations."

Once the groups seemed done, Ianara asked each pod what their destination was to be. Khem, Mayaland, Tibet, Sirius, the Pleiades. Each group seemed harmonious, ordered to one place, each one different. Except Megan. When she answered that she was to go to Avalon, to Megan's surprise Ianara turned to Thuya. "Is she to take the sentinels?"

"Three," Thuya answered. "Each pod that stays on earth is to take three sentinels. They are too powerful to keep together in the coming darkness."

"She's our most powerful seer," Daphyll whispered. "She will return home with us."

Ianara accepted Thuya's word. She turned to the whole group again. "Take as many of our tools as you can. Pack a few clothes, food, tools. The elders will come with me to prepare the Fire Stone."

After an hour of work, the pods going off planet were called to the Crystal Matrix Chamber. It took a double complement of workers to send them, but they got there safely. But two hours later, the earth broke open. Lava flooded the volcanoes and flowed down the slopes toward the city. Buildings fell, floors shook. And the Fire Stone could no longer be used. They'd have to travel by ship.

Megan went back to her room to gather her personal belongings. She took a few sea shells from her childhood collection, pillows, and her favorite dress, then ran back to the temple. The place felt empty and hollow, just a room. The Fire Stone had been sung to sleep and sealed.

Ianara made her way across the rippling floor, walking like a sailor. "We've packed the sentinels. Are you ready?"

"Did you ever find out?" she asked. Another quake hit, and the two women grabbed each other to stay upright.

After it died down, Ianara answered her. "We only know he is still on earth. May you find him again, Megan."

Tears welled in her eyes, but she brushed them away, remembering what her guide had said. Now, she had to save herself and their child. At least she had that. "Thank you for everything. Good luck."

Two men she did not know shouldered the three sentinels and they walked to the harbor guarded by soldiers. People screamed at her as they made their way to the ship. "You're leaving us to die." "Fix the Fire Stone and stop the quakes." "Take my child with you. Oh, have pity."

Megan ducked her head. She hadn't even seen her family—her cousins, her mother's sisters and brothers, her grandmothers. She had no idea what was happening to them. Somewhere deep inside she knew her parents would travel west and that she would never see them again. Tears ran, but she trudged ahead. Duty, that was all that was left.

Others had been ordered to Avalon, and once the ship was loaded, they set sail. As they pulled away from Eden, the whole city came into view. It was ablaze. Rubble had replaced buildings. The trees were black skeletons. She looked toward the high hill where the Queen's palace stood, and the Temple of Poseidon where she'd first heard Govannan's voice. It had fallen—all of it. Then the water seemed to be rushing out, and it took the ship with it.

"Raise sails," the captain shouted. "Man the oars."

The ship made it out to the open ocean. Megan watched from safety as a monster wave rose above her lost home and crashed over it, putting out fires and sweeping the remaining people of Atlantis into the sea. Had Ianara made it out? Herasto and Daphyll? She would never know.

GOVANNAN SAT against the wall in this new cell where he'd been locked for two days. He'd gotten a glimpse of the house when they'd first arrived in the predawn grey—a stone and glass mansion surrounded by gardens and an orchard. The lowing of some kind of animals came across the rolling hills. He looked forward to a room with a view, to sunlight and the flowers he smelled on the wind, but once again had been taken below ground and locked away in the dark, damp bowels of the house. One small, grated window looked out to a metal retaining wall, at least bringing in some air, if little light. The food the guard provided tasted faintly of some kind of metal. Limp, lifeless vegetables, lumps of muscle meat, and a strong brown drink that set his heart racing. He could imagine what Oria would say about it.

He explored the room for weaknesses in case he'd need to escape, but if this man's idea of hospitality reflected anything about how the people in this mysterious place thought, he could have difficulty with basic necessities. Making his way back to the portal could prove dangerous if not impossible. Add to all this the fact that the Matrix Stone Cagliostro used on this side lay on its side at the bottom of the ocean. Even if he got to it, how would he activate it?

Which brought him to another puzzle. Where had Cagliostro's pod of workers been? They had emerged into the murky depths alone, with no back up. Maybe his team hadn't had time to gather. That was the only answer he could think of. In Atlantis, Cagliostro had acted on impulse, jumped without harmonizing with the more subtle dimensions, an act that a few days ago he wouldn't have been able to imagine. The imbalance resulting from this had manifested as quakes in Eden. He hoped his own guild had healed them by now.

His mind continued to function like flotsam caught by a strong current. Thoughts and emotions flooded him unbidden and they were hard to dismiss.

His focus waned when he got tired. His stamina just wasn't what it had been before the jump. Even his memory was spotty. He'd completely lost his awareness of the One. He knew it was there, an underground stream, only because it always had been, because it was the very fabric of all life. He yearned to reconnect to this cosmic ocean of consciousness that had always supported him before, so he did the only thing he knew to do. He spent long hours meditating, trying to clear out the imbalance that the hasty jump had caused, then exercised in his cell as best he could. Good food and pure water would have helped. But these his captor denied him. At times he doubted his decision to go with Cagliostro. But the madman would have returned, creating worse havoc. Govannan tried to reconcile himself to his task. He waited. He imagined that Cagliostro was still recovering from the transport, just as he was.

On the third day, the guard, whose name he now knew was Mueller, brought him upstairs into the dazzling sunlight to a room where Cagliostro sat at a desk. Behind him stood a golden icon. Govannan pushed down his complaints and pointed at the statue. "A striking piece of art."

Cagliostro glanced behind him, as if he'd forgotten about this glorious artifact. "Oh, yes. Amen, the Hidden One. But it isn't this statue that concerns me."

Govannan's guess that his captor had been ill proved true. The dark circles under his eyes were gone. He sat straight as a young tree, his blue eyes intent, his silver hair hanging down his back in a ponytail. He was bright and full of vitality. But it was the vitality of a python, cold blooded and intent on its prey. He got up, walked around the desk. He took Govannan by the arm, then sniffed, frowning at him.

"I hope you'll excuse me," Govannan said in a flat voice, "but my room does not have a bath."

Mueller, who stood stiff as the wood of the door, broke his pose and gave him a sharp glance.

"If you agree to help me," Cagliostro said, "all the amenities shall be provided." He stopped in front of a glass display table.

"But this is why I came with you," Govannan said. "To help you."

Cagliostro turned with a snarl. "Let's drop the pretense that you're here voluntarily, shall we? I forced you to come with me because you kept interfering."

"It has never been my intention to hinder you." Govannan spoke slowly as if trying to quiet a rattle snake.

"And yet you did. You stopped me even when we entered the crystal again." Cagliostro's voice was mild, but his eyes blazed like diamonds in the sun.

"I don't know what you mean," Govannan said.

"I'll give you one more chance." He turned to the image hanging on the wall. "Tell me how to get to this place."

Govannan studied the painting, hoping to find something familiar in it. He'd seen elements of the image in several locations—tall crystal spires, glass domes—but not this exact combination. He turned to his captor. "Why do you think I know? It is your picture, after all."

Cagliostro began to pace. "I remember this city in Atlantis. Exactly as it's depicted here. But the Tuaoi Stone does not take me there."

"How do you communicate your destination to the crystal?"

Cagliostro stopped, the look of hope in his eyes so vivid that Govannan felt a stab of pity. Cagliostro's face flushed. "All I need from you is information."

Govannan spread his hands. "Of course. This is why I asked." He realized his hands were shaking. "May we sit down? I haven't slept well."

Cagliostro surveyed his dirty clothes with a look of distain. "If you must."

Govannan sank onto an armchair, grateful for a soft cushion that didn't poke into his hip bones. He closed his eyes to gather his thoughts—and to scan Cagliostro, who caught him at it and put up an impenetrable shield. At least impenetrable in Govannan's present condition. He opened his eyes and gave Cagliostro an appraising look. *Very well*, he thought. *The only way out of this situation is to heal this man.* Then he spoke as if to a student, "Tell me your procedure for transport."

His captor raised an eyebrow at Govannan's tone of voice. "Once I enter the stone—"

"How did you manage to get the stone to open?"

"By using the proper tones." Cagliostro looked at Govannan as if he'd just now begun to doubt his intelligence.

"And you did this alone?"

"Of course."

"You'll excuse the question, but on Atlantis we never risk a transport without a full compliment of Crystal Matrix singers. The work is too delicate."

Cagliostro snorted. "I'm beginning to think that Atlantis does not live up to the legends about it."

Govannan opened his mouth to continue his questioning, then heard the word 'legends' echo in his mind. He remembered Cagliostro saying that most people didn't believe in Atlantis. He felt a revelation sweeping toward him, but he fought it off, like that moment when a swimmer realizes a strong wave is upon him and he struggles to escape it. But the ocean always wins. Implacable, the realization crested and spilled over into his mind. That night Cagliostro had not taken him to a different place. He'd taken him to a different time.

Govannan's face drained of all color. He grabbed the arms of the chair, grateful for its support.

"What?" Cagliostro snapped.

Govannan moved his head around slowly, peeking at the room, as if hesitant to confront it directly.

"What is wrong with you?"

"What year is this?" Govannan asked, his voice thin.

A cruel smile broke over Cagliostro's face. "Your civilization disappeared 11,500 years ago."

"How?" he whispered.

"The volcanoes. The earth opened up and your island sank beneath the waves." Cagliostro sneered, as if this should be self evident. "The island was geologically unstable. A stupid place to build."

A dark pit opened up inside Govannan's gut. Tears flooded his eyes and overflowed, making clean tracks through the smudges of dirt on his face. His body shook and he made no attempt to contain his weeping. Cagliostro made a noise of disgust, but Govannan only covered his face with his hands and continued to sob. His beautiful city, all his friends, and Megan, the light of his heart—all gone. And he was marooned in the time the Star Elders had warned him of. Only it was worse, much worse than he could ever have imagined.

After a moment, he heard Cagliostro's voice. "But I can take you back. I can take you back before the end—" he paused "—but only if you help me."

Govannan shook his head. "No."

Cagliostro leaned across the space and hissed, "You dare refuse me?"

"You have destroyed it."

"What are you talking about? It's right there, on the other side of the Fire Stone." He stood up and shouted. "It's the only place the damn thing will take me to."

"We caused the earthquakes."

"What are you talking about?"

"The Crystal Matrix Temple balanced the earth's energy. We used those volcanoes for energy, heat. For—" Govannan shook his head. He couldn't tell this man those secrets. "We controlled the tension in the mantle through the Fire Stone." He looked at Cagliostro and his heart filled with the fire of that sacred mountain. "But you tore that balance to shreds when you went through time. Such an operation requires the most delicate attention. You've killed thousands of people."

Cagliostro laughed. "You're trying to tell me that I caused the fall of Atlantis? Don't be ridiculous." Cagliostro turned to his guard. "Take him back to his cell. Let him think about his options."

Mueller took Govannan by his arm and pulled him up. Govannan stumbled along next to him, blind to all but his grief. Mueller tossed him in his cell where he huddled in a corner and wept, wishing only that he could throw himself into the ocean and join his friends and family. When his eyes dried of their own accord, he built up the image of Megan as he'd last seen her, dressed in Pleiadean finery, her young face soft with joy and radiant with wonder, and he said his goodbyes, told her how he would have made love to her on all the worlds he'd ever visited, then imagined their children, born one by one, nurtured, loved, instructed. He saw those children growing up and going out to make their way in the world. He remembered his family, his friends, the other workers in the Crystal Matrix Chamber—and he said goodbye one by one. When he'd finished, he stretched out on the stone floor of his cell and offered his life to the Mother of All.

24

Michael sat in the living room of the Glastonbury house catching Garth up on his hunt for Atlantean crystals. "We never found the current holder of the Roerich artifacts, but received reassurance they were safe." The slanted rays of the afternoon sun hit his face and he squinted.

Anne got up and pulled the shade down, then turned on a few lamps. Arnold perched on the edge of an overstuffed chair, refusing to relax.

Michael looked at him. "Tell them what you found."

"The Illuminati have sent an agent to find them, but she's still investigating the false leads set up by Franz's group. But Cagliostro's the one who bears watching." His smile made him look like a wolf.

"He always bears watching," Garth muttered.

"He turned up back on Bimini right after the theft in India, which confirms our suspicions. Then he took some engineers from Black Ops out into the Atlantic. The next day he went out with only his bodyguard. Early the next morning, I took these." His laptop sat on the coffee table and he turned it around.

Garth and Anne leaned forward to peer at the screen. Ghostly silver shapes stood in the water. Something lay in the sand. "What's this?" Garth asked.

Arnold touched a button and a close up of the large crystal laying on its side came on the screen.

"That is the Tuaoi Stone," Michael said.

"Bloody hell." Garth put on his glasses to see better. "Are you certain, now?"

"I estimate the crystal to be over thirty feet tall," Arnold said. "Could be more. It's hard to tell how much of the base is buried without more sophisticated equipment. About twelve feet thick."

A low whistle came from Garth.

"Then I made a mistake." Arnold shook his head. "It's common practice to skip a day between extended dives, but not our Alex. I thought it would be safe for me to go see about the Roerich fragments, so I left the next day. But Cagliostro went out again. That night."

"What did he do?" Garth asked.

"We aren't sure," Michael answered. "We didn't hear about it until later. But the following evening, he flew to England. Cagliostro's holed up at his ancestral home."

"That's it then." Garth stood up in his excitement.

"What?" Anne asked.

"That's what I've been sensing. The feeling there's a door ajar. Remember me telling you?"

She nodded.

"He's used it. He's reactivated the Tuaoi Stone," Garth said.

"Maybe," Michael said, "let's think it through. What's likely to happen?"

Anne reached for the laptop and punched a few buttons. "Here's one thing."

Michael and Garth sat in front of the computer. Arnold walked behind the couch and leaned over the back.

Bermuda Triangle Claims Another Victim
Nassau

A fishing boat was reported missing two days ago just off the coast of New Providence. The search turned up nothing. No bad weather had been reported. Locals speculate that the famous Bermuda Triangle is to blame.

"I was out late that day," a fisherman who asked not to be identified reported. "We saw that funny lightning and dark clouds came up out of nowhere."

Michael looked up from the screen at Anne. "What paper is this?"

"*National Inquirer*," Garth said. "Isn't that—"

"Anne," Michael protested. "Be serious."

"Who else is going to report it?" She put a hand on her hip.

"But we don't know if it actually happened." Michael shook his head in dismissal.

"The local paper reported the same ship missing," she said.

Michael turned back to Garth. "What else?"

"Oh," Anne's eyebrows arched. "So, you admit that's something."

Garth hid a smile behind his huge hand. Arnold shrugged. Michael turned back to her. "OK, so a boat has disappeared. What else?" he repeated.

"It could be this is what's affecting White Spring," Garth said.

"But you said it's been running erratically for a few years now." The glint in Michael's eyes almost overcame his caution.

"Yes, but over the last couple of weeks it's been much worse. Then in the last two days, it's gushed and then dripped—" he scratched his beard, his gaze turned inward "—almost on a schedule."

Now accustomed to his long silences, they waited. After a few minutes, he looked up. "I think the Tuaoi Stone is cycling through some kind of energy fluctuation. Opening and closing some sort of gate. Maybe the Tor is in sync somehow, and it's showing up in White Spring."

"But I thought Glastonbury had a telluric link with Jerusalem," Michael said.

Garth nodded his approval, then held up his index finger. "And Atlantis."

"We need to put together a team of divers to lull our giant back to sleep," Michael said.

"Good man." Garth stood up. "I've got email addresses at my house."

Arnold looked up. "No email. Do you have phone numbers?"

"Well, yes," Garth said, "but people can also eavesdrop on phone calls, you know."

"Not on my watch," Arnold said.

"I'll just go and—"

The house shuttered. The lamp in the hallway swung like a pendulum from its cord. A few books fell from the desk in the office. Everyone stood stock still. After half a minute, everything settled down again.

"What was that?" Garth asked.

"An earthquake?" Michael looked around, frowning.

Anne walked into the office to turn on the radio. The front door burst open. Arnold ran into the hallway and pulled a revolver.

"Garth, the spring—Easy on." Bran stood in the hallway, hands in the air.

"He's all right, Arnold," Anne said.

Arnold tucked his gun away. Bran looked from him to Garth, who asked. "What's happened?"

Bran gave a little start, remembering his mission. "It's the spring. The water's stopped."

GOVANNAN HAD LAID himself on the earth, offering his life to the Mother of All, but it seemed She had other plans. As his body grew cold and his breath more shallow, a tiny seed of light glowed to life, as if She had blown on an ember in his chest. He reached to find the source of this sensation and his hand brushed against the small crystal point the Sirians had given him. Then, something answered the call of that crystal. A stream of energy reached out and touched him. Something deep, quiet, and immensely powerful.

He lifted his head and looked around, but saw only darkness. The touch took on weight and shape. He began to sense something out there in the darkness, some distance away, but there. Faint at first, ephemeral as a dream, then growing stronger. A pulse, an energy song, a heartbeat. Yes, a portal.

Govannan lifted his face toward the sky that he knew was still above him and asked for help, for the intervention of the Divine Ones, for a miracle. If somehow, beyond all hope and reason, he could get to this portal, then perhaps he too would do the unthinkable. After all, the worst had already happened. Thousands of years ago. He would travel back in time. He would go back to Eden and stop this destruction. At the very least he would save Megan. Or see her once again.

He walked over to the grated window and began to sing to a tiny spot of rusted metal. He sang of dissolution, of loss, of decay and despair. He poured his grief into that metal, and it began to crumble. Then it turned to dust. Govannan rested his hand on the grate, gathering his strength. Then he pushed. It gave way with a creak. He waited. No footsteps came, so he grabbed the ledge and pulled himself up. The slick metal of the window well gave his fingers no purchase. He jumped. On the third try, he caught the top of the well. A sharp edge tore his fingers open, reopening a wound, but he ignored the pain and hauled himself up to the ground.

He laid on the wet ground, reveling in the moisture, even the goose flesh from the chill. The portal pulled at him, a homing beacon. He got to his feet and loped across the lawn, heading toward it.

THAT AFTERNOON, Anne sat in the back of the Assembly Hall with Michael. The room buzzed with talk and tension. Even the peace of Glastonbury Abbey on the other side of the wall did nothing to calm the crowd. She leaned her head against Michael's shoulder, slightly queasy. Michael said his head ached and Garth had been snappy. The quake had disrupted Glastonbury in more ways than one.

Joanne Katter walked up on the stage and raised her hand for silence, but the best she got was a lull in the din. "Please everyone. We're here to heal Bridget's Spring."

"White Spring," someone shouted over the crowd noise, "and it belongs to the god." Everyone turned to look. He ducked before people could see him, but most of them were neighbors and knew who had spoken.

"Thank you, Glenn," Joanne said, "but we need to cooperate if we're going to get anything accomplished."

"Perhaps we need to acknowledge everyone's views," came a mild voice.

Anne recognized the well dressed man who she'd seen in the crowd at White Spring the first time there'd been trouble.

Joanne conceded this with a dip of her head. "Right you are, then." A door banged in the back of the hall. Garth and Bran came in with a few other people. Half the room cheered. The other half shook their heads and muttered. They sat in the front.

"Come up, Garth," Joanne said, a clinched smile on her face. "I'm sure many people will want to hear your perspective."

Garth stood up. "Thank you. But first, may I suggest we hear from Dr. Manly? He's been into the cave to assess the damage."

"Cave?" Anne whispered.

"You know, Merlin's Crystal Cave?" Michael asked.

"I thought it was a legend."

"It's real," he continued in a low voice. 'I just didn't know you could still get into it."

Dr. Manly mounted the stage. "With the permission of the British Heritage Foundation and the township of Glastonbury—" he began in a sonorous voice.

"If you've got the right connections, I guess," Michael said in her ear.

"—we went into the cave as soon as we could after the quake yesterday. This disturbance registered 4.5 on the Richter scale."

"That's nothing," came an American voice.

"Which our friends—" he emphasized this word "—in America are quite accustomed to, thank you." The interruption was quelled. "I am happy to report that there is no structural damage inside the Tor, as we had feared."

A general hubbub followed this. Dr. Manly waited for a moment, then spoke again in a voice that penetrated through the hall, but still seemed mild. Anne remembered Grandmother Elizabeth teaching her how to do that in political meetings. She regarded Dr. Manly with renewed interest.

"This leaves us with the problem of why no water flows through White Spring." He turned to the well dressed man toward the front. "We had wondered if the problem was with the pipes the Victorians installed, but found they are still intact."

The man nodded. Anne remembered that's what he'd been concerned about before.

Manly continued. "We shall have to replace them in the near future, but our immediate problem still remains. White Spring flows from the top of the aquifer. We think the quake shifted some rock, but that the water will work its way through again."

"How long?" someone shouted.

"It's difficult to know."

The crowd had quieted somewhat, although comments and side conversations still continued. Now shouts erupted. "No." "This science is bunk."

He spoke through the heckling. "I've pulled a few strings and the Royal Air Force has agreed to fly over and do some ground penetrating radar. This should give us a more complete picture." He smiled, expecting gratitude, but the crowd seemed ambivalent. He gathered himself up again. "Once this is done, we'll have a better estimate of when the water will return."

More shouts erupted. "We can't wait." "We need to do a ritual."

Garth had arrived on the stage and his size alone seemed to quiet people. He thanked Dr. Manly, then Joanne took over again. "Now the caretakers of Chalice Well have something to share with us." A man and a woman took the stage and reported that Red Spring seemed not to have been affected by the quake.

A woman dressed all in green behind Anne and Michael kept telling her companion what the problem was. "More people need to connect with the faery realm. We must balance with the Under World."

"We're planning to meet tonight," the man beside her answered. "We'll petition Gwyn."

Garth shouted over the racket. "We all agree that spiritual work must be done. Joanne and I have agreed to hold a joint ritual tomorrow." Both cheers and jeers went up. "We invite all groups to come. We need a concerted effort to heal the spring."

Shouts and questions rang out, and Garth tried to answer them all.

"Let's go back to the house," Michael said. "I'd like to see what Arnold's spies know about Cagliostro."

"I'd like to take a nap," she said. "I'm exhausted." On the way out the door, Anne spotted a vagrant huddled in a corner. Something about him pulled at her memory. His avid eyes and air of power were at odds with his torn clothes. A smudge of red that looked like blood spread across his cheek, but copious braids covered much of his face.

Anne tugged at Michael's shirt. "Do you see that man?"

"Just another crazy," Michael whispered. "The townsfolk will feed him."

"It's not that. I think I've seen him somewhere."

"Probably hanging around the spring. Let's go."

GOVANNAN WATCHED THE TALL, blond woman walk out the door. Her resemblance to Pleione was so strong it brought tears to his eyes. The portal still pulled at him, but the commotion had drawn him to this meeting. And the desire to blend in. Mueller must be looking for him by now. Cagliostro still had the translation crystal, but it was clear something was wrong in this town—something metaphysical. The room twanged with psychic power, mostly ill trained, at least by Atlantean standards. A few adepts sat around the room or stood on the stage, tranquil pools of finely honed senses. The woman who'd noticed him had power, exceptional ability even, but it flickered around her like a novice's did. One master who sat in the middle of the room eyed him from time to time, nodding when Govannan happened to catch her eye.

A man with matted hair sidled up to him and said something. His breath and clothes reeked. Govannan shook his head, hoping to convey that he didn't understand. The man rubbed his stomach, then mimicked eating. Govannan nodded vigorously. The man gestured for him to follow. They walked out through a courtyard, then crossed the street. Govannan stuck close to his new friend who dodged the speeding vehicles with aplomb. Safely on the other side, they went through down a covered walkway. The smell of food made Govannan's stomach gurgle, but they walked past the restaurant and sat at an abandoned table in an open eating area. One group of people cast hostile glances at them. Another conversed cheerfully with his new friend. Once they stood up to go, the vagrant moved to their table, gesturing for Govannan to follow. He started to eat what they'd left.

Shocked, Govannan stood to enter the restaurant and get a fresh plate, but his new friend shook his head and pulled on the shirt Mueller had given him. He was getting used to these funny clothes. The man pushed a plate with some greens and long, yellowish sticks toward him, then mimicked eating again. Govannan shrugged. He'd just have to make the best of things in this strange time. He picked up one of the sticks and bit into it. A little oily, but satisfying. The unfriendly people stood to go. Once they were out of sight, the vagrant grabbed their leftovers and brought them to their table.

Once they'd eaten the food left by three tables, the man stood up and gestured for him to follow. He wound his way up the hill, stopping behind a bakery to check for handouts, getting some round metal objects from people on the street or shopkeepers, which seemed to make him happy. Govannan tried to be patient, but as they made their way up the street, the magnetic draw of the portal grew stronger, lulling him into a mild trance. He allowed himself to be pulled along in the wake of his new friend, afraid that alone he might draw attention or do something that would put himself in jeopardy. Soon they were walking along a street with houses built right up to it, cars roaring by belching out the ubiquitous exhaust, his new friend jabbering away at him.

Then it hit him. It was like walking into a temple, but there were houses, roads, vehicles, people walking, then stopping and putting boxes in front of their faces. A chaos of activity, and it seemed few recognized the power pouring from the place in front of him. Then he saw the hill, the slopping terraced sides. The work of Atlantis—a sign of his old home. On top of this great portal stood a tower, a lone finger pointing to the sky. Tears ran down his face. His friend patted him on the back and talked some more, then took him by the hand and led him past a stone wall and around a corner.

A knot of people had gathered on a small terrace. They spilled out into the street. His friend walked up to a large metal box, lifted the lid and started poking through what looked like garbage. Govannan followed the power of the portal to a squat, stone building where the people milled around. It seemed they did recognize the energy after all. They just didn't know what to do with it. He made his way through the crowd over to a wall reinforcing a hillside and searched until he found a place where the ground peeked through. Placing his hands flat on the earth, he closed his eyes and the portal opened his sight. Glorious crystals and geodes filled the hill—long points shot up from the ground or hung from the ceiling above a flat body of water. But something was wrong, the energy was blocked. Some being in a deeper frequency had set up a wall to stop—what? He allowed his consciousness to sink deeper. Yes, there it was, a loop. That fool Cagliostro had created a time loop. He wasn't surprised. Wasn't this the fallen time? Hadn't consciousness waned? But he could close it—after he went back home. He'd do it tonight, while the town slept.

Relieved, Govannan settled down with his back against the stone of the building and closed his eyes. Someone put a warm blanket over him. He looked up into the smiling face of a woman with long brown hair. She spoke with his new friend for a while, pulled a blanket out of her pack for him, then left them alone. The crowd began to thin as the sun set, and his friend made a make-shift shelter for them. He unrolled some bedding and patted one side, offering it to Govannan. He lay down beside him and closed his eyes, pretending to sleep. Just when he thought the coast was clear, another knot of people would arrive. He'd sleep a while, he decided, and wake up deep in the night so he could do his work unimpeded.

Govannan dreamed that he sat at a long table with a host of laughing beings, that he ate the most delicious food he'd ever tasted and drank wine that had captured starlight. A dark haired man who lived among them took out a harp and sang a song that mended for a time the gaping wound that was his heart.

25

Caitir listened to the last of her mother's story, which she'd heard many times before—how they'd sailed through a world dark with volcanic ash, then found the village in Avalon destroyed by high waves. Miraculously, the vigil hut had survived, and the stand of yews. Many of her friends had been washed out to sea, yet the Lady Winifred had survived, but changed, already tuning to the other world, sometimes blind to this one. When the skies cleared, they realized the earth had tilted. The stars were askew in the heavens. They rebuilt the village, and soon discovered that the seasons were more pronounced, the summers hot and wet, the winters so cold as to freeze the rain and bring snow instead. Even later they learned that they aged more quickly. Their minds became a jumble and it took much more effort to do the spiritual work that before had come like breath. But worst was that Megan had never seen Govannan again.

Caitir also listened to her mother's lungs filling with fluid. Megan coughed and coughed, but got no relief. Fever replaced chills, then fever came again. She would not live through the night. Her mother would be gone by the time she returned from this final initiation that would prepare her to take her mother's place as the Keeper of the Key. Caitir fought back tears. She would miss her crotchety old ways, miss watching her own children climb on their grandmother's lap, heedless of her rank.

Megan took another ragged breath, then said, "The time has come. Go to the sentinels, sing the song that I have taught you, and the Tor will open for you." These last words filled Megan's withered face with a luminous awe.

Caitir leaned forward and took her mother in her arms. Truly, she was as light as a bird. "Thank you for—" then her voice broke.

"For what? I have done what any mother would do. You know this yourself."

Caitir nodded, tears streaming down her face, her shoulders heaving with her sobs.

Megan patted her just as she had when she'd been a child, sobbing her eyes out when she'd found a dead bird or scraped her knee. "There, there, child. I will be as close as a thought." Suddenly, the frail form straightened and her voice deepened. "Go now."

Caitir scrambled up and pulled her cloak around her. She looked once more, but all she saw was the Morgen, the eyes filmed over, the face imperious. Her own mother had vanished.

Outside, the smells of flowers filled the late spring night air. She walked, head down, to White Spring where she bent and washed the tears from her face with the sacred water. She stayed there, gathering her intention for this ceremony. She would begin a long line of women for whom the golden era was only a fable, not a memory. Then Caitir stood, squared her shoulders and walked into the mouth of the cave.

A CLAW GRABBED Govannan's shoulder and hauled him away from the golden world he'd gone to in his dream. He opened his eyes to Cagliostro's face contorted with rage. "How dare you? How dare you try to get away from me?"

Govannan understood him, which meant he'd brought the translation crystal.

"Do you know how long I've searched? Do you know how difficult it was to find the Fire Stone, to learn to use it? And for what, you ungrateful son of a bitch?"

Govannan stared up into the eyes of the man who'd hauled him through time, destroying his home in the process, and who now had tracked him down when he was on the verge of escape. What he saw chilled him to the bone.

Cagliostro glazed eyes slid away from his. They looked through him, into a world his fevered imagination had concocted. His mind had come unhinged. And his madness had set loose a deeper, darker power, an instinctual intelligence, like a domestic cat gone feral.

"Stand up. You're coming with me." Cagliostro reached down and jerked Govannan up with an unnatural strength unleashed by his madness.

"Don't hurt me, man." Govannan whirled around to see Mueller pulling his new friend out of his nest of blankets. "Don't hurt me." The vagrant crouched, his hands protecting his head.

Govannan cursed himself for delaying. He should have gone ahead. Even with people around, he should have opened the portal and gone home to Atlantis, to Megan. Now it was too late.

"Inside," Cagliostro commanded.

Govannan shook the door. "It's locked."

"You can talk," said the astonished vagrant.

"Shut up," Cagliostro snarled. He grabbed the handle and jerked the door off its frame.

Govannan stared. What had happened to this man?

Mueller pointed his beloved piece of metal at them both. "Inside."

The vagrant raised his hands. "Don't shoot me, man. I don't want to die. Please."

"I said shut up." Cagliostro's tone sealed the man's mouth.

They walked into the darkness of the well house, stumbling down a short flight of stairs onto a flagstone floor. Cagliostro switched on some kind of torch and shone it around. Stone walls, aqueducts and black wrought iron steps flashed out of the dark.

The raw power of the place beat like the wild heart of a stag, opening Govannan's shriveled scenes like a morning glory in the first rays of the sun. He threw his head back, his mane of hair slapping his shoulders.

"You must take me to the city. I have to find her."

"Who?"

Cagliostro groaned. "The woman with the red hair."

"I don't know what you're talking about," Govannan said evenly.

318

A howl of agony rose from Cagliostro. "Now." He walked to the back wall and pointed. "Here."

"What do you want?" Govannan repeated, but Cagliostro turned to Mueller. "It's here." Mueller took out a pick axe and swung it at the wall.

"Man, what are you doing?" the vagrant yelled.

A few more swings opened a hole in the wall large enough for them to crawl through.

Yes, thought Govannan, *yes. Deeper. We must go deeper.*

"Stay here," Cagliostro said to Mueller. "Don't let anybody in."

"What about me—" the vagrant turned white when he saw Cagliostro's expression.

"Watch him. Kill him if he gets in the way."

SOMETHING WOKE ANNE. She listened, but heard nothing except the ticking of the grandfather clock in the hall downstairs. Michael slept, his breath deep and even. An eerie light filled the bedroom. Terrified to look, more terrified not to, she sat up. They were everywhere—hounds, white with red spots, red ears, red paws, and those uncanny blue eyes, eyes that were lit tonight with an otherworldly glow.

The female who had visited Anne before stepped forward and licked her hand. Then the hound walked through the bedroom and out into the hall, the rest of the pack flowing around her. They glided down the steps, moving like ghosts. The female stopped and looked back at her, then whined. One eerie note.

Anne shook Michael, but he slept as one under a spell. They were here to help, she knew this. She'd have to go alone. Anne jumped up and threw on the clothes she'd left at the foot of the bed, then followed the female. The pack waited in the downstairs hallway, their red tongues lolling from their open mouths. When the third step squeaked under her weight, they flowed into the kitchen, then turned and poured down the basement steps, their nails making no sound on the wood. Anne followed, oddly calm. She knew already what she'd find. She walked to the back of the basement, ducked her head and entered the tunnel. The ancient oak door stood open. A faint light glowed from inside. The pack streamed through the open door, the female waiting for Anne. Her heart pounding, she followed.

MEGAN'S CHEST rattled with each painful breath. Suddenly, the room grew brighter. A light had formed in the middle of the room, so bright it should hurt her eyes, but she found it soothing. She struggled to raise her head to call the healer, but the room was empty. Was she out of her body already? Was this the other world beckoning her? Then she saw him—Govannan as he'd been, his shoulders roped with muscle, his hair braided with shells and beads. He reached his hand out to her. Her long dead lover had come for her.

"Get up, silly. It's time."

"Govannan." Megan sat up. "Is that you?" Somehow she rose from her bed and staggered forward, but he was gone. She pushed the door open, panting with the effort, and called his name into the dark night. He didn't answer.

But then a light flashed amongst the trees. She stumbled toward it, but when she arrived at the spot where the light had been, it was gone. Then it reappeared farther into the forest. She leaned against an old oak, panting until she could move again. Megan struggled through the woods, the light leading her, until she came to White Spring. She fell to the ground. "Govannan," she called, but her voice was only a wisp of sound. She lay there, her body half in the stream.

I'll catch my death, she thought, then started to laugh. She'd done that already. Megan took a sip of the sacred liquid of the spring, then splashed her face. The water sang in her frail body, giving her the energy to rise again.

Now the light glowed inside the mouth of the cave. But this was Caitir's night, the eve of Beltane, the night she sat vigil while the others had made their way to Avebury for the ceremony, now a journey of two days. The Crystal Cave belonged to her daughter tonight.

A dark haired man stepped from the light, his hand out, the same man who had led her to the table of the faery court the night she'd sought her first vision here as a young girl. "Come," he said. And she found she could walk easily.

GARTH SAT bolt upright in bed. He'd only just gotten to sleep after hours of meetings, then meditation with Bran and his group. It was happening, now. His body, mind and spirit sang with power. He had to get into the Tor. He threw on his clothes and rushed down the hill to Anne's house. The front door was locked. He tried his key, but it no longer fit. That's right, she'd changed the locks after the burglary. Garth pounded on the door, the stained glass with the red and white roses rattling in its frame. After a minute, the light in the hallway came on and Michael appeared, his hair sticking up from sleep, his eyes squinting.

He flung open the door. "She's gone. Anne's gone," he shouted.

Garth went straight to the kitchen where they found the door to the basement open. "I knew it."

"What?"

"They've come for her."

"The Illuminati?"

Garth shook his head. "Follow me."

The two men rushed down the stairs and Garth headed to the back of the basement. At the end of the small tunnel, the rounded oak door stood open.

Michael stopped dead in his tracks. "But . . ." He turned to Garth.

"The ceremony has begun. Let's go." And he ducked through the low entrance with Michael on his heels.

Garth had never used this entrance to the cave before. A few feet in, the tight tunnel opened up. A few more steps and they came to a spiral staircase leading downwards. Garth started down. Michael followed with no hesitation. The stairs took them to a larger tunnel, the remnants of an ancient cave. A stream bed, still damp, led deeper into the hill. They followed it to a fork and heard voices coming from the left.

CAGLIOSTRO'S TORCH revealed packed dirt walls interlaced with roots. Deeper in, the soil gave way to black rock. A faint light glowed at the end of the tunnel, calling to them, and they all moved toward it without any need for coercion, each drawn by a promise, a hope, a memory just now surfacing. The light inside the cave brightened. Cagliostro let his torch slip from his hand. They entered a large chamber. In the middle knelt a woman. Her long, red hair fell in lustrous waves down her back.

A strangled cry sprang from Cagliostro and he ran forward. "I've found you." He reached for her, but she recoiled.

"Who are you?" she demanded. "What are you doing here on this sacred night?"

"Don't you remember me?" Cagliostro grabbed her arm.

"You have violated the sanctuary of the Lady of Avalon."

Cagliostro looked into her face, then snarled with rage. "What have you done with her?" He moved behind her as quick as a snake strikes. A flash of silver showed a knife at her throat. "I asked you a question."

"Let my daughter go."

They all looked to find an old woman standing in the entrance, her long, crooked finger pointing at Cagliostro, her eyes filming over, a nimbus of power surrounding her.

Govannan took a step toward her. "Be careful. He's dangerous."

Her eyes cleared. She stared. "Govannan?" The hope in her voice tore their hearts.

There was something about that voice. Govannan looked at her more closely.

"Nobody move." Cagliostro moved the knife closer to the woman's throat. A thin line of red appeared. "Where is she?"

"Who has brought this weapon of iron into my domain?" This voice touched something deep in each of their minds. All eyes turned to a tall, blond being who stood where a wall had been before. Behind him thronged a host of laughing beings, their clothes rich in velvet and silk, their hair filled with flowers, ribbons and gem stones. Some carried bows and arrows, others horns, still others harps. Behind them stretched a green lawn and farther in the distance a forest of trees the like of which could never be seen on earth.

A pack of white hounds with red ears and tails streamed from the entrance to the chamber up to this being, their tails a blur. They howled, a sound that brought dread to every human present. A woman came running after them, then stopped dead when she saw the host of faeries, her eyes wide. Two men ran in behind her. One called her name, and she went and stood between them.

All gaped at the spectacle before them.

Except the old woman. Even in the presence of the fae, she tottered closer to Govannan. With each step, she grew stronger. And younger. "My love. What happened to you? You disappeared, and then—" Tears flowed down her face.

The faery host listened, their faces intent. And their eyes, always their eyes.

The years fell away from her with each step toward him. Govannan's heart gave a lurch. "Megan?" He took a faltering step toward her. "How did you—"

She drew closer still. "You disappeared. Was it him?" She pointed to Cagliostro, who stared at her. "Was it this man who stole you from me and ripped a hole in time itself?"

"Yes," Govannan said. "But what has happened to you?"

"Father?" The red-haired woman held by Cagliostro leaned toward him, heedless of the knife. She looked at Megan. "Is this my father?"

The tall, blond faery turned his attention back to Cagliostro. "Brother?" he asked

Cagliostro looked as if he were a gong that had been struck. He blinked.

"Do you not know me, brother?"

Cagliostro stared at him, dumbfounded.

"Do you not know yourself?"

And then he too began to change. Something in his face. His chin seemed longer, his ears took on a slant, and his eyes. His eyes cleared. "Gwyn."

"Gwyn ap Nudd." Garth stepped forward. "The Lord of the Faeries. It is an honor to be in your presence."

Gwyn swung his magnificent head around and smiled at Garth. "My friend who has guarded this place. It is I who am honored."

"But—" Megan pointed to the being who had been Cagliostro. "I saw you ride out with the Wild Hunt."

The white and red hounds swarmed around Cagliostro and licked his hands.

Laughter floated from behind the faery host, the smell of flowers wafted through the air, and the sound of bells. The host parted and a light appeared amongst them. Then a shape formed in the light and the most beautiful faery of them all stepped forward, her skin alabaster, her lips mulberries, and her hair—red curls the color of flame. She put out her delicate hand and called him by name. "Gwythr ap Greidawl."

Cagliostro dropped the knife with a clatter on the stone floor of the cavern.

"What have you brought me, my love? You rode out only this morning, but I have missed you sorely."

Gwyn smiled at her as if this weren't quite true.

"My love," said Gwythr who had long ago named himself Alexander Cagliostro in search of a worthy name. Tears streamed from his eyes. "It seems much longer than a day." He walked toward her, touched her hand, and the transformation was complete. The loss, the confusion, time itself fell from him. With a shake of his head, his tears turned to laughter. "It seems more an age."

Gwyn reached a hand out to her. "Blodeuwedd," he cried, the yearning thick in his voice.

But she had eyes now only for his brother, who turned to him and said, "Now is my time to rule."

Gwyn's face darkened dangerously, but the couple walked away, their hands intertwined, their faces close, whispering to each other. Gwyn watched them go.

"What's happening?" Anne whispered. "Who's Blodeuwedd?"

"The Maiden of Flowers. There is a faerytale that on May Day, two brothers fight for her love," Michael said.

"A faerytale?" she smiled. "Then it must be true."

Blodeuwedd and Gwythr disappeared beneath the trees. Gwyn gave himself a shake. After a moment, his face relaxed and he turned his attention to his guests. "Caitir, Lady of Avalon."

She stepped forward.

Gwyn stretched out his hand and she seemed to know what to do. She took a necklace from around her neck and placed it in his hand. He closed his hand over it for a moment, then opened his fingers. The crystal, all aglow with rainbows, gradually cleared. She placed it around her neck again.

"This key will see you through the dark times to come. Call upon me and I will aid you."

She dipped her knee to him, then stood straight.

He surveyed them all. "Now, you must all return to your own times."

"But I have no home to go to, my Lord," Govannan said.

"And I have just left my death bed," Megan added.

Gwyn surveyed the two for a moment. "Then you may stay with us."

"My Lord, how could we accept such an honor?" Govannan began.

"I insist," the Faery Lord said.

They bowed their heads, then turned to their daughter, whose eyes shone. Govannan embraced her. After a moment, she pulled back and he held her at arms length. "You are the light of my heart," he said. "If only I could go back and see you born. Be a father to you."

Caitir shook her head. "It is well that I have met you—and enough that you two can finally be together."

Megan took her hands. "Keep the stone and the story. Pass it on. Keep the teachings of Avalon."

Tears of joy sparkled in her eyes. "I will, Mother."

"And remember, we are just here, inside the Tor."

Caitir turned to walk out of the Crystal Cave, but paused when she passed Anne. They both touched the crystal around their necks, as if one looked in a mirror and the other faithfully reflected her.

Anne smiled. "You will succeed."

Caitir frowned, confused for a moment.

"Your vigil through the darkness," Anne explained. "You will bring us to the light."

Caitir reached out and touched her face. "Thank you, daughter." Then she walked out of the cavern.

Gwyn turned to Garth. "You have earned a boon. What would you ask?"

Garth spread his hands. "You know my heart, Lord."

Gwyn's laugh warmed the cavern. "Then it is done." He stepped aside, a mischievous smile on his face, and behind him stood figures of light. One stepped forward, and her features formed to become a tall, willowy woman with reddish blond hair in her prime.

"Cynthia," Garth cried. He ran to her, picked her up in his arms, and twirled her around. "I thought I had lost you."

"How could you lose me?" she answered, then he stopped her words with his lips.

Gwyn turned to Anne and Michael. He stretched out his hand. Understanding, they slid their crystals from around their necks and laid them side by side in his palm. He closed his fingers over the stones, then looked deeply into their faces. "But you two have more to do before the light is assured." He returned their crystal keys.

"Thank you, my Lord," Michael said.

Anne dipped her head. Her family had taught her how to treat royalty.

"There is one more thing." Gwyn smiled at them, his expression playful. "On Samhein, we hunt the souls of the dead. But on this night, the eve of Beltane, souls wishing to be born come through our realm." He placed his hand over Anne's womb. "A great being is coming to you."

"Oh," Anne murmured. The reason for her nausea and fatigue now came clear to her.

"You mean?" Michael began.

"Guard this one well," Gwyn said.

Then the great being turned and walked across the green lawn with Garth and Cynthia.

In the distance, close to the forest stood another form. He waved and his face suddenly became clear.

"Thomas?" Anne ran forward, but a look from Gwyn told her that she was not invited to enter faeryland.

"Remember," Thomas called, "we are just here, inside the Tor."

And with a snap, the fae and their guests disappeared. Anne and Michael stood in the dark womb of the Tor, holding each other. Dark except for the nine Sentinel Stones that stood around the perimeter, glowing faintly.

"A baby," he breathed into her ear.

She nodded. "Do you think these sentinels are safe?"

Michael nuzzled against her. "They've been here for eleven thousand years. I'd say so."

"Good. Let's go home."

They walked out of the cavern into the tunnel where more light reached, from what source they couldn't tell. They found the stairs, climbed up and went through the rounded, oak door into the cellar. The door closed behind them and locked itself.

Anne regarded it for a long moment. "I guess we can't sell this house."

"No kidding," Michael said.

Outside, the sun had risen. Suddenly ravenous, they walked into town and bought pasties at Burns the Bread. They went down to the end of High Street and bought coffee, then sat outside at a table, watching the perfectly ordinary events of a Glastonbury morning unfold around them. A man watered the flower boxes hanging from the second stories of the buildings with a long hose. The pigeons pecked at their feet. Tourists began to mill about. Another store opened its doors.

They returned home to a great jubilation. White Spring gushed, and the pipe from Red Spring just across the small lane had joined with her mate. Red and white water poured forth for all to drink. People went back to their houses and returned with jugs to fill. Life was returning to normal.

That evening, when the Beltane Fire burned bright in a tall pyramid on top of the Tor and the celebrants danced around it, Michael and Anne walked down to White Spring and watched the water gush from the pipes.

Anne turned to him. "That was some vacation."

He laughed and took her in his arms.

Get A Free Power Places Novel &
Free Short Story

Building a relationship with my readers is the very best thing about writing. I occasionally send newsletters with details on new releases, special offers and other bits of news relating to the Power Place series and my other books. And if you sign up to the mailing list I'll send you this free Milton content:

1. A free copy of the first Power Places novel, *Under the Stone Paw.*

2. A free copy of "The Judgment of Osiris," a short story set in Egypt.

You can get your book & story **for free** by signing up at https://dl.bookfunnel.com/a8u8t9wm9w.

Enjoy this book?
You can make a big difference

Reviews are the most powerful tools in my arsenal when it comes getting attention for my books. Much as I'd like to, I don't have the financial muscle of a New York publisher. I can't take out full page ads in the newspaper or put posters on the subway.

(Not yet, anyway.)

But I do have something much more powerful and effective than that, and it's something that those publishers would kill to get their hands on.

A committed and loyal bunch of readers.

Honest reviews of my books help bring them to the attention of other readers.

If you've enjoyed this book I would be very grateful if you could spend just five minutes leaving a review (it can be as short as you like) on the book's Amazon page.

Thank you very much.

About the Author

Theresa Crater brings ancient temples, lost civilizations, and secret societies back to life in her visionary fiction. She is the author of the Power Places series as well as stand-alone novels. Her short stories explore ancient myth brought into the present day.

For more information:

www.theresalcrater.com

theresa@theresalcrater.com

Also by Theresa Crater
Have you read them all?

In the Power Places Series

Under the Stone Paw

Anne Le Clair, a successful, young attorney, has always managed to remain free from her family's gothic past—until now. When she inherits her eccentric aunt's antique necklace though, she finds no escape from its secrets. Anne is immersed in a crash course of forbidden wisdom, secret societies, and her family's own legacy. She soon discovers that her aunt's necklace is one of just six powerful "keys" that, when combined with the other five at the appointed time, unlocks the legendary Hall of Records. However, another group, the shadowy Illuminati, is working behind the scenes to uncover the same powerful secrets—and make them their own.

Buy *Under the Stone Paw*

Beneath the Hallowed Hill

Anne Le Clair travels to Glastonbury with her fiancée, Egyptologist and mystic Michael Levy, to investigate a house she inherited from a mysterious aunt…only to find trouble waiting. One of Avalon's sacred twin springs is failing. Together, Anne and Michael try to restore the water flow, but discover there is much more at stake: the Illuminati master Alexander Cagliostro has activated an ancient crystal tower, tearing a hole in time which threatens much more than one sacred spring. Meanwhile, in ancient Atlantis, Megan, priestess of the Crystal Matrix Chamber, flees the destruction of her world carrying with herself a vital artifact.

Buy *Beneath the Hallowed Hill*

Return of the Grail King

The long-awaited King Arthur returns to be reborn in the 21st century, but an old enemy from the past rises to stop him. Anne and Michael must return to Arthurian England to rectify an old mistake.

Buy *Return of the Grail King*

Stand-Alones

The Star Family

Jane Frey inherits a Gothic mansion filled with unexpected treasures. A prophecy claims it hides an important artifact – the key to an energy grid laid down by the Founding Fathers themselves. Whoever controls this grid controls the very centers of world power. Except Jane has no idea what they're looking for.

Buy *The Star Family*

Historicals

School of Hard Knocks

When Maggie Winters is asked to perform an exorcism on a young child, she finds the problem traces all the way back to the tragedy that ended her own childhood. Will appeal to readers of The Secret Life of Bees and The Help. "Crater's prose is accomplished and her story engaging." Kirkus Review

Buy *School of Hard Knocks*

God in a Box

It's the guru invasion of the 1980s. After spending her life savings to fly to Europe and become a meditation teacher, Stacey is told to go home. Lesbians are not welcome. She's lost the love of her life already. Will she lose the other half of her dreams now?

Buy *God in a Box*

Acknowledgments

I would like to thank T.L. Morganfield for her critique and Ark Redwood, the head gardener at Chalice Well in Glastonbury, for his corrections about the garden there. All mistakes are mine. Special thanks to Stephen Mehler for his unflagging support, and to my mother for everything.

RETURN OF THE GRAIL KING

The Power Places Series

Theresa Crater

An Excerpt

Prologue

Sand drifted down from the cave ceiling and settled on Hashem Sayeed's blue cotton shirt. He straightened as much as he could and brushed off his shoulders. Ali and Moustafa paused in their digging, hunched under the low dirt ceiling. They listened.

Silence.

Hashem gave a nod, picked up his spade, and went back to cleaning the earth from around a large stone. Ali and Moustafa filled sacks with dirt they'd cleared. They'd been digging this tunnel for a few months, working their way at a steady downward angle, and finally found rock. Behind rock, there was usually a tomb. In a tomb, artifacts. Ancient statues. His family could hawk the small figurines of the gods and *ushabtis* to the tourists, such as they were. The Giza Plateau had been practically empty since the revolution. Nothing like the old days when you could barely shoulder your way through the crowds. But things were picking up again.

Hashem stabbed his spade into the red earth, venting his frustration and hunger. He hoped for a large sculpture, perhaps two or three. Rings with gems, ancient necklaces. Maybe even gold. Something for the black market to tide them over for a year or more. Until the rest of the world realized Egypt was safe and came back. He'd sell this house, buy something in Abu Sir, put his feet up, and watch his grandchildren play in the pool he'd build. Just like those big hotels down the street from his house. He smiled and shook his head at this. The crooks in the black market never paid a fair price, but what choice did he have? At least they would eat.

His spade pushed through the dirt into emptiness. A rush of musty, stale air pushed through the opening.

He rocked back on his heels and shouted, *"Alhamdulillah."*

Ali threw down his shovel. "What?"

"A tomb, son. *Inshalla.*"

The three crowded close, pulling the earth away with their hands, pounding at the hard places with the spade. Once they'd cleared a large enough spy hole, Hashem shined his flashlight through. He pushed his face up, moved the beam of the light around. Something flashed in one corner. He angled the light toward it. Gold glinted in the darkness.

"Alhamdulillah," he shouted again.

Moustafa pushed his face to the hole, pointed the flashlight around, then looked back at his brother. "We've found gold."

"What is it?" Fatimah's voice came down to them from the hole in the back of the kitchen where they'd dug.

Hashem crawled toward her and stuck his head and shoulders out. "A tomb."

She threw her arms up. *"Alhamdulillah."*

Hashem reached up, and she leaned down to throw her arms around his neck. This time she didn't make a fuss about how dirty he was. She poured him a cup of water and he drank it thirstily, then crouched and crawled back down the passage.

Ali had already doubled the size of the opening. Hashem kicked the small pile of debris to the other side of the tunnel. They'd clean up later. He picked up the shovel and dug as close to Ali's knees as he dared. Moustafa disappeared into the house and came back with a hammer and another spade.

After another fifteen minutes of digging, the hole widened enough to allow a man to pass sideways. Ali and Moustafa stepped back. "You first," Moustafa said. "It was your find."

Hashem clasped his hand to his heart. "There will be enough for us all, my brother."

"Inshalla," they both answered at once, but this time more from habit, because they had seen the gold and the statues and the gleam of a painted wood coffin in the corner.

Hashem stepped in. Fatimah couldn't wait any longer and came down to watch. She passed in a lantern. The light bounced off a large gold statue, hands folded in front. The head gave off a bluish tint. Finely chiseled feathers covered the body and the graceful lines of a many-tiered menit encircled its neck. The hands held a staff topped by a djed pillar and an ankh.

"Ptah," Hashem breathed. Even he recognized this god.

As if in response, the jet eyes of the figure seemed to shift in the light.

Hashem pulled back with a start. The others had crept in as he stood mesmerized by the statue. To his right, Ali reached out and gingerly picked up a bowl from a carved niche in the wall. He turned it upside down and held it to the light of the lantern on the ground next to his father's feet. Translucent yellow, thin and flawless. Finest alabaster.

Moustafa leaned over the coffin in the corner and rubbed the wood with the edge of his beige shirt. He could just make out features. It looked like a man's painted face, probably somebody important since this whole tomb seemed to hold only one mummy.

A loud rumble came from below their feet. Then the growl of rock filled the chamber. Hashem grabbed Fatima and rushed for the opening, Ali and Moustafa close behind. A cloud of dust rushed toward them, clogging their noses. Grit burned their eyes.

Hashem pushed his wife up the passageway, but the floor tilted. Fatima screamed and fell. Hashem took a breath of air and grit, trying to shout, but the ceiling fell in before he could let out a cry.

Above ground, the wall of the house crumbled up to the third story and slid into the pit. A huge plume of dust rose along with the screams of children. Then silence, followed by the barks of the neighborhood dog pack.

Lights switched on in the surrounding houses. Neighbors swarmed into the streets, pulling their clothes on as they ran. But they were too late. Where Hashem's house had stood, the mouth of a cave showed black against the greying horizon. The people gaped in silence for a moment, not believing their eyes.

The lone voice of the muezzin from a mosque several blocks away lifted into the coming morning as if in blessing.

Chapter 1

Michael Levy quietly closed the book he'd been showing to Anne and tucked the alpaca throw around her now sleeping form. She'd been doing that a lot this late in her pregnancy—just dropping off in the middle of a conversation. He gently pushed the soft wool under her rotund belly, tight as a tick who'd feasted undiscovered. He frowned at the unbidden thought. This was his child he was thinking about after all. Boy or girl—they'd elected not to know.

He picked up the 1458 edition of *The Book of the Sacred Magic of Abra-Melin the Mage* and replaced it inside the small glass case they kept it in. The Le Clair library, filled with rare books and ancient manuscripts, not to mention all the important texts of esoteric literature, could content Michael for the rest of his life. Except he wanted to add some books on Egypt and archaeology. Michael had left his position at the Metropolitan Museum when he and Anne married. The Le Clair fortune made him not just secure, but able to do the kind of collecting he'd always dreamed about. He stayed involved in his field, though, consulting with his colleagues at the Met and Smithsonian, the Natural History Museum, and occasionally the British Museum. Another dream come true.

He returned to his seat by the fire and reached for coffee, but found nothing. How many cups had he already had this morning? Should he ring for some? He still couldn't get used to having servants, but Grandmother Elizabeth told him she wouldn't get rid of excellent workers whose family had been with hers for several generations just to satisfy his plebeian sensibilities. "Besides, the economy is still in recovery," she'd added. That he'd even considered calling a servant for coffee told him how much he'd already assimilated.

His cell phone vibrated across the table. Grateful it was on mute, he grabbed it up before it woke Anne and walked out into the hall, closing the door quietly behind him. The name on the screen surprised him.

Azizi Tau. The guide and security expert Michael always added to his entourage in Egypt. Second only to Tahir Nur Ahram, the indigenous wisdom keeper also trained in Western archaeology and Egyptology.

Michael took a few more steps away from the library door and answered. "Hello, my friend. What a surprise!"

"I'm glad I caught you," Azizi said. "Have you seen the news?"

"No. What's happened?" Michael walked back down the hall to a family room that had a television.

"A house collapsed this morning on the edge of the Giza Plateau. The family was digging underneath the foundation for artifacts—"

"Like everybody," Michael quipped.

Azizi gave a short laugh. "Yes, except this time it got a bunch of people killed. Only the family on the top floor survived, a niece and her children. The husband was in the tunnel though."

Michael switched on CNN, but they were covering US politics. BBC World Service News showed a crowd of soldiers circling a blocked part of the road that ran next to the Sphinx enclosure. A large group of people milled around in front.

"That's terrible." He waited. Azizi had not called to tell him this news.

"The military has cordoned off the area. The thing is, the collapse opened a huge underground cavern. We've found tombs on the periphery, but further in are ceremonial chambers. Lots of artifacts."

"Exciting." Michael grimaced at his enthusiasm. "Except for the tragedy."

"Of course." Azizi's tone was dismissive. Egyptians took births and deaths much more in their stride. Sometimes Michael appreciated their more philosophical view.

"We need you, Michael. Even with the stability of the new government, the Antiquities Department is still recovering from the Revolution. The

President didn't want to just reappoint all the old crew."

"Amazing he cares about the appearance of corruption."

Azizi didn't answer immediately. Michael chided himself for speaking so openly. People in Egypt had to watch their backs again. Be careful what they said about the new regime. "The President is doing an excellent job," he said for any listening ears.

"Yes, he is," Azizi parroted back.

"I'd love to come, but we're expecting a baby."

"Mabrouk. A son? Is he your first?"

"We don't know if it's a boy or girl. The baby hasn't been born yet, but Anne is due very soon."

This silence was different. Clearly Azizi thought that was plenty of time, plus what did birth have to do with fathers?

"I could probably come for a couple of days. That's all," Michael found himself saying to bridge this cultural gap. The find intrigued him, but he wondered how Anne would take this.

"Excellent. I will book a room for you in the Mena House."

"Thank you, Azizi."

"When can we expect you?"

"Day after tomorrow, I suppose. I'll text to confirm."

"Of course you should go." Anne waved her hand at him as if to dismiss him already. "I'm fine. Honestly, you and Grandmother treat me like I'm some fragile Ming vase. Women have been having babies for thousands of years now, in case you didn't know."

Michael mimicked shock. "Is that so?"

She repeated this every time he asked about the trip during the day and while he packed the next morning.

"I promise not to take long." He headed toward the closet for a couple more shirts to add to his suitcase, but Anne caught his arm when he walked by the bed and pulled him to her. She planted a sloppy kiss on his cheek. He turned his head and found her lips, touching delicately at first, but she deepened the kiss, locking her arms around his neck. She leaned back, taking him with her.

Michael caught himself before he fell, steading himself with a hand on either side of her face. He stared down into those sapphire eyes, his torso just brushing her pregnant belly, then settled behind her and laid his hand on her stomach. The child stirred, then gave a kick. Michael pulled his hand away, but Anne took it and held it against the ripple beneath the skin.

"It doesn't hurt when he does that?"

"No, only when she gets mad if I'm sleeping on my back. Then she kicks until I wake up and move."

He pushed his face into her waves of blond hair at her neck. "She must have a temper."

"He's stubborn, like you." She turned in his arms. Her kiss was genial.

"I'd better get going," he said, but didn't move.

"Don't worry. We'll be fine. We'll wait for you to come back."

"It's just that—"

"You should go."

"It's a first for me. Not wanting to go to Egypt."

She laughed and pushed against his chest.

Michael kissed her forehead and headed into the bathroom to check for last-minute toiletries. He usually kept a travel kit packed, but had been home for the winter holidays and hadn't planned on traveling until well after the baby was born. He threw in an extra tube of toothpaste and slipped a packet of homeopathic tablets to help with jet lag into his front pocket.

Back in their bedroom, Anne held up the lid of his suitcase. He tossed in the toiletries bag and she zipped the case shut. "I left you a surprise."

They walked hand in hand down to the car.

The Le Clair family private jet pulled in next to a larger Gulfstream with the Oman flag painted on the side. Uniformed soldiers stood on either side of the tail of that plane, their guns holstered on one side, swords gleaming in scabbards on the other. Michael nodded at them as he disembarked, but neither moved a muscle. The sun burned down and the temperature had been reported at 95 Fahrenheit, hot for late January.

Azizi had sent one of his helpers to expedite the visa process. A bored guard finally stamped his passport after waiting in line for half an hour, and they headed out to the terminal. Michael grabbed a cup of coffee before they jumped into the waiting Nissan. Azizi's helper seemed young, so Michael didn't ask him any questions about the situation. He tuned out the young man, who pointed out the tourist sites along the way as if this was Michael's first trip. He indulged the kid, thinking it was good practice, and watched the Presidential Palace give way to the Mosque of Muhammad Ali and the long stretch of the cemetery. Soon the pyramids rose in the distance. The driver turned off the Ring Road and fought the traffic next to the canals. A herd of horses and one huge water buffalo stood in the middle of the canal, their owner washing them off. Further down plastic bottles and trash clogged the surface. They kept driving and the water cleared again. Village life buzzed around him, but his eyes were getting heavy. On the plane, he'd reviewed secret files about the Giza Plateau from several mystical organizations. The possibilities of what had been uncovered intrigued him.

When they entered the village of Nazlet-el-Samman, Michael pressed his face up against the window. A wooden fence blocked the site, but the dozen men in military uniform carrying SIG 552s marked this as the spot of the collapse. They'd gotten that fence up fast.

The black sedan pulled into the driveway of the Mena House and a bellhop dressed in a black-fringed vest and sporting a matching fez stepped up to open his door. Michael tipped the guy—he'd gotten generous since the marriage—and stepped through the metal detector which buzzed. The guard casually waved him in, never budging from his seat.

Azizi threw up a hand to catch Michael's attention, and he walked over to the bar just off the lobby. "I've already checked you in," Azizi said. "Come have something to drink. Relax."

Michael rubbed at his gritty eyes. "I thought this was an emergency," he said.

"We've got permission from the Antiquities Department to go in after dark. They want to limit visibility as much as they can."

Michael ordered tea, hoping it would wake him up. Outside the window, the pyramids soared into the blue sky, golden and indomitable. "What do we know so far?"

Azizi's smile was conspiratorial. He leaned forward, speaking in a quiet voice. "You won't believe it. Looks like a big ceremonial court with Osiris standing in the middle. It's surrounded by smaller temples. We've been able to get into the Anubis sanctuary. May be a Sekhmet shrine next to it, but they were still shifting rock when I left."

"Hmm, think the others will be Anput and P'tah?"

Azizi squirmed in his seat like a kid at Christmas. "I think there's more than four. The smaller temples might circle the large Osiris statue in the middle. We've hit the mother lode." Oxford educated, Azizi's English sounded like the upper crust of England, but his vocabulary was sprinkled with American slang. "There are stairs up and down. Might be a shrine for each major group of Neters." Neters was the ancient word for Egyptian gods and goddesses.

"What do you need me for?"

Azizi glanced around the bar. "This might be the major ceremonial site the traditions have always talked about."

"Maybe, but the question remains."

"There's more. You'll see."

"I should go over to the house. Say hello to the family."

"Tahir will meet us at the site tonight. Get some rest. We may be at it all night."

Michael glanced wryly at his tea, but the caffeine had barely scratched the surface of his fatigue. He wondered if he was coming down with something.

After agreeing to meet Azizi at eight o'clock, Michael followed the labyrinth of hallways to his room in the main palace building. He loved staying in the old section of the hotel, with its sudden steps up or down, checkered carpeting, and honey-colored paneling. When he arrived in his room, he found a gilded headboard on the bed in the shape of a round mandala. Too bad Anne wasn't with him this trip.

He showered and unpacked, finding Anne's surprise tucked between his shirts. It was a picture of the last sonogram, taken from an angle that left the child's gender unidentifiable. She'd written "Come back soon, Daddy," on the picture. He tucked it into the corner of the gold frame of the mirror and checked his watch. He had two hours before going to the site. He set an alarm and lay down on the bed.

Sleep came immediately, and a dream. Towering Neters whispered to him, looming dark forms, their faces hidden. Try as he might, he couldn't make out the words. The alarm sounded and he woke, still tired. He grabbed a quick snack, then headed outside.

Azizi lounged on the front wall and stood when Michael came out. "Let's take the short way."

They walked up the hill in front of the hotel. Azizi showed his ID and pass to the guard and they made their way up to the parking lot in front of the Great Pyramid. Across the now empty paving stones, a cluster of aspirants dressed all in white waited near the door of the giant structure to be let in for their private session. Azizi and Michael slipped through the shadows over to the causeway and walked down toward the Sphinx, her cone shaped head just visible in the growing dark.

"Looks like Cayce might have been right," Azizi said casually.

"What? But—"

"I know, I know." Azizi held up a hand. "You said you'd opened the Hall of Records already, that it was a spiritual place and not physical. But there is a hallway in the uncovered temple that goes over to the Sphinx toward a chamber." He paused for dramatic effect. "Right beneath the right paw."

"How can you tell?"

"It matches the ground-penetrating radar done a few years back. That crack the Antiquities Director made fun of?"

"The 45 x 45-foot perfect square? The crack was in his head."

Azizi laughed. "The hallway goes straight toward it."

People just couldn't let go of the Hall of Records, Michael thought. But maybe there was something stored in that square room. Still, he'd known deep down they'd opened Cayce's famed hall last time. And it had not been artifacts or lost technology from Atlantis. It had been an exalted state of consciousness—powerful enough to bring a huge energy surge into the earth's grid. Many things had changed for the positive afterwards, but the dark forces had redoubled their efforts.

"How about the staff of Osiris?" Michael asked.

"The real one that's supposed to open all the secret chambers in Egypt?"

"The very one."

"I think the Sayeed family already did that for us."

"The Ring of Isis?"

Azizi shook his head.

"Or the Seeing Stone from the great oracle of Ammon in the Oasis."

"But that's way south."

"It's never been found. Perhaps it was moved. Hidden away here in the North."

Azizi patted him on the shoulder. "Who knows what we'll find, my brother? Who knows?"

They walked in silence, the sand soft beneath their feet. A group of men waited close to the new fence near the ragged hole in the ground. Rubble from the house sat on the side. The front stoops of adjacent houses had been boarded up. Michael could only guess how these people got in and out of their residences now. The street up to the new fence was empty. Maybe the army had evacuated the whole neighborhood.

Michael spotted a tall figure in a flowing woolen galabeya, a white turban on his head. "Tahir!" He sprinted forward and grabbed him in a rough hug.

"Michael, I am so glad you came. Who knows what we will discover." His eyes gleamed.

A man with a muscular build and sporting a traditional beard stepped out of a knot of soldiers. "Azizi, is your group ready?"

"Yes. Eiham, this is Dr. Michael Levy, curator of the Egyptian collection at the Metropolitan Museum in New York."

Former, Michael thought, but decided not to correct him. "Pleased to meet you, Eiham." They shook hands.

"You know Tahir Nur Ahram, of course." Azizi nodded toward Tahir.

"Everyone knows Tahir," Eiham said. "Shall we go down?" Without waiting for an answer, Eiham walked behind a pile of rocks twice the height of a camel's head and picked his way down the steep drop. The cave ceiling closed over their heads. Electric torches lit the way forward.

"They've been busy," Michael pitched his voice for Tahir only.

"Very," he answered. "Many trucks."

Michael knew this meant the top black market dealers had already had their pick. They'd leave some things for the museums and universities to study, but given the difficult economy, Michael imagined the site would be more picked over than usual. What they'd left stopped the group in their tracks.

In front of them stretched a level area, blue and white marble tiles showing here and there between piles of sand and rock. In the middle rose an enormous statue of Osiris, his crowned head stretching maybe twenty feet, almost to the top of the cavern, his hands folded in front, the crook and flail resting on either shoulder. Dust still covered the head and shoulders, but the gold gleamed beneath it. The eyes seemed to shift as Eiham played his flashlight over the statue.

"Amazing, yes?"

"Beautiful," Michael breathed.

"The house stood there." He pointed the flashlight up, illuminating a gutted structure, stairs rising up to a precariously perched bedroom, the door to an armoire open showing what looked like children's clothes. "We think they discovered this tomb."

Eiham moved his light down on what now looked like a cave pockmarked with niches. One wall was painted with typical feast scenes. A wooden sarcophagus stood unopened and several gold statuettes littered the ground. That these had been left told Michael how rich the find was.

They turned back to the towering statue of Osiris. The piece dominated the cave, standing like a good shepherd ready to guide his sheep—or goats in the case of Egypt. Michael walked around the statue, marveling at the careful etching in the folds of his garment, the inlaid turquoise and coral in the crook and flail held in his crossed arms. "It's a miracle this statue survived. It looks untouched," he said.

"Over here is the Anubis chapel." Eiham walked to the west, behind Osiris, but Michael was drawn to the south where the workers had just cleared another entrance.

He walked across the even tiles, avoiding a pile of rubble near the wall, and stood in front of the chapel entrance. Inside, the great lioness regarded him quietly, her lotus staff blossoming just at her heart. This Sekhmet had a gold disk on her head.

Eiham gave out a low whistle. "Would you look at that?"

Michael stiffened at Eiham's intrusion. He'd rather be alone with Tahir down here. Even Azizi's presence was a bit of a distraction. Eiham had no metaphysical training. Azizi had studied some, but he was a natural. He'd probably been a member of a mystery school in a past life. Now, he was down-to-earth, concerned with making a living for his growing family, as Michael would be if he hadn't married into money.

Michael snapped a picture of the newly revealed Sekhmet, apologizing to her for the impertinence, but he feared the disk that topped her head would disappear. At least he'd have evidence. One look at Azizi was all it took.

"Eiham," Azizi called from near the ramp. Thankfully, the man walked toward him. After a brief discussion, Azizi called out. "An hour?" his voice echoed off the walls, setting the large space reverberating.

"That would be excellent," Michael said in a softer voice. The sound carried as if he held a microphone.

"*Shokran*," Tahir said.

"Yes, thank you," Michael said.

Michael stood in front of Sekhmet and steadied his breathing. He stepped over the threshold of the chapel and dropped to his knees before her, silently asking her permission to search the area and for her protection. She stood quietly for a long moment, regarding him. Michael felt the same urge he always did before this great mother. He stood and leaned his head against her staff, his forehead resting between her breasts. She was the same height as the Karnak statue.

Be prepared, my son. A great test awaits you.

Michael wondered what it might be. Resisting the wealth that lay all around him? Documenting the find before the black marketers stripped it clean? Perhaps he'd discover something entirely new, unknown to Egyptologists before now.

Go West.

He bowed his head to her and walked toward the Anubis shrine, hardly hearing Tahir tell him he would try to get through the crack and enter the chamber to the East.

Anubis stood in the shadows, his dark skin barely reflecting the light of Michael's flashlight. He held a gold ankh in his left hand. His *was* staff gleamed dark mahogany. The jackal head peered down at him, quartz crystal shining back from the iris. This ancient technique made the eyes come alive, giving the viewer the feeling of being watched.

Michael stood in front of the statue, silencing his mind, waiting. He intoned a sacred sound, letting it fill his body and the chamber.

Nothing stirred.

He intoned the sound again, willing himself to patience. Michael listened as the tones filled the room, ringing like a bell at first, then softening as the vibration stretched out, thinned, and disappeared, leaving silence.

Something took a long, shuddering breath. Then the breathing steadied. Became regular and deep.

Michael opened his eyes. The statue's chest rose and fell.

The Great Opener of the Ways shifted in the dark.

Reached out his left hand and pointed the shaft of the golden ankh at Michael.

Michael steadied himself internally, then grasped it.

The Neter stepped down from his pedestal and led Michael back into the yawning dark cavern behind the chapel.

Made in the USA
Coppell, TX
11 February 2020